Eyes of War

by Janna Nickerson

A Hidden Talent Press Book
Missoula, Montana

Copyright 2006 by Janna Nickerson
Second Edition

Eyes of War

A Hidden Talent Press Book

P.O Box 9052
Missoula, MT
59807

www.iysofwar.com

Cover by Theo Ellsworth
www.artcapacity.com
theoellsworth@hotmail.com

ISBN:
0-9776114-0-X

Printed in the United States of America 2006

Acknowledgements

There are so many people who helped me with my goal, all of whom I am so thankful to, it is difficult to convey my gratitude. They have helped me to do something that was not only a dream but have given me something to be proud of and to show the world what I can accomplish.

The greatest thanks must go to my family (Dad, Bryan and Grandma and Grandpa P.) for their undying support and faith in me. Mom, if it wasn't for you, I wouldn't be able to do this, you read it, corrected it and told me your opinion. Without that I wouldn't have the courage to go on.

Bob and Lisa, thank you for taking the time out of your day and reading my book either to check it or just for enjoyment. Your encouragement, advice and enthusiasm gave me that extra confidence in my book and my writing skills.

Patty, thank you for reading my book and making sure the grammar and spelling was all where it needed to be. Most of all thank you for taking time out of your summer to read my book. I appreciate that and the compliments you have given me, they mean millions.

Ms. Cole, I don't think I would have been able to go through the self publishing process without your willingness to help me in getting PageMaker up and ready. You helped me with the layout, scanning the cover and map, showed me what to do and let me work in your class even when you had other classes going. You put so much time and effort into this, I have no way of telling you how lucky I am to have a teacher like you.

Mrs. Rothwell, it all begins with you. Your class was the class that really pushed me to write. For that I can't even begin to say how much I am indebted to you. You gave me something so precious, the desire to write a book and finish it, that I'm truly at a loss for words.

Manuela, thank you for your interest in my book and belief in me, it means more than the world. Also, thank you, you and Olivia, for letting me base two characters on you. Even if those characters grew into two different people, they started with you.

Barbara, thank you for your help and support with the marketing of my book. If it weren't for your help, my book wouldn't be going anywhere very quickly. I've learned so much from you, thanks doesn't seem like enough.

Of course, thank you Theo for the wonderful, amazing and thoroughly eye-catching cover. The time you put into it is apparent and you have my deepest thanks for it.

All of these people and many I have not named who played minor but important roles in the self-publishing of my book have showed me such kindness that I would have to live for thousands of years before I felt like I have given you each what you have given me. Thank you. I must also thank all my friends for showing the enthusiasm that they did. It means more than you can imagine.

Janna Nickerson

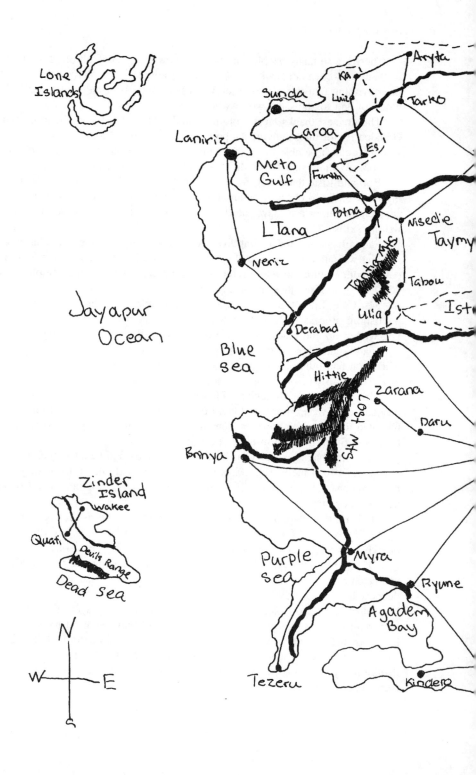

"There are powers awakening
in this world that you would do
well to fear."

~ Queen Eliza of Caendor

Beginnings: ALD 3900 SD April

Silence filled the night air of the Northern Kingdom. Across the land, the hum of voices was hushed to frightened whispers and the chirping of crickets died. Dogs huddled under bushes, trembling in fear. Children clutched their mothers, as tears of terror rolled down their cheeks.

As people and creatures lay quiet, a deep rumbling came from within the earth. The rumbling grew to a roar and the ground shook, waves of grass and soil sweeping across the country. Balls of fire began raining from the night sky, illuminating the land in an orange glow. The seas sloshed upon the shores and the oceans boiled. Snow fell in places that had never seen water and lush forests dried up, crumbling to dust.

Across the land, people fled from their homes, as fire fell from the sky and the earth rolled in anger. They ran for safety, but none could be found. Crying out in panic, they screamed curses at the gods.

In the palace of Caendor, within the Tower of the Light, the Queen of Caendor shrieked in pain as a contraction ripped through her body. She collapsed on the floor. "Richard," she gasped to her husband, "the baby is coming. She will not wait."

The King ran from the room, calling for servants to bring blankets and water. It was their first child and the King was fearful. Very few babies were born at the beginning of a new Age. It was a time of chaos and death. Those that were born were cursed.

The King found several servants and ordered them to follow him. When he returned to the room, the servants went to work, making sure the Queen was comfortable.

Gazing down at his wife, the King sighed. "I have a terrible fear for our child, my wife. Babies are not born in times such as these. A new Age is here and the Prophecies are being proven true as I speak. The balance of power is tilting and our daughter will soon be at the center of it. Ruling or running, it does not matter, she will have a great role to play in the future." The King looked up. "If the priests are right, the Dragons and the Warlord are coming." He paused, his brow furrowed in concentration. "We will not test our daughter in the Art of Magic."

Miles from Jariran, as fireballs fell and the earth rumbled, another woman was in the throes of birth. Her hands grasped the sides of the bed, pale and glistening with sweat. A woman sitting at her side ran a wet cloth across her forehead. "It will be all right. The baby will be born soon. Not much longer."

Standing across from the bed was a man, the father to the unborn baby. He was gazing out the window at the turmoil spilling through the land. "When our son is born, we will not test him to see if he has any Talent."

Through shivers of pain, the to-be-mother asked, "Why not?"

"I do not want him taken from us."

"One day he will be," the other woman said. "The gods will take him from you."

The father stared out the window. "I know but not before he is ready."

Over a sea and across a nation, another birth was in the making. The pregnant mother cried in silent agony and her husband grasped her hand, wishing to ease her pain.

"The pain will pass, my love," the husband whispered. "He will be born soon."

The woman breathed heavily. "Why did I do it? Why did I trust him? I do not want him to be born! He's not even your—I can feel his evil! It is poisoning me!"

The husband squeezed her hand. "I know, love, but he must be. The Lord of Darkness is watching over him. And no matter how much we want to destroy your son before he can destroy others, we cannot. He is protected by the forces of Evil."

"Why am I cursed?" she wailed. "I have done nothing to deserve a baby that will wield such evil. Nothing!"

"The gods are moving the pieces and we are but pawns, my love. We can do nothing."

The woman wept as she gave birth to her son.

While the terror reigned and the births began, the Priests of the Light watched from their temples, eyes filled with prophecy. One of the priests turned to another. "They are coming," he said.

His companion nodded. "And soon our land will be naught but ashes as they wage their war."

 C3   C3   &O

ALD 3919 SD April

A rooster crowed as the morning sun crept up over the horizon, flooding the land with light. Dew sparkled on leaves and grass in the soft orange glow of the sun. Animals crawled back into dens and birds began their morning song.

People awoke to another day they would spend in the fields and shops. Shepherds blinked away sleep as they went out to check on their livestock. People of all shapes and sizes moved about the land. The smells of bread, wine, incense, cooking meat, linen, wool and other various items floated in the air around towns. Fishermen walked down to the rivers and hoped to bring in a catch. Wagons started to roll into the many cities of Caendor, loaded with goods. Shoi, magic users, ambled down streets, carrying books through the throng of people in major cities, their robes twisting around their feet. Ladies, their carriages pulled by the finest horses, held silken kerchiefs to their noses, keeping away the smell of commoners. Lords trotted their horses up and down the cobblestone streets of the cities, dignity flaunting itself in the way they sat. Women carried baskets of food or laundry and little children raced among the adults. It promised to be a good day.

ଔ ଔ ଔ

People say that the town or city in which they live is the most beautiful. But everyone agreed that the city of Jariran exceeded all others.

Obsidian walls, six feet thick, surrounded the city. The city gates, decorated in bronze, gold, and silver welcomed weary travelers. Temples to the Light, with designs engraved into the rock, dotted the city. Fountains of all creations, from black stone to crystal, stood in plazas and gardens, blossoming fresh water. Red, blue, orange, yellow, purple, pink and white flowers, growing out of brightly painted pots and gardens, swayed in the gentle breeze. Trees heavy with blossoms or green leaves filled parks and outlined the squares. Small palaces glittered in the light, making the city look like a large diamond in the sun. White stone houses surrounded the marble walls of the Palace. Inside the marble walls, the Four Towers, with golden teardrop tops rose up into the air making the viewer tilt his head back until it hurt to see the top. An even larger tower rose up out of the marble walls. The stained crystal glass forming the teardrop top gave off flashes of blinding light when hit with the sun's rays. The Tower of the Light earned its name. For more than a thousand years kings and queens ruled from that tower and brought peace, riches and victories to Jariran and all the other cities, and villages in the country of Caendor. The palace itself was breath-taking. Golden doors lead to the inside of the palace walls. Hanging gardens covered the sides of each wall, some even crawling up the Four Towers. Fountains spouted clear water into pools where yellow-orange fish swam about lazily. Balconies led to the rooms of the King and his family. Jade statues of kings and queens long past lined up along the stone path leading to bronze doors worked with gold. Inside those doors, gray-white pillars filed up and down the Hall. A long red and gold carpet led the way to the throne room, several levels up in the Tower of the Light. Servants in red and black livery scuttled around the Hall fulfilling chores or carrying out orders of the King.

Jariran was a powerful capitol. Caendor was a large and powerful nation, but even the strongest nations can fall.

Chapter 1

A Princess

On one of the balconies Princess Janevra, Heir to the Throne, Princess of the Tower of the Light, Daughter of the Nation Caendor, and Child of the King, leaned over the rail and looked out across the city, ignoring her mother, Queen Eliza of Caendor, as she read from a thick red book.

Janevra sighed quietly. Her mind was anywhere but concentrating on her mother's words. She was thinking about magic, wondering why her parents had never tested her to see if she had any Talent. She knew her mother despised shoi and her father didn't care for them. But every child, save the very poor, were tested to see if they had any Talent.

"Janevra, are you listening?"

"What? Oh, I'm listening, Mother. What were you saying?" replied Janevra, turning around. Straight auburn hair that fell past her shoulders outlined a freckled face. Naturally curved reddish-brown eyebrows and long dark eyelashes gave her wide-set green eyes a commanding presence. Full lips suppressed a smile. A blue silk dress clung to her slender, strong body. The neck of her blue dress stopped above her bosom but not enough to be called modest. Around her neck hung a necklace of pearls and diamonds. Slender fingers smoothed out a dress that didn't need to be straightened.

"Janevra, how can I tell you Caendor's history when you do not listen? You are the future Queen of this country. You need to know its past so you do not repeat preceding rulers' mistakes."

"Mother! I already know all of this. I've known it all since I was ten."

The Queen shook her head. Her gray hair, that still held a few blonde strands, was piled up on her head, holding her crown in place. Paints and oils had been masterfully applied to her cheeks and eyelids, emphasizing her delicate bone structure even more. Her face looked anything but delicate at the moment. Her light blue eyes could have melted ice as she looked her daughter in the eye. Or tried to. Her daughter was four inches taller than her mother's five feet six inches.

"You will sit down and listen or I will get your father," her mother said calmly.

Janevra could not resist a little laugh. "Mother, you know as well as I that Father does not approve of these lessons you give me. He won't do anything."

"Then behave yourself. It is rude not to listen while someone is trying to teach you."

"I've read that book three times in the last two years. I know it by heart. There is nothing in there I don't know."

"Don't presume you know everything, Janevra."

"I'm not saying I know everything. My point is that I have been trained to be a ruler ever since I was born. It's something I don't understand," Janevra said.

The Queen frowned. "Don't understand?"

"Yes. In Caendor, a woman can never rule without a man. It has been the law for Ages. You know this. Why teach me when I must get married and hand over all power to my husband?"

"You don't want to be educated?" the Queen asked.

Janevra sighed. "No. I want to be and I'm very glad that I am. But I am not naive, Mother. My education has extended far into areas most women in Caendor are never allowed to know. I only want to know why."

"Someday you will know why I've gone to such lengths to make you one of the most educated persons in the Northern Kingdom. Very soon, things are going to change. I'm preparing you."

"To rule without a king?"

"Yes."

"What does Father think of that?"

"He promised me long ago that I would have complete control over your education. He has disapproved of it many times, but he is a man who keeps his promises."

Janevra sat quietly for a while. "How did you know to prepare me to rule? What is going to change? Why did you teach me things I should never know?"

The Queen looked at Janevra, fear and worry etched across her face. "You need to know how to be the greatest ruler of all time. You need to know how to fight and win. You need to know how to sacrifice personal desires and not feel angered because you must. You need to know this and everything else that I have trained you in if you are to survive the coming years. You cannot rule until then."

Janevra gazed at her mother through narrowed eyes. "I know how to rule a country, Mother. You've forced it on me since I was born. I know how to fight for my country and lead the people into battle. You had me trained to be a master of the sword and hold my own with other weapons. No other woman of privilege in Caendor knows what I know when it comes to war. The only thing I do not know is why you are afraid to let me rule. Most children are co-regents with their parents when they turn eighteen. What are you afraid of that's holding you back? The Priests of the Light? I know their power was once greater than yours before I was born. Are you fearful of them regaining that power? I have not been tested in the Art of Magic. For all I know, I could be a shoi, a magic user. They hold no sway over me even if I did have the Talent, if that's why you are worried. If it is not that, what are you afraid of, Mother? What powers do you see that I do not?"

"There are powers awakening in this world that you would do well to fear, my daughter, especially considering your lineage and power. However, my fears do not concern you or your father." Not yet, her tone seemed to imply.

Janevra lifted an eyebrow. "You are keeping secrets from Father?"

The Queen snapped her book shut. "Our lesson is over." Then, more quietly, "One day you will know the truth, Janevra. If I die before I can tell you, then search for the Knives of Thorn. They hold the secrets to our past. Go back to your room, the trials will begin soon and don't mention any of this to your father."

Janevra frowned as she turned her back to her mother. Her mother was worried and terrified about something and Janevra wanted to know what it was even if it meant provoking her mother. *I wish you could tell me what it is you see and fear, Mother,* she thought. *I know, what ever it is, I can fight it. I love my people, and I would die for them but I need to know what enemy I am going to face. I need to know what you know.*

Janevra closed the door behind her and proceeded down the hallway. She was halfway to her room, after taking the round-about way, when she came upon two guards dragging a prisoner through the hall. She lifted her dress and ran after them. "Stop!" she shouted, reaching them and holding up a hand.

"My Lady?" one of the guards asked.

"What are you doing with this man?"

The guards glanced at each other. "Ah...taking him to the captain for his beheading," one of the guards answered.

"What is his crime? I'm sure since his penalty is death, he must have done something horrible. Is he a murderer, a rapist, a conspirator against the King?"

The guards shook their heads. "No, my lady," they murmured.

Janevra put her hands on her hips. "What is he then?"

"A thief," one said.

"A thief? When has my father beheaded a thief?"

"Never, my Lady." They lowered their eyes, staring at the floor.

"Is this the captain's doing?" she demanded.

They nodded.

Janevra frowned. *One day the captain will go too far in disobeying my father's wishes.* "Let him go."

The guards bent down and untied the thief's wrists. The thief rubbed his arms, gawking at Janevra.

"I would run, sir. I may have saved your life, but the captain is not a man who likes losing." Janevra pressed two gold chips into the thief's hand. "Buy yourself some food and leave Jariran for a few days."

The thief bowed low, pressed his lips to the floor and dashed off. The two guards watched him go.

"Now," Janevra said. The guards faced her. "I want one of you to make sure the thief leaves and I want the other to deliver a message to the captain for me. Tell him I know he is disobeying my father's wishes. It is wrong to kill those who have done nothing but try to survive. If he attempts to kill another innocent man and I hear of it, he will be held responsible."

The guards bowed, their armor creaking. They set off at a march down the hallway.

Janevra waited for them to turn the corner before continuing to her room. *Who does the captain think he is, deciding that those who only steal to survive should be killed?* She was furious.

Walking up a flight of stairs, her anger cooled and Janevra was satisfied in saving at least one man from the captain. Maybe today at the trials she would save another.

Once inside her room, she slipped out of her high-heeled shoes. She set them on her bed and walked barefoot out on to her balcony. Leaning against the stone rail, she watched the city below her.

Janevra sighed. *I wish I could be normal. Live a normal life, one where I could marry the love of my youth, have children, work hard and be happy. No, I will never have that. My parents will make me marry some fool lord and I will be stuck being the Queen to a king who holds no love for women. Not that I don't want to help people. It's just that I can't live how I want to. I have no control.* She couldn't do many things that others took for granted. She had never been in the city without curtains surrounding her or guards blocking her view. What she wanted to do was go into the city where people wouldn't see her as the princess, just some commoner.

Janevra turned away from the balcony and moved towards a chair where she sprawled in a most improper manner. *What does my mother know? What is her fear? I can see it in her eyes whenever she looks at me.*

"Princess, if your mother saw you she would have a fit."

Janevra smiled and looked up at her maid. "I know, Sariah. Thanks for cleaning my clothes and putting them in the wardrobe."

The gray haired maid walked out on to the balcony. "It's my job, Princess, no need to thank me." Sariah's red dress and white apron gave the woman a homely appearance and her blue eyes brightness.

"*Eyath hmya'nxe olqo'ehz lmotwje,*" Janevra replied.

Sariah raised her eyebrows. "My Lady?"

"You should always thank. I just finished learning elven," Janevra said.

Sariah frowned. "I don't see why, 'tis a dead language, miss. No elves ever lived anyway."

"I think they did. I found a book that taught me the ancient languages and since I have nothing else to do, I might as well learn." Janevra smiled. "'Learning is the power that makes all things possible, Lady Thysi,'" Janevra quoted.

Sariah shrugged and went back into Janevra's room, hanging up several dresses in Janevra's wardrobe.

Janevra followed her and plopped down on her bed. She propped herself up on her elbows.

"Can you tell me a tale of the old days? Please?"

The old maid looked up from dusting a bookshelf. "Aren't you a little old, Princess?"

"Yes, but I do love to listen to your stories."

Sariah smiled. "Alright, miss, if you say so. Let me see… In the Fifth age, called the Age of the First Dragons or the Third Battle by others, two young people arose. They grew up in a world of Evil, but their hearts remained pure. It's believed they were gods in disguise, come to rid the world of the Evil that was power. In order to destroy the Evil, they gathered together the people of the Northern Kingdom to fight. It was the year ALD 3200 FD DD when two young people, a man and a woman, became the Dragons. The name was created because of their awesome ability in the Art of Magic and the way they commanded the love of the people. They had incredible power in magic and challenged the Warlord of that era. The battle was fought in the Gangga Pass. Good verse Evil, Light verse Dark. The battle was waged for three days. At times, the Light held the upper hand only to be thrown back down by the mightier power of the Dark. Many lost their lives, but good triumphed. The Dragons, who had managed to survive the battle, became the High King and Queen of the Northern Kingdom. Peace prospered even after their death and the Northern Kingdom became strong once again. But like all things, it came to an end. In the year ALD 3800 AD, Evil yet again tried to conquer all. It failed when the nations of the Northern Kingdom banded together and fought the Fourth Battle against Evil. When the war came to an end a new age arose out of the mists of destruction and the Hundred Years of Prophecies began. Then in the Year ALD 3900 AD on the first day of spring, the Second Dragons were born and the year became ALD 3900 SD. No one knew why the Dragons had been born for Evil had not shown its fingertips. But the time comes again when Evil grows and the Dragons' power is once more demanded to conquer the Evil and throw everlasting light across the world."

Sariah turned back to her work.

"That was good but a little vague and it sounded like a history lesson," Janevra said, staring up at the ceiling, dreaming. She had always wished to live in the times when history was made.

"Forgive me, Princess. The stories of the Prophecies and the Dragons are always vague. Your parents saw to that. They didn't want their rule stolen from them. When you become Queen you will understand the fear of having your power taken from you."

Janevra looked up at her maid. "What of the stories before? The ancient stories about the past? Are those as vague?"

"You should know that, Princess, with all your history. Most of them are vague. Many things get lost in time, many important things."

Silence settled and Sariah hummed gently to herself.

"I wish something interesting would happen around here. Such as battles and stunning victories."

Sariah rounded on Janevra in barely contained fury. Her eyes were sharp. "Don't ever let me hear you say that again. You don't know what you're talking about."

Janevra bit her lip. "Sorry."

Sariah softened. "All is well, Princess. You'll understand what I mean some day."

Janevra frowned. "Why did my parents not test me to see if I had any

Talent in magic? Every child is tested, except the very poor. What were my parents frightened of? History shows the Priests are usually powerful shoi. They can come in handy during war."

Sariah winced and faced the princess. "You were born in the Year of the Dragon and you were born on the first day of spring, a day when magic is at its strongest. Your parents were afraid that you would be taken from them and raised in the Hall of the Shoi. At that time, the priests had more power than the King and Queen and your parents did not want the shoi to get more power. It threatened their rule."

"But now there seems to be no tension between the two," Janevra observed. It made no sense. Why did it not continue?

"With the birth of the Dragons and the prophecy being proven, the priests have had more pressing matters."

"Prophecies? Have the Dragons truly returned?"

"Don't waste your time, Princess. It's just a bunch of pig wallow if you ask me." The maid left the room, her wide skirts rustling.

Janevra picked a book off a table near her bed, still wondering of the Prophecies. She found where she left off and started reading, deciding that she would look into the Prophecies some time soon. She walked onto the balcony.

"Calahadar was an ancient city, now in ruins. It was that city that created the Great Sword of Hadar out of Black Iron and the fiery metal furipyr, a metal forged only in the deep mines of Huyak, the Dwarven capital. Also created in Calahadar was the white ball perched on top of the White Staff of Jayapur, forged of furipyr. The greatest city of time fell to the forces of Evil in ALD 2801 AD AE. It was the last stronghold of good before everything fell to the Shadow.

Janevra shuddered. She could almost feel the icy reach of the shadow caress her back. *Perhaps I should wish for peaceful times instead of war,* she thought and continued to read.

"The city was built by the elves in the Age of Magic. It was believed that the elves were trying to create a city that would never fall into ruin or be destroyed by the forces of Evil. In their attempts to create an immortal city, they also discovered an amulet called the Hawk, the Hand and the Eye that had the power to bring men back to the Light. The amulet's other powers have long been lost. Many say it was the amulet that stole elven immortality but when asked about this, the elves said, 'the Ancients stole our gift from Fate and Time. They stole our immortality and used it to hide and protect the Books of Power. We will never reclaim our gift. The Books are lost as are we.' Many attempts over the centuries have been made to find the Books of Power but all have failed. None know where to look but the promise of the ultimate power that lies within the books is enough to drive men mad in search for it."

Closing the book, Janevra gazed down into the city, her eyes landing on one of the beautiful temples of the Light. From her perch, the white stone of the temple flashed in the sun like a thousand jewels. She had always wanted to see if she had any Talent in the Art of Magic, but her parents had forbidden her long ago that if she were ever to test herself, they would disinherit her. She figured that since she did not have any siblings, they could not disinherit her. It would be the downfall of her family's dynasty. *One day I'll test myself, and I'll see what hidden powers I have that my mother fears.*

Somewhere within the palace, a bell tolled, it's ring spreading through the palace like a soft breath of air. Janevra groaned. Every day she had to attend the trials and listen to the prisoners' plea for their lives. She knew by some instinct which ones lied and which ones spoke the truth.

Her father had made a law several years ago that commanded everyone of royal blood to listen to men's pleas when they were accused of certain charges. Those of royal blood then decided if the man was innocent or guilty. The least amount of people of royal blood needed on a trial was three. Since there were only three in the ruling family, Janevra had to be present. She did not mind the trials, but the amount of men the guards brought in who were actually innocent was appalling. There were way too many and that meant the true thieves or murders escaped.

Janevra hurried into her room, quickly setting her book back in its place on her bookshelf. She hastily slid her feet into her shoes and ran a brush through her hair before pinning it up in a bun.

Running out her door and into the anteroom, she collided with a young guard coming to tell her that her presence was required in the Tower of the Light. They fell down in a helpless heap.

The guard jumped up, his face rigid in terror. "Princess! I- I did not see you! I'm so-so sorry, Princess." Panic made his voice squeak.

Janevra got up, a little dizzy. "No, no, it's alright. I was not paying attention." She looked up at him and smiled. "Next time I will be more careful."

The young guard blushed to his hairline. He mumbled something, but Janevra did not catch it. He bowed low and held the door of the anteroom open for her.

Janevra thanked him, walking swiftly down the hall. She was half way to the Tower where the trials were held, when she passed a white robed man wearing a bronze belt. The man, a priest, noticed her and bowed low. "Princess," he said.

"Sir," Janevra said, curious. She had never seen a priest in the palace before. "What is your business here in the palace?" *If my father has finally agreed to see them, this means their respect is once again rising. I wonder what this means.*

The priest clutched a scroll in his hand. He glanced down at it, clearing his throat. "I had a meeting with the King, Princess. The Priests of the Light are eager to show that we have no intention of taking away his power. More pressing matters are concerning us at the moment, and we do not have the time to dally in political matters."

"What matters, sir?"

"The Priests of the Light are searching for the Dragons. We need to find them soon, Princess, before the year's end. Without them the Evil that will rise in the south will conquer the Northern Kingdom unhindered."

"Sir, if it is the will of the gods, do you not think the Dragons will be found when the gods will them to be found? History has proven to us that the gods twist the realm of mortals to their liking. What would stop them from waging their undying war against each other?"

"I believe your words hold truth." The priest eyed her shrewdly. "You will be a great Queen, Princess. One who will rise above the other leaders of this nation. Yours will be the name that goes down forever in the history books of all the nations. It is a pity you have not been tested."

Janevra smiled. "When I am Queen, I will command all men and women to be tested in the Art to see if they can become shoi and the Second Age of Magic will dawn."

The priest of the Light nearly clapped his hands in joy, his face creasing into happy wrinkles. "A great cause for a great Queen, Princess. But I warn you, when you are Queen, this will not be the same land you know now. War is coming." The priest bowed, turned on his heel and continued down the hall.

Janevra stared at him, his words ringing in her head like the tolling of the palace bell. *War is coming.*

Shaken, Janevra walked down the hallway, slowly making her way to the Tower of the Light.

Reaching the bronze doors that lead to the inside of the Tower of the Light, Janevra gently pushed them open. She looked up at her mother and father as they sat up on the dais, the golden thrones at their backs.

War is coming.

Chapter 2
A Peasant

Mat Trakall wiped the sweat from his forehead, leaning upon the shovel. He surveyed his work, grimacing to himself. *One person can only do so much,* he thought.

He bent down to his work, the warm sun of spring beating down on his back. Digging several holes, he went back over them, sprinkling the seeds into them.

It was late in the year for planting, but the winter had been long and had killed all their seeds planted in the ground last fall. The seeds would grow, but it would be a small harvest, barely enough for his family to get by.

As he planted the seeds, anxiety welled up in him. *What if we don't have enough?* Mat thought. *What if the harvest is so poor we can't get by? We only have two pigs we can kill and our cattle are too thin to butcher.*

What will happen to my family? Mat paused in his work. *Maybe I could become a soldier in the King's Army. That would surely pay for my family. It would support them in the hard times. Or maybe I could take up a trade. I like building. Maybe I could go Jariran and work in the wharf there and build riverboats for the King.*

Mat shoved the worrisome thoughts from his mind, focusing on his work. Dig, plant, and cover, over and over again until the whole field was planted. It would take him all day.

Mat worked through the hot hours of the day; sweat drenching his homemade shirt and breeches. His hair clung to his head and dripped with sweat. He looked up for a moment, judging the distance he had covered. *I'm almost done.*

As he finished, he thought of the gossip he had heard his mother and father talking about. It dealt with war in the east and strange things roaming the land at night, things such as sylai and rogui, creatures from a bard's tale. Yet he failed in believing that war and sylai were real as he failed to believe the talk concerning the Dragons and Warlord. Things like that only happened in the stories.

A shadow fell across Mat. Looking up into the hazel eyes of his father, Mat shook his head. "Father, you should be in bed. You're sick. Mother will put up a fit if she sees you."

His father, a big man with dark brown ringlets for hair and slumped shoulders, laughed heartily before coughing himself to silence. "Don't worry, son, your mother won't catch me. She's gone to the neighbors to see if they need anything in the city that you can pick up when you go tomorrow."

Mat felt a thrill run through him. He had never been to Jariran before and the excitement of setting foot in the city made his blood run.

Mat's house was twenty miles away from Jariran. His father was a farmer of wheat who usually made the trips to the city. Considering his father was coming down with a sickness and in no mood for traveling, Mat finally got his chance to travel to the most beautiful city in the world. The one bards told stories of and children dreamed of seeing. Jariran, the City of Jewels.

"What's the city like, Father?" Mat asked.

His father smiled. "You will see, son. Words cannot describe its beauty."

"Words cannot describe it or you do not know the words to describe it?" Mat jested, a grin spreading across his face.

His father cuffed him softly over the head. "Respect your elders, son. One day you'll be one and I won't be around to protect you from little children's jests."

Mat laughed with his father, enjoying the moment.

Shaking off the last bit of mirth, Mat finished the last row of wheat, his father watching him placidly. His work done, Mat carried the shovel and bag of wheat seeds back to the house.

"Father," Mat called over his shoulder. "Have you noticed strange footprints in the dirt lately? When I came out this morning, there were tracks that were made by some type of creature all over the place. I tried to figure out what kind of animal made such tracks but I couldn't."

"Tracks? What kind of tracks?" his father asked, walking behind Mat.

"They were odd, almost like a human's but larger, wider and they only had four toes. You could tell by the impressions in the dirt that those creatures were carrying something heavy. The only thing heavy enough that I can think of to imprint the tracks like that would be armor. Very thick armor, Father."

"If you see any more, show them to me. I think I know what they are."

"What do you think they are?"

"I will tell you when I know for sure, son. No use upsetting you."

Mat leaned against the house, waiting for his father to catch up.

His father came up, looking worried and older than usual. "Mat, I have something I need to tell you." He sat down on a bench next to the house, motioning to the seat next to him. Mat obeyed and waited patiently as another coughing fit took his father.

Clearing his throat and issuing a short cough, Mat's father looked down at him, pain hidden behind his eyes. "It is not easy for me to tell you this, Mat. It's a secret I've carried with myself since my father died. Your mother doesn't even know of it."

Mat winced. Secrets were deadly. He knew from experience. He had once, seven years ago, gone with a group of friends to the Caendor River to swim. It was a hot summer day and they had all finished their chores. As they splashed in the river, one of Mat's friends dared him to set fire to the old farmhouse a half mile down river. Mat had declined and gone home soon after that. The next day, news reached his family of a fire spreading down river at a fast speed. Men and women worked side by side to control the fire before it reached the small town not far from the old farmhouse. Sadly, the fire, helped by gusts of wind, destroyed the town and eventually died out a mile away. Several people were severely burned, and soldiers from Jariran were sent out to find the culprits. Mat knew it was his friends who had started the fire, but when the soldiers came to his house, he denied that he knew who did it. He did not want his friends to suffer the punishment of prison, which tended to end in death. The soldiers never found the perpetrators but the guilt of lying destroyed Mat. For weeks, he was nervous of someone discovering the truth and blaming him for covering up for his friends. His mother noticed something was wrong and confronted him about it. He told her everything. His punishment for lying was harsh but later she said keeping the secret, as much as it tormented him, saved the lives of his friends.

Mat's father sighed. "I should tell you the more important of the two. I—"

Mat held up his hand. "Two? You've kept two secrets from Mother?"

His father shook his head. "She knows one. As much as I regret doing it, she deserved to know even if it did hurt her." Taking a deep breath, his father continued. "I told her a month before you were born and she took it poorly, as I expected her to but—"

Shaking his head, Mat stood up. "I don't want to know, Father. I don't want to know either of them. Secrets tear people apart and I like things the way they are."

Mat's father smiled forlornly. "I understand your fear. But hear this, my line ends with you. You will not have a son or a daughter to carry on our blood. You will die before you can create a child. Our race will continue, but not our direct blood. One of my secrets lies in our blood and who our ancestors were."

"How do you know this?" Mat felt a shiver crawl down his back. "Why do you believe that I will not survive to have a child?"

"You were born on the day of Dragon Birth, Mat. No matter what you want to do, destiny will make you do what it wants you to do. The gods have once again dipped their hands into the masses of humanity. Our times are at an end, and it all starts with you, my son, you and two more people somewhere in the world. It is you who will dance to the strings of the gods, while making all other living things dance on the strings you create. When you were born, I kept you, selfishly, from taking the Test of the Robe. I did not want you taken from me, Mat. I knew if you took that test, the priests would steal you from me." His father sat quietly for a moment. He looked up at Mat in anguish, a wheeze from a suppressed cough whispering from his lips. "Do you wish for me to continue?"

Mat sunk back down on the bench. "Tell me." The things his father was saying kept turning over in his mind and one thought kept resurfacing. *Who am I?*

"I have powers and strengths unfathomable to the shoi. I have powers I have not even discovered yet. One day you will find your powers and the two in the world who are equal to you in strength. I do not wish to burden you with this knowledge but I must say it. You are—"

Mat's mother's shrill voice carried to them outside. "Mat! Where is your father? Tell him to get in here this instant! He is sick and in no condition to be outside!"

Mat smiled weakly as his father slowly got up and went indoor. "We will talk when you come back from the city, my son," his father said as he walked through the door.

Leaning against the house, Mat pondered what his father had said, trying to figure what his father was trying to get at. The only thing he could decide on was that his father was not who he said he was and knew things that very few people knew.

The sun was beginning to set, casting orange and yellow into the white clouds. The buzz of insects arose from the dusk as night creatures took the place of daytime creatures. The smell of food drifted to Mat through the open window, making him aware of his appetite.

"Look, boys, it's Mat Trakall," a voice yelled.

Mat twisted just in time to fend off three young men trying to slap him on the back in greetings. Their slaps were always a little harder than necessary.

"Hello, Jordan, Irrik, Breon," Mat said.

All three young men were around the age of Mat. Jordan was the tallest of the three with straight blonde hair, thousands of freckles and much too skinny to be healthy. He had a long nose that twitched whenever he was irritated. Irrik was the opposite, pudgy and round with twinkling brown eyes and red cheeks. Breon was Mat's height, had large green eyes and tied his long brown hair back in a ponytail. He had a small scar on his forehead from his sister who had pushed him into a table when he was five. They all wore old and patched clothes, the common garb of a farmer. Mat and his friends had known each other since a young age and lived in the same area, each sons of farmers.

They sat down on the bench but Irrik took a chair next to the bench, insisting he didn't want to break the bench with his added weight.

"Mat Trakall, goes to the big city," Jordan said, punching his friend lightly on the shoulder.

"Gods, I wish I could go," Breon said. "Apparently the goddess of Light doesn't favor me." He grinned up at the sky, shaking his head.

"I don't want to go to the city," Irrik said. The other three stared at him, causing him to shift uncomfortably. "Everything I love is here."

Jordan and Breon laughed.

"You never want to go?" Mat asked. "It's an adventure."

"I don't like adventure. I would get lost," Irrik insisted.

"Crazy," Mat, Jordan and Breon chimed together.

Irrik rolled his eyes. "It's not that I would never go, but I would only go if I could see the Princess."

Breon let out a low whistle. "Gods, she's beautiful. What I wouldn't give to see her."

Jordan sighed dreamily. "The Princess of Caendor, the woman who has captured my heart. I will marry no woman but her!" Jordan proclaimed.

Mat laughed. "You're going to live a lonely life, my friend."

Jordan smiled. "If only dreams could come true."

"Do you think you will get to see her, Mat?" Irrik asked. "I would be so envious if you did."

"If I ever see her, it would be when the sky becomes a thousand colors," Mat said dryly. "And when the stars fall."

Jordan patted Mat on the back. "It could happen."

They settled into a compatible silence, each thinking about the dreams they had had of the Princess and her famous beauty.

Breon shattered the silence with words of war. "I heard my parents talking the other night about war. They said the time is coming."

"What time?" Irrik asked.

"They said Evil is rising in the south and creatures are once again springing from the abyss. They come to this land to wreak havoc until their master is discovered and calls them to him. When that day dawns, the Dragons will be found and the Warlord will wage his war."

Jordan snorted. "You listen to too much gossip, Breon. Your mother is known to be a gossiper. She probably made it up."

Breon shrugged. "It doesn't matter if she made it up. I've decided to enlist in the army."

"Why?" Mat asked.

"My brothers want the farm. I don't. I've decided it's time for me to move on, live somewhere else. I've been thinking about joining the army in Istra."

"Why Istra?" Irrik asked. "They are a weak country."

"I believe my mother's words. Caendor is going to fall, and I will not be here when it happens."

Mat shivered at Breon's words. "Don't speak of such things."

Jordan frowned at Breon. "I think he's right, Mat. Caendor has been powerful too long, and with the talk of war, I fear the end is coming." He paused. "I'm coming with you."

"I won't," Irrik declared. "Not unless something actually happens."

"What of you, Mat? Will you come with us on our adventure?"

Mat shook his head. "I can't. You all have siblings to care for the farm. My parents only have me. I would be deserting them if I left."

Jordan nodded, glancing at the dark sky. "We should be going. I know I have to get up early tomorrow, but we will see you when you get back from the city, Mat, then you will tell us all about it." Jordan shook his head and said, "I wish I was going to the City of Jewels."

Jordan, Breon and Irrik left, disappearing into the dark, the only thing betraying them was their laughter. Mat smiled after them but drawn by the promise of food, Mat stood up and went inside, joining his parents for a delicious dinner followed closely by bed.

 C   C   D

Mat sat up in bed, yawning. He rubbed the sleep from his eyes and slipped a shirt over his head. He stared out his window for a few seconds until remembering what day it was. With a whoop, he jumped out of bed, tugging on a pair of pants. Running out of the room and down the creaky hallway, he nearly collided with his mother.

"Oops. Sorry, Mother." He planted a kiss on her cheek and quickly brushed past her. He reached the kitchen where he sat down and started eating the breakfast his mother had laid out. He bit into an apple, savoring the burst of flavor blossoming in his mouth. With a ravenous appetite, he dug into the rest of the food on his plate.

His mother came back down the hall carrying a basket of his dirty laundry. Mat saw the basket she was carrying and quickly got up to take it from her. His mother pulled away from him. "I'll do your chores today, dear. There's no need for you to waste your time. You only have two days in the city. You should spend all the time you can there. Jariran is such a beautiful city."

Mat hugged his mother. "Thanks." He sat back down and continued eating.

His mother went outside for a moment and dumped the clothes in a large bucket of water. It was best to let clothes soak for a while to get out all the dirt.

Walking back into the kitchen, she smiled at her son. "Now, don't forget to buy some wool for me. You know I need some to make more shirts for you and your father."

Mat smiled around a mouthful of bread. "I won't."

His mother ruffled his hair. "I know, dear."

Mat looked up at his mother. "Is Father going to be alright? I heard him coughing again last night. It sounded awful."

His mother looked pained for a moment but she quickly masked it. "Yes, dear. He'll be fine. He's a strong man."

"If we had any extra money I would buy him a tonic from the priests."

His mother chuckled. "I know, dear. But your father's a tough man. He doesn't need a potion to make him better."

"I know. But Father's getting old. He's not as healthy as he could be." Mat glanced at his mother. He didn't mention that she was getting old too.

His mother sat down at the table. "Mat, don't worry about your father or me. We know how to take care of ourselves. Just because we're not as young or lively as you are doesn't mean we need help."

Mat nodded and took another apple from the bowl in the middle of the table. He looked at it for a moment, tossing it between his hands, before slowly eating it. He cursed to himself silently. He wished that their farm wasn't failing and they had enough money to buy necessities, like proper clothes and something to help his father. Maybe even enough to fix up their old, crumbling house. *If I could only make some money*, he thought.

His mother patted him on the back. "Mat, dear, you'd better get moving. Like I said, you don't want to waste a minute." His mother bent down and kissed him on the cheek.

Mat heard his father coughing and his mother left, hurrying to her husband's side. With a bound he got up and quickly cleaned his dishes, handing some tidbits to the small dog that lay in the corner of the kitchen by the fire.

"I'll be back in a couple of days," Mat yelled down the hall to his mother. He hopped out of the house, closing the door behind him. He stuck his hand down one of his pockets to make sure he had money and,

feeling the cool coins, started off. He finished the apple, tossed it into a
bush and unintentionally wiped his hands on his pants.

Mat walked down the dirt road, his feet kicking up dust. The sun rose
in the sky, yellow and shining.

Hearing the sounds of a wagon Mat looked over his shoulder. A wagon
was moving down the road, rather quickly too, and in the direction of
Jariran. The wagon, pulled by a strong horse, approached and Mat waved
to the driver who smiled in return. Taking a few quick steps he jumped into
the back of the wagon as it passed him, knowing he would get to Jariran in
several hours rather than at dusk.

Mat hung his feet over the edge of the wagon and laid his head on the
one of the barrels the wagon driver was carting.

His mind at first drifted to the words of his father from yesterday but he
pushed them aside and focused on legends of the past. The legends told of
the ancient battles fought between Good and Evil, when powerful kings and
queens had ruled the land and fought for freedom. As a child, even still as a
young man, he daydreamed of adventure where heroes walked the land and
grand armies fought. He wished he lived in those times when legends
formed. He could have been a solider instead of a farmer. He could have
fought in battles and traveled to lands far from here. He could have been a
name in history.

Mat sighed. The chances of him ever going farther than Jariran were as
slim as him meeting the Princess of the Tower of the Light, the Daughter of
the Nation Caendor.

Mat shifted, his bones jarring from the bumpy dirt road. He closed his
eyes and let the sleep come.

A beautiful woman drifted into his dreams. A woman with flowing
brown hair and gray eyes, whose red lips sparkled and body glimmered.
The woman smiled at him, an aura of light surrounded her being.

A man just as beautiful appeared next to her, but he was dark and evil
radiated from him. He frowned at Mat and reached out his hand, touching
Mat on the cheek. The cold fingers slid down his face and a warm liquid
followed in their place.

Mat jolted awake. He reached his hand up to his cheek, searching for
the blood, but his cheek was unmarred. Realizing that the wagon had
slowed, he looked around. It was noon and wagons were everywhere.

Mat, eyes wide in wonder, stared at the large black walls of Jariran. He
tilted his head back to look up at the gate as the wagon was pulled into
Jariran, a line of merchant wagons in front slowing down the process.
Guards stood next to the grand gate, watching for the suspicious traveler.
Once the wagon entered the walled city, Mat jumped off and gasped. He
had heard stories about Jariran being the most beautiful city in the world.
He never had believed them till now.

Trees and potted plants were everywhere and filled the air with the
scent as sweet as spring and filled with the promise of a wonderful summer.

Tall white buildings towered above the streets, clothes hanging from the windows and flowerpots perched on the windowsills. Temples to the Light and their tall towers rose above all buildings and laid a comforting coat of care and love over the city. The Library of Jariran could be seen from where Mat was standing, it's golden roof magnificent in the sunlight. The Tower of the Light and the Four Towers surpassed all in height and splendor. The Four Towers, ending in golden teardrop tops looked like sentinels over the city, watching their citizens. The Tower of the Light, it's teardrop shaped, stained glass top spoke of Caendor's power, majesty and good deeds all in one simple glance. It was the tower that ruled the nation.

Finally dragging his eyes away from the Tower of the Light, Mat made his way through the street. He passed shops and tried to get a look inside but too many people were trying to get in and out. Women with dresses displaying too much and flirting with handsome men gave him second looks, some even going as far as to wink at him.

He shook his head as the seventh woman winked at him. He wasn't that good looking was he? As he walked by a store with glass windows he caught a picture of himself. A tall and lean nineteen-year-old young man looked back at him. Semi short, curly, dark brown hair needed a brush. Hazel eyes appearing soft and hard at the same time were positioned below black eyebrows. Normal lips and a perfect nose completed his image. Maybe he was a little on the handsome side. But not too much. Not like those lords who looked in their mirrors all day preening themselves like birds.

Turning, a man in ragged clothes with a filthy beard ran into him. Mat and the man crashed to the ground. The man, not bothering to apologize, struggled up and ran, leaving behind a purse.

Getting up, Mat spotted the purse and bent to pick it up. Peeking inside he gasped. In the purse were four golden rings, a pearl necklace and a silver bracelet. Looking around he caught sight of the man and was about to run after him when he was pushed over into a puddle of muddy water. Shaking his head, he tried to get up when he was thrown back down on the cobblestone street. He looked up. A man in black clothes with a silver lion on the front leaned over him. A sword was pointed at Mat's throat. The man's blue eyes shone murderously and a sneer twisted his mouth. The man, who Mat assumed was an officer, reached down and hauled him up, ripping the purse from his hands.

"Well, little thief, to the palace with you, where the King will decide your fate. He'll be pleased to meet the man that has been raiding the jewelry stores of late." The officer snickered. "I hope he beheads you."

"What?" Mat yelled, outraged.

"Don't lie, boy. You stole the purse. Worth three thousand gold chips. You'll go to the King for your trial."

"I didn't do it." Mat tried to control his temper but it was leaking over the edges.

The officer grabbed Mat roughly by the collar. "I said don't lie!"

"Let me go! You have no right to accuse me of stealing!" Mat struggled wildly in the officer's grasp.

The officer smacked Mat in the face. "Quiet! Under the rule of the King I have the right to throw you in prison without a trail! Be careful or I might do just that."

Mat glared. "Do it."

The officer looked astonished. Obviously no one had demanded to be thrown in prison.

"Throw me in prison. It's where I belong, right?"

A cruel grin slowly spread across the officer's features. "Yes. Thieves like you deserve the scenery of the prison walls. I will throw you in prison."

Mat looked around and saw an audience had gathered. He lowered his voice when he spoke next. "But you can't do that can you?"

The officer's eyes darted around, seeing several dozen men and women watching him. The officer snarled. For him to stay in the good will of the public eye he had no choice but to give Mat his trial.

The officer motioned to two of his patrol, ordering chains.

As Mat's hands were forced into the cold metal chains, Mat strained to hear the words the officer was speaking to one of his men.

"—kill him if he gets free. I know he stole—"

"—yes, sir."

"—not right to be walking the streets—"

"—vermin—"

One of the patrolmen shoved Mat. "Get moving. We don't have all day."

Mat didn't try to argue anymore. He knew it was useless. Hands chained, he let his thoughts wander as he began walking. *What will happen to me? What about my parents?*

He held his head up high as he was led through the streets like a criminal. People stepped aside as his guards marched down the avenue. Some people gave him disgusted looks, others pity. A few even went so far as to ask whether he was getting a trial.

Mat shivered. *Why does this have to happen to me? I only wanted to see the city, not the dampness of a prison wall or the King himself. I prefer not to meet the King, especially have a trial ruled by him. Even if I am not found guilty, rumor will spread and people will start wondering if I am a criminal. My parents will be disgraced and will probably double my workload. I wish they would just throw me in the dungeon.*

Mat looked up as the cobblestones beneath his feet changed to white stone. His captors were leading him through a garden, a very beautiful garden filled with fountains and exotic plants. His gaze traveled up to the shimmering stones of the palace. The Tower of the Light stood above all, luminous and dazzling in the afternoon sun. The stained crystal windows that made up its top cast rainbows of color into the sky. It was the pride of the people of Caendor. Mat stared up at the tower, his head craned back. For a spilt second of time, he thought he saw a beautiful face reflected in the glass of the tower's top. A very beautiful face indeed, a face that was as ageless as time itself. He had seen that face before. It had been the face in his dreams. To him it seemed like the face of a goddess. The face disappeared as quickly as Mat could blink yet it left him with a feeling of security, as if his mother was watching over him. It was in that moment he knew the goddess Tghil was with him.

His guards took him through the bronze doors of the palace and into a long hallway filled with marble pillars. They walked the length of the hall and up a flight of stairs, and several more flights of stairs. As they topped the fifth flight, Mat's guards were out of breath. His guards took a minute of rest before they grabbed Mat roughly by his upper arms and dragged him up four more sets of stairs. By the time they reached the top of the ninth set, Mat's guards were wheezing. They stayed at the top of these stairs until their breath was conquered. They proceeded down a hallway lined with portraits of past kings and came to a set of golden doors. Thereupon, the golden doors were opened and Mat entered the room to the Tower of the Light.

Chapter 3
Trial

Janevra sighed as the thief went on with his story. He's innocent! she wanted to scream but knew her mother would disapprove.

Her father sat on the throne, black hair and mustache gleaming faintly, with broad shoulders up straight and green eyes intent. The crown on his head glinted in the light, rubies and diamonds sparkling. The Queen sat off to the right, and Janevra sat to the left.

Marble pillars lined the throne room and a fountain spouted water near the dais where Janevra and her parents sat. The ceiling was made of stained crystal windows, making the top a circle, and filling the room with colored lights. The room itself was a thousand paces long and a hundred paces wide. The floor was tiled in a light gray that, in the center of the room, created a silver lion, a gold sun and a blossoming red rose. Guards stood next to large golden doors, and servants awaiting orders lounged on soft pillows.

"…And therefore I say guilty," her mother finished. Her mother turned, sitting neatly in her chair, and fixed Janevra with a look.

It was her turn to say if she thought the man in front of her was guilty or not. Groaning inwardly, Janevra stood up to voice her opinion. "This man is accused of stealing bread? For what reason did you steal the bread?" Janevra asked.

"This man…" the corporal trailed off as the Princess glared at him.

"Corporal, I was addressing the man who is the whole point of this trial. When I address you, corporal, I expect you to answer but when I ask the man on trial a question, I want his voice, not yours. Now, sir, why did you steal the bread? I want the truth," Janevra said.

"Um…I-uh…" the straw colored haired man began. Stopping to take a deep breath, he blurted it all out. "Me lady, me family of eight is very poor. Me job, cleaning the docks, don't pay too well. Me wife just gave birth and is very weak, because she's not having the right amount of food. I didn't think that one loaf would matter. If you do not think I'm telling the truth, kill me, but I know I stole for a good 'eason."

Janevra smiled triumphantly. "This man stole because he did not have enough food for his family, not for himself. He wanted to help those he cared for. I say he should not be killed or put in prison for any long time, perhaps a day or two. And once he is out, we should give him enough money to last him a year. We should also find this man a better job, where he can get paid enough to take care of his whole family. His wife and new child should be seen by a priest and be healed if possible. If anyone should be blamed, it should be us, for we did not watch for signs of starvation." Janevra finished to a room of complete silence.

Her parents were wide eyed and the man on trial began to weep, showing his gratitude.

Her father stood up, his six-foot height seeming to fill the large throne room.

"If this is true, which I believe it is, a day in prison for this man and, corporal, make sure this man's family is taken care of."

"Majesty, could I say something to the Lady Janevra?" The King nodded his head, and the prisoner went on. "Me Lady, for saving me life and me family's, I'm forever in your debt. I can't tell you how thankful I am. Me Lady, when you become Queen, I know you will be remembered as a great Queen, one who ruled her country with a firm hand and belief in her people." The man swept a deep bow and turned to go.

As the door closed behind the guards, Queen Eliza twisted toward her daughter, fury plain on her face. "How dare you! You are not the Queen yet, Janevra. You will be—" the Queen cut off as the King snorted, his black mustache hairs blowing outward.

"Eliza. I know you're mad, dear, but shouldn't you be proud that your daughter handled this so well? Janevra is not a child anymore and you and I are not young. She will be Queen sooner than she thinks and all you do is get mad at her when she knows perfectly well what she is doing. You saw her take control. She knows when people are innocent and when they're not. She was a queen there. Did you see the guards when she finished speaking? They weren't certain whether to fulfill the order without my saying or to stand and wait for me to speak." The King's broad shoulders began to shake in laughter. "Their faces…" he held his sides as his laughter strengthened.

Janevra smiled in spite of herself. Her father had never said anything like that around her before. He never laughed around her for that matter. Janevra started to giggle, earning a look from her mother. Janevra only laughed harder.

"Look at you two! You should... " the Queen smiled, eyes looking victorious. "Pull yourselves together before the next prisoner is announced."

Janevra stopped laughing, but it took an effort, her face going red in the process. The King's laugh died, but it looked like he was biting his tongue to stop. Both of them regaining composer, the Queen called for the next prisoner. The guards hesitated.

"You will never do that again, Eliza. It is my call to whether or not we will see another prisoner," the King murmured darkly. The Queen paled. Then much louder, the King said, "Bring in the next one."

"Your Majesty, this one was caught stealing from a jewelry shop. The worth of what he stole was over three thousand gold chips," the guard announced.

A tall youth was pushed in, his hands chained. As the youth approached, his head bent, Janevra felt something within her connect to him, as if her destiny lay with him and that if he should fall, she would too. The hairs on the back of her neck rose.

The King motioned for Janevra to speak first.

Pride flooded her as she stood up.

The youth kneeled at the foot of the dais and looked up. Janevra's breath caught. He was the most beautiful man she had ever seen. A man should *not* be that beautiful! As she stared at him, a feeling of pending disaster filled her, and she realized that she needed to save him from whatever crime he had committed.

Taking a deep breath Janevra spoke. "Sir, please tell me, in your own words what happened and why, if you did, steal all this money."

"I didn't steal it, Princess." The youth spoke with a voice filled with some inner power, Janevra noticed as he watched her confidently. He faced three royals, all overpowering, and he glared at them fearlessly. "I was looking inside a store window when a man ran into me. I fell and so did the thief. He dropped his purse as he got up and ran. I picked it up and was going to return it to him when the officer pushed me down, Princess."

"Are you new to this city?" Janevra asked, her stomach doing cartwheels.

"Yes, Princess. I live a half a days ride from the city. I'm a farmer and in the city to buy wool for my mother. Usually my father goes to town, but he is sick and needs rest."

"Why don't you have a priest tend him? Some priests can heal a man, and he will be better before the day is out."

He glowered. "Our farm is failing. We don't have the money."

"Oh." Janevra was taken back. Sometimes she forgot that others were not as fortunate as she was. *What? Did you think he was prince?* a little voice in the back of her head said mockingly. *Can't peasants be that handsome?* "What is your name?"

"Mat Trakall, Princess."

Janevra studied him for a long time, forgetting where she was. He was so handsome. His eyes were breathtaking and his body…Janevra gave her head a shake, pink staining her cheeks at the thought. Coming to her senses, she took a breath and spoke. "Mat Trakall is innocent. No man or woman could make up a story like that in the time it takes to get up here and tell it without stuttering. I would like to propose that Mat stay in the palace and become my servant." She flinched as his eyes flared at her. *Why did I say that? I have no right to say that. But I saved his life. He could be a little grateful for that.* "I will pay you well, Mat. It is the least I can do for having you so wrongly accused. After a month or so, I will let you go and you can use the money to help your farm. For your father's sake, I will let you send some money to him." She was glad she was helping him but the most important thing was that he had been in the city.

Sitting back in her chair, Janevra tried to catch her breath. *No man should be that beautiful,* she thought again.

The King stood. "I believe my daughter is right. He is innocent. And since she wishes it, he shall be her personal servant. This day of trial is over."

The Queen roared to her feet. "No! Never! I will not have my daughter served by some street miscreant! It is unthinkable! Impossible! I will not have it!"

Janevra's eyes flared. "He is not a miscreant. Did we not just prove him innocent?"

The Queen faltered for a moment and then said, "It does not matter. He is still a peasant and I will not have my house soiled by his feet."

The King cleared his throat. "Eliza, dear—"

"Quiet, Richard! This time you are out of place! It is my job to see that our daughter is safe and taken care of and this peasant jeopardizes her safety. There is something in him I don't like!"

Janevra put her hands on her hips. "I am capable of taking care of myself, Mother. We are not living in your day where civilians wanted to see the death of the King and Queen. No, we are living in my time, where peasants are accused wrongly and unfairly just because of who they are. Those we treat cruelly should be given food or money for the problems we caused them. I've been to many of these trials, Mother, and I know that most of the men and women we see in here are innocent. This young man is no different. Our officers threw him down in the street and marched him through the city like an animal. He deserves our apology."

The Queen shook her head furiously. "I still will not have it! A peasant in your rooms? It's horrendous! Think of all the rumors that would fly around! Our family would be in disgrace!"

"Is that all you care for, Mother, how you appear to others? Is that all you worry about, trying to uphold the family name? I am ashamed. How can you even worry about that when we have people starving and others without homes? The least you can do is give a boy a chance to be all he can be."

The Queen opened her mouth to protest when the King held up his finger. "Eliza, our daughter has proven a point. We have insulted this young man with accusing him of theft and I think we owe it to him to let him live in luxury for a while. It is the *least* we could do."

The Queen glared at her husband and sat down on her throne, her arms folded across her chest. Her face was stony and she looked like a little girl who had wanted candy and had received nothing.

The King turned to his daughter. "Mat Trakall may be your servant as long as you see fit, my daughter."

Janevra hid a smile behind her hand.

Walking down the stairs of the dais, she told the guard to unchain Mat.

"Please come with me, Mat. We can talk when we get to my rooms." Janevra spoke with as much calm as she could muster.

CB   CR   BO

Walking down the hall, colorful wall hangings lining the corridor, Mat puzzled over all that had just happened. The Princess was the most beautiful young woman he had ever seen, but he didn't understand why she wanted him to be her servant. When she had first said that, he had been angry. Then he had thought how lucky he was that he got to spend time with her, the Princess of Caendor and earn money for his family. It was an opportunity of a lifetime. Feeling happy that he could save the farm and help his father, Mat noticed that they had come to a stop in front of large ivory doors. Two guards opened the doors and Janevra glided in, Mat following.

The Princess's room, he guessed.

Inside, chairs sat around a glass table, and straight ahead of them were wooden doors inlaid with roses. Walking through the wood doors, Mat's breath caught. The room was not only huge but also lavish. An ebony four-posted canopy bed fit for four people stood to the left. Further on, past the bed, silk curtains revealed a white balcony. A large mirror and table were off to the right and an expensive rug covered the floor. A wardrobe, with one door ajar, sat near the bed. Two chairs stood in the middle of the room, facing each other, with a crystal table between them. A bookshelf covered one wall. Books about the past and ancient scrolls filled the shelves. A door was next to the bookshelf, leading into a bathroom with a washstand.

Janevra motioned for Mat to sit in one of the chairs.

"I'm sorry that I had to make you a servant, Mat. It was really the only way not to get you killed behind my father's back. The captain kills people he does not like when they are put back on the streets. I will try to get you back to your family as soon as possible. And don't worry, I'll pay you well for the problems you've been caused."

"Thank you, Princess," Mat replied. "I can use the money."

"Call me Janevra."

"Call me my lord," Mat said, grinning at her.

She laughed, the sound like silver bells. She smiled at him and then became serious. "Do you know the city well enough to show me around?" Janevra asked. "I've never been there."

Mat frowned, scratching his head. "This is my first time in the city. I know my way for the most part... but I don't know how I'm going to show you around with all the guards."

"Guards? I'm not going to have guards around me. My parents aren't going to know that I was in the city."

Mat jerked, panic overwhelming his senses. "What? You've never been in the city, you aren't going to tell your parents and you've picked me to show you around? I barely know you." Mat scrubbed a hand through his hair in puzzled frustration. *I could get hanged for this,* he thought, rubbing his neck tenderly.

Janevra smiled. "That's the plan."

"No. What if we get caught? I will be killed for sure. This is... is..." Mat stopped, swallowing, at the irritated look from the woman sitting across from him. "Uh... maybe we could work something out."

The princess nodded.

Mat raised an eyebrow. *She's bossy! I bet she gets her way a lot. No doubt spoiled rotten too.*

She must have read his mind. She glared at him. "I do not get my way all the time, Mat Trakall! Matter of fact, I rarely do! Do you know how hard it is when everyone thinks you're stuck up and spoiled? Even though I don't know a lot of people beside the ones that live in the palace, they think I'm spoiled, because I'm the princess. Other girls, who are of noble blood, only want to be my friend because I'm the *Princess.*"

Mat held up his hands in defense. "I didn't mean to offend you, Princess. I'm sorry." He did feel bad. Usually he kept from judging people before he knew them.

"You are forgiven. But let me tell you this. It's hard to be a princess. Everyone expects you to be perfect. My parents want me to know every-thing, when all I want to do is have fun for once in my life." Tears threat-ened to trickle down Janevra's face. "Now try to see me like you do other people and not as a princess."

"I didn't know that it was like that. I thought you were... perfect," Mat muttered, trying to express his apology.

Janevra smiled but it looked pained. "I'll show you where you will sleep, and tomorrow we will plan how and when we will go to the city."

Janevra walked out of the room, Mat following and thinking of the day's events.

 G   Q   Z

Mat rolled over in his bed, not wanting to get up. He had gotten the best night sleep he had ever had. The silk sheets of the palace were paradise compared to his home-woven wool blankets.

Mat's room was small in relationship to the princess's, but it was the largest he had ever slept in. A washstand stood below an antique mirror in a small adjacent room that also held a copper bathtub. A chair sat by one of the windows in the room. The window overlooked one of the many courtyards in the palace. A wardrobe with new clothes in it was next to his bed. Two paintings hung on the wall above his head, scenes of lords hunting in a mountain wilderness.

Mat groaned as sunlight filtered into his room. "Let me sleep," he murmured.

He lay in bed for an hour, letting the time tick to afternoon. Finally getting up, he walked over to the washstand and splashed his face with the ice-cold water. Drying off his face, Mat ran fingers through his hair, brushing it quickly.

He had decided that he liked Janevra, even though she had a temper at times and she was too trusting. He had just met her yet she insisted he take her into the city. Any other man would have taken advantage of her. *She's lucky I despise men who do that to women,* he thought.

Dressed in a white linen shirt and dark green trousers, Mat walked out into the hall.

Janevra's room was right down the next hall. Luckily, he was close or he would have become lost in the many hallways of the palace.

Arriving at the Princess's room, he knocked five times as she had told him to do.

"Come in."

Opening the door Mat slipped in.

The princess was sitting in a chair in the anteroom wearing a short sleeve green dress with a low neck and an earth colored necklace encircling her throat. Her hair was piled up high and her green eyes were bright.

"Good morning, Mat," she said.

"Good morning, Princess," Mat replied.

"Come out on my balcony and talk with me about the city." The princess smiled at him, a beautiful smile.

Janevra stood up, and Mat followed her out onto the balcony, suddenly wishing that this day would never end. *At least it will be a great story to tell my children. If I have any,* he thought darkly.

The sun was near its zenith and the clamor of the city could be heard even from the high reaches of the balcony.

Janevra, her dress swirling around her feet, gracefully moved over to the edge of the balcony and sat on the railing.

Feeling uncomfortable and unexpectedly aware of his simple upbringings, Mat sat at the end of a high backed chair draped in silk. He shifted his weight from one side to the other.

Janevra clapped her hands together, smiling. "Mat, tell me, what's it like?"

"What's what like?"

"Your life! You have no obligations other than that to your family. You can be whom ever you want to be. You can be a merchant, a farmer like your father, a soldier, a craftsmen, anything! I, as the sole heir to the Throne of Caendor, can only be the Princess and once my parents hand over the throne, Queen. I cannot have adventures like you can. I cannot choose my life. It was chosen for me."

Mat stared at Janevra, surprised by her enthusiasm about being anything other than a Royal. "Well...my life is hard. Money is scarce and my parents only had one child so that makes work in the fields even harder. I'm always trying to find new ways to make money. I even considered becoming a soldier and send them the money I was paid. I wouldn't mind working in the wharf. I like building things, but both of those jobs would require me to spend more time away from my family. I can't do that; they're both old and my father's sick. Sometimes I wish I were born into a different family, a richer one, where life wasn't so hard but that takes away everything that I do care about. As much as I struggle, the life that I'm living is good. My parents love me, we have a home, in good years, decent pay and there's always food. Even if I have to work hard to get there, it's worth it." Mat realized he was pouring his heart out to Janevra, but he couldn't stop. "The taxes are never too harsh, and we've been lucky in not having any plagues sweeping the land, or else I would be alone. I suppose, once my parents are too old to work, I'll take a wife and start my own family. Perhaps I could be a merchant or craftsmen but that takes money and time, things I don't have. In the end, I see myself as a farmer trying to make my way in this country."

Janevra watched him somberly. "Any fears of this life?"

"Being forgotten," he said bluntly. "You don't have that problem. You will be a face in the pages of time, but me? No, I will be the 'masses' and never be remembered a hundred years from now."

"If you don't strive to be great, you never will be," Janevra said.

"Yes, but greatness also depends on the circumstances. In times of war, greatness is needed. In times of peace, greatness is needed for those who hold the right position, like royals or nobles. In our time, Princess, there is not room for a 'great' peasant."

Janevra's eyes flashed. "I think greatness can be achieved by anyone during any time, no matter peace or war time."

Mat shook his head. "Of course you would think that. You, who has everything, do not know what it's like to work for something you want, as I must for everything. In order for me to be great, a miracle or disaster would have to occur, and I do not foresee either one."

"I see what you are saying, but there are ways for a peasant to become great without a miracle or disaster. Those who have the Talent in the Art of Magic can rise very high in life and achieve a great deal. Do you have any Talent, Mat?"

Mat shrugged. "I don't know. My father forbad me to get tested. He said shoi were never to be trusted."

Janevra frowned. "In what year were you born and on what day?"

"I was born After the Light and the Dark in the year thirty-nine hundred on the Day of Dragon Birth, the Age of the Second Dragons." The look on Janevra's face alarmed Mat. "What? What is it?"

Staring at him with curiosity and wonder, Janevra said, "I was born on the Day of Dragon Birth in the year thirty-nine hundred. My parents never had me tested either. My father wanted total power of the country and was suspicious of the priests and my mother feared them." Janevra's wonder turned into delight. "When we go into the city tomorrow, we must go to one of the Temples and get tested! It would be great fun!"

"I don't know. If our parents…"

"Oh, Mat, they won't know. More than likely, we don't have any Talent."

"No. No, I would bet we do. We were born in the beginning of an Age on the Day of those said to destroy the future Evil. More than anyone we should have some Talent. You know what people say, people with great Talent are born at the beginning or end of an age." He didn't add the other part to that saying, the part about being cursed.

Janevra grinned mischievously. "Well then, if we do, we won't tell them."

Mat sighed. *I guess I'll have another secret to keep. Wonderful.*

Leaping off the railing and back onto the balcony, Janevra motioned for Mat to come stand next to her. Mat obliged and they watched the city for a moment.

"Princess, errr…Janevra, why do you want to go to the city without guards, and with me, a stranger? What are you trying to accomplish?" Mat asked, his face reddening from asking the Princess such a direct question.

Janevra faced him, her green eyes alight with challenge. "I don't know the people, Mat. I've never met them. You are the only one I've talked to or have attempted to know. When I become Queen, I still would not know them, what they thought or believed. I would be a horrible Queen. I believe the Queen needs to know her people like she knows the lords and ladies, so she can rule justly while bringing joy. To do this, I need to be part of the people. I need to know them and understand them, and I can only attain that through being among them. That is why I need you. You are a commoner, and you know the people. I need you to teach me how to

be one of them and show me what their lives are like. When we do go to the
city, I will also need you to help me search for someone we can trust,
someone who would be willing to help me by sending me reports about the
general mood and feeling of the city. To be the Queen I want to be, I need to
do this and to do that I need your help. I will not demand that you help but I
am asking for your help. Will you help me?"

Mat nodded, his throat clogged with emotion. *She will be a great
Queen, better than Caendor has ever seen.* Mat was proud that she had
asked for his help and felt equal to her, even though he was not supposed
to.

Janevra gave him a dazzling smile and kissed him on the cheek. Mat
blushed crimson.

"Thank you so much, Mat. I promise you will not regret helping me,"
she swore. "In fact," she said, running back into her room and coming back
out with a piece of parchment and a quill with an ink bottle, "you will write
your parents and tell them the good news." She sprinted back into her room
and ran out again with a large pouch that clanked together with the sound of
money. "Along with the letter, you will also send them twenty-five gold
chips."

Mat felt his knees go weak. "I can't accept that much money. You're
the Princess and I am your subject. I should not expect to be paid to help
you."

"Ridiculous. You will take the money."

Mat was not inclined to argue further.

Janevra handed him the parchment and quill. "You do know how to
write?" she asked quizzically, eyeing the paper.

Mat nodded. "My father taught me."

Janevra frowned. "Do you know where your father learned? Not
many peasants I've heard of know how to write."

"No, but he is very intelligent. He probably figured it out on his own.
In fact, when he taught me, I learned most of it on my own."

"That's strange. I didn't think most farmers knew how to write and
read. Those that I have talked to during the trials can barely speak correctly. Where did your father learn, because there's no way he could teach
himself?"

"I don't know, Janevra. I'm sorry."

Janevra waved a hand. "It's fine, just write a quick letter of explanation." She sat down on a chair, waiting for him.

Mat picked up the quill and dipped into the inkwell. He felt Janevra's
eyes on him as he took the quill in his left hand and began to write.

"Dear Mother and Father,
   *I don't know how to tell you this, but I'm staying in the palace. The
Princess Janevra is hiring me to show her around the city and I'm going to
get good money for it, enough to last us a year or so. You are probably*

wondering how I met her. It's a long story, but the short of it is that I was accused of stealing, which I did not do. I was brought up to the Tower of the Light for my trial where I was proved innocent. There the Princess took me as her servant. She told me after that she needed my help. That's how the Princess of Caendor employed me. I'm sorry I can't come home, but I think this money will help us greatly and the wheat I planted does not need any care until harvesting season. Get well, Father. I'm sorry, Mother, but I can't get wool. Maybe with this money, you can buy some quality linen and make a new dress for yourself and new pants and shirts for Father and I.

With love,

Mat

Mat set the quill in the inkwell, blew on the paper, and rolled it up. Janevra handed him a purple ribbon, and he tied it neatly. Handing the letter to Janevra, she gave it to a guard who had appeared some moments before he had finished writing.

"Take this to the Trakalls. They live twenty miles south of here and own a wheat farm." She handed him the money. "Give this to them too and make sure they get it." She tossed him another bag. "Your pay for carrying the letter and remaining quiet."

The guard bowed, leaving Mat and Janevra alone. Janevra propped her elbows on the balcony railing, her auburn hair falling out in small wisps.

Mat stared at her. *Such beauty,* he thought. *It's amazing she's not married or has a dozen lords hanging off her every word. I bet during festivals she's not lacking in dancing partners. Festivals!* Mat cursed. "Princess, the Festival of the Stars is in two days. Will I be able to be home by then?"

Janevra shrugged her shoulders. "You're not a prisoner, Mat, you can leave whenever you want. It is your choice."

"I think I will stay," Mat said a moment later. "I will never see the city again. Why not stay for the festival?"

Janevra laughed. "I'm glad you're staying. You can come to the ball with me."

"Ball?" Mat shivered. "I don't know about that. I'm not fond of lords and ladies. Besides, won't they know who I am?"

"No. I'll say you're a friend visiting from far away. I'm the Princess, remember. They'll believe anything I say."

Mat grinned. "Such power."

Janevra punched him lightly on the arm. "Do not mock my powers."

Mat lifted his hands in mock defense. "I'm sorry, your greatness."

They dissolved into laughter.

As they clung to each other in laughter, the Queen glided into the room. After a stifled scream, she flew towards them. "Janevra! What are you doing?"

Mat sobered immediately, stepping back from the Queen and Janevra, watching the event.

Janevra kept laughing, ignoring the Queen.

"Janevra!" the Queen snapped. "I warned you about that boy!"

Janevra stopped laughing and gave her mother a cold look. "Is laughing forbidden, Mother? Can I not laugh with a friend?"

Mat lifted his head higher. *So we are not strangers anymore but friends. "All it takes is laughter to create friendship," his mother would always say,* Mat mused.

The Queen, her extravagant purple gown covered with laces, ribbons, and frills, clutched the fabric in white hands. "I will not tolerate this, Janevra! You cannot be seen with a peasant in your rooms! All those men who want to marry you will think you are ruined by this commoner!" The Queen's blue eyes shot out sparks, her voice rising with each word.

"We've talked about this, Mother. Stop bringing it up," Janevra said, her voice like a knife's edge.

The Queen stomped her foot, a sight that almost made Mat start laughing. *I never figured a queen would stomp her foot and pout.*

"Janevra, you need to change how you are acting. It's dangerous as a Princess to be throwing fits and demanding toys!"

Mat bristled, near to shouting at the Queen.

Janevra saved him the anger. Her green eyes flared up like fires and her jaw clenched in fury. Her cheeks grew red and her mouth twisted into a dark smirk. "Toys? Is that what you think Mat is to me? He is my friend, Mother, and he will probably be my only true friend in life," Janevra said quietly. As quickly as she spit fire, her whole demeanor change to sweetness. "Why are you here, Mother? What do you want?"

The Queen's face was tight. "Your father wants you at dinner tonight and Mat is to accompany you. Make sure he wears something nice." The Queen turned, her back rigid, and left. The door to Janevra's bedroom slammed shut behind her.

Janevra scowled after her mother and muttered a curse. Mat choked. He didn't know the princess could have such coarse language.

"We need to get ready for dinner, Mat," Janevra said, turning and going into her room.

Mat followed her. "What am I going to wear?"

"If you go back to your room, you'll find some appropriate clothes in your wardrobe. I'll come and get you when dinner is ready."

Mat thanked her and left, walking quickly back to his room. Once inside, he closed the door and strode across the room to the dresser. He pulled out a clean linen shirt, a dark blue coat and black pants. He wiggled out of his other clothes and slipped into the new ones. He looked at himself in the mirror, adjusting the coat slightly. "I'll never look this good again in my life," he said sourly. "It's the only good thing about being a lord, the nice clean clothes that feel like silk."

Mat sat down on the bed, careful not to rumple the coat or pants. He must have fallen asleep because he woke up to someone pounding on the door.

Stretching, he got up and opened the door.

Janevra stood before him, wearing an elegant turquoise dress with a low-neck line and long sleeves. She had a small silver crown perched on her head and a pearl necklace. Her hair fell down her back in waves.

Mat's breath caught. "You're beautiful."

Janevra, red springing to her cheeks, smiled shyly. She quickly overcame it and bustled into his room. "You cannot go to dinner like that." She pulled out a chair. "Sit." He sat and she started brushing the dark curls. "If my father is gracious enough to invite you to dinner, you need to look like a lord at least."

As she brushed his hair, she went over her plan for tomorrow and the trip to the city. "We should leave not too long after sunrise and we can stay the entire day. If I'm careful, my parents should not worry about not seeing me tomorrow and no one will miss you, not to be offending, but they won't. Once we reach the city, I don't know where we will go, but remember, I need to find someone I can trust to bring me information. There," she said, looking at him in the mirror. She had brushed his hair so that it was shiny and hung around his head in perfect curls.

"Ah," she said, smiling. "You're handsome." He didn't have time to respond to her compliment, because she was already out the door, motioning him to follow.

Shutting the door, Mat and Janevra walked down the hallway. Having no idea where he was going, Mat dropped behind her slightly and let her lead.

They came to a large ebony door held open by a guard. Janevra swept in, Mat close on her heels.

Mat found himself in a large room with a dark wood table for four loaded with food. Large paintings decorated the walls and a chandelier hung from the ceiling. The King and Queen, each wearing dark purple, sat at the ends of the table. Janevra took a seat on one side, indicating for Mat to sit across from her. Hesitant, Mat sat down.

Through two courses, the King and Queen talked to each other, making a point of ignoring Mat and only occasionally including Janevra. Glad to be quiet, Mat ate his food with the will of a starving man. His mother was a wonderful cook, but Mat had never tasted food this good in his life. "The gods bless me," he said, staring down into another course that was apparently the main dish.

While the main course was eaten, no one talked and an uncomfortable silence descended. However, once the meal was done and their wine glasses refilled, the Queen turned her eyes on Mat for the world like a predator watching its next meal.

"Tell me, Mat, what is your father like?"

Janevra and the King gave the Queen odd looks, but Mat answered. "He's a simple man, a farmer, Your Majesty. But he knows how to read and write. He taught himself," Mat said with pride.

The Queen nodded. "Yes. Interesting. What is his last name?"

"Trakall."

The Queen paled. "Trakall, what an odd name. Where does it come from?"

"I don't know, Your Majesty."

The Queen smiled. "I happen to know. It's a very old name, like the name of my family. It goes back to the Age of the four Dragon Overlords. I wonder, does your father have fear for your future?"

Mat frowned. "He has mentioned his worries, Your Majesty, but nothing a normal parent would not fear."

The Queen nodded but her eyes said she knew he was lying. She stood up suddenly. "Come, Richard, I'm tired."

The King thanked Mat for coming to dinner and left with the Queen.

Janevra winced. "I apologize for my mother's behavior. She's been acting odd lately and fearful of things she will not tell me."

Mat cracked a yawn, trying to stifle it beneath his fist.

Janevra stood up. "Bed for you, my friend."

"Yes, bed for me," Mat mumbled.

Janevra laughed and they left the dining room.

They walked back to Mat's bedroom in compatible silence.

"Remember," Janevra said. "Tomorrow morning we go to the city."

Mat nodded and wished her good night, closing the door once she left. He fell into bed with a sigh, letting the silken sheets pool around him like water. Sleep was soon to follow.

Chapter 4
Two Girls

Caya de'Ralla rubbed the smooth stone between her hands. The big blue stones mined in Istra had always been her favorite. She set down the stone and tugged at her sister's dress. Her sister, Lousai, put down the black stone she was looking at and joined Caya in the street.

Jariran, the City of Jewels, amazed Caya. Everything was clean and beautiful. The people were friendly and chatted to strangers as if they were relatives.

Caya de'Ralla was a twelve-year-old with a long pointed nose and crooked teeth. Lengthy, light brown hair was knotted and a long purple bruise lay on her left cheek. Her puffy blue skirt had a big rip on the bottom and her once white blouse was turning a light brown. Bitten fingernails were near black and her one shoe turned her walk into a hobble. Smudges of dirt on her face gave her the appearance of a beggar.

Her sister, thirteen-year-old Lousai de'Ralla had big brown eyes and long dark wavy hair. Her freckled face had the appearance of a day-dreamer. Thin lips and a somewhat pointy chin made her look almost pretty. Her clothes, a white blouse and tight red skirt, had wrinkles in them.

Walking down the stone street, they peeked inside shop windows and bent down to smell potted flowers.

It promised to be a good end of the day. The sun was close to setting and there wasn't a cloud in the sky. People walked around with smiles and large purses, probably wanting to buy a gown or nice coat for the Festival of the Stars two nights hence.

Coming upon an inn with a sign saying The Drinking Woman, Caya glanced at Lousai and grinned, an idea setting itself in her mind.

"Do you want to have some wine?" Caya's smile split her face in half.

"What? How can you think of that?" Lousai's eyes grew bigger with each word. "Remember what Pa said? It's bad for you and will make you sick."

Caya's smile broadened as she stuck a hand in her pocket, pulling out two copper chips. "Just enough for two drinks."

Turning to walk into the inn, Lousai caught Caya's arm. "You're going to get drunk after one sip, Caya. What if Ma and Pa find out? Or Jarin, or Teaa!" Lousai squeaked.

Caya wiggled free of her sister's grasp and waved a hand, walking into the inn. "They won't find out." Shaking her head, Lousai followed her sibling.

"If you get drunk, I'm not responsible for you. You can wobble your own way back to the inn," Lousai muttered. Caya ignored her.

Inside the inn, men sat at tables drinking and gambling. A round barkeeper sat behind a bar polishing a mug. Serving girls filled up empty cups and brought food to their customers. A black fireplace looked cold and empty.

Strutting up to the bar, which was a foot too high, Caya reached up, putting her two chips on the sticky counter.

"Two drinks, please." Caya smiled.

The barkeeper, turning around said, "Coming right up."

Caya twisted toward her sister, grinning like a fool.

Lousai, rolling her eyes, sat down at a table by the window.

Taking the chips, the barkeeper put down two mugs filled with a white cream. Gripping the mugs firmly in her hand, Caya walked over to her sister and sat down.

Lousai peered at the mugs with a smile staining her lips, a knowing light shining in her eyes. Caya lifted an eyebrow at her sister, her eyes narrowing. "What?"

Lousai shook her head. "Try it."

Picking up one of the mugs and taking a deep breath, Caya took a swig. Her eyes bulged. Choking and sputtering Caya jumped up and ran over to the innkeeper.

"This isn't wine! It's milk, very creamy milk! I paid for wine! My sister and…" Caya glanced at her sister. Lousai was sitting at the table, drinking contently, a smug look on her face. "Okay. *I* wanted wine. How come you gave me milk?" Caya asked the barkeeper, her pride hurt.

The barkeeper shrugged. "I'm stocking up for the festival and I'm not about to waste good beer and wine on a scrawny child."

"But I asked for wine and you gave me milk! I demand my money back!"

The barkeeper laughed. "You asked for a drink, girl. You did not say what kind of drink you wanted. Therefore I do not have to give your money back."

Growling, Caya walked stiffly back to her table and a giggling Lousai.

"Milk! Can you believe he gave me milk?" Caya said, outraged.

"You asked for it."

Caya glared at her sister. "I was misunderstood."

Lousai giggled in answer, her mug empty, and a milk stain on her upper lip.

They sat there awhile, watching men coming and going. But their attention was caught when a woman walked in. She had long brown hair and gray eyes. She was stunningly beautiful and every man in the inn turned and looked. An aura of power seemed to glimmer around her and her body moved with a gracefulness not of this world. Her clothes were exotic. At first glance, her white shirt and black trousers looked nothing out of the ordinary but when you looked closer the foreign look became obvious. Both items of clothing seemed to shine and show the observer other worlds. Nestled at her throat, tied to a silver chain was a pink pearl that looked out of place. The woman's gaze traveled around and her eyes settled on Caya and Lousai.

She came over to them, her gray eyes twinkling with some inner amusement. "May I sit?" the woman asked. She had a strange accent.

Caya nodded, interested. She had never seen a woman like this before.

The innkeeper came up and took the woman's order, which consisted of a spiced wine and a roasted duck.

Sure, she gets wine, Caya thought.

As the innkeeper walked away, the woman folded her hands and looked at Caya and Lousai. "Now, children, would you like to hear a story?"

Lousai looked up, more interested now. Caya sat on the edge of her chair.

The woman's eyes twinkled again with an inner secret as they both nodded. "Now then. Lets see, a story." The woman rubbed her chin. "Ah, yes, a story of elves, hmmm?"

The two girls nodded again. Elves were always interesting to hear about. Perhaps because they weren't real made them so fascinating.

"The elves are a magnificent race, even after their immortality was stolen. They treasure life and everything it gives. They have a connection to all living things; they can feel the pain of a dying tree or the joy of a flower receiving sun for the first time. For the acceptance of living things they were given long lives, up to four thousand years. Life seems to flow by them, most never live their lives. They don't fulfill it. With their tilted, almond shaped eyes, they can see much further than us and can even penetrate the dark of night.

"Elves are a pure people. Because of their goodness and long lives, they have taken the responsibility of recording the world's past. Even though they are historians they are fearful of change and slow to act. Or so say the storytellers who do not know the elves. This is where my story begins, from the account of an elf who lived long ago and saw the birth of the Six Nations.

"This elf was old enough to have witnessed the immortality that was stolen from the elves. He did not live long after his immortality was stolen, but he lived long enough to see to what use the Ancients put the elven immortality. His account says the Ancients created a sword, an axe, a bow, a knife, a spear, a staff and a shield, each to represent the Six Nations and one to represent everlasting peace.

"The Sword of Steel and Power was given to the Men.

The Axe of Stone and Force was given to the Dwarves.

The Bow of Wood and Stealth was given to the Elves.

The Knife of Bronze and Swiftness was given to the Little Peoples.

The Spear of Flint and Greed was given to the Goblins.

The Staff of Redwood and Strength was given to the Ogres.

The Shield of Iron and Peace was given to all the nations for ever lasting peace among them."

"These Seven Relics of Ancient Bysiniium, so called by the Ancients, were used to seal away the Books of Power which the Ancients had long ago discovered. It was these Books of Power that led them to their destruction because of the Evil the books contained. The Ancients feared this Evil so they added one more ward to keep the Books of Power hidden, so no race could be destroyed by power and greed as the Ancients themselves were. They created the Harp of Song which was later broken by the God of the Dark." The woman stopped and sipped at her wine, which a serving girl had set down at the end of the story.

"Is that it?" Caya asked, disappointment on her face. "That wasn't a story, it was the beginning of a story."

"Yes, but that poem at the end will help you greatly in the months to come."

Caya was still disappointed. "Is that the only story?"

"Oh, no, I have another story to tell you before you leave. It's not a story, truth be told but another poem that fits."

The strange woman swallowed the rest of her wine and began.

"The long eared people, long forgotten, Elves in name their arrows
white flame.
Roughly bearded, stone dwellers, and axe blade are Dwarven trade.
Small and child like is fame, thief and pocket picker are the little
ones blame.
Once of beauty, now of beast, first of beings, Ogres a race never
told their knowledge lost among wings.
Live for death, die a death, forget the peace it brings no sleep in
Goblins eyes.
Bold and daring, greedy and jealous are the Men, a collapse to all
yet a hope that will not fall."

The woman smiled, obviously pleased with something.
"Is there any more, ma'am?" Lousai asked.
"Hmpf, no," she said, eating some duck, the grease on her fingers.
"Thank you miss, for the stories."
The woman nodded, not listening.
"Let's go," murmured Caya. "She's funny."
Stepping out of the inn, they turned left towards the Central Plaza
where their family was staying in a tavern called The Rich Merchants Inn.
The cobblestone street was empty and people were closing down their
shops.
Caya rubbed a hand across her check, trying to scrub the dirt off.
Lousai smoothed her wrinkled skirt as best she could. Their mother would
not be happy that they missed dinner and then turned up looking like a pair
of beat up tomcats.
When they reached the inn, the sun was setting, throwing yellow,
orange, red and purple in the sky.
Coming to the door of the inn, both girls glanced at each other. Would
they get in trouble for missing dinner?
Lousai, shrugging her shoulders, walked in.
The common room of the inn was big with a stone fireplace to the right.
Square tables scattered the room, each of them full with men drinking and
gambling. Serving girls walked around carrying trays of food and wine.
The innkeeper, a round woman with her hair pulled back in a tight bun,
waddled up to them.
"Girls, Mistress Adea does be mad that you missed dinner. Just
thought to warn yeh." The innkeeper had a look of sympathy on her face.
"Lousai! Caya!"
Whirling to the staircase, both girls flinched.
Their mother, a robust woman with a handsome face walked towards
them, her wide skirts sweeping the floor. A frown twisted her face making
her look like a bird of prey. Her brown eyes looked hard.
The innkeeper made a full curtsy, murmuring a quick "mistress Adea" to

their mother then walked away.

"We will talk upstairs," Adea said, her mouth tightening.

Marching up the wide staircase to the right of the fireplace, Caya took a deep breath, preparing for the onslaught of words.

Arriving at the door to their room, the largest room in the inn, their mother jerked the door open and directed them in.

Walking in, Caya saw their father, Joea, sitting in an armchair with a pipe clenched between his teeth. He was a tall man with a rich black beard and broad shoulders. His red-gold coat and baggy black trousers told he was a very well-to-do merchant.

Sitting next to their father on a stool was their brother, Jarin, a twenty-four-year old youth with blonde hair and a skinny frame. He would soon marry a woman he had met five years earlier while in Jariran alone. He was preparing to move out and into the city to build a home and set up a shop; selling items from all around the world. Wearing a dark blue coat and green trousers he was plain, but looks can always be deceiving.

Standing next to one of the five beds, Teaa, their twenty-two year-old sister, was inheritor of the family business since Jarin did not want the merchant life. With long black hair, full lips and a pale face, Teaa was pretty. Wearing a tight silk dress that revealed a nicely curved body, she attracted the attention of a lot of young men.

Caya and Lousai went over by their sister, but their mother stood at the doorway, hands on hips. Caya winced. *We're dead*, she thought.

"Where did you two go?" Adea asked quietly, her mouth pressed tightly together.

"Ah…we a… went on a walk," Lousai said carefully.

"A walk that took you four hours?" their father pointed out.

"We did stop for a drink," Caya murmured, lowering her head.

"A drink?" Teaa said in a soft voice.

"You two were drinking?" Adea yelled in horror and outrage. "You know what your father and I think of drinking!"

Jarin scowled at his mother like it was obvious. "Mother, calm down. They didn't drink wine, only milk. If they did drink wine, you would be able to smell in on their breath. They spice their wine in Jariran."

"Oh." Adea sniffed. "You still have no reason to miss dinner and come home lookin' like a pigsty. What's your excuse this time?" Their mother arched an eyebrow.

"Ummmm." Lousai shrugged. "It's odd but…oh well. You see we were walking when this mean looking guy came up to us and stole all of our money and punched Caya. She was trying to get away when she tripped on her skirt and fell, ripping her dress and making her shoe fall off. The guy must've had his fun 'cause he left."

Caya frowned. That wasn't what happened. What had happened was they were walking along and she had stepped in a pile of poop and her shoe had gotten stuck forcing her to take it off. As for the purple bruise, she had been trying to play one of her jokes on Lousai by scaring her. She had gone up ahead, hiding behind a corner. Hearing footsteps and expecting Lousai to come around the corner next, she had jumped out and hit her face right on the sharp edge of a cart. She tumbled backwards and tripped over her skirt, ripping it along the bottom. Her blouse had already been a light brown from playing in a haystack earlier that day. And for her hair, well, it was always knotted just like Lousai's clothes were always wrinkled. The matter of the money was something Caya was glad her sister was keeping from their mother. The money was not stolen, only ill used. They had lost the money in a small game of dice with a few orphan boys. Caya still believed they cheated. *One of them probably had the Talent and used it to turn the dice in their favor*, Caya thought.

Going along with Lousai's story, all Caya did was nod her head vigorously in agreement.

Their mother sighed. "I'm glad you two weren't goofing off and getting into trouble. Now into bed, both of you, you've had a long day. And tomorrow we start trading and selling in the Grand Plaza. Two nights from now is the Festival of the Stars. And you know that people all around stay up all night and celebrate the day when the King of Caendor won the Battle of the Iwo Mountains, ending the First Battle. Do you remember the story? No? The battle was won on a clear night in the beginning of spring against the peoples from the Nation Angarat, less then two thousands years ago. Angarat was the first pawn of the Dark Lord. Before Caendor had established the dynasty that still holds power today, Angarat was a thriving nation with no enemies due to its dark influence, an influence that began moments after Kard became the God of Darkness, still intent on his quest to conquer the world. He crafted Angarat into the strongest nation and kept it strong through the small wars that broke out between the other nations, the wars that dropped the number of nations from fifteen to eleven. He kept it strong and powerful for four hundred and eighty years, keeping all other nations weaker. Tghil, the Goddess of Light, once more working behind the scenes, picked Caendor as her pawn. She slowly strengthened it to match Angarat's power over the four hundred and eighty years. After almost five centuries, Kard had Angarat make it's move. At that time, Angarat had control of the lower half of the Iwo Mountains. But once the High Lord Arin became the King of Angarat, Angarat's power and land began expanding. Soon they controlled much of the lands in the south that now belong to Caendor and Selkare. Angarat continued to expand under the control of King Arin. The King of Angarat was under the power of the God of Darkness, Kard, and could not stop Angarat's conquering. Finally two large armies met in combat in the Iwo Mountains, Angarat's army verses the only other nation that could defend itself with equal power, Caendor. The winner of the battle, the King of Caendor, made the borderline between Caendor and Angarat the Iwo Mountains. But the nation Selkare interfered and said that since Angarat had been terrorizing Caendor and Selkare for some time, they should not be allowed the land of the Iwo Mountains. Therefore Angarat was made strictly a small seaport nation, with no land near the mountains."

Teaa rolled her eyes. "Enough with the history lessons, Mother." Teaa turned to Caya. "You know she's not telling you stories."

"They are stories to us," Caya retorted.

Lousai sat on her bed. "Tell us a story about the Six Nations, Mother."

Adea smiled at her daughter. "Long ago, when the Six Nations ruled the land with a fair hand, the first fingers of darkness touched the land. A young man arose to power in the Human Nation. He became so powerful that he built an army, something never before done within the Six Nations. Without any warning he conquered the nations of the ogres and goblins. But a young woman born in the Light gathered her own army and challenged the authority of Kard the Destroyer. They fought. Neither side won. The Little People disappeared, followed soon by the Dwarves and Elves. Where they went was forgotten in the ages of time. The goblins retreated to the lower Gangga Mountains where they were killed by some creatures of the Dark Lord. The ogres, only three, lived and still live on the Atay Islands in dying peace. The humans took control of everything the other nations left behind. No one knew what happened to the Destroyer and the woman who challenged him, Tghil. Some say they became the Light and the Dark, but that myth still needs to be proven. We use their names for our gods for unknown reasons but if perhaps Tghil and Kard, the two humans who fought each other, are our gods, then many parts of our history which we throw aside as myth or rumors, are true."

Lousai snorted gently in her bed, wrapping the blanket around her. Caya kissed their mother and snuggled down into her own bed.

Adea turned the lights off and slipped into her bed, stretching out along side her husband.

"Goodnight," Teaa said as she rolled into the linen sheets of her bed.

Jarin's snore soon filled the dark room.

C3 CR ЮO

The next day dawned fresh and clear.

Lousai crept out of bed. She slipped out from under the warm covers of her bed and put on a plain yellow shirt and a gray skirt, tying a belt around her waist. She ran her fingers through her hair to brush it and tiptoed over to Caya's bed.

"Wake up," she whispered.

Caya gave a start and her eyes flew open. Her brown eyes looked around, not seeing.

"Caya, it's me," Lousai said, shaking her sister gently.

Caya's eyes cleared and her face lit with fear. "I dreamed we had to leave our home and an evil man took over the throne of Jariran."

Lousai sniffed. "It didn't happen."

Caya got out of bed and put on pants and a shirt. "Come on. Ma and Pa will be up soon."

"Just a minute," Lousai muttered, scrawling a quick note to their mother and father.

They quietly left the room and closed the door, walking down the creaky stairs leading to the common room.

The common room was empty except for a serving girl sweeping the floor.

The serving girl, a young woman named Tica with dark blonde hair, smiled at them. "Ya'll up early."

Caya shrugged. "We wanted to look around some more."

"The city is beautiful in the morning. Ya just be careful and stay out of the Nobles Square."

"Nobles Square?" Lousai asked, curious.

"All the nobles live there. They don't like it when us common folk go walking on their stone."

Caya was by the door. "We'll be back in two hours if our parents happen to ask."

Lousai followed her sister. "Bye."

Tica waved and went back to her chores.

It was a beautiful day outside. The sun glittered on the buildings and turned the trees a bright green. The sky was clear of clouds and a warm breeze blew through the street.

Many people walked the streets of Jariran. Women carried baskets of clothes or market goods. Men jingled purses and swaggered down the street. Little children ran among the adults, giggling. The city guard patrolled, questioning anyone doing something suspicious.

Caya and Lousai turned south in the direction of the Grand Plaza.

Dodging an unusual amount of people, Caya became impatient. "Let's take the short route."

Lousai stopped walking. "Short route?" She prayed her sister didn't get them into more trouble.

Caya grinned mischievously. "Follow me."

Lousai groaned as she hurried to follow Caya down an alley.

When they reached the end, Caya put her hands on one of the walls. She grasped something, but it seemed as if she was holding on to air.

"What are you doing?" Lousai asked.

"Just watch."

Caya then lifted her feet off the ground. It appeared to Lousai as if Caya was hanging in mid air.

Lousai gasped. "Magic! Where did you learn that?"

Caya started climbing. "I didn't. Some of the thieves must know magic, cause they put it here."

Lousai looked up at her sister, eyes narrowed. "Now, how would you know that?"

"It doesn't matter does it?" Caya said, glancing down at Lousai. "Hurry up."

Lousai bit her lip. She put her hand on the wall and felt the weavings of magic, but other than that, the texture was indescribable. Throwing caution to the winds, she grasped the weaving and pulled herself into the air. She looked up at Caya, as her sister reached the top of the wall.

"Hurry," her sister whispered down to her.

Lousai grunted and slowly pulled herself up the wall. When she reached the top and was pulled over the edge by Caya, she blinked. It was bright.

Standing up, Lousai looked around. The view was incredible.

They were standing on one of the higher buildings but the temples obscured the view in some places and the Theater, College and Library did the same. It was still dazzling. The buildings sparkled in the sun's light and down below them they could see the fountains sprouting water. The Tower of the Light was the most stunning. Its teardrop top caused everyone to tip their heads back and its many colors were eye blinding. The Four Towers surrounding the palace walls seemed to add to the majesty of the Tower of the Light.

Caya cleared her throat impatiently.

Lousai stopped daydreaming and followed her sister.

When they came to the next building, Caya stopped and picked some rocks off the building top. She threw them across. They seemed to skid in mid air and then float there.

Caya grinned. "Thieves and magic make brilliance."

She stepped onto air and when Lousai thought she was going to fall, Caya's foot hit something solid. She continued to walk the space between the buildings.

Lousai, instead of waiting for her sister to cross all the way, put her foot on the magical bridge. Her breath caught as she landed on the weavings of magic.

"Just walk straight," Caya said.

Lousai prayed to the Light as she started walking in what she hoped was a straight line.

In the time it took her to cross the mere ten feet between the buildings she was pale and sweating.

Caya rolled her eyes as her sister joined her.

They passed over five more invisible bridge-like structures before they reached the Grand Plaza.

They looked down upon the plaza's design and sighed. It was Caendor's flag. The design on the plaza could not be seen from standing on it but from their view, the flag seemed to flutter. The picture, made of splashes of water, yellow flowers, and red diamonds, created the flag of Caendor.

Lousai's eyes were drawn to a young woman standing on the outer edge of the plaza. The woman was clothed in a violet colored dress. A man was standing next to her. Power seemed to radiate from them. She lost track of time as she watched them and didn't move until her sister shouted at her.

"Come on or Mother is going to kill us," Caya said, already across the first magical bridge.

Lousai jumped up and quickly followed suit. They sprinted across the rest of the bridges praying that they wouldn't fall. It was harder climbing down the magical wall weavings, but they managed it and were soon on the steps of the Rich Merchant Inn.

The inn had some customers in it already and a glance around told them that their mother was not up yet.

They sat down at a table in the back.

The serving girl, Tica, came up to them. "Ya do be lucky. Mistress Adea isn't up yet." Tica swept off, called by one of the customers.

They both sighed and Caya pulled out some dice from her pant pocket.

"Want ta play Foxes and Birds?" Caya asked, also pulling out cards.

Lousai nodded. Foxes and birds was her favorite game.

They had just passed out the ten cards when the strange woman and man Lousai had seen in the plaza walked in.

Chapter 5

Into the City

Janevra awoke with a start. What had awakened her? Dawn was still a half hour away. Getting up, she went over to her wardrobe, picking out a violet dress with half sleeves, and a black belt. It was the plainest dress she owned. Studying herself in a mirror by her wardrobe, she nodded to herself. The dress was perfect for the city. It wasn't too tight or so puffy that she couldn't walk, but just right, and maybe a dress that a rich merchant or minor noble would wear. Walking across her room and over to a larger mirror, Janevra ran a brush through her hair.

Not bothering to put on shoes, she went outside onto her balcony to watch the sunrise.

She couldn't wait to get out into the city. She hoped she could meet someone she could trust. If she didn't, she would have to go into the city again tomorrow. *I need someone in the city to tell me what is going on in Caendor's capitol and what rumors are flying around. I must find someone!* she thought.

Leaning on the rail, Janevra looked down at the city as the sky in the east started to lighten. It was going to be another warm day.

Janevra looked up at the sky and noticed shooting stars were everywhere and strange colors were starting to fade. *What is going on?* She wondered. This had happened last night too. She had just come from showing Mat his room and noticed strange colors on the floor in her room.

She had gone outside and to her amazement stars were shooting across the sky. Different colors were creating patterns in the midnight heavens. It was a phenomenon that had stolen her breath away.

Coming back to the present, she suddenly got a feeling she was not alone. Twisting around, Janevra saw it was Mat. He was sitting on a wooden chair with the best linen making a soft seat and backrest.

"How long have you been here?" Janevra demanded.

"I'm sorry I woke you up coming in, but I figured that if you wanted to go to the city today, we might want to leave soon. When do your parents get up?" Mat replied, shielding his eyes from the sun as it filled the sky.

"I don't know…two hours after the sun has risen. And I usually sleep four hours after sunrise," she said.

"That means we have four hours until we have to be back."

"No. I talked to my parents yesterday and told them that I'm going to spend some time working on my speech that I have to give to the nobles during the Festival of the Stars. They know not to disturb me while I'm working. I finished that speech last night." She grinned at Mat.

"Is that the dress you are going to wear?"

"Yes."

"It'll work but keep your hair down and you'll look like a well-to-do merchant. But if you put it up you will look too noble," Mat said standing up.

He was wearing a white long sleeved shirt made of fine linen, and black trousers. He looked very nice wearing those clothes. *When doesn't he look good?* she asked herself.

Getting out of the Palace was easy. The servants didn't look up from their chores and when they did, it wasn't their job to look after the Princess. The problem came when they had to leave the palace grounds that were guarded by ten men at the front of the gate, and twenty patrolling the walls.

The lieutenant on guard duty, whom Janevra knew well, was in charge of all who entered the palace and who left it.

"Princess," the lieutenant bowed. He was a darkly handsome man, probably only twenty-five. His name was Dhamom.

"Lieutenant Dhamom, let me pass," Janevra said.

"Apologies, Princess, but I cannot let you. You are not allowed to pass without a proper escort."

"Can I trust you, Dhamom?" Janevra asked.

The man nodded, crossing his hands over his chest, a sign of loyalty.

"I'm planning to go out into the city for a day with my servant. I have never truly been into the city before and I would like to see it prior to becoming Queen. Wait." Janevra put up a hand, keeping the lieutenant from speaking. "I know it's not what royalty should do. But being kept in that palace for most of my life and never having been into the city, without curtains surrounding my carriage, so no one can see in or out, is boring. I will not let anyone know who I am. All I will be is a rich merchant with her friend, walking the streets of Jariran." Janevra looked Dhamom in the eye. "You must swear that you and your guards will not tell anyone about what happened here today."

"Princess, I swear." The Lieutenant swept a bow low enough for an empress.

They stayed at the gates until every guardsman swore on the death of their fathers that they would not tell even the Lord of the Dark.

Walking out of the gates and into the housing of the nobles, Janevra's heart started beating fast. White stone houses had flowers of every sort hanging out the windows. The cobblestone street had a fountain in the middle of it and trees were growing along the side of the walkways, right up against the housing. There weren't many people out, except some servants. It was still too early for nobles to awake.

They walked across a wide but short stone bridge with a glittering stream underneath and trees and flowers growing along side. Green grass sparkled in the sunlight. It was a beautiful park. They had left the noble housing and were now entering the Grand Plaza, the largest plaza in Caendor. A glass fountain in the middle of the plaza was shooting water out of the hands and mouths of two dancing girls, who were dressed in clothes that only covered their breast and hips. One side of the plaza lead to a small park, statues of jade and jasper lined the cobblestone path. On festival nights, sweethearts would sit on the benches, watching the stars and talking of the future. On the other side of the plaza was a large market place where traders from all over the world come to trade their goods. People of all colors, shapes and sizes bargained for foreign items, talked of the upcoming Festival and simply just walked around, enjoying the serenity and beauty of the city.

The plaza was breathtaking. Tiles without any design on them were beautiful yellow. Red tiles formed roses. Blue tiles created splashes of water. White tiles copied the stars and green tiles were vines encircling the outer tiles and the base of the fountain. Only visible from a high point, like the top of the palace, the plaza made a stunning picture. The white, red, yellow, blue and green-formed squares surrounding the fountain produced Caendor's flag, the silver lion in abstract color.

Janevra had seen the plaza from her balcony, and knew it was gorgeous from high up, but it was breathtaking standing on it and looking at the design.

"Come, Janevra, you can't stand here all day," Mat said, taking her out of her daydream.

"Um… where do you think we should go?" she asked, still staring at all the people.

"Did you bring any money?"

"Some, about a hundred gold chips."

"A *hundred gold* chips? Do you know how much you could buy here in the city with that much? You could buy a whole inn and still buy food to

feed your customers for a week and not to mention buy a new wardrobe."
Mat's eyes were so wide Janevra thought they might pop out, which would
be a shame because he had very pretty eyes.

"Sorry," was all she said.

"Here, give me the money, at least it will be safe." Mat held out a hand.

"Okay, but if you lose my money…" Janevra smiled sweetly at him.

"Where do you want to go?" Janevra asked him again, handing Mat the
gold chips.

"Why don't we start with the area I was in before I was taken to the
palace? It's by the Central Plaza," Mat said, tying the gold chips to his belt,
hiding it under his coat.

Walking through the Grand Plaza, Janevra couldn't help but notice how
happy she felt to finally be in the city. A little dance was put into her step.

Coming upon a large market place bordering the Grand Plaza, Janevra
stopped and stared. She couldn't believe all the different types of items and
foods sold in one place. Back at the palace she had a lot of foreign imports,
like ebony and glass tables, but never really thought people living in the
city had access to them.

Motioning for Mat to follow her, she walked into the market. Merchants yelled out prices and buyers clutched purses. Pulling Mat along she
walked up to a man selling a rich scented perfume. He was probably a
wealthy man considering the cut of his red gold coat and black trousers.

"My name is Joea de'Ralla, seller of the richest perfume." The man
bowed deeply.

"Pleased to meet you," Janevra said, her court manners coming
naturally to her.

"Pardon, Lady," Joea said, running an expert eye over her clothes, "you
look so familiar…"

Janevra sighed. *I can't lie.*

Mat came up beside her and elbowed her in the ribs. She elbowed him
back.

"Sir, before I say anything please still treat me like a normal person.
This man here is Mat, one of my only friends," she said tilting her head
towards Mat, "and I'm—"

"Sir, just a second please," Mat said, interrupting her. "I need to talk to
you."

Moving a little ways away from Joea, Janevra glared at Mat.

"What was that for?" she whispered fiercely.

"Do you really want to tell him who you are? Do you know how fast
word can spread?" Mat growled.

Janevra lowered her eyes. "I dislike lying. I…" she trailed off.
Turning back to Joea she said, "Sir, I would like three bottles of perfume."

Janevra paid the man ten gold chips. Perfume was expensive.

Walking out of the market area, they continued on their way.

Janevra frowned to herself. *Why did I listen to Mat? He doesn't control me. But I listened. Maybe it is because I thought he was right. I can't decide my feelings for him either. He is so very good looking, smart and nice to talk to.* She shook her head. *What am I doing? He is my friend and cannot be anything more.*

Janevra was so deep in thought she didn't see Mat stop in front of a tavern named The Rich Merchant Inn just outside the Central Plaza.

"Janevra?" Mat said as she continued walking.

"What?" she said turning around.

"Don't you want something to eat? Breakfast?" Mat asked.

"I am rather hungry," Janevra said, walking back to Mat.

The inn had a large common room, with a lot of tables, and a large fireplace by the stairs, probably leading up to the rooms.

They picked a seat by one of the windows. A pretty serving girl came up to them. Her hair was a dark blonde and her lips were ruby red. Her red dress was very low and drew Mat's eye.

"I'm Tica. What would ya'll like?" the girl asked, glancing at Mat.

Janevra saw Mat return Tica's glance, and she bristled like a mad cat.

"I will have your best breakfast," Janevra said grinding her teeth.

"I'll have what she's having," Mat said winking at the girl.

When the maid left, Janevra smiled her best smile, portraying nothing of how she felt.

"You like her, don't you?" Janevra said trying to keep her temper.

"No, but she did have a very nice body and a ..." Mat stopped as if just realizing to whom he was talking.

Janevra put her elbows up on the table, looking at Mat like a bird would a worm.

"I didn't mean it that way," Mat said, eyes going wide in fake innocence.

Janevra's lips thinned. "I saw that look you gave each other." She sat back in her chair, arms folded across her breasts, tapping her foot on the ground. She didn't look at Mat and kept her mouth shut. *You fool!* A voice screamed at her. *What are you doing? Friend, remember!*

The food came quickly but it brought trouble back.

Tica was carrying the food and ended the silence between them.

"Ya know, I'm free after my shift," Tica purred. "Maybe we could get together."

Janevra's temper snapped.

"Miss... whatever your name is, get out of here, so I can enjoy my late breakfast in peace."

"Lady, I don't care what ya say, it's his choice. Are ya busy tonight?" she asked Mat again, ignoring Janevra.

Mat glanced at both of the young women. It was hard for him to answer. Tica was very close and her low dress revealed most of her milky white bosom. Mat's face reddened.

"I'll make his choice for him. No," Janevra said calmly, her eyes daggers.

Tica sniffed. "Well if he changes his mind, I'll be here." Tica smiled at Mat and left.

"Why did you do that?" Mat asked, biting into a piece of meat, his face red. "It's not my fault you're jealous. Don't take it out on me. I can handle myself. I don't need your help. You don't even know what I like. You can't tell me what I can and cannot do!"

"Jealous? Me?" Janevra laughed without humor. *I am* not *jealous!* "You didn't even know what that woman was planning to do to you."

"And you know?"

"Mat, all she wanted was one night to have you in her bed, one night to call you hers. After that she would not even pay attention to you. You are a very handsome young man, and most women won't let the chance go of sleeping with you."

Mat smirked at her. "How come I don't believe you?"

"You forgot that I'm a young woman and I would not let the opportunity slip away if I was her."

Mat nodded, blushing, and cleared his throat.

Janevra looked down at her food. It was fried potatoes and some kind of meat. She had lost her appetite long ago and pushed her plate away. Waiting for Mat to finish, she looked around the room at the other people.

At one of the tables, two girls, not that far apart in age, were playing a game of some sort. One girl had knotted hair and the other had clothes that were wrinkled. Sitting at another table were four men. One caught her looking at them and got up. He walked over to her.

He was a fine looking man, near middle aged. He had black hair and blue eyes. His only fault was a scar running from his left ear to his chin.

She stood up.

The man smiled at her, running a hand through his hair.

"Why was ya lookin' at me?" he said and she wrinkled her nose, as she smelled the wine on his breath. He was drunk. She detested men like him. She despised them. They were disgusting.

"I was looking around, but I was not looking at you," Janevra replied calmly, lifting her lip repulsively.

"Yes ya were."

"I was not."

The man moved closer, grinning.

"Get away from me," she said in a low voice.

Mat looked at her and got up, getting in a fighting stance, daring the man to continue. "Leave her alone, sir," Mat said, moving in between the man and Janevra.

The man pushed Mat aside. "Get out o' my way, boy."

Mat balled his fists but Janevra held up a hand. "I can handle this, Mat." Mat backed away. "Leave, sir." Janevra leaned away from the man. He was making her eyes water with his wine infested breath. The spice they had put in the wine was too much.

"Why?" the stranger said, leaning closer.

"I don't want to have to hurt you."

By this time most of the people in the inn were watching, the two girls abandoning their game.

"What can you do?" the man laughed.

"You'll find out if you get any closer." Her hands balled into fists. When she was a little girl she had been taught by one of the guards of the palace how to fight with her feet and hands.

The man stepped closer. It was close enough to embrace her. He wrapped his arms around her waist.

"Get away from me."

"No. I think I'll have fun with you. I like young, pretty, women."

Janevra swung her arm and punched him in the face. Hard. The man stumbled backward, surprised, but he quickly regained his footing.

He rubbed his jaw. "Ya'll pay for this!" he spat and ran at her.

She was ready. When he was close to colliding with her she moved to the side and brought her leg up, flipping him over.

The man fell into the table and didn't get up.

She cautiously walked toward him. He was still conscious, but his face had a red mark on it and his lip was bleeding.

"You're lucky you didn't try to kiss me," she muttered so only he could hear. She turned toward Mat, whose mouth was hanging open.

Dusting off her hands she said to the innkeeper, "I'm sorry about the mess, I'll pay for it to be cleaned up." She handed the innkeeper five gold chips from her pocket, and turned to go.

"Lady, wait."

Janevra turned around at the sound and a woman with gray hair that fell to her waist was coming towards her, wide skirts sweeping the floor.

"Yes?"

"Where did you learn to fight like that?"

"I can't tell you."

"Please tell me, I want to know," the gray haired woman said. "I...have I met you before?"

Janevra shook her head. "Do you have a place where we could talk?" Janevra asked. *Why did I say that? I don't know this woman! Is it happenstance that I blurted that out or because the gods interfered? Things have been strange lately. First meeting Mat who happened to agree to show me around the city and now a woman who might agree to help me learn more of the people of Caendor. The gods must be interfering.*

"Yes, follow me. Caya, Lousai come on," the women said to the two girls staring at Janevra.

Janevra and Mat followed the women up the staircase. When they reached the top, red carpet lined the floor and numbered doors were all along the hall. Glass lamps hung from the wall, filling the hallway with a warm glow.

Arriving at a door numbered twelve, the woman brought out a key and opening the door, walked in. The two girls trailed after her.

"Come on," she said.

"Just a minute, ma'am," Mat said. "I need to talk to her."

The women nodded firmly and shut the door.

Mat turned to Janevra. His eyes were full of so many emotions that Janevra couldn't decide what he was feeling or what he wanted to talk about.

"I'm sorry."

"For what?"

"For looking at the girl and thinking of things that I shouldn't have thought of."

Janevra stepped closer to him, her stomach doing flips. "I'm not sorry for yelling at you." He was so close to her.

Mat laughed. "Janevra, where did you learn to fight like that?" Mat inquired. "You fight well."

"When I was young one of the guards at the palace taught me how to fight and use different kinds of weapons. He thought it was vastly amusing to watch a girl learn how to fight even though my mother ordered it. But that hurt! I did more damage to myself then I did to that man." She rubbed her hand.

Mat grinned. His arms encircled her waist and her hands his neck.

This feels right somehow, Janevra thought. *Oddly right. But nothing can come of it, only pain. I cannot allow myself to get close to him!*

All they did was hug.

"One more question, Janevra. Are you going to tell them your real name?" Mat said pulling away from Janevra.

"I think so. I believe that we can trust them," Janevra said, her hand on the doorknob. Mat nodded reluctantly.

Opening the door, they walked in. The room was large and held five beds and two armchairs. The windows were open and a breeze was coming in. Four people were in the room.

"This is Lousai and Caya," the woman said, pointing to the two little girls. "And this is my oldest daughter, Teaa. My name is Adea de'Ralla. My husband, Joea, is a merchant. I have a son, Jarin, who is somewhere out in the city getting ready for his wedding," Adea said. The woman was very formal. "I don't know what made me talk to both of you. I'm not interested in my girls learning how to fight. I don't understand why I asked you to come up here. It was as if the gods had something to do with it."

Teaa stood up with her blue dress appearing like a second layer of skin. She walked over to the window. Mat's eyes followed her but quickly snapped back to Adea.

Lousai and Caya peered up at Mat, faces curious.

"I am Mat Trakall, a farmer." A grin spread across Mat's face.

Janevra took a deep breath. *How am I going to go about this? I guess the best way is just to blurt it out.* "What I say you must swear you will not tell anyone." They all nodded. "I'm Janevra, Princess of Caendor, Heir to the Throne," she said.

Caya's eyes grew big and round. Lousai squeaked. Teaa twirled away from the window and stared at Janevra, mouth hanging open. Adea gasped and suddenly remembered herself and curtsied.

"B-b-ut you don't even have a guard," Teaa stuttered.

"That is why you must not tell anyone. I have never been alone to the city before this day and that is why I came," Janevra said. "Mat knew his way around the city well enough for me to take the chance."

"Princess, why did you tell us?" Lousai asked as she gawked at Janevra.

"Because I need some people in the city who I can trust and have as friends. It seemed as if I could trust you. I took the opening that I had. Sometimes the gods deal us the cards we want."

"Milady, you can trust us." Caya smiled, showing crooked teeth.

"I hope I can." Janevra paused, looking at each in turn. "Now what I'm about to say, you don't have to do, but listen to what I'm going to tell you first. I will pay you well to do this. In return for your help I will give your son, Jarin, a wedding that a rich noble might have. I will also buy your family a nice house. I'm doing this because I need information about the city. I need to know this because as future Queen I need to be familiar with what's going on in my own city. I also want friends, but hopefully that will develop over time. Here's what I will want you to do if you agree. Your family will listen to the rumors and people's opinions. You will then meet Mat somewhere and tell him what you heard. He will then tell me. But one of you is going to need access to the Palace to be able to give Mat the information."

Teaa came over to Janevra and curtsied. "Princess, I will gladly work at the Palace."

"I will assign you a guard that I trust. He will protect you when you need it. I'm sure you will find him quite attractive." Janevra winked at her and Teaa grinned in return.

Mat shook his head as if to say "Women!"

"Princess, me and Lousai will be spies," Caya said, eyes going bright.

"Caya, it's Lousai and I," Adea said sternly but her heart was not in it.

"Can we, Princess? Please?" Caya hopped up and down, disregarding her mother.

"If it's alright with Adea." Janevra looked at Adea.

"Can we, Mother? Please, please, please!" Lousai begged.

Smiling, Adea bowed her head in allowance.

Lousai squealed in glee.

"Adea, you and your husband can talk to your customers. Jarin doesn't have to work until after he is married. For the pay, I'll give you five gold chips every time you report, plus five more for helping."

"Princess, we'd be more than willing to help you," Adea said.

Teaa smiled and ran a tongue over her lips. "I can't wait to go to the Palace. I've always wanted to go there. When do I get to go?"

Adea looked at her daughter sharply. "Teaa, where are your manners?"

"I'm sorry."

"It's fine, ma'am, I can understand why she is so anxious to go." Janevra smiled, laughter bubbling up. "Teaa, you can come to the Palace tomorrow morning. I'll tell the guards to let you through and I will tell the lieutenant to escort you to my rooms. There I'll inform you of your job. Caya and Lousai, you can start tomorrow on gathering information. Adea, you can start at any time. And please tell Jarin as soon as possible about our arrangement."

Mat coughed.

"I'm sorry, but I need to go. Here are ten gold chips for helping me. And thank you again for your help. Until next time," Janevra said as she walked towards the door.

"It was nice meeting you," Mat called from the hallway.

Lousai and Caya waved goodbye as Mat shut the door behind Janevra.

"I'm glad that worked out for you, Janevra. Where do you want to go next?" Mat asked as he started to walk down the hall.

"I would like to visit some of the Temples of Light, but what do you want to do?"

"I wouldn't mind doing that, although I would like to see the Great Library of Jariran. I hear it's amazing."

They walked out of the inn and back into the bustle of the city. The bright sun and noise overwhelmed them after the faint and quiet room. The sun was high in the sky, indicating that it was time for the mid-day meal. Puffy white clouds dotted the sky, occasionally concealing the sun from view and allowing the citizens a moment of relief from the blistering heat.

Mat took Janevra's hand in his own. "What temple do you want to see?" he asked. "I know you mentioned it yesterday but I forgot."

Janevra smiled at Mat. He was so handsome. "The Temple of the Light near the Library."

They walked down the cobblestone street, until they came to the second right where they turned down the street.

Up ahead was an enormous building, made from black granite and inlaid with white marble. It was the Theater, the largest one in Caendor, and the most beautiful. A block away from the Theater was a large structure made of white stone. Broad stairs lead to four huge, white pillars. Two glass fountains stood on either side of two ivory doors. Along the sides of the temple were carved shapes and unknown symbols. A lush garden lined the perimeter of the building. Saying prayers or going about their chores, white robed Priests of the Light walked around or sat by one of the crystal fountains in the garden. The sun caused the fountains and the temple itself to sparkle with a clear white light.

Powerful feelings overcame Janevra when she caught her first real look at the temple. It was a feeling of awe and strength. She felt like she could do amazing things. There was one more feeling, but she couldn't quite get her hand on it. It made her palms sweaty and her mouth dry. *Is it fear? No. Why would I be scared of a temple?*

Mat grinned mischievously. "Should we go in and see if we have any Talent in the Art?"

Janevra smiled, and rubbed her hands together like a child at the Festival of the Stars.

At the base of the steps, Janevra glanced at Mat. He looked back and squeezed her hand, as if telling her it was okay.

Why did he do that? she thought. *I must look a little nervous.*

After walking up more than fifty steps, she had lost track after forty-one, they were stopped by an elder priest wearing a white robe. He was a bald man, with slightly humped shoulders and a very wrinkled face. On his right middle finger, a greenish blue stone was attached to a golden circlet.

"How do you do, my lord?" the priest inquired politely.

Janevra almost glared at the man. She was not used to being addressed after the men. Being the Princess, she was always first asked how she was. It did not matter whom she was with unless it was her parents.

"Fine, sir, and you?" Mat replied with an aristocratic bearing. She wanted to punch him.

"I'm as good as I can be at my age, my lord. Please excuse my rudeness but may I ask why have you come to the Temple of Light? Perhaps you have come to pay your respects to Tghil?"

"We have come here to..." Mat looked at Janevra for help.

"Sir, we have come here to find if we have any Talent," Janevra said.

"You did not take the test when you were younger?" the old man frowned to himself. "But you probably didn't if you were born in the Year of the Dragon. You are the right age for it, and if you were of a poor family you wouldn't have had the money and if you are of the royal family..." the priest mumbled most of this to himself, forgetting their presence for a time.

"Sir?"

"Huh? What? Oh yes. Come this way." The old man waved to them to follow.

Mat gave Janevra a questioning look. She shrugged her shoulders and followed the priest through the large ivory doors.

The inside of the temple was more breathtaking than the outside. Large marble pillars held up an arched top. An obsidian fountain sat in the center of the temple. At the far end of the structure was a huge carving of a woman with gray eyes. The figure had long brown hair that fell over her breasts and her full lips were painted red. The statue wore a lilac dress with a low neck. A pendant hung around her neck, the sign of the Light upon it. The sign was a sun with eight lightning bolts pointing away from it. A staff was clutched in one of the smooth jade hands. The top of the staff was glowing a bright white. The other hand held a sword of some sort.

Janevra stood there, staring at the statue of the goddess, until Mat came up and pulled her towards the waiting priest.

The priest looked at them for a long time before saying, "that is the statue of Tghil, as you know, our Goddess." He looked at them a little longer. "Are you sure you want to be tested for a shoi?" The old man stared into their eyes, searching for something.

"We want to be tested, sir," Mat said.

"Mat, you don't think the King and Queen would mind? I know we talked about not telling them, but I don't like keeping things from them and since I wasn't tested when I was younger—" Janevra gasped.

The priest's eyes bulged, and he squeaked in astonishment. Mat looked at her surprised, but he didn't say anything.

"P-Pr-princess, what are you doing here?" he screeched.

"Quiet! I don't want other people to know that I'm here." She took a deep breath. "I'm here for no reason. I just wanted to see the city." The man started to bow. "Don't waste any court courtesies on me. Just continue as you were."

The man swallowed. "Yes, my lady, um-uh...you said you both wanted to be tested for a shoi?"

They both nodded.

"Well then, my lady, I suppose you already know of the Prophecies?"

"Prophecies? What Prophecies?" Mat blurted out, bewildered.

The priest blinked. "You don't know the Prophecies?"

"I'm not from a rich family," Mat said.

"I asked my maid about them, but she said they were of no importance," Janevra said.

The priest's chest puffed out. "What? Not important...ah, I see. The Prophecies have been forgotten," the priest said sadly. "Would you like to hear them after your test?"

"Excuse us, sir, we need to talk," Janevra said as she pulled Mat aside.

"I really want to find out what these 'prophecies' truly are. But do you really think we should be tested as shoi?" she asked, second-guessing herself, swiftly aware of the possible trouble the results might cause.

"Why not? It won't hurt. We did decide yesterday that we should," Mat replied. As an afterthought, he murmured, "I don't know about a test. I hope it's not hard."

They walked back over to the priest.

"We will be tested for shoi," Janevra said.

The old man wrinkled his nose. "Follow me."

"Why do we have to take a test?" Mat asked, sounding as if he was on the verge of panic.

"To see if you are the Dragons. If the sphere glows a pure white light, you will be the Dragons."

Janevra scoffed, like *they* would be the Dragons. The Dragons were prophesied to come in the world's time of need. When the forces of Dark grew powerful once more, magic of unbelievable strength would be needed again. Considering that Evil was not in power anywhere, the Dragons were not needed. So why bother testing them?

They followed the priest down a long hallway with twin copper doors at the end. Along the walls of the hall were tapestries with pictures of the past and scenes of long ago battles.

They were lead into a small circular room. It was empty except for a round table. On the top of the table was a glowing sphere floating in mid air. It was the only source of light in the globular room.

"Stay here," the priest commanded.

He walked around to the other side of the table and murmured a few unintelligible words.

Noise suddenly burst in the room and a voice sounded. "THE DRAGONS ARE PEOPLE WITH THE HIGHEST MAGICAL POWER IN THE WORLD. TO BE A DRAGON, ONE MUST FULFILL THE FIRST PART OF THE PROPHECIES. WHEN THEY ARE FOUND, THEY SHALL FIGHT IN THE FIFTH BATTLE AGAINST EVIL, AGAISNT THE WARLORD TO SAVE THE WORLD FROM DESTRUCTION."

The noise stopped, leaving Janevra and Mat momentarily deaf.

"Who is this warlord?" Janevra questioned, rubbing her ears.

"He is the one who is supposed to defy the Light. He does not follow anyone, but the darkness within him, which is fed every day as the Lord of Darkness turns his heart blacker than the god's heart itself."

Silence settled in the room like a giant weight.

"This is why we must find the Dragons," the priest said solemnly. He looked up at Janevra and cocked a finger at her.

Janevra moved forward slowly, expecting something to happen.

"Lay your hands on the globe, Princess."

Janevra did as she was told, and immediately felt a warm sensation flood her body. The orb glowed brilliantly white before dying down to an eerie whitish green.

"You're not the Dragon," the priest said in disappointment. "I have one year left to find the Dragons or the year of the birth, as the Prophecies say, will be wrong and that would be the end of all things."

Janevra took her hands from the globe. "What do I do now?" she said, looking directly at the priest. "Why was it green?"

"You will become a shoi, if you wish. As for the green light it means that you have an extraordinary large power in the Art of Magic. If you did become a shoi, you would be among the strongest or the strongest." The priest sniffed, not liking the idea of someone being stronger than him. "It is your turn," he told Mat.

Mat moved forward and laid his hands on the sphere. The globe blazed a white light, and then flickered to the same green Janevra's had.

The priest looked like he was close to fainting by the time Mat moved away from the globe. "Another Green," he murmured. "This cannot be. Two of the most powerful types of shoi in one day! And they came together!" He shook his head. "I'm only a Blue, and I'm the top shoi in Jariran." The priest looked up at Janevra and Mat. His astonishment did not last long, however, quickly changing to a business like manner. "Before I tell you the Prophecies, a brief telling of shoi rank is in order. The Test of the Robe, the test you have just passed, is an important event in the life of each shoi. It informs the to-be shoi of his or her rank, and their Talent. If a light brown glow comes from the sphere it means that the person's Talent is small and they probably will not continue life as a shoi. These colors range from yellow, orange, red, bronze, gray, and blue, with green being the least common. Red and bronze are typical colors and are thought of as rather strong. No matter your strength, every shoi wears a white robe with a colored belt showing their Robe. White is the color of the Dragons and not allowed in the Robes. Black is left out for one reason. It means that the shoi has become Evil and does not worship the Light. Instead he or she worships the god of Darkness, and is considered an outcast by fellow shoi.

"After the Test of the Robe, the to-be-shoi will become an apprentice to one of the shoi of his or her Robe. When they complete their training, they are given the *lapis lazuli*, a stone of a greenish-blue hue flecked with gold. The stone is then handed to a jeweler who makes a necklace, bracelet or ring. In any nation this stone is a symbol of a shoi and the person is to be held with the utmost respect." The priest paused, his face falling. "At least, we used to be held with the utmost respect everywhere. Alas many kings and queens fear our power and that we might try to take it from them. I am afraid it is not like it used to be. With the coming of the Dragons, I'm sure our standing will change for the better but until then, we are only thought of as Priests of the Light who decided to pursue the Talent of Magic." He gazed wistfully past them for a moment, hope burning in his eyes.

The priest stepped away from the table. "Welcome to the Temple of Light. Since Green Robes are rare, I don't know who is going to teach you. You can probably teach yourselves. For a forewarning, you may not be as knowledgeable. However you might learn things a master could never teach you."

"We'll teach ourselves," Mat said confidently.

"Another thing you should know when studying magic is that shoi do not have to memorize spells. A number of shoi do memorize most spells, especially the harder ones, for it makes it easier. Words in magic not only make casting the spell easier but also more powerful. In this world, magic is a matter of concentration. As a shoi, you must think of the spell or weapon you want and think of it in life. You will then be able to create your spell. You might think this is very strenuous but actually it's not. A shoi will only get tired after using magic for a long period of time, such as a day. When this happens, the shoi faints or is not able to use magic for a certain amount of time. When too much power is used in a small time period, the same effect can happen. It takes apprentices a while before they can control so much power and for a while they say words with their magic. Even for shoi of your caliber, you will still need to utter words in the beginning. Any questions?" asked the priest.

"How did you know it was a day?" inquired Janevra.

"A Green attempted to do an experiment that would have killed him but he survived after a full day of using magic. Instead of death he got a headache. It never used to be this way. About twenty years ago we would tire after several minutes of use. Ever since the Birth of the Dragons, things have changed."

"Besides the magic, how have other things changed?"

The priest shrugged. "Pieces of our past that have been hidden for centuries are revealing themselves. Stronger shoi are joining our ranks. We are closer than ever to decoding the full Prophecy." The priest shivered as if he was afraid of what was going to happen. "Odd things happen in the Age of the Dragons." The priest mumbled something to himself and then smiled. "Anything else?"

"Yes," Mat said. "When we want to summon our magic, do we think of what we want and then we get it?"

"Essentially, yes," the priest said. "It's much more complicated than that. Magic is something that is all around us but living on another plane of existence if you will. Those who are stronger in mind, body and soul, who have a will and a desire, and have been given the gift of being able to reach into the plane by Tghil, can reach into this plane where the magic resides and summon it to them. Once they have summoned their magic, all they must do is imagine what they need, want or wish to accomplish and the magic will make it so. In the old days, magic was used for war and sometimes this plane of existence would actually merge with our world for a moment and cause chaos. It happened in the Last Battle of the First Dragons when they fought the Warlord at the Gangga Pass. So much magic was used, the land became littered with unexploded shells and creatures of the magical plane. The Pass is haunted by creatures that cannot get back to their own world, and they seek revenge."

"Can you tell us the Prophecies?" Janevra asked, eager.

"Ah…yes…I forgot…we shall go to the Hall of Shoi. I'll feel more comfortable there," said the priest as he walked out of the room. Janevra and Mat followed.

The Hall of Shoi was located to the left of the statue of Tghil behind gold doors. The hall was long and had a table stretching from one end to the other. Chairs lined the table. Large glass windows filled the room with light.

"Please sit down."

Janevra and Mat sat opposite the priest.

The priest cleared his throat and began speaking.

"In times of need, the Dragons are born. First to destroy the Evil that was power. Second to stop the Evil that will be power. The time comes again when the Dragons will be upon us, gods in disguise.

"The night of their birth will be fire and hell. Burning balls of flame will fall from the heavenly night sky. The grounds will shake and rumble. New seas will be made and mountain ranges will appear. Rivers will flood and some will empty. Deserts will freeze and glaciers will melt. All will happen on the Day of Dragon Birth. One man, one woman. Each will lead a life so different from the other. When they meet, stars will fall. The Lord of the Dark will be awakening. A trench shall open up in the East Sea, binding the abyss to the world. Good and Evil will assemble in the star lit sky and throw the colors of shoi across the world for eight days. All will be undone. All will be set for the Dragons to rule the world again.

"One shall make the Ile, the Children of the Plains, one nation with the golden sun on right arm. One will unite the Forgotten People, the ones of the Lost Mountains, the Lone Islands and the Forgotten Valley with a white lightning bolt on the right arm.

"The Talents of the Ancients will sing in their blood and together in power they shall form the Dragons and be the Dragons. The Dragons will come with the morning's dawn, in a time of need, on wings of hope, they shall begin their quest.

"Together they will unite the People of the World. They will bring together the small people and the large. Nothing will be easy. Everything won will have a price. The answer will appear in blood in the skies of midnight black when the Dragons use their power against Evil. The World will be in the hands of Children."

The priest looked at Janevra and Mat.

"I do not understand parts of it," Mat said.

Janevra did not speak. She was a bit disturbed by the talk of war and Evil.

"The priest whose duty it is to study the Prophecy has not deciphered the whole manuscript. It is very unfortunate that he has not. I fear that the time is near. If you happen to look at the night sky, stars will be falling, and the sky will be filled with all the colors. This means that the Dragons have met."

"I've seen that too. It was beautiful, but it unsettled me. As it is, we need to get going, sir. My parents don't know I'm here. Do you have any books we can borrow, sir, for studying?"

"As a matter of fact, yes, I do." The priest snapped his fingers and four books appeared in front of him. "These are books for the Green Robes to study from. This one has the Prophecy in it if you want to study it," he said holding up a dark blue book. "It was nice to meet you Princess and you, Mat. Good day." With that the old priest clapped his hands, disappearing with a pop.

Janevra looked at Mat and picked up the books. "I want to learn how to do that."

"Come on, let's go," Mat said, as he took Janevra's arm and pulled her out into the hall.

When they came out of the Temple and into the full blast of the sun, they squinted as they walked down the many steps of the temple.

"Could we go to the Library?" Mat pointed across the street at a huge building.

"Of course."

They walked down the street a ways, turning west and coming upon rich gardens.

Above the gardens, high over their heads was the Library of Jariran. It was a building made of pure marble and limestone with a roof of gold. The top of the library ended like that of the Tower of the Light, a teardrop top.

"Information about the last five ages of the world. No other place has a library of this sort. No one has this much information. If it were ever to burn, a lot of knowledge would disappear," Janevra said, her head turned upwards.

They walked up the stairs to the library. They opened the smaller door of copper, built into a larger pair.

The smell of old parchment and books flooded their senses. It took their eyes a minute to adjust to the small amount of light. Once they could see again, they stared in amazement. Books covered every wall, every shelf. Scribes sat at tables and scratched away at the parchment. Several lords and ladies were looking for books.

"Wow," Janevra whispered, looking at the shelves of books and scrolls. It was stunning.

"Haven't you been here before?" Mat asked, not taking his eyes away from all the books.

"No, the Palace has its own library. I was never permitted here."

They walked around the Library for two hours, looking, sometimes reading.

One book caught their attention, but they had no time to check it out for the sun was starting to set. The title was "Before the Dragons." It was an old book, its pages age worn. The most interesting thing was the date. It was ALD 2125 BD SA, meaning After the Light and the Dark, the year 2125 Before the Dragons, the Second Age.

When they exited the Library, they watched the sun set for a moment before setting off. It had been a long day for both of them and they had become closer as the day passed.

"Home is it?" Mat asked her.

"I guess. I wish we could have stayed longer in the city. I had such a great time." Janevra sighed.

They walked down the street with one last look at the Temple of Magic. It was beautiful with the slowly darkening sky behind it and the colors of the sunset making the temple appear like a burning square of fire.

"We better hurry back, or your parents will catch us," Mat said.

They dashed through the streets, brushing against people and muttering hasty apologies. They ran past the Theater and made a sharp turn. The Palace was before them.

They slowed down as they reached the guards. Janevra fanned her face, hoping to get rid of the flush that had rushed to her cheeks. She quickly smoothed her hands over her dress to straighten it.

Mat wheezed beside her as they walked over to Lieutenant Dhamom.

"My Lady, you look... flushed," he said glancing at Mat.

"We were running to get here quickly. We forgot the time. Oh, Lieutenant! It was so wonderful in the city," Janevra said with excitement, clapping her hands together.

"I bet it was," Dhamom said dryly. "What is that, Princess?" he said, glancing at the books Janevra held in her hand.

"Nothing that concerns you...Open the gates, but just a little. We don't want to attract attention."

The lieutenant signaled to two of his guards. They swung the iron gates open slightly.

"Lieutenant, tomorrow a girl named Teaa will require entrance. I want you to let her in and show her to my rooms," Janevra ordered.

"Yes, Princess," said Dhamom, bowing to her as she swept past.

Mat followed her, not getting a bow but a glare from the lieutenant. Mat scowled.

Janevra inhaled deeply. She loved the smell of the gardens. It was so pleasant and reassuring. The gardens were full of different flowers and exotic trees and plants. Two paths lead through the gardens that branched off from the twelve-foot wide stone road.

Janevra and Mat made it all the way back to her rooms without any troubles.

Janevra tossed herself into a chair, threw the books on the floor, and smiled at Mat as he sat down in the other chair. "That was so entertaining! Thank you so much!" She jumped out of her chair and kissed Mat on the cheek.

Mat blushed and looked away from Janevra.

Janevra sat back down, pulling the perfume from her pocket and setting it on the table. Mat intrigued her. He could be so predictable and then at other times surprising.

An awkward silence filled the room. Mat shifted uncomfortably.

"I hope we can go to the city again," he said breaking the silence. "It was—" Mat cut off as the Queen opened the door. Her wide yellow silk dress filled the doorway. She was smiling and her face did not darken when she saw Mat.

Mat bowed hastily, jumping out of his chair.

"Mother...what brings you to my room?" Janevra frowned looking at her mother. Her mother's appearance was never a good thing.

"It's so wonderful dear! It's all I've ever wanted for you! I cannot wait," the Queen said, running over to her daughter. The Queen hugged Janevra fiercely, squishing her daughter to her bosom.

"Mother, get off! What can't you wait for?" Janevra demanded, wary.

"The son of the High Lord Darquin, Lord Ravften, asked for your hand in marriage and your father agreed. It's so…what's the matter my daughter? Ravften is the most handsome lord in the Palace. You should be delighted!"

Janevra frowned, looking at the floor. Her fingers tapped her hips. Not Lord Ravften. He was arrogant and had a dark side. She hated him.

She looked up at her mother, determination on her face. "Mother," she said slowly, choosing her words carefully. "I'm not going to marry him, I don't love him. He only wants to marry me because I'm the Princess. I don't want to have a marriage like yours and Father's." Janevra stuck out her chin, her father's stubbornness setting in.

"What?" The Queen took a step back.

"I'm not going to marry him."

"Yes, you are, dear," the Queen said, her voice calm.

"No, I won't. Why are you forcing this on me when it was you who has prepared me to rule alone?"

"I have my reasons. But you are going to marry him no matter what you want! Your father said that he wants Ravften to be the king after him. The marriage date is in eight months. Good night!" The Queen stormed out of the room, slamming the door behind her.

Janevra turned in rage and ran out onto the balcony. She sat down on a chair, her head in her hands. Tears rolled down her cheeks.

She looked up as Mat walked towards her, concern on his face. "I ca-can't marry him! I-I hate him. I…" she trailed off as a new group of tears spilled out of her eyes. She buried her head in her arms.

"I'm sorry. I don't want you to get married either."

Janevra looked up at him, her tear stained face shining in the diminishing light. She stood up and flung her arms around him, crying into his shoulder.

"Thank you," she muttered into his shirt.

"For what?" Mat asked putting his arms around her.

"For saying that."

"Oh." Mat lifted her chin with his hand. He gently wiped away her tears. When he took his hand away, he stared at her.

Janevra flushed under his look. Slowly she felt the seed of rebellion grow within her and her face hardened.

Mat frowned. "Janevra, promise me that you won't do anything you will regret later?"

"I cannot promise that…shall we study those magic books?" She looked up at him in all innocence.

"I suppose," he said, relenting.

Janevra went inside to get the books. She came out quickly, carrying a book and a candle. She found Mat leaning on the rail of the balcony talking to himself. She stopped to listen.

"Why am I so upset that she is getting married? And why don't I want to go home? My family needs me! Mat, you are fool!"

Janevra smiled. "Some people think it's not good to talk to yourself."

Mat whirled around, his face a brilliant red. "Do they?" he croaked.

Janevra laughed and sat down in a chair. She pulled her knees under and looked very unladylike. She propped one of the books up against her knees. It was a thick book with a beaten up cover. The title was *Fire, Light and Words of Command.*

"Listen to this... '*Mobuia pyjjia...glowing ball of fire.*' Do you want to try it?" Janevra asked.

"Why not?"

Janevra concentrated, closing her eyes, as the priest had told her. Suddenly the feeling of something strange and alien filled her. It was the plane of magic. Following the priest's instructions, she pictured a small ball of flame floating in her palm.

Opening her eyes she saw a small flame in her hand. Mat's was identical.

"Oh...wow...I didn't think it would work. This is amazing! And we didn't say the words," Janevra said amazed.

For the rest of the night the two practiced different spells. They learned spells that could lift an object up and fly towards them. They learned things such as heat spells. They mastered light, which made them able to shoot it from their fingers and zap things, leaving a person tingling. Mat found this out when he bent to pick up another book. Janevra accidentally shot a line of yellow light at him. Mat had yelped, his hands clasping his bottom while Janevra giggled.

They finished the book but had been too tired to move and had fallen asleep in the chairs.

Before falling asleep, Mat murmured a question that would have disturbed her if she had not been so tired. "Why is it so easy?" he asked.

Janevra, in return, only murmured, "I don't know."

Chapter 6
Marriage

Janevra awoke six hours after sunrise. Rubbing her eyes from sleep, she stood and stretched, working out the sore spots from sleeping in the chair.

Mat lay sprawled in the chair next to her, snoring.

Janevra walked into her room and shut the door. The servants had filled up a copper tub, knowing she would want a bath come morning. Stripping, she felt the water. It was cold. Using a heat spell, she warmed the water.

She washed herself quickly, using soap to clean off the dirt and sweat from yesterday.

Feeling clean and refreshed, Janevra wrapped a towel around herself. She pulled out a low cut neck, dark blue dress. She slipped into it.

Brushing her auburn hair, she studied herself in the mirror. Tonight was the Festival of the Stars. And it was ruined by the fact that she had to get married. But she wasn't going to get married if she could help it. *Never will I marry that fool of a lord.*

She sighed and walked back outside. Mat was still snoring.

Janevra rolled her eyes. Men. She walked over to him and poked him. He snorted.

She poked him harder.

He slapped at her hand and grunted. Still sleeping.

She went behind his chair and watched him for a moment.

Darting back inside, she came out with rouge and eye color. She hadn't done this for a long time but it was so fun. Sometimes her child inside got the best of her common sense.

It only took her a second to dab some rouge and eye color onto his face.

Grinning, she stood in front of him. *Wow, he would be an ugly woman,* she thought, giggling lightly. *Now its time for the fun.*

"MAT! Wake up!" she shouted.

He woke with a start and fell out of the chair.

"Wha...Wha oing on?" he asked groggily.

Janevra snickered. This was so much fun.

Mat shook his head and looked up at her. "Er...hello." He stood up.

Janevra laughed harder.

"What? What's so funny?" he asked bewildered.

Janevra stifled another burst of giggles with her hand. He looked like a confused and very ugly woman.

"There is a tub in my room. You can go and wash if you want."

"Okay." He looked at her, perplexed, and walked into her room, shutting the door.

Janevra sat down, not able to contain her laughter anymore.

A yelp sounded from behind the door and she dissolved once again in giggles.

Half an hour later Mat came out. He was standing very straight and his lips were in a thin line. He had very pink cheeks where he had rubbed to get the rouge off. He walked over to the railing and stared straight ahead.

"Mat, it was only a joke." Janevra glanced at him, uncertain.

"I don't care."

"Now if you can't..." she broke off as Mat laughed. "What?"

"Do you think you could try a little better next time? Like put me in a dress or something? That was pathetic," Mat teased.

Janevra joined him in his laughter. She *would* try better next time.

"Mat, I need to go and talk to my father regarding the marriage. Will you come with me?"

"For moral support, of course I will."

Janevra walked ahead of Mat. It was impolite for a servant to walk next to or ahead of a royal.

Going up a flight of stairs and turning around several corners, they made it to the King's room. Janevra tapped once and walked in.

The room was large with huge windows at one end. Intricate paintings lined the walls. Chairs and tables holding vases of flowers sat here and there.

The King was sitting in a high backed chair, sipping wine.

"I was wondering when you were going to come and talk to me," said the King, twitching his mustache.

Janevra exploded. "Father, I don't want to get married to that—that *lord*! I can't stand him! I can't marry him, Father! I won't marry him!"

Janevra snuck a peek at Mat. He was standing behind her, stunned. She grinned inwardly. It was probably a shock to him to see someone shout at the King. Turning her attention back at her father, Janevra set her jaw stubbornly.

"Daughter," the King said, standing up, his presence seeming to fill the room. "You will marry him, because it is best for the kingdom. He is smart and he will rule this kingdom with a firm hand."

Janevra felt heartbroken. She was about to retort back when someone knocked on the door.

"Come in," said her father as he sat back down.

A tall man entered. He had black hair and well muscled arms. His bright morning blue eyes could have charmed a baby bird from its nest. His dark blue coat and black trousers emphasized his eyes even more. He was good featured, Janevra had to admit, but she always got shivers down her back when the man entered a room she was in.

"My Lord King." The man bowed in the doorway and swept past Mat. "My lady, what a pleasure it is to see you this early in the morning. I believe my day just became brighter."

Janevra's lip curled. "Good morning, Lord Ravften."

Ravften turned his attention back to the King. "Majesty, I came to talk to you about the marriage."

"Yes, so did Janevra." The King twitched his mustache in amusement.

"Then we can set the date, my King," said Lord Ravften.

"My mother has already set the date, Ravften." Janevra practically spat his name and her green eyes blazed hotter than a forge.

"Well then, since that is settled, Majesty, may I talk to my future wife?" Ravften asked, his voice cheerful.

"Why certainly, my lord. I'm sure she will let you talk to her in her room. I must attend some important matters with my generals."

Janevra glowered at her father.

The way back to Janevra's rooms was very uncomfortable for her. Her back was rigid as she walked and she could feel Mat's eyes on them as he walked behind them. Ravften talked idly about the festival and court gossip, unaware of the discomfort of the others.

They reached Janevra's room and entered the anteroom.

Janevra sat down in a chair and called for a servant to bring wine.

Ravften sat in the chair next to her, motioning for the servant to pour the wine and leave.

"Why didn't you just send this boy to get the wine?" he asked.

Janevra watched Mat bristle. "This *boy* is Mat," Janevra replied tartly, turning her green stare back to Ravften.

"It has a name? In that case, leave, Mat, your presence is not wanted," Ravften said.

"Mat is not going anywhere unless I ask him to," Janevra said her lips forming a tight line. "Mat, could you please wait for me in my room?"

Mat walked into Janevra's room and closed the door.

"Thank you, Janevra, but in the future, as my wife, you will do as I say. And when I want something, you will do what I want," Ravften said smugly.

"I am not your wife nor ever will be."

"But you still will do as I tell you. I am the heir to the throne."

"You are not the heir."

"If I am not, then why did the King pick me as your husband? If you were the true heir, he would have said you could pick your own husband. However, since women cannot rule alone in Caendor, he picked me," Ravften said, tapping his chest.

Janevra glared at him. "Why do you want to be king, Ravften? I know it's not only for the power. What are you planning?"

Ravften laughed deeply. "Are you afraid of what I might do to your precious country, Princess?"

"I am afraid you will destroy it and raze this city to ashes."

Ravften looked at her, his blue eyes bright. He lifted his hand and the wine glass floated towards him. He grasped it delicately and took a sip.

Janevra's breath caught. "You know magic? How? When did you learn?"

Ravften set down the glass. "My father has always had an interest in claiming the throne one day, but he was too weak to do anything. He made sure I was ready to be crowned king and he especially made sure I had hidden talents to help bring me the throne."

A sense of dread overcame Janevra. She rubbed her forehead, wincing. "My parents. What did you do to them?"

Ravften smiled cruelly. "One of my many Talents in the Art is charming people. I find I can get whatever I want when I use a little magic."

"You enchanted them!" Janevra rose, furious.

Ravften waved his hand. "Only your father. Your mother loves me so much, I didn't need to do anything. The only thing I need to make me the next true King of Caendor is your hand in marriage. Marry me, my love," he cooed.

"If you want this throne so badly, why didn't you enchant me? That would have been the easiest way to go."

"I couldn't," Ravften said, a note of anger seeping into his voice. "At first I thought you were a very powerful shoi, warded against any invasions of the mind. But I have never seen or felt you summon magic. Then I guessed that at your birth, your parents had a shoi put a spell on you that would protect you against those with darker intentions. I checked the history books to see if any such thing had been done and I couldn't find anything, only pages concerning the King and Queen's fear of shoi. My curiosity in this matter has not been satisfied. Why can't I enchant you, my sweet? What powers do you have? I would like to know of them before our marriage so I can put them to good use. And you will marry me, your parents will make sure it happens."

"I will not marry you. Now leave my room," Janevra said standing up. She didn't think she could break the spell he put on her parents, she wasn't learned enough in the Art to challenge a full fledge shoi. But she would hold off the wedding until she could overcome the magic he had put on her father. Then Ravften would be sorry.

Ravften stood and met her eyes. "No. I do not think I want to leave yet. I want to have some fun with my future wife. When the war comes, I won't have much time to spend with you."

Janevra's eyes widened as Ravften moved close to her.

"Get away from me." Janevra moved out of her chair and put her back up against the wall of the anteroom.

"No." Ravften's face was very close, the wine on his breath heavy and spicy.

Janevra tried to push him away but he caught her hands and pinned her against the wall.

"If you go along with it, you'll have fun," he breathed.

She struggled more and was about to use a spell when he kissed her and moved one of his hands down the front of her dress. Her concentration snapped and she screamed, but the sound was muffled against his lips. Janevra tried to push away but he was too strong and he pushed her against the wall, kissing her. He rubbed his hands across her breasts.

ભ   ભ   ૪ઝ

Mat waited in Janevra's room. He had his ear pressed up against the door, listening to their conversation. When nothing was spoken in a long time, Mat opened the doors and saw Janevra up against the wall, Ravften touching her.

"Get your hands off her!" Mat yelled and charged at Ravften.

Janevra saw him coming and pulled her leg up between Ravften's legs. Ravften dropped her and doubled over in pain. Janevra, wrapping her arms around herself, ran into her rooms.

Mat hit Ravften in the stomach, hard.

Ravften was knocked down on the floor but he stood quickly. He spread his fingers out and Mat went flying into the wall.

Dazed, Mat shook his head, realization filling him with horror. Ravften was a shoi. He summoned his own magic, feeling the powers of another plane filling his blood. Envisioning a wave of air, Mat aimed his fingers at Ravften but a shield reflected his attack.

"The servant boy knows some magic. How impressive," Ravften sneered.

Mat clenched his jaw, letting the mocking words flow over him. "Janevra will never give you the throne."

Ravften laughed. "I will be King of Caendor and I will not let some peasant boy stand in my way." He pointed his finger at Mat, a thin line of fire shooting out of it.

Mat quickly erected a shield. It was a weak one, but it did the job. The fire Ravften had shot at him slowly melted into the shield. Mat, gathering more magic into his being, shoved a ball of air at Ravften. Ravften failed to notice what was happening and flew against the wall.

Mat grabbed a glass of wine as Ravften slid down the wall. Ravften was about to stand when Mat hit him over the head with the wine glass, using a hint of magical strength. Ravften slumped, passing out, jagged shards of glass in his head.

Mat called for a servant to come and get Ravften, telling the servant, "Lord Ravften had too much wine and passed out."

When the anteroom was cleaned up, Mat went into Janevra's rooms. He found her on her bed, crying.

"I hate him!" she screamed at her pillow.

"Janevra, I'm sorry. I shouldn't have left."

Janevra looked up at Mat, her face red and wet. "I hate him."

"Why don't you go to sleep? You'll feel better." Mat closed the door and went out onto the balcony. He stared down into the city, letting his magic go slowly.

What have I gotten myself into? Court rivalries, evil men trying to take the throne, dangerous captains, fearful queens, and a princess who is the center of it all. Not to mention Prophecies becoming true and rumors of a future war. Mat shivered. *My father was right, things are happening that don't bode well for the future.*

Chapter 7
The Festival of the Stars

Janevra slept for seven hours, while Mat sat on the balcony and thought. During that time Teaa had come and Mat told her all that she needed to know and do. It wasn't much. Janevra wanted Teaa to act as a maid in the Palace and deliver the information from Caya and Lousai to her and then tell Janevra what Teaa herself had heard.

When Janevra came out, she had changed into new clothes. It was a dark red gown that spread out slightly after the waist with a low neck and sleeves that stopped at her elbows. A pearl necklace was around her throat. Her hair was piled on her head into a beautiful arrangement, which Mat could not name. She had a silver crown with rubies and pearls on her head. She seemed to have forgotten the ordeal.

"What's the occasion?"

"The Festival of the Stars is in two hours. You should get dressed too." She tossed him a red coat with gold leaves working their way up the sleeves, and black trousers.

How could I forget? he thought, and then glanced at Janevra. *Question answered.*

Mat dressed as Janevra waited for him. The red coat fit snugly and the trousers were a little bit too big but he didn't say anything to her as they walked to the Great Hall together.

"What is this speech you must give?" Mat asked as they made their way down a staircase.

"You'll see," was the reply.

"Okay then…what are we going to do?"

"First, I am going to give my speech and most likely the lords and ladies will dance." At this she rolled her eyes. Apparently she did not care for dancing. "Then I, as the Princess, have to ride through the city and wave to the people. There is usually a parade and fireworks. Then we dance again in the Grand Plaza."

"What about eating?"

"Oh, everyone eats when we go into the city. That's why people look forward to this festival…everyone bakes something and brings it to the Grand Plaza."

"I thought you hadn't been to the city before yesterday?" Mat said, cocking his head at her.

"I haven't. Being nineteen, I'm finally able to attend. My parents would not let me until I turned nineteen. Besides, I can't talk to people with them knowing it's me. People would never tell me how they felt about the King. They would lie in hopes of pleasing me with some fake happiness. "

When they reached the Great Hall, it was decorated in banners of all the lords and ladies. Three thrones sat at one end of the hall at which sat the King and Queen. People were already dancing to the sweet slow music.

Applause erupted in the Hall as they walked in. Nobles stormed around Janevra and Mat, women in beautiful dress and men in charming coats.

"This is my friend, Lord Mat Trakall. He is visiting from the country."

This seemed to suit them. They asked him questions and wondered where he stood on the political platform. Janevra had to answer most of the questions. Occasionally he got to answer a few on his own when Janevra let him. But Mat was sure they knew who he was. Or at least the men did, the women just fluttered their fans at him and smiled seductively.

When they finally got to the front of the Hall, everyone quieted down.

Janevra stood in front of her parents, facing the audience. Mat moved around until he was in the front of the crowd, looking up at Janevra.

"I'm sure that by now you have all heard of the marriage. Unfortunately Lord Ravften is not here today, for the reason of too much drink, I daresay." Janevra glanced at Mat and a smile twitched around the edges of her mouth. "I'm glad he is not here today due to the fact of the announcement I am going to make. My mother has set the date in eight months. I would like it in four years for the reason being, do you not think that your princess should be more educated and more mature before she gets married in order to help her husband?" At these words the ladies chuckled and the men snorted.

"But don't you agree?" Janevra repeated.

There was a loud "yes" and then clapping.

"One more question. As part of the people of Caendor, do *you* think that Lord Ravften is a suitable husband for me and a good king for this country?"

The Hall was filled with murmurs.

Mat had to smile despite himself. Janevra was clearly trying to show her father what people thought of Ravften and no doubt praying they did not like him.

A lady Janevra's age, with black hair and a yellow silk dress spoke up. "I do not think Lord Ravften would fill the requirements needed." Some applause sounded.

A middle-aged man spoke. "I think that he would make a fine king. Yet I wonder what you think, my Princess?"

"I think he would be a *fine* husband and king."

A scattered applause broke out at this, while others frowned and shook their heads, hearing her sarcasm.

"Thank you, everyone, for your time. And now I think its time for the party," Janevra said, smiling with brilliance at the crowd.

Music from somewhere started up again and the lords and ladies chose partners to begin a dance that would have had Mat in circles.

Janevra motioned Mat to come with her up onto the dais.

He went up, if reluctantly, beside her and murmured "nice speech" in her ear. She wrinkled her nose at him.

The King smiled as Janevra curtsied and Mat bowed. The King was wearing a black coat inlaid with silver lions on the collar and his crown was perched on flat, black hair that was sprinkled with gray.

"That was a very well planned little speech you had there, my daughter. But you are still marrying him."

"I know, I know," Janevra said, as she sat down. Mat stood next to her.

The Queen, wearing a lavender silk gown with her hair tied up in a bun, her crown placed neatly on her head, looked disapproving at Mat. "My daughter, you seem to have accepted the fact that you are getting married. Am I right in saying so?"

"Yes, Mother, you are," Janevra smiled, but it was a forced smile according to Mat.

Her mother seemed to believe this and nodded. "However, why wait four years, Janevra. You are easily the most educated woman, you're probably more educated than most men, in the Northern Kingdom. You can't learn much more."

"I have my reasons, Mother," Janevra replied.

The Queen sighed. "At least you're marrying him."

"My Queen, would you like this dance?" the King said, turning to his wife.

"Most gladly."

They walked off together and into the crowd of twirling people.

This gave Mat the chance he wanted.

"Janevra, I have already asked you this question. *Are* you planning something?"

Janevra looked at him then nodded her crowned head.

"What?"

"You will know soon."

And she wouldn't say any more.

They sat silently for a while.

"Mat, will you dance with me?"

"I thought you did not enjoy dancing."

"I don't but my parents expect me to dance. They don't think it is right for a princess not to dance." She waved her fingers around, clearly disgusted.

"In that case, I will most gladly," Mat said in a low voice like that of the Queen.

Janevra laughed.

Arm in arm, they walked down the stairs leading to the dais.

As they reached the dance floor Mat stopped. "Uh…I don't know the steps," Mat said, biting his lip.

"Don't worry, I'll show you. It's not that hard." Janevra smiled at him.

Janevra tried to show him the easy way by simply doing the common foot movement for any dance, but Mat kept stepping on her feet or bumping into other people.

"Janevra, I can't do this. You have to be born a noble to do this," Mat said throwing his hands up into the air.

So they went to the edge of the dance floor and watched the dancers twirl in their beautiful clothes and colors.

The music stopped soon after and the King stood up on the dais. "Lords and Ladies, I think it is time for the parade."

Applause erupted as did un-lady and gentlemen-like cheering.

Janevra poked Mat in the ribs. "Come with me. We need to get to the carriage before everyone starts to leave."

Mat followed Janevra out of the Great Hall, and through the front doors of the Palace. And there waiting for them was a golden carriage, pulled by four large white horses. There was not a top on the carriage.

Mat jumped in, pursued by Janevra, the carriage wobbling with their added weight.

The man in the front, wearing black attire, flicked his whip and the carriage started to move.

They drove through the gates and were hit with a burst of noise.

It seemed like the whole city was there. Children hopped up and down waving to the carriage. Young women swayed when they walked, attracting the eyes of young men. The elders applauded as the carriage went by. Everyone was wearing their best.

Lights had been put up in the trees lining the street, lighting the way for the parade. Flowerpots were standing on windowsills, their blossoms hanging over the edge.

Mat looked behind him and saw jugglers juggling torches and knives. Mythical creatures, made of linen, such as dragons and unicorns walked the street, making the children go crazy with glee.

Mat turned around, conscious of all the eyes on him and Janevra. He glanced at Janevra. She was waving to the people and they cheered harder. A young girl came up to the carriage at a run and gave Janevra a flower. Janevra smiled and lifted the girl up into the carriage, setting her on her knee. The girl laughed in excitement.

Mat, waving now, helped another child up into the carriage. The boy, perhaps six, cocked his head at Mat and asked, "R you her sweetie hart?" Mat, blushing furiously, shook his head.

Janevra was having a wonderful time. She let the children ride with her for a short while before letting another take their turn.

The parade, Mat had to admit, was short but fun. They stopped at the Grand Plaza where more people were dancing to the type of music Mat had grown up with. He felt more at home than he had in days.

Mat jumped out of the carriage and helped Janevra down, even though she didn't need it.

The center part of the plaza was filled with dancers, while the edges of the plaza had tables of food. Jugglers were at one end, attracting a crowd of children.

"Janevra, will you dance with me? I promise it will be much more enjoyable than how the nobles dance," Mat asked.

"I don't know the steps." Janevra looked at him uncertainly.

"You don't need to, just let me lead you." Mat took her by the hand.

They walked onto the plaza. Some people noticed Janevra and bowed or curtsied. Others paid no attention to them.

"What do I do?" Janevra asked him, her face glowing with joy.

Mat moved forward and took hold of her hands. "Just let me do the leading, you follow."

Janevra nodded.

Mat waited a second before starting, getting with the beat. He first spun her around in circles, stopping her suddenly. He then went into a complicated step, trying to slow it so Janevra could grasp the steps.

He stopped when the music stopped.

Janevra fell against his chest, breathing hard. She looked up at him. "Where did you learn that?"

"At home."

"It was very enjoyable. But I don't think I can do that again for a while. I'm dizzy," she said as she tried to catch her breath.

Mat helped her off the dance floor and she walked over to a wall, leaning against it.

Janevra gazed at him for a long time. Mat blushed. She was the most beautiful and powerful woman he had ever met and he felt equal to her.

"You have hazel eyes," she said at last.

Mat looked down at her, into her eyes. She had green eyes with flecks of gold. By the Goddess of Light was she beautiful with her cheeks flushed from dancing.

Mat leaned close to her. "Janevra, what are you planning to do?"

Janevra sighed. "I'll tell you but..."

"But what?"

"You mustn't tell anybody."

"I won't."

Janevra glanced at him. "I'm planning to leave the Palace."

"What? You can't do that. You're to be Queen."

"I know but—"

A cough sounded near them.

Mat turned and saw Caya and Lousai.

Caya, with her crooked teeth, was wearing a short maroon dress that stopped at her ankles and surprisingly did not have a rip in it. Her hair appeared to have been attacked by a brush, but it wasn't the brush that won.

Lousai was outfitted in a blue dress, but it was long and had a bow on the back. Her dark hair was curled and hung around her shoulders.

"We have news, Princess," said Lousai grinning. "But if you want us to leave you alone we will."

Janevra lifted her eyebrows. "How long have you been listening?"

"Oh...we only just got here," said Caya.

Janevra smiled at them. "What news do you two have?"

"We have some. There is rumor of you getting married," said Lousai squinting at her. "Is that true?"

"Yes," said Janevra, a frown fluttering across her features.

"That man you are getting married to, Lord Ravften, nobody likes him. People have seen odd events such as lights of strange colors lighting the sky at night. The King of Angarat is said to be gathering an army. And it is rumored that the Prophecies, which the old remember, are coming true. War is coming, they say," Lousai smiled, pleased with herself.

Janevra handed her five gold chips from her purse.

"Caya, Lousai, can I talk to your parents?" Janevra asked.

"I don't think so. Mother and Father said they wanted to be left alone," said Caya, grinning. The grin split her face in two.

"Can you find Teaa and tell her I want to talk to her tomorrow?"

"You bet," Lousai said, snickering. "If she's not busy."

Lousai and Caya ran off towards the jugglers.

Mat turned to Janevra. "Would you like to dance?"

Janevra smiled at him but shook her head. "No, I want to visit your parents."

Mat was taken back. "What?"

"I want to meet your parents. You talk about them with such love, I can't help but want to meet them. You don't mind going do you?"

"No. I just hope they don't die from the shock of having the Princess of Caendor coming to their home." Mat looked at Janevra for a moment. "How will we get there?"

Janevra's eyes glittered with enthusiasm. "Magic."

Mat lifted an eyebrow. "Magic? How will we get there?" Mat asked again, his attention distracted for a moment by a man juggling fire. He shook his head and brought his attention back to her.

"We will transport ourselves. I know it sounds difficult, but it's not. It's explained in one of the books we borrowed. All we need to do is to summon our magic and think of the place we want to go. Of course, since I don't know where we are going we will have to hold hands. I don't think we can do it by ourselves until we've had training from an actual shoi, but together I think we can."

Mat felt unease creep into his mind. "I don't know, Janevra. We're not that practiced in the Art."

Mat felt Janevra summoning her magic. She reached down and grasped his hand. "Summon your magic," she ordered. Mat summoned his magic, feeling the power slide along his body and drawing him into its sweet embrace. Janevra smiled at him, her eyes glowing with power. "Think of your home, Mat. Think of the wheat fields." Mat thought, closing his eyes, his mind going back to the field in which he had spent so many hours of his life.

The ground dropped from under them for a moment before returning.

Mat felt Janevra's hand drop his. He opened his eyes and gasped, the magic leaving his body. They were standing in the middle of his father's wheat field. The lights of the house, glowing in the dark, twinkled merrily. He was surprised his parents weren't asleep.

Glancing down at Janevra, Mat smiled at her. "I guess we know how to transport now."

Janevra patted his arm. "In the end, we will know much more."

Hand in hand, they made their way to Mat's house. Mat peeked in the window before he opened the door and noticed that his friends, Jordan, Breon and Irrik were inside, talking to his parents over mugs of warm cider. Mat opened the door, his face alight with joy when his parents looked up in astonishment and then ran over to him, each giving him a tight hug.

"Come in, dear," his mother said. "We shouldn't keep you out in the dark like that." Her eyes grew wide when Mat stepped into the light and she saw his perfectly tailored coat and well made trousers. "Mat, dear, palace life is treating you well, I see."

Mat grinned and accepted hugs from his friends. As they all sat back down again, Mat said, "I have someone I want you to meet. She's the one whose idea it was to come here." Mat leaned back out the door and took Janevra's hand, leading her into the house. "This is Princess Janevra."

The looks of surprise were enough to send Mat into a fit of laughter, but he managed to keep his mouth closed.

Waiting for his parents and friends to overcome their astonishment of seeing the Princess of Caendor, Mat looked at her and saw her in a new light. He could not keep from staring like the rest of them. Her dark red gown was glorious on her and made her look more like a Queen than a Princess. The silver crown laid upon an arrangement of hair accented her face so that she seemed even more beautiful than she really was, or perhaps it showed her true beauty. Her green eyes shone with delight and her red lips were pulled back in a smile, showing perfectly straight white teeth.

Mat grinned down at Janevra. "Janevra, this is my mother, Nyevia Trakall.

Janevra reached out her hand and grasped Mat's mother's calloused hand in her own. "Lady Trakall, I am pleased to meet you. Mat talks about you so much," she said, her words sending his mother into a deep blush of delight.

"No, Princess, I am not a lady," his mother replied humbly.

"Anyone who raises such a kind and intelligent man as Mat is a lady in my mind," Janevra smiled, withdrawing her hand from his mother's as Nyevia absently began to dry wash her hands in nervousness.

His mother bustled into the kitchen. "Well, this will not do. I will not have the Princess in my house if I cannot prepare a decent meal for her." She busied herself taking out pots and food items.

Mat laughed and turned Janevra to face his father. "Janevra, my father, Timon Trakall."

Janevra greeted his father formally, bowing slightly. Mat's father, not the least bit flabbergasted, smiled warmly at Janevra. "Princess, what an honor it is to have you in my house. You and Mat together makes my heart warm. I never thought I'd live to see the day when my son met his equal. I have never felt such power before," he murmured, gazing at the two of them with awe before quickly covering up his words with, "You would do an old man much happiness if you gave him a kiss on the cheek."

Janevra laughed and bent down, brushing her lips against Timon's cheek. His father turned as red as a cherry and hurried to join his wife in the kitchen.

Mat pulled out a chair for Janevra, but before she could sit, Jordan, Breon and Irrik jumped to their feet, clamoring for Mat to introduce them to the Princess.

"Janevra, the one that looks like a twig is Jordan. The one in the middle who is holding the mug of cider is Irrik and the other is Breon. Boys, this is Princess Janevra."

Jordan stepped forward first, his eyes drinking in the sight of her. "Will you marry me?" he asked.

Janevra looked at him in surprise then leaned forward and kissed Jordan fully on the lips. "In another life and time perhaps," she whispered to him.

Jordan touched his lips, and then turned to his friends. "She kissed me! Me! The Princess kissed me! Oh, the glory!"

Irrik came up to Janevra next. She was taller than him but his round face glowed in pleasure. "Princess," he said. "It is an honor to meet you."

"The honor is all mine, Irrik," Janevra said, extending her hand and shaking his fat one.

Irrik, his eyes dazed, turned and moved over to Mat. "Oh, gods," he squeaked. "The Princess!"

Breon bowed low before Janevra. "Princess," he said taking her hands in his and kissing it gently. "You have no idea how jealous of Mat I am right now."

Janevra pleased them all with her laughter.

Stepping back, Breon took a seat, shifting his sword. Mat frowned. "Breon, why do you carry a sword? Do you even know how to use it?"

Breon looked up. "I'm leaving for Istra in a few days. I was saying goodbye to your parents. And yes, my oldest brother was a soldier for three years. He taught Jordan and me how to use a sword."

Mat turned to Irrik and Jordan. "Are you two going too? I see you also carry a sword, Jordan."

Jordan nodded. "I decided to go to Istra with him. There is nothing for me here but dirt."

Irrik shook his head. "My place is with my family."

Janevra, concern on her face, looked at Jordan and Breon. "Why do you wish to leave Caendor?"

Breon scraped a bow. "Jordan and I believe war is coming. We want to leave. We told our parents to come with us, but they think we are crazy. I pray war does not come but I *know* it will."

Janevra clutched her stomach, sitting down hard on a chair. "War is coming," she whispered. "That is what the priest told me, but I've known it for a long time. Too many odd things have been happening." Janevra looked up, so fearful Mat bent down and embraced her. She wept into his shoulder, mumbling. "All the rumors are true. Lousai and Caya, Ravften, the priest, my mother. They were right."

Mat's mother came into the room, followed by his father. "What's the matter, dear?" his mother asked Janevra.

Janevra looked up, tears on her cheeks. Mat's mother rushed forward and pulled Janevra into the kitchen where both women talked in low tones.

Mat's father watched them go before turning to Mat. "What did you say?"

"It was not Mat, sir," Breon answered. "It was me. I told her war is coming."

"She needs to know the truth, poor girl. She will be Queen in such dark times."

"You believe this talk of war and darkness, Father?" Mat asked, astonished.

Mat's father looked at him sharply. "And you should too, my son. It will be you who leads the armies against the darkness. It will be you who fights in the war." Mat stared at his father but his father waved his hand. "Enough of this dark talk, my son. I am pleased indeed to see you with the Princess. I always suspected, but I was never quiet sure. Do you love her?" his father asked abruptly.

Mat gaped. "Love her? I barely know her!"

Mat's father slapped him on the back. "Your eyes will clear sooner than later, my son."

Jordan, Irrik and Breon laughed at Mat's confusion, but they all nodded and agreed with his father.

Talk fell to Mat and his life at the palace.

"Lord Mat," Jordan said, bowing, "what is life like at the palace?"

Mat punched his friend on the shoulder. "I am no lord, Jordan. Life there has been treating me well. It's amazing how many things go on in the palace and how most of it revolves around Janevra."

"She is the heir, Mat," Irrik said. "The future of this country rests on her shoulders."

"I know." Mat struggled, trying to find the words to explain but gave up. "Father," he said, "how is the farm? And how are you? Is your sickness gone?"

"The farm is doing well, my son, and I am doing much better. The cough seems to have receded a little and I'm feeling almost normal."

Mat eyed his father. His color did look normal but there were rings

under his eyes and his face seemed hollow. "Father, maybe you should
come back with Janevra and me. In the city, I can take you to a priest. They
are sure to heal you."

"No, Mat, I will not have one of those priests touch me. They know too
much already."

Mat was about to ask what they knew when his father frowned. "How
did you get here, Mat?" he asked.

So the truth is unveiled, he thought. "By magic."

Jordan, Irrik and Breon gasped. "What?" they echoed together.

"Janevra and I went to the Temple of the Light yesterday and had
ourselves tested in the Art," Mat explained.

"Did you?" Mat's father said, creases lining his brow. "What Talent do
you have?"

Mat fidgeted. "Janevra and I were both tested to be greens. From the
reaction of the priest, it's a very strong position in the Art."

Mat's father's eyebrows shot up. "Greens? Now that is surprising. I
would have thought— never mind. Did they ask you to join their order?"

"No. I think they were too intimidated by Janevra and our strength in
the Art."

Mat's father sighed, sitting down in a chair and relaxing. "That is
good. That is very good."

Jordan patted Mat on the back. "A shoi, huh? You can use your magic
to make the wheat grow. I can see it now! Mat the Magical Farmer!"
Jordan hooted with laughter.

Mat glanced at his friend. "Maybe I will cast a spell on you that makes
it so you can't talk."

Jordan shut his mouth, edging away from Mat in mock horror.

"Would you, Mat?" Irrik asked. "Jordan can get so annoying."

"No, I wouldn't use my magic to hurt my friends." A small sigh went
around the room and Mat looked at his friends carefully. "Just because I
have a strong Talent in the Art, doesn't make me different from what I was
before," Mat said, hurt that they would be fearful of him. *I haven't
changed!* he thought. *Yes, but you are changing,* a voice sneered in his
mind.

Mat sat down. "Look, Jordan, Breon, Irrik, I won't ever use my magic
to hurt you. The only thing I will ever use it for is—"

Screams sounded from the kitchen. His dog let out a bark and stopped
with a yelp. The five men rushed into the room, Breon and Jordan brandish-
ing their swords. The scene that met their eyes caused fear to rise up in their
throats.

Janevra and Mat's mother were standing near the fire, Janevra shielding Mat's mother. In the doorway, the door hacked to bits, stood an ugly
creature with long greasy hair and sharp pointed yellow teeth. Its body was
covered in black armor and a wickedly curved sword was held in its hand.
Several more were standing behind it, in the darkness, burning torches held

above their heads, black eyes squinting into the house. The dog lay dead on the floor.

The creatures, called rogui in the stories, stalked towards Janevra and Mat's mother. Before Mat or his friends could react, Mat's father darted between the two, his hands held out in front of him. "Stop!" he shouted, commanded so powerful in his voice, the rogui paused for a second before bringing its sword back and leveling it towards his father.

Mat thought his father was going to die but suddenly a fiery sword was held in his father's hands. In one movement the creature's and his father's sword met, sending bursts of flame everywhere. Several of the sparks landed on the ceiling and took hold. As the fire spread slowly, Mat's father dropped back and ran the creature through, slaying it instantly. In the next instant, his father raised his hand and a stream of water rushed forward, landing on the flickering flames and extinguishing it.

In shock, Mat stared at his father. *My father knows magic?* he marveled.

The other rogui in the doorway roared and stormed into the room. Mat's father faced them, joined by Breon and Jordan.

"Mat, get your mother and the Princess out of here!" his father shouted, locked in combat with a rogui.

Mat dragged Irrik with him.

"How do we get out?" Mat's mother asked.

Mat's eyes darted around and landed on the chimney. "Quickly, Mother, dump that pot of water on the fire! We're climbing up the chimney!"

His mother grabbed the pot and dumped it over the flames, steam rising and hissing.

"Hurry!" Mat shouted.

His mother stepped into the fireplace, helped by Janevra. They slowly disappeared up the chimney.

Mat turned to Irrik. "Will you fit?" he asked.

Irrik shook his head, fear alight in his eyes. "No, I can't."

Mat grabbed two butchering knives and handed one to Irrik. "If anything comes at you, defend yourself!" Irrik nodded, setting his back to the wall, his eyes watching Jordan, Breon and Mat's father battle the creatures several feet from him. Three rogui lay dead on the floor, dark blood seeping from their bodies and spreading over the ground.

Mat looked up the chimney, glad to see his mother and Janevra almost out. He turned back to the fight, picking up another knife. Praying he did not hit a friend, he threw it, amazed to see it protruding from the throat of a rogui battling Breon. Breon smiled briefly before his attention was directed to helping Jordan.

"Mat!" Janevra screamed from the chimney. Mat looked up, unable to see anything but the starry sky at the end. "Mat, help us!" Janevra shouted from the roof.

Sticking the knife in his belt, Mat reached up into the chimney and

grasped an uneven brick. He pulled himself up as quickly as he could, soot
and dust blackening his skin and clothes. He was almost to the top when a
scream sounded below him. Glancing down, Mat saw Irrik fall into the fire
pit, a deep gash across his throat. Blood spurted from the wound, and Irrik's
life slipped away. A rogui dragged the body away before coming back and
looked up the chimney. The rogui screeched and started climbing up. Mat
redoubled his efforts, and climb over the top of the chimney into a scene
that stopped his heart.

His mother lay against the chimney, an arrow sticking from her
shoulder and blood seeping from a wound across her abdomen. Janevra,
balanced precariously on the roof, held a rogui sword, trying to keep three
of the horrible creatures at bay. Two already lay dead on the roof. Soot
stood on her face like war paint and her once beautiful gown was ripped
and in tatters. He noticed that a large piece of the fabric was wrapped
around his mother's head.

A deep growl echoed behind Mat and he turned, the knife in his hand.
The rogui's head popped up and Mat jabbed the thing in the eyes. The
creature fell back, screaming, falling back inside the house to land in the
fire pit with a sickening crunch.

Mat rushed to Janevra's aid but before he could reach her, her sword bit
into the flesh of two rogui and they dropped to the roof, rolling down and
landing on the ground. She was already paring with the last one, the clang
of metal sounding in the night air. Neatly sidestepping a powerful swipe of
the rogui, she brought her sword up and thrust it into the creature's back.
She wrenched her sword out and kicked the rogui in the ribs, sending it
over the side of the roof.

Wiping the sword on her ruined dress, Janevra hurried over to Mat,
tears in her eyes. "I'm so sorry, Mat…your mother…the arrow came out of
nowhere…they were waiting for us."

Turning, Mat knelt by his mother's side. He pressed his fingers to her
throat, searching for the beat that told of life. Finding none, he cried out.
Janevra rushed to him, gathering him in her embrace. Mat felt his heart
clench tightly in his chest, sobs heaving from him. "Why, Janevra? Why
did they come?"

Janevra shook her head. "I don't know, Mat, but your father is down
there, as are your friends. We must help them before you can weep."

Mat brushed the tears from his eyes. "You're right."

Janevra and Mat crept down to the side of the roof, peering over the
rim. The sounds of fighting came from inside the house. Glass shattered
somewhere and a harsh scream tore from someone's throat. Mat tensed,
ready to jump from the roof, but Janevra grabbed his arm. Wildly, he
looked at her. She brought a finger to her lips and pointed towards the
wheat field. A dozen rogui, weapons in hand, waited on the border of the
field, their black armor glittering in the night.

"Let me go first," Janevra said. "I have the sword."

Mat made to argue except she had already swung down from the roof, landing gracefully on the ground. Bending down, she took another sword from a dead rogui and moved towards the group of rogui.

"Janevra!" Mat whispered desperately. "What are you doing?"

Ignoring him, she pointed her sword at the creatures. "Fight me!" she challenged.

Mat watched in horror as five of the creatures broke off and charged, unsheathing their weapons, and howling in glee as they ran to kill the lone human.

Janevra greeted the rogui with a clash of metal and blood. Two of the rogui died before Mat could blink, his heart in his throat. Another died from a slash across the face. That left two. Janevra twirled her swords in front of her, forcing the rogui to give her a wide berth. The swords left her hands and both thudded into the chests of the rogui. Janevra pulled her swords from their bodies, as calmly as if she did it every day.

Mat swung down from the roof, rushing to her. "Are you hurt?" he asked.

She shook her head, and handed him a bloodstained sword.

"I do not know how," he said.

"Learn quickly, then," Janevra said, moving into a fighting stance. "They are coming."

Mat looked up and saw the remaining seven rogui dashing at them, weapons raised high.

Before the rogui were upon them, Mat's father, carrying his flaming sword, jumped between them. Jordan and Breon came up behind Janevra and Mat, watching in awe. Mat's father darted between the rogui, his sword burning like a beacon and dealing out a fiery death.

"Help him," Mat demanded of his friends.

Jordan shook his head. "He's in the battle rage. He would kill us too."

Mat's father parried and thrust, a wild grin splitting his face. A high-pitched scream that sounded like an animal screech tore from his throat as he danced around the rogui. When the last one fell, Mat's father stared around in disbelief and collapsed on the ground.

Running to his father, Mat fell to his side. "Father," he cried, "are you hurt?"

Mat's father laughed weakly. "No, but I will not last too much longer on this earth."

Mat frowned, confused. Janevra and Mat's friends stayed back, letting Mat have time alone with his father.

"My son, my time has come. Even we cannot live forever. I'm glad you found Janevra before this happened. I always knew you and she were the ones."

"You knew this would happen?" Mat shouted, bothered by his father's words.

"I suspected. Sometimes my powers, as much as they are a gift, are a curse. I am so glad you inherited different powers. The gift of foresight is one I would not wish on even my most hated enemy." His father smiled, reaching up and touching Mat's face. "Goodbye, my son." His father's eyes stared past him, glazing over.

Mat sobbed, burying his face in his father's neck. His parents were gone, taken from him. Both of them. In the same night. He was alone and he had nowhere to go. Crying, tears running down his face, Mat cursed the gods and their malicious plots. He cursed the Evil that chose to rise up again and he cursed himself for letting them die.

He didn't remember how long he had been there, holding his father's body and crying until Janevra came up and pried his fingers from his father's body.

"Mat," she said. "Please, we need to bury him."

Mat nodded. "What of my mother?"

Janevra hugged him tenderly. "Jordan and Breon finished digging the graves. We've put your mother and Irrik in them. We are waiting for you, so we can put your father with them and cover them."

Mat nodded again, numb. Jordan and Breon came over, picking up his father's body and carrying it to the grave. They set him in tenderly and began covering the graves, Janevra working along side them. Mat joined them, tears blurring his vision.

When they finished, Jordan set up a wooden headstone for each that was created out of the backs of the chairs. Breon said a few words, tears trailing down his own face. Janevra summoned her magic and created flowers, laying them on the graves. Mat could only watch, his heart empty.

Jordan and Breon dragged the rogui bodies from the house, tossing them into a pile. Janevra helped them, hauling the ones from the field to the pile and throwing her swords in with them. She summoned her magic once more and set the pile of bodies on fire.

The stench of burning flesh smothered the air, leaving all four choking for breath.

Janevra came up to Mat. "Mat, what of the house?"

"Burn it. There's nothing for me here."

Janevra looked at him, but he didn't raise his eyes to meet hers. She turned, and he felt her summon her magic and set the house on fire. He heard a shout and Breon came running towards him. "Mat! You must see this! Before the house burns down!"

Mat let Breon drag him to the front door where Janevra and Jordan were standing. "Look," Breon said. Mat looked up, squinting, trying to read by the two moon's light.

Inscribed into the front door were three lines of words.

"War is coming,
The Warlord is coming,
We are coming, die."

Staring at the words, Mat trembled. "Janevra, quick! Summon your magic!"

Janevra, startled, summoned her magic. Mat grasped her hand and commanded Jordan and Breon to take their empty ones. Summoning his own magic, Mat envisioned Jordan's farm.

The ground spun underneath them before stopping and leaving the four standing in front of Jordan's house, or what was left of it. The light of the two moons lightened the sky and showed the skeleton of the house, it's beams still burning. Seven bodies lay in front of the house. Jordan broke their circle and ran to his family. He fell to the dusty ground, looking into the faces of his dead parents and siblings. His broken cries poured over Mat as Mat fought to control his own emotions.

"Mat, three are missing," Breon said. "Jordan had eight siblings. Three are not here."

Mat, Janevra and Breon hurried over to the ruins of the house, shifting through the rubble.

Janevra let out a yell, and pointed to the floor. Mat and Breon ran over as Janevra bent down and pulled on a ring that was connected to the floor. The trap door opened, and the moons' light spread into the darkness of the hole. Three faces stared up at them, tear stained and fearful. Two of the faces belonged to twin fifteen-year-old girls. The other belonged to a twelve-year-old boy. Mat called to Jordan. Jordan came running and hugged his siblings as they climbed out of the hole.

The three began the tedious work of digging shallow graves and burying the dead. Jordan, his pain somewhat healed from finding three siblings alive, helped them dig, even though his sisters and brother wept.

Mat and Janevra summoned their magic again, grasping hands with everyone. They transported themselves to Breon's farm. Breon wept in joy when he saw that his house was not yet burned. Mat made sure they wasted no time in collecting Breon's parents and three siblings before transporting themselves to Irrik's farm. Much to Mat's dismay, they found the farm in ashes and no sign of Irrik's family.

Mat and Janevra decided to take them back to the palace where they would outfit the family to go to Istra, where Breon and Jordan had planned to go. Where it was safe.

Janevra gave each person a hundred gold chips from the Royal Treasury, new clothing for each and horses, much to the anger of the Queen. Mat said goodbye to his friends, his heart heavy with the loss and sorrow. At the mid of night, his friends left the palace gates, heading for Istra. Mat watched them go, wishing he could leave this land that promised future war but knowing his place was with Janevra.

Chapter 8
The Warriors of the Tar-ten

Deivenada of the Edieata gazed up at the statue of an ancient battle djed. He held in his hands a battle spear and the battle sword, a curved blade with a bejeweled handle, his weapons that all Ile named *khrieths*. His eyes watched the distance intently. Sighing, Deivenada ran a hand along the base of the statue. He had been the Djed, the leader of the Edieata in the Third Battle. It was said he had the blessings of all four gods of the Ile. The storytellers said, "Tiysar was blessed by the gods. Aystarte gave him the power of war and luck, Mayita blessed him with truth, Mandoulis bestowed upon him the power of the sun, and Reshef-sia gifted him with the power of divine knowledge of all things. Reshef-sia even gave him the knowledge of strategy in battle."

Deivenada's eyes traveled to the four temples behind the statue of Tiysar. *Gods of the Light, bless my people. The Yria'ti has foreseen hard times ahead and she swears her magic never fails her. Let us get through these new times with glory and peace.* She bowed her head to the temples. *The Yria'ti mentioned last night at the village gathering that the Dragon of the Rising Sun is in our future. Mandoulis, sun god, is this true? We will need your guidance, my gods, because war is coming.*

Picking up her *khrieth*, a spear with a foot long blade, Deivenada turned and made her way through the market place. Even though her village was small, the market managed to seem filled with people.

A young man with blue eyes and a shaved head, hurried towards Deivenada. "Deivenada," he said, clutching a curved sword in his hand, also known as a *khrieth*. "Your brother told me to tell you he went hunting. He said the djed wanted some fresh meat for the festival tonight."

Deivenada smiled. "Thank you, Etad. Do you know where he went hunting?"

"He mentioned the glade near the waterfall."

"Thank you. Is Zenerax with him?"

Etad shook his head.

Deivenada thanked him once more and set off in search of her brother. It was dusk and it was never safe to be out in the woods alone, especially with the growing threat of the Nekid and the rumors of war.

Slipping out to the village, Deivenada crept into the woods, careful not to make a sound. She slithered through the trees, unheard and unseen for a quarter of a mile before coming to a stop. She had stopped at the glade, still concealed within the protection of the trees.

Deivenada peered through the bush, and smiled when she saw her brother. Her brother was a youth of twenty-two summers. He was tall, with a muscular body. His blonde-red hair was messy and his sharp blue eyes were locked on his target. A tattoo of a sun was on his left arm, drawn onto his deltoid muscle. A spear was in his hand.

Deivenada herself looked much like her brother. They had the same angular features even though she was two summers younger than he. She had long red hair braided in two-dozen braids, tanned skin and gray eyes. She carried the same tattoo as her brother. The *khrieth* she carried with her lay propped up against a tree.

Caught up in the excitement of the hunt, Deivenada did not notice the shadow detach itself from a tree to her right.

Her brother crouched down behind a tree, taking aim at the doe. He let the spear fly and it ran into the body of the animal, killing it instantly.

Deivenada went to jump up and run to her brother when she was tackled from behind.

The force of the other body threw her into the decaying leaves of the forest floor.

The person, or thing, grabbed her arms and pulled them behind her back.

"Get off me!" she yelled, her leather clothes rubbing uncomfortably against her skin.

A chuckle sounded above her. "Fine."

Pressure was released and Deivenada got to her feet, brushing herself off. She looked up into the morning gray eyes of a youth her age. It was Zenerax, her friend and hopeful future husband. He was tall like her brother and well muscled, with brown hair. On his bicep was the same tattoo she and her brother wore. The tattoo showed that he was of the Ile class Warrior of the Tar-ten. She herself was among the elite warrior group.

Deivenada smiled. She somehow managed to glare at him at the same time. "You always do that to me. One of these days it'll be you scared out of your skin."

Zenerax kissed her lightly on the lips.

"Come, I think your brother needs help with his kill. It's getting dark," Zenerax said.

Dei located her spear and picked it up.

Hand in hand, they found her brother skinning the deer.

"Want some help, Kayzi?" Deivenada asked.

"Yes, I..." her brother trailed off as he looked up at them, his gaze going past them.

They turned around and looked up at the sky. It was glowing with colors that were twisting and turning, changing into different forms in front of their eyes.

They stared in silence, not believing.

"The prophecy," Deivenada whispered, voicing the thought of the others. "The Dragons have been found. The Ile will soon be united under the Dragon of the Rising Sun and brought to victory. Gods hope it is so."

"Only when the day comes will I believe it. If he can unite us and stop the Nekid in their killing then he truly will lead us to victory," said Kayzi.

"I hope the Nekid stop taking our land and don't come any farther even without the help of the Dragons. I do not feel like spilling the blood of the Tar-ten." Dei touched the knife in her belt and ran her hands along her spear. She did not like spilling the blood of her people, but if the goddess of war, Aystarte, willed it, she would fight and she would kill.

Dei glanced over at Kayzi. He was her only living relative. Their parents had both been killed when they had lived in a border village. The Nekid had attacked, killing everyone. Deivenada and her brother had escaped and made their way to a mountain village. They had made camp one night below the Gangga Mountains, and when they awoke spears were at their throat. Zenerax and a friend had come upon them sleeping and not knowing who they were, had been ready to attack. A quick explanation from Deivenada had cleared things up, and they were welcomed in the village. This had been three years ago.

Over the years, Zenerax, Kayzi and Deivenada had become friends and a relationship had formed between Deivenada and Zenerax.

"We had better get back. The djed will be wondering what happened to us and why we aren't celebrating with everyone else," said Kayzi. "And what of the deer?" Kayzi twisted to look at the deer, but it was gone. He straightened, his eyes going to the dark forest and then to the colors in the sky. Maybe it would be better to stay.

"We should go, Dei," Zenerax was saying.

"Can't we stay and watch for a while? This is history. Our lives will be different forever from this point on," Deivenada begged.

Kayzi nodded. "She's right. Our lives will be different."

Zenerax sighed. "Why not?" He lay down in the grass, Deivenada next to him. She snuggled up against his chest, feeling pleased. She was watching the Prophecies come true and her beloved would be with her throughout it all.

The colors in the sky flashed a bright blue and purple light, with tints of green, swirling around. They appeared like streams, running and twisting through the stars. But the white streams that appeared stunned the watchers with their brilliance.

Everything was silent. The trees were not whispering, and the grass was not moving. Everything was silent, and maybe that was why Zenerax heard the snap of a twig.

Zenerax suddenly became tense. Dei jerked her head up, feeling his tension.

He signaled her to be silent. Crawling in warrior style, he crept through the grass and into the trees.

Dei waited, listening for any sound that might tell her where Zenerax was, or where the danger might be.

A yell sounded to her right and all was quiet.

She waited, Kayzi next to her. *Why is it taking him so long to return?*

Dei started to get fidgety. *What if Zenerax is hurt? What if he is dead?* Dei shuddered, not wanting to think about it.

She couldn't take it any more. Dei grabbed her spear and ran towards the shout. She sprinted through the grass. Kayzi gave a yelp and was soon running after her.

Dei's heart pounded in her chest as she slowed to a walk just outside the forest. She looked back at Kayzi; his eyes were wide and alert.

She walked into the forest, her body rigid. She looked every way, searching for Zenerax. She passed by dark, mysterious trees, and bushes that appeared like a Nekid warrior crouching for an attack.

Dei could feel Kayzi behind her, breathing quietly. Her eyes were wide and alert. She could hear the pounding of her own heart the silence in the forest was so pure.

A rock whizzed out of nowhere, hitting her brother on the head. Kayzi crumpled to the ground. But when she turned around to go to him, his body was gone.

A hand seized her from behind, putting a long knife up to her throat and clamping her hands behind her back. Her spear was kicked under a bush. A cold feeling crawled up her spine, tingling with fear and darkness.

She struggled once before the blade was pushed closer to her throat.

The voice that spoke next was cold and full of a hate that forced her skin to ripple in shivers. "Where do you think you were going, uh? It's not safe to wander around this forest anymore, girl. You're going to get yourself killed. And a pretty thing like you, it would be a waste. I might just kill you now. I would take great pleasure in hearing you scream." It had a rough accent as if her language was difficult.

The thing holding her turned her around, and she got her first good look at her captor. Her breath caught in her throat and her heart skipped a beat.

It stood five and a half feet tall with large muscles covered by black skin. A spiked armor was it's clothing with straps holding iron flats. It had hair on its head but only a little and most of it was stringy. Needle sharp teeth filled its mouth. Its black eyes were glinting out from under a helmet. A sword was strapped to its back and a number of knives were around its waist in a belt. Small bags also hung around the waist; one was dripping a green liquid. Probably poison.

Dei's eyes went wide in terror, and her breath sucked in. She instantly regretted it. The horrible stench of the creature clogged her nostrils.

The thing smiled. "I am of the Xquwernaghtoisylaivien. But that's too hard for you pathetic humans to say. Call us the sylai, killers of the night, night hunters, or even the creatures of hell. My master prefers that one." The sylai looked at her, licking its lips with a black, snake like tongue.

"Your master? Who is this person?" Dei was finally able to say, her throat clogged from the smell.

"Person? My Lord is no mortal. He is the Great god of the Dark, the Lord of Dark Magic, Lord of Evil." The sylai puffed out with obvious pride.

Dei's legs trembled. The God of the Dark was known for battles that he started between Good and Evil in the past. The battles killed thousands. Good had always triumphed, except once, in the Second Battle, and Evil had ruled the world for four hundred years. The realm of Evil had stretched from the Cyrain Plains, past the Iwo Mountains and to the Jayapur Ocean, controlling all of Caendor, Selkare, Angarat, Istra, Caroa, and Taymyr. The Dragons, a man and a woman of great magical power, had been born to rid the world of Evil, thus creating the Third Battle.

There were four battles between Good and Evil. The Prophecies said that the next Dragons would be in the Fifth Battle and it would be the bloodiest.

It was believed that the armies of the Dark, which would march in the Seventh Age, were made of creatures with sinister hearts, men with cruel plans and people with the want of power. *This creature fits the belief well,* Dei thought.

"What are you going to do with me?"

"Eat you," the sylai said.

Dei's eyes grew wide but she held in her scream. She did not want to please this creature with her cry.

The sylai drew a knife, dripping in a green liquid. Before it could gut her, a rock cracked upon its head, and the sylai crashed to the forest floor.

Two figures leaped out of the brush. Zenerax and Kayzi.

Zenerax ran towards her. "Dei, are you all right?" He swept her up in an embrace.

Dei coughed. "I'm okay, but you might want to kill him."

Zenerax turned around, pulled out a knife and plunged it through the beast's chest. A gurgle sounded from its throat, and a red fluid flowed from its mouth, drenching Zenerax's knife in blood. The sylai sneered at Zenerax, reached out and started pulling Zenerax towards him. It growled low in its throat.

Dei moved quickly. She rolled across the ground to the bush her *khrieth* had fallen under and came up, her spear neatly slicing into the head of the sylai.

Zenerax pushed himself away from the body, the body tumbling to the ground with a gentle thud. The head rolled along the ground for a few feet before a foot stopped it.

Zenerax, Dei and Kayzi looked up and into the black eyes of another sylai.

"Oh…damn…this isn't good," Zenerax said. He crouched low, his *khrieth* parallel to the ground.

The sylai did not have time to move as three spears drove into its body, quivering. The creature dropped to the ground, blood spilling.

"Those were sylai," Dei said slowly. "They come from the world of death." She went over to the sylai and nudged it with her foot. Deciding it was truly dead, she pulled out the spears and handed each to its owner.

"We know. We heard what it said." Kayzi swallowed, as if remembering a bad memory. "I didn't think they existed. Are they allied with the Nekid?"

Dei shrugged. "I do not know. All it said was that it served the Lord of the Dark."

"If there are more of those things, there is going to be no peace tonight," Zenerax said.

Dei looked up at Zenerax as he spoke, horror dawning in her eyes. "We must fly."

Leaving behind the two bodies, they ran. Branches whipped against their faces, blades of grass cutting into their legs. They ran. They ran faster than they had ever run in their lives, but they were not fast enough.

The smell of smoke clung to the air. The three came upon the clearing to their home, and found ashes and burning bodies.

Dei gasped, her hand flying to her mouth. Zenerax came up behind her and held her as Kayzi sunk down to the ashy ground in desolation.

Skeletons of wooden huts stood naked against the starry sky. Wisps of smoke drifted out of the ruins. They walked into the center of the burned village. Small flames flickered here and there, lighting up the charred remains of people who had been laughing that morning. The four temples to their gods, Aystarte, Mayita, Mandoulis and Reshef-sia were blackened by the fire and crumbling from where sylai axes had bitten into the stone. The tomb to their leading family was desecrated. Their leader, the djed, had been hung from a post, his body flayed until his skin hung in ribbons of flesh.

"A spell book," Dei whispered, pointing to a book lying on the ground. Picking it up she said, "The lights we saw in the sky were the working of magic. There are no Dragons." She threw down the book in rage.

"At least the people defended themselves," Kayzi said, nodding to a spearhead lying in the ash. "I wonder if anyone is alive." He muttered a quick prayer to Mayita, the goddess of truth, that his words were true.

"No one would be alive. These things kill all and leave. They live to kill."

Dei nodded, she knew the stories told by the older Tar-ten. These sylai were in them. They had been told of what sylai did to villages. The sylai killed all that they could find. At the end they did a sweep, killing the ones who hid by magic. No one was left alive, not men, women, elderly or children. "I know the stories, but we still must try," Dei said. "The gods curse us if we don't try."

Zenerax shook his head. "I know from what I see that there are none alive. The bodies, they are all about us. Burned and slashed. Maybe some live but I doubt it." Zenerax clenched his jaw.

"We must find the survivors," Dei said thrusting her chin up.

Zenerax nodded.

The three spread out, turning over bodies of the dead and feeling for a heartbeat.

Dei threw up once after turning over the body of a young child, her face frozen in terror, a long gash across her neck.

Dei walked into a hut, looking at the bodies of a family strewn about the floor. She went over to a body of a child girl, and knelt down beside her. Dei coughed from the smoke, but when she looked down again the child's eyes were open, tears leaking out.

"Oh gods! Zen! Kayzi! Come quick!" Dei yelled. Pounding feet sounded behind her, announcing the presence of the two young men.

"What?" Kayzi asked huffing.

"The girl, she's alive. Help me get her to stand."

Kayzi and Zenerax lifted the girl up by her arms, making her stand on her feet. "What is your name?" Dei asked softly.

"Aska," the girl whimpered. Aska's blonde hair drooped about her shoulders in knots. The oval face held fear.

"Aska, I'm Deivenada and that's my brother Kayzi, and that's Zenerax. We're here to help."

"Where are my parents?" the girl whined.

Dei looked at Zen and Kayzi who shook their heads. Dei sighed.

"Aska, your parents are dead."

Aska threw her skinny arms around Dei's waist and wept.

Zenerax was about to turn away to go and look for more survivors, but he heard the girl whisper, "Mother, please come back."

"Come Aska, we must look for more survivors. I'm so sorry, but we must not cry now," Zenerax said gently.

"He is right, Aska, we can mourn later. If we wait too long, we have no hope of finding others alive."

Aska nodded, still clinging to Dei's pant legs.

Two hours later found Dei, Zenerax, Kayzi, Aska and seven more souls, sitting in the center of the village.

Dei looked at the seven new people. They were all between the ages of twelve and twenty-two, Aska as the youngest and her brother as the oldest. All the people were in good enough physical shape to run and hide or fight. Weapons had been scavenged from the ruins of the village and the survivors clutched the spears and swords desperately.

"We need to leave," Zenerax said making everyone jump. They had not built a fire but the two moons above illuminated the ground.

"Where would we go?" asked a young woman named Biqua.

"We would go to the City of the Daaguwh," Dei said calmly.

Shocked silence followed her voice.

"Why?" asked a youth of fourteen summers.

"Because the Edieata are friends with the Daaguwh, and soon will be enemies, if they aren't already, of the sylai," Zenerax said quietly. "We must remember we already have the common enemy of the Nekid and they are massing in the north."

"The Daaguwh are our only hope now. It will be a long journey, but we will survive," Dei said.

"Why not go to the other villages of the Edieata?" asked Etad, a youth one year younger than Zenerax.

"Because we are not strong enough as a nation to defend ourselves. And hopefully the others will know to go there too," Kayzi answered.

"Before we leave, we must try to warn all the other villages," Dei said.

"I agree," Zenerax said.

Kayzi twirled his spear between his nimble fingers. "We should see if any horses were left. I know we must leave the chariots but horses will be a great advantage if we happen to run into any sylai."

Etad held up his hand, waiting until Kayzi acknowledged him. "I was hiding near the stables. The sylai destroyed the stables and killed the horses."

Dei groaned. "We travel to the city of the Edieata on foot and pray they are still standing."

Eleven people, the last surviving of the Mountain Edieata, set off to find help in a city that might already be burnt. They traveled through dense forests, their sure feet carrying them swiftly and as silently as ghosts. Weapons, salvaged from the wreckage of their homes, decorated their bodies. Long spears with curved blades and curved swords were slung over backs or lashed to waists. Red knol, a form of paint, was dyed on their faces, a sign of war. A black smear was on their foreheads, which told of the deaths the young warriors were avenging. The unquestioned leaders of the small band ran at the head. Dei, Zenerax and Kayzi, faces set in determination, led the small band east fifty miles to the nearest Edieata town, praying to the gods that the town still stood. During the nights they slept, but many stared up at the sky as it filled with brilliant colors and shooting stars. The Dragons have met, the colors said. Prepare yourselves. Throughout their travel, they knew the sylai were not far behind them and were pushed to run faster at times when a sylai scout was spotted in the distance.

Four days of running and foraging for food in the woods brought them to the Edieata town of Sia'lyra near dusk on the fourth day.

Seeing the short thick walls of the town with the four temples to their gods looming above it, Dei collapsed against Zenerax in relief.

"We must move quickly," Kayzi said. "If the sylai are not here now, they will be soon. We need to warn them."

Dei led the small group to the wooden gates of the town, looking up at the guards standing several feet above her head.

"What business do you have here?" a guard asked.

"We ask entrance," Dei replied.

"We would lend entrance to any Edieata. What news do you have of the west? Rumors have been spreading lately and news would be welcome to our ears," one of the guards said, idly toying with a knife.

"We were attacked by sylai four days back. Those that you see before you are the only survivors of the Mountain Edieata," Zenerax said, his features set in stone.

The guards on the walls moaned and a few wept openly.

"The Nekid, were they with the sylai?" someone asked.

Kayzi shook his head. "We did not see any, but we have our suspicions."

Dei nodded at her brother. "Yes, and we fear the sylai are coming here. They were not far behind us, maybe half a day. They wish to destroy us before the Dragon of the Rising Sun can unite us with the other Ile nations."

Three of the guards scaled down the wall and into the town, yelling to prepare for war. Dei, Zenerax, Kayzi and their followers were ushered into the city, the wooden gates closed and barred behind them.

One of the guards grabbed Dei's arm. "Will you fight?" he asked, eyeing their armored bodies.

Dei nodded curtly. "All but the youngest." The guard thanked her and went back to ordering the town to prepare for war.

Dei, suddenly anxious, called for Aska and Twoin. Two young children bounded over to Dei, their faces pinched with worry. "I want you to hide in one of the houses near the far side of town. If we need to escape, we will leave by those doors. In fact," Dei said, motioning to a fourteen-year-old youth called Jeikou, "Jeikou will protect you if anything happens."

Jeikou hurried up to Dei. "Yes, djed?"

Dei frowned over the use of the title but let it be. "Will you protect Aska and Twoin until the battle is over or we must flee?"

Jeikou bowed his head, unsheathing his sword. He grasped both children's hands in his own and took them to safety at the far end of town.

Dei watched them go, worried. Zenerax came up behind her, putting his arms around her waist. She leaned up against his chest, enjoying the warmth and security his body created. "Do not worry, love, they will be safe," Zenerax said, kissing her on the cheek. "Come, we must prepare."

"They are going to attack! We don't have time!"

"They will not attack until night, like they did last time. They are creatures of the night, darkness is their element," Zenerax said, taking her by the hand and bringing her to a small table that had been set up to hold red war knol.

Dei and Zenerax painted the battle stripes on each other's faces as men and women around them painted their own faces. Several were stripping and donning their war clothes.

Off the battlefield, most Ile warriors dress in white linen. Even if caught unprepared, white linen allowed for easy movement and is light enough it would not weigh the wearer down. They always carried their spear or sword with them.

It was a tradition among all the Ile, that when in battle they cover their faces with red paint or knol, a sign of war. They would wear high tied boots made out of animal skin and the clothes would be dyed tan so they could blend into the tall golden grasses of the plains, slipping in and out of view like ghosts.

Men and women Ile who chose to fight were called Warriors of the Tar-ten. These men and women had one tattoo on their left deltoid muscle showing their status as a warrior and future followers of the Dragon of the Rising Sun. Every Warrior of the Tar-ten carried a dirk, short knives, bow and arrows and a spear or sword. In battle, the women painted red knol in two lines under their cheeks, one across their forehead and two more vertically on their cheeks. Men of the Tar-ten wore red knol in three diagonal stripes on their cheeks when in battle. All warriors trained in hand-to-hand combat and specialized in most weapons, which consisted of spears, knives, bows, staffs, darts, and swords. They wore leather pants tucked into high boots and some form of shirt for the women that was usually tight, so it would not get in the way during a fight. Men tended to go shirtless into battle.

As Zenerax finished putting the last touches on Dei's face, she caught sight of a man and a woman dressed in long white linens. Dei rushed over to them, bowing her head. "Yria'ti, I must warn you, the sylai have magic users with them."

The man and woman bowed their heads in acknowledgement. "Thank you for warning us, Tar-ten. We shall spread the word." They left, sweeping through the throngs of warriors with an air of command. Dei saw them confront the djed, who quickly ordered the Yria'ti to prepare defenses.

Women and men Ile who were not warriors, but had magical abilities, were called Yria'ti. They had the ability to cast spells and use them in battle. When someone was discovered to have a magical ability they were given the choice to become a Yria'ti or learn the ways of the warriors. After that they were taken to the Temple where all Ile magic users went to study the ways of magic under older mentors. Each Yria'ti was valued and all were in high ranks once they passed the Test of the Yria'ti, which is much like the outsiders Test of the Robe.

Zenerax came up to Dei, turning her so she faced him. "Dei," he said quietly. "Be careful tonight. I don't want you to get hurt."

Dei smiled. "I won't, but I worry for you."

Zenerax laughed and bent down to kiss her. "Then we shall stay side by side. If one is injured, the other can protect them."

"Dei, Zenerax," Kayzi said, appearing next to them. "We need to position ourselves on the walls."

They followed Kayzi, making sure the Mountain Edieata came with them. Up on the walls, they drew their bows and notched their arrows, waiting for the fall of darkness and the attack.

The djed of the town came up to Kayzi. "Are you their djed?" he asked.

"I am one of them. My sister and Zenerax," Kayzi pointed at them, "are also the leaders."

The djed was a tall Ile, with his long yellow hair pulled back and clasped with a bone. His eyes were small but were lighted with a keen intelligence.

Dei and Zenerax moved closer to Kayzi in order to hear the djed's words. "The Yria'ti have thrown a magical field over the town, so we cannot be bombarded by magic, but the shield does not protect us from the arrows or other weapons of the enemy. When the enemy shows themselves, the order will be given to fire the arrows. Do not light your arrows with fire. I do not want them to see when our arrows hit them. Once the first five volleys are fired, the gates will open and the chariots will ride out. I want you three to lead those on foot behind the chariots, so we can engage in open war. I do not want this to become a siege. We don't have enough food to survive one."

"What if we cannot defeat them?" Kayzi asked.

The djed cast an annoyed look at Kayzi. "Then you will lead my people to safety like you did with your people. Take them to the next town and raise the warning."

"What of you, djed?" Dei insisted.

The djed lifted his chin, his eyes like jewels in the star lit sky now swirling with colors. "The Yria'ti foresaw it long ago that I would die in a battle when the Mountain Edieata came to warn us of attack. She said never will I serve under the Dragon of the Rising Sun, but I will create the escape so those who will can reach him." The djed made sure they understood before heading back to his place above the gates.

Dei's gaze followed the djed carefully. "Why do we open the gates?" she asked. "It is inviting disaster."

Zenerax looked down at her, his painted face alight with the thrill of battle. "Do not worry, love. The will of the gods cannot be changed. It will be as they wish it."

Dei sniffed. "Sometimes the gods don't see."

Zenerax ignored her last comment and turned to the woods. Dei came up next to him, watching.

For an hour the Tar-ten and Yria'ti waited. As the colors grew brighter and the falling stars more frequent, the two moons rose above the Cyrain Plains, drenching the land in silvery light. It was then that the first torch was seen through the dense woods that ended three thousand paces before the town walls. More and more torches were lit, dancing in the shadows of the trees. The noisy armor of the sylai creaked and banged as they readied themselves for battle. Harsh cries and growls were heard from the trees and soon a harsh chant issued from the creature's mouths, rolling over the lines of Ile as they stood to defend their town and those who could not fight.

The signal was given for the archers to draw their bows. The sylai, a thousand in all, stepped from the trees, and clanked their weapons against their armored bodies. The sound boomed over the town and children hidden in the houses began to scream.

Zenerax glanced back. "We should have evacuated the city when we had the chance."

Dei winced and pulled her bow up, aiming for a sylai. Zenerax and Kayzi followed her example. *"A'shaing te kra de naum!"* Dei whispered. Today is a good day to die.

The command to fire was given.

Dei let her arrow fly, another one quickly notched. The night arrows fell upon the sylai. Many bounced off the hard armor. Those that found flesh dealt death and brought screeches from the charging sylai.

They continued to aim and shoot, their arrows hitting and missing. Sweat poured down Deivenada's face, trailing down her neck and back. Reaching back for another arrow, her hand grasped nothing. She slid her bow into her quiver and picked up her spear. Jumping from the wall and landing soundly on her feet, she watched as the gates were opened and the chariots rolled out, archers and warriors loaded onto the back.

The sylai were five hundred paces away. The chariots aligned, two dozen in all. A horn sounded from the wall and the chariots charged. Dei looked up at Zenerax and Kayzi. They jumped down from the short wall and joined her. All along the walls, the Tar-ten jumped, landing on their feet, spears and swords at the ready. They stepped away from the wall. That was when the magic of the sylai hit them.

Dei crumpled to the ground, everyone around her becoming dizzy and weak. They too fell. Charioteers, aided by spells laced into the wood of the chariots were not affected by the magic and joined the battle with the sylai.

Dei struggled trying to regain her footing, but she felt as if she was drowning in a sea of water. Her breath came short and terror filled her eyes. She felt what seemed like a hand grasp her heart and clench it painfully. Screaming in pain, Dei tried to fight the magic, but it was to no avail.

As quickly as the magic was upon them, it was gone, thanks to the Yria'ti working their magic on the wall tops.

Dei sprung to her feet and let out a scream. She leveled her spear and charged into the melee. Zenerax ran next to her and gave her a grin before they melted into the battle, back to back, their spears dancing around them and dealing out swift death.

She never had time to think or feel, just react. She flowed from move to move, dancing around the sylai gracefully. Her face, streaked with blood and dirt, was hard, trying not to let in the emotion.

Kayzi fought next to them, his spear in one hand and a knife in the other. The knol on his face was smeared and it looked like blood.

The clang of steel on steel rang over the battle. Screams and battle cries filled the night air, as did the cries of the wounded.

Blood spurted on Dei's face as she sliced off a sylai's head. More blood ran along her arms as she dug a knife into another creature's stomach.

Ile and sylai fell, never to stand again.

Dei, Zenerax's warm back against her back, drew a knife and threw it. It landed in the throat of a sylai. The creature gurgled and collapsed. She bent down, ripping her knife from its throat only to throw it into one that was approaching her brother from behind. Her brother gave her a wild grin of thanks before turning his attention to another sylai.

Bringing her spear up to defend against a sword as it was swiped down, intending to cut her in half, Dei looked up into the black eyes of a sylai. The creature used its superior weight to force her to her knees. Screaming in rage, Deivenada bent, trying to force the creature off. The creature sneered at her, breath smelling of dead animals blasting her in the face. The creature brought out it's free hand, and pulled a knife from her belt. It reached its hand back, ready to gut her, when a spear blade cut through its neck. The head of the sylai landed on Dei as she fell backwards from the sudden release of pressure.

Scrambling back and away, she was yanked up by Zenerax. "We must go," he said. "The battle is lost."

Dei looked over the field of battle. Dead Ile and sylai lay entwined. All of the chariots were overturned, their wheels spinning slowly. Spears and arrows stuck out of the ground. Blood covered everything and the smell of death clung to the air like a sickly perfume. A few scattered skirmishes were still being carried out but for the Ile that still fought, the outcome looked bleak. Carrion birds already feasted on the dead, their squawks and bickering dishonoring those who lay still.

Dei, Zenerax and Kayzi sprinted for the gates of the town. The djed order the gates opened and let them in, along with a few other survivors.

"Get the people out!" the djed shouted down at them. "Get them somewhere safe!" The djed unsheathed his sword and jumped down on the other side of the wall, his battle cry sounding in the silencing aftermath of the battle.

The few survivors, along with Dei, Zenerax and her brother, ran through the town, collecting children and warriors who had chosen not to fight. The elders they came upon refused to go with them. Instead they armed themselves and marched to the front gates.

Dei called for Aska, Twoin and Jeikou. They came out of a house, frightened. Dei herded them to the back gates, mentally counting the original eleven. Relief swept her when she found they were all alive.

The gates were opened and over two hundred Edieata crept into the night, led by Dei, Zenerax and her brother. Over half that came with them were warriors. Turning south, they ran, heading towards the next town.

For seven days, they ran, all of the children and warriors fit enough to do so. It was in their blood to run. At night they slept, eating the meager food they brought or found. On the fifth day, they came across another band of refuges, fleeing towards the Edieata city. They joined forces and fled, trying to spread the warning.

At noon on the seventh day, they reached the next town. As they peeked over a hill, they stopped. The town was in ruins, burned and destroyed like Dei's village had been. Prayers to the gods were said quietly and they moved down the hill into the wreckage to look for survivors. They spent the day searching and found a group of men and women, nearly thirty strong, preparing to follow the sylai and take revenge. Without much persuasion, the group joined Dei, Zenerax and Kayzi. With the added group, the moving band of Edieata numbered four hundred.

In the two weeks it took them to reach the Edieata city, they passed through nine more villages and each time they were too late. It became obvious to them that the army of sylai they had fought was not the only army moving through the land. More survivors joined them and by the time they reached the city, which was thankfully still standing, their numbers were over five hundred.

At the outskirts of the city, they were attacked by two scores of sylai. It was their second battle with the sylai and that was when one of the original eleven died.

Dei had given strict orders for Aska to remain behind. But the little girl had been drawn to the sound of fighting and moved from her safe area toward the clearing and the location of the battle. When she reached the battle scene, it was chaos. Aska had turned to run when a sylai saw and killed her with a poisoned knife.

After burying the dead, they had moved into the city that was already prepared for war. They were given orders to help defend and were placed on the tall walls surrounding the city. The Djed of the Edieata gave the orders to Dei, Zenerax and Kayzi to lead the survivors out if the city should fall. This time Zenerax insisted that the city be deserted and those who were not fighting moved to a series of caves northwest of the city. The Djed had agreed and had sent over five hundred Ile into the caves, a large portion of them children and other Tar-ten who swore to protect the children if the worst should happen.

Dei looked over the countryside, tears in her eyes as she thought of those who had died. She was standing on the wall, waiting, once more, for night to fall and the battle to be begin. Zenerax was behind her, his hands massaging her back. Their weapons were propped against the battlements.

"Zen, if we fail tonight, we have a long journey to the Daaguwh city."

"I know, love. And if we do fail, we will be the Djed of the Edieata. I hope we can lead our people to safety."

Dei turned and embraced Zenerax. "Do not worry, my love. All will be well." *I pray to the gods all will be well.*

Dei sat in Zenerax's arms, looking out over the city. It was not a large city, maybe it held two thousand men and women. The only large features were the white stoned temples. Engraved upon each temple was the sign of the Light, a blazing sun with eight lightning bolts shooting out from it. Even though the Ile believed in four gods, the gods simply represented different parts of the Light. One represented war, another truth, one sun power, the power of the Light, and the other knowledge. They represented all things important to the Ile.

"Do you remember, heart of my heart, when we first fell in love?"

Dei looked at Zenerax, blushing. "I will never forget. You and my brother were dueling for practice and you beat him. I said, "I'm not surprised you beat Kayzi. He's not as good as I." Then you, after much silent urging from Kayzi agreed to duel me." Dei's blushed deepened. "I was winning until you kissed me on the lips and threw me off guard."

Zenerax laughed, a deep rumbling in his chest. "Yes, I was a little thrown off by that kiss too. But it was so tempting. You were so intent on revenging your brother's honor, you looked like a fiery goddess ready to smote her undeserving follower. I remember that after I won, you called foul and demanded a rematch."

"I deserved one! You cheated!"

"Ah, but I beat you in the second duel anyhow."

"I was worried you would kiss me again."

"Worried or hopeful?"

"Worried. You are such a horrible kisser."

"Am I?"

"Yes."

Zenerax bent down and kissed her long and passionately on the lips. He pulled back and his touch seemed to linger on her lips. Dei stared at nothing for a moment then shook her head and smiled. "You're not bad."

Zenerax laughed and caressed her cheek. "I am so lucky to have found you. I believe that love is one of those things not everyone gets and those who find it must honor it."

Dei nodded, resting her head on his shoulder. "We are lucky, so very lucky." She looked up at him. "When will you ask me to marry you again?" Three years ago, Zenerax had asked her to marry him. He had gone through all the rituals and had even asked Kayzi for his permission to marry her. Upon asking her, she declined because she wasn't ready for marriage. She was only seventeen but had promised she would say yes the next time, having no doubt that their love would continue.

"I will ask you when the time is right. I would ask you now but we are on the run and do not have the time to stop to get married. I would ask you every moment of every day if you would marry me, my love. I would, but it is not the time."

"When will be the time?" Dei asked, wishing she had said yes three years ago.

"When our people are safe and war is not a threat."

"Dei, Zenerax, we need to get into position," Kayzi said, running up to them. Night had fallen and magical torches were lining the walls. The army of the sylai, estimated to be over two thousand, sprawled out before them, large siege machine slowly being wheeled to the front line. Huge fires blazed in the plain below and sharp sounding horns filled the night air.

Kayzi, after informing them of the plan, turned and left. The Djed had appointed him the job, along with several other Tar-ten to protect the gates and make sure the sylai could not get through.

As Dei and Zenerax notched their bows, two hundred archers, bows straining in tension, joined them. Dei had strapped her spear to her back, and a dozen knives lined her belt.

Below them the sylai loaded rocks onto catapults. As soon as the rocks were in place, they burst into a magical flame.

"Why are we up here?" Dei asked. "They are going to destroy the city."

Zenerax smiled grimly. "I know, love, but we do not command the forces here, only those who came with us."

"Our arrows cannot even reach that far, Zen. We're ineffective up here. Why did the Djed station us up here?"

Zenerax shrugged, frowning. Wrapping cloth around the tip of his arrow, he dipped it into the magical torch. Once the arrow caught fire, he notched and pulled the arrow back until the red fletching touched his cheek. He sighted along the arrow, aiming carefully and taking in the slight breeze that blew across the wall top. Letting the arrow fly, the tip lighted by fire, they watched as it *thunked* into a catapult. The catapult burst into fire as the sylai hurried to douse the inferno.

"The Yria'ti have dealt with the problem of distance, it seems," Zenerax said, laughing as he watched the catapult crash to the ground, the burnt timbers useless.

Heartened by this turn of events, the other archers lit their arrows, aimed and loosened. The arrows zoomed up, arching and then the points turned down, thudding into the wooden planks of the catapults. Many of the catapults burst into flame but not before the sylai managed to set loose the burning rocks.

"Get off the wall!" Dei shouted, dragging Zenerax along the wall as boulders blazed towards them. The other archers scrambled to get away. Some laid flat on the wall, hidden by the battlements, others sprinted to the stairs, hurrying to get down.

Zenerax tackled Dei from behind, a boulder whizzing overhead and smashing into a building down below. The walls shuddered as rocks pounded against them. A roar ripped from the throats of the sylai and Dei knew they were running to take down the gates.

Dei and Zenerax scrambled up, running along the wall, dodging piles of rock and dead Tar-ten. They reached the stairs near the gates and looked down in horror as Tar-ten braced their bodies against the gates and sylai hammered on the gates with a battering ram.

Reaching back and grabbing an arrow from her quiver, Dei aimed down and shot her arrow. A sylai screamed, falling to the ground with an arrow growing from his neck.

Zenerax grinned reassuringly at her, drew an arrow and fired.

Another sylai dropped.

Aiming carefully and shooting, their aim helped by the light from all the fires, more sylai fell, dying.

Dei was the first to run out of arrows. As she searched among the rubble for something to throw or shoot, Zenerax shouted. Dei ran to him.

"What?" she screamed, fear filling her stomach.

Zenerax pointed down. Dei followed his finger and groaned. More sylai were coming and the battering ram had been rolled to the side. Then something implausible happened. The gates opened and the sylai stormed into the city.

Zenerax made to go down the stairs and fight, but Dei caught his arm. "Our duty is to take everyone else to safety." Zenerax looked at her, uncomprehending for a moment before he nodded. They ran across the walls, bellowing for a retreat to the caves. Kayzi caught up to them, blood covering his body.

"Kayzi, are you hurt?"

Kayzi shook his head. "It's not my blood."

Unrelenting, they ran along the walls. When they reached the far gates, they climbed down the stairs and opened the gates. They guided Tar-ten, who had been assigned to help protect the children if the battle went bad, out of the city. Only three hundred would stay behind to fight and give the others time to escape.

Dei glanced up as a temple exploded into fire. They waited a moment before closing the gates and running into the woods.

Exhausted and tired, they reached the caves, where over a thousand Edieata waiting for them. Putting aside their weariness, they ordered everyone out of the caves, and at a slow run, they left, making their way north to Dagau. The children who were too small to run were carried on backs and a few who were injured were carried between two warriors.

By dusk of the next day, they were miles from the city. Dei, Zenerax and Kayzi ordered a short rest before they moved on. No one complained, the desire to reach the protection of the Daaguwh lands was too great.

In one week they crossed the border, where they rested for a day.

Dei soon forgot what it was like to not move. All they did was run or walk, never stopping for anything but food and rest. Weapons weighed down the warriors and the gathered food weighted the children. The days melted together. The strain of leadership in the beginning wore on all three, but by the time they were near Dagau, the strain lessened and they were able to lead their people without fear or stress, only the simple determination of leaders to keep their people safe.

Two weeks later, Dei, Zenerax and Kayzi along with a thousand other Edieata found themselves outside the city of Dagau, the feeling of security filling the hearts of most for the first time in a long while. Now all that was required was an audience with the Daaguwh Council, so they could ask permission to stay within the Daaguwh lands.

Chapter 9
Elven Warrior

Qwaser Silverglow of the Elves took up his bow and pulled an arrow from his quiver. Wood slid against leather.

He took aim at his target, a hole in a tree, keeping both eyes open. He let the arrow fly. The arrow stood quivering dead center in the hole.

Qwaser sighed and rested his head against the trunk of a large oak. Why was shooting an arrow so easy, when he could barely ask a girl to a festival the village was planning?

Qwaser was nine hundred years old. He looked as if he was twenty, with short brown hair that did not cover his ears and startling bright green eyes. He had been born in the Fourth Age, during the Second Battle. He was roughly around the height of five-ten and good looking by elven standards. A necklace with a hanging black crystal was tied around his throat.

Qwaser notched another arrow and fired, scarcely noticing that it hit the dead center of the tree. His mind was elsewhere, focusing on elven maidens and the upcoming festival. *Why can I never seem to get a girl to go with me to a ball or festival?* he thought. *Hasaxta can walk up to a lady he doesn't even know and ask her to dance and she always says yes. Maybe it's because I prefer to hunt and be by myself. Or that I'm always getting into trouble by going to the outer limits of the kingdom in search of adventure or maybe it is because I'm here in a village just outside the Elven Nation's boundaries, because I spoke to a human, making me an outcast. Why is Tghil against me?*

Qwaser had been living in the village for three years now and he was starting to wish he was back at court, with his mother, father, and brother, and never had laid eyes on the human girl. The law forbad him of course. He had a five-year sentence because of his encounter.

He remembered it so clearly.

 og   oe   ਠ

Qwaser was in the outer limits of elven land, exploring the area. His brother and Hasaxta were with him. They had decided they wanted to hunt the wild goose in the area. It was believed the goose were extra plentiful and it would not hurt the populations if one or two were taken for a meal.

Growing bored with his friend and brother's attempts to shoot something, Qwaser moved off, alone, stalking through the forest.

The forest was filled with the sounds of life. Birds flittered from branch to branch, chirping and singing their songs. Insects buzzed in the air and large butterflies, dazzling the watcher with their colors, quietly flew through the air. Squirrels nibbled away at nuts and pinecones, while deer nosed through the leafy floor of the forest, searching for edible plants.

Qwaser slipped his bow into his quiver and then swung it over his back. He walked for a while before noticing that the woods were starting to thin. Intrigued and mindful he was near human territory, he slowed his pace and crept cautiously forward.

Reaching the end of the woods, he stopped, parting the tree branches and looking out. Vast rolling plains spread before him, covered in the tall green grasses of summer. The blue sky touched the plains at the horizon and Qwaser had a sudden urge to walk towards that horizon and into the unknown.

Suppressing the desire to do so, he occupied himself by stepping out of the woods and into the open, a dangerous place to be for an elf in times when elves did not exist in human minds.

On the whispering breeze came the soft melody of a song. Qwaser moved silently to the song, his senses heightened by the threat of possible danger. *What is it?* he thought, as he lowered himself to the ground, parted the grass and looked out.

Sitting on the ground, gathering berries from a bush, sat a young human girl. Long blonde hair that hung in curls splashed to her waist. Her sweet voice continued to sing, telling of a lost love. Her pink dress and white coat were out of place on the plains. She carried no weapons save for a knife sheathed at her belt.

Qwaser stood up, looking down at her. He had never seen a human before and he kept noticing the differences. She did not have elegantly pointed ears like he, nor almond shaped eyes and delicate features like that of most elves. Her body was neither naturally lean nor small boned, but he supposed her way of life made her as thin as he was. Freckles dotted her cheeks and nose.

As if aware that someone was watching her, she turned and looked up into Qwaser's bright green eyes. She frowned. "Who are you?"

Qwaser, like all elves, knew the language of mankind. "I'm Qwaser Silverglow of the Elven Nation."

The girl rose to her feet and Qwaser was surprised that she was almost his height.

"An elf, huh?" She didn't seem shocked by this but instead seemed to accept it as if she had always suspected but was never sure. "I am Cadinyss, the daughter of the blacksmith of Zarana. You can call me Cadiny." She smiled and held out her hand.

Qwaser shook it before withdrawing his hand. "What are you doing out here? It's unsafe to be alone."

She shrugged her small shoulders. "I can take care of myself." She looked up at him through her long eyelashes. "Why are you here?"

"I was hunting and grew bored. Your singing caught my attention, so I followed it. I was not expecting to find a human."

"Why not? You are in Caendor, the strongest human nation of this

Age. What did you think you would find?"

"I do not know." He looked back at the woods. "I should be going."

"Why? I want to learn about your people. Stay, please."

"It is against the law for an elf to talk to a human. I must go or I will have to face the consequences of speaking to you."

The human laughed, shocking Qwaser. He didn't think they were capable of laughter. The stories always portrayed humans as ugly, mean and dull creatures. This girl was everything but ugly, mean and dull.

The girl sat down on a rock and pointed to the one next to her. "Sit," she said, command in her voice.

Qwaser, more interested than anything, sat down and watched her closely. "I want to learn about your people. Will you tell me?"

The girl grinned. "Why not? I live in Caendor, which is ruled by a king and queen. Their daughter, the Princess Janevra, will inherit the throne when her parents deem her worthy. Lately the Priests of the Light have been searching for the Dragons, fearful of the prophecy being fulfilled before they find the Dragons." Qwaser nodded. The elves had the same prophecy as the humans. "I don't know what else to tell you, Qwaser Silverglow."

"Your Priests, do they know magic?"

"Most of them. I have some Talent of my own." She looked at him, filled with pride. Suddenly a pink flower appeared in her hand and she handed it to him. "How old are you?" she asked.

"I am almost nine hundred years old, and you?" he asked, accepting the flower.

"You're old. I'm sixteen."

Qwaser stared at her. She had only lived sixteen years? He wondered briefly how humans managed to survive at all with such short a lifespan.

The girl stood up, picking up a basket full of berries. "I should be going," she said. "My father wanted me back before noon." She smiled at him and hurried off through the grass, calling to her horse. The horse came galloping up and she rode off, waving as she disappeared down a hill.

Qwaser stood and walked back into the woods where his brother and Hasaxta jumped down from the trees, their eyes cold.

"Why, Qwaser?" his brother demanded. "You know the laws."

When they had returned home after a month of travel, his brother and friend had informed his parents and his parents, acting under the law, reported what had happened to the King. A trial was held and Qwaser found himself an outcast for five years in a small elven town.

                              ෪   ଔ   ଷ

Shaking his head, Qwaser left the past. It was no use. What was done, was done.

He sighed. He had better get home if he felt like saying goodbye to

Brytaya before she left. She was leaving very early in the morning, so early
he would still be dreaming. Brytaya was an elf just like him, always getting
into trouble. She had been sent out a year after he had come, because she
too had talked to a human. She only had to be an outcast for two years. He
would miss her. She was a dear friend of his, but she seemed to have a dark
secret, something that she would not tell him even when he pressured her.

He went over and pulled the arrows from the tree.

He kicked leaves as he walked through the forest. Why was everything
that he did not want to happen happening? With the Dragons having met
but not found and him in the middle of nowhere, he would never have an
adventure in his life or fulfill his dream of fighting next to the Dragons in the
Fifth Battle.

Qwaser shuffled onto a well-worn path, kicking up dust.

He glanced up at the sky, now starting to dance with colors. Oranges
and reds intertwined. Yellows and greens flowed from one spot to another.
Purple and blue formed patterns that only the shoi and the gifted of the
Plains people could read. White, the brightest of all, seemed to flow like
water across the black sky. Stars twinkled behind the colors; painting a
picture no artist could paint.

Lights in the distance told him he was nearing his goal. He picked up
his pace and started to run.

He was barely breathing hard when he got to the edge of the village.
The last light of the day was diminishing over the mountains.

The village was small, probably only over two hundred people living in
or near by. The village was made of beautiful white stone houses, each
holding a family. Gardens surrounded every house and trees filled with
white flowers grew along the elven streets, near their windows and in the
courtyards. The trees added a sweet perfume in the air and when the wind
blew gently, the blossoms fell, looking like little fairies dancing in the wind.
During the day, the village the elves called Andaon, after the Elven prince
who had died during the Second Battle, was full of trading. Smells of all
kinds roamed the streets, as did sounds. The blacksmith making horse-
shoes, the potter setting out new pots, the baker drawing people to its door
for fresh bread and the weaver positioning beautifully made blankets.

The elves of the Northern Kingdom were a race that cherished every
plant and animal. They only took what they needed, never more, like
humans did. They lived in harmony with nature and kept beautiful gardens
of unknown splendor growing in their land. The magic that they used for
this was a wild magic, a magic that lived in the heart of all living things.
The elves, the ones who could use this magic, brought this out of the plants
to make them grow into pictures of fairytales.

Reaching a small white stone house, Qwaser opened the door and the
scent of roses drifted over him. Brytaya made incense and had made a
fortune selling it in the village. She loved herbs and was somewhat of a
healer.

He found Brytaya sitting by the fire, watching the flames flicker. He set his bow and arrows by the door.

Brytaya had bound her raven black hair up into a bun. She was short, her head only reaching to his chest. But he loved her like a younger sister.

"Hello, my friend. How was shooting?" Brytaya said, standing up and turning towards him.

"I had good aim today," he said closing the door behind him.

"Did you know that I was hoping you would not have come back for a while?" she said, walking over to him, the smell of roses engulfing him.

"No. Why?"

"I was making you a fare-thee-well gift."

"Oh. Do you want me to leave?" he asked.

"No, it's okay," she waved her hand in front of him. "I finished it."

She pulled a small bottle out of a pocket in her blouse. The bottle had a clear thick liquid in it.

"What is it?" he asked. She was always tricking him with some sort of thing. One week after he had met her, she had given him a vial of a green liquid. She said it was a formula to use for his arrows that would make them more flexible. She had battered her lashes at him and begged him to put it on his arrows. Who could resist doing what she wanted when she acted as if she was going to have a tantrum? It turned out to be incense, and his case of arrows smelled of strong perfume for a month. He had learned not to trust her completely.

She laughed. It was a low sound, like a bell. "Don't worry. I'm not trying to trick you. It's a healing potion for large cuts. Seriously!" she said as his eyebrows rose. She handed him the vial.

"Thank you, Brytaya. And this is for you." He pulled from his tunic a small red and blue stone he had found one day in the forest and a rare herb.

She smiled at him as he handed her her gift.

"Thank you, Qwaser, I will treasure it always." She stood on tiptoe and hugged him, planting a kiss on his cheek.

"I was hoping…" Qwaser began but stopped as a crash shook the house.

"What was that?" Brytaya whispered.

More noise floated to them, the sound of fighting.

They crept to the door. Qwaser opened it a crack, and gasped. The village was on fire and battle was raging in the Green. He opened the door further.

Ugly, grayish beasts ran about, flailing axes and swords, cutting open screaming elves. Greasy hair covered their heads. Sharp pointed yellow teeth protruded from the creatures as they snarled and their bodies were covered in black armor. Charred wood reached his nose, along with the odor of death.

Too late did he realize his mistake in opening the door. Two rogui came towards him, bearing spears.

"Quickly, Brytaya, hand me my arrows."

Brytaya stepped back and grabbed for his bow and arrows. She thrust them to him.

Quickly taking aim, he fired. An arrow jutted from one of the beast's foreheads. The other, yelling in rage, charged forward.

Qwaser notched another arrow and shot the rogui, hitting it in the chest. Blood flowed from its mouth as it gurgled a harsh prayer to its god.

Qwaser stepped out of the house, Brytaya close on his heels and holding a sword.

"Where did you get that?" he asked her.

"I've always had it, a gift from my father."

"Do you know how to use it?"

She nodded, and as if to prove it, ran the rogui sprinting towards them through its middle.

Blood drenched her sword, staining it red.

Back to back they went, one shooting arrows and the other fending off attackers with a sword.

Qwaser had never been in battle before and he felt queasy at the sight of all the blood and guts.

"Qwaser... help..."

He turned around at the sound of Brytaya's voice. What he saw threw him into a frenzy. He picked up her sword and swung it at the rogui's head. The rogui had one moment to know what was happening before it was beheaded, and toppled over backwards with a crash.

Qwaser felt the sword go through bone and shivered. Blood spurted on his arms and chest from the beast's neck.

He dropped the sword and went to his knees next to Brytaya, cradling her head in his arms. A knife was sticking out of her middle, seeping blood. Her hair had fallen out of its bun and was covering her features.

"Brytaya," he whispered, pulling her hair out of her face.

"Even...the potion...I gave you...won't heal....me. I hope ...you...like it."

"I do! I love it. Don't leave me, Brytaya. You can't!" His tears landed on her face.

"Promise me...you'll—" she took a deep rasping breath. "Promise me you'll fight for the right cause...when the Fifth Battle comes...and find...someone who cares...for you as much as I did. I hope you find the...Dragons...and fight for them...I...." Blood dripped out of her mouth. Her eyes dimmed and then clouded over in death.

"Brytaya! No!" he screamed, still holding her body close. "Damn you!" he shrieked at the approaching rogui.

Filled with anger and despair, he picked up Brytaya's sword and ran at the creature, blood filling his eyes in battle rage.

At the sight of him the rogui stumbled backwards, trying to get away, but was still slashed and killed.

Qwaser moved forward, killing and injuring everything that was not elven.

Smoke stung at his eyes, and sweat trickled down his shirt. Dirt was smudged on his face, streaked with blood.

The remaining rogui fled back into the forest, yowling in anger at the lone elf that seemed to have no fear, only rage and hatred.

Qwaser slumped to the ground, breathing in deep grateful breaths. He licked his dry lips and stood back up.

The battlefield was strung with wounded and dead. Moans and wails carried through the air and to his ears. But what scared him the most was that he had killed something and felt nothing but rage and loathing.

He was one of the only ones not wounded or dead. Moving around the wounded, Qwaser ended their life if it was too fatal, bandaging those who could be helped. He killed any live rogui he found.

In the end, only five elves could get up and walk, and be thankful for life.

The remaining five, including Qwaser, were young, and had had practice with weapons before.

"We need to bury our dead. We must dig a trench to fit over one-hundred," he said to the weary group.

"I agree," said the only women survivor. She was Qwasers's age, with long honey hair and bright blue eyes. "When do we tell the King? Now?"

"No, I think we should bury our dead first then tell the King," replied a youth.

During the eight days it took to dig the trench, they were attacked one more time by a small group of rogui, reducing their group down to four and killing all that had been injured.

The bodies gave off a horrible stench and soon they could barely breathe. They worked quickly to finish the trench, wrapping the bodies in linen they had scavenged from the ruined homes and laying them in the grave. They used a large, flat rock as a crude headstone and carved words into its surface.

The stone planted on top of the grave read:

"Those who died here are the first to die of Elven blood in the Fifth Battle. They were killed for no reason. Innocent elves were cut down where they stood. We hope that every passerby fights for the right cause and joins the Dragons."

The last words on the stone were the last words of a dying elf, Qwaser thought, bitter tears sliding down his cheek as a small ceremony was performed by the last elves.

A hot discussion on what to do soon erupted after the ceremony.

"We need to leave. The King must know about this."

"But we need to get help from other nations, too. We cannot fight this war alone," replied the woman, whose name was Kalioa.

"No! Humans won't help us," said a boy named Tasawer. He was a skinny youth only six hundred years old. He had a remarkable resemblance to Brytaya.

"Oh yes, they would, I know they would," said a boy the same age as Tasawer named Danlk.

Qwaser, who had yet to speak, spoke. "I think we should go to the humans for help. I have met one before. They are just like us, in trouble and running from the dark," he whispered softly. The battle had changed him and he was filled with hate. "I can only go because I cannot go back to the city and I can speak their tongue better than any of you. I am not wanted anyhow and I don't care to go back home. I will go by myself. I will travel to Jariran to get help and find a way to bring our people back into the world. This isolation of ours must end or it will be our doom."

The others gaped at him, and then slowly nodded their heads in agreement.

The next morning was cloudy and smoky. No birds sung, no wind murmured in the trees, nothing was living, except four elves, with misty eyes, staring down at a grave filled with loved ones.

"I'll never forget you. When we meet again, we will fight in battle together," said Qwaser.

"And I will not forget you, Qwaser," said the honey haired Kalioa.

"Good-bye, my friend, I hope you get help, for your sake and ours," said Tasawer.

"I know we only just met, but I have grown to respect you. Kill some rogui for me, huh?" said Danlk.

"I will, Danlk. Tell my parents where I went, will you? And tell them to pray that the Dragons are ready to lead armies into battle. Don't forget to prepare the King for whatever may happen when I return or with whom I might return."

Qwaser hugged everyone once more, then turned and only looked back once to wave goodbye.

"I hope he makes it," said Kalioa, fingering the pendant around her neck.

"Oh, he will, I know he will," answered Danlk.

"He is brave, and for the world's sake, I hope he is on the side of the Dragons come the Last Battle." Tasawer gazed after Qwaser.

They turned their backs and began to walk towards the city.

Qwaser, his body covered by a black cloak, moved quickly away from the ruined town, trying to leave behind painful memories. Brytaya had been one of his only friends in his long life. Many of his friends had come and gone, moving on to other things. Perhaps it was Qwaser's rebellious nature that turned them away and his constant desire for adventure. Where most elves wanted peace and quiet, Qwaser wanted heart-pounding excitement. Hasaxta and Brytaya were the only ones who had stayed with him in his search for glory and exhilaration.

He arrived in Zarana six hours later. Making sure to cover his ears with his cloak and conceal his sword and bow, he walked down the street. Needing a place to stay but having no money, he wondered if he would be able to find Cadinyss's house.

"Excuse me, sir," Qwaser said, stopping a man on the street. "Do you know where I can find the blacksmith?" *I hope to the goddess Tghil there is only one,* he thought.

The man looked at him suspiciously before nodding his head slowly. "You're not far. Go two more blocks and turn right and you'll find the blacksmith."

Qwaser thanked him and hastened down the street, turning right once he passed two blocks. He stopped, looking down the street and spotting a sign with an anvil and hammer upon it.

Qwaser reached the door and walked into a small room with a counter. An open door showed a back room where the forge was located. Voices came from the forge area, two men's voices. Waiting patiently for one of the men to come to the counter, Qwaser leaned against the wall.

"Yes, Father, I know," came a voice, and through the door walked a young man in his early twenties.

The young man spotted Qwaser and jumped. "Sorry, sir, I didn't hear you come in. What can I do for you?"

Qwaser moved over to the counter and leaned across it. "Does Cadinyss live here?"

The young man scowled at Qwaser. "Who wants to know?"

Qwaser's bright green eyes flared with annoyance. "I do and if she happens to live here would you please go and get her so I can speak to her?"

The young man looked Qwaser over. "You're not the father, are you?" His gazed traveled up and down Qwaser's body. "You're about the right age and she did say the father was fine featured."

Taken aback, Qwaser shook his head. *What kind of world have I jumped into?* he thought. "Just get her," Qwaser snapped. "Or I will find her myself."

The young man darted back into the forge.

While he waited once more, Qwaser put his hand under his cloak, touching Brytaya's sword. *I will avenge you, my friend. I will join the Dragons and kill as many rogui as I can. But no matter how many I kill, it will not be enough to avenge your life which was so unfairly taken from you,* Qwaser thought.

The young man came back into the room, a mug of wine in his hand. He handed it to Qwaser saying, "My sister will be down in a moment." He left Qwaser to his drink.

Qwaser stared down into his drink, swirling the contents in the mug. He brought it up to his nose and sniffed. Coughing, he set it down on the table. *What kind of foul concoction is this?* he thought. *It smells like a sewer!*

"Don't like your beer, I see," said a voice from the forgery doorway. "It's a good thing you don't. My brother makes it strong. That's how he likes it."

Qwaser looked up and saw Cadinyss standing in the door, hands on her hips. Her stomach was bulging slightly from a five-month pregnancy and her blonde hair was hanging down over her shoulders. Her face was older and Qwaser was amazed how much she had changed in three years. She regarded him curiously.

Moving into the room, she stood behind the counter. "Do I know you? My brother insists that you are the man that got me pregnant, but I know he left town when he found out what happened. So, who are you?"

Qwaser pulled the hood from his head, letting her see his pointed ears. "I'm Qwaser Silverglow."

Cadinyss blinked, staring at him before suddenly smiling and running around the counter to embrace him. "Qwaser! How good it is to see you! You have no idea how glad I am!" She took his hand. "Come, we shall go upstairs and have some tea and you can tell me all that has happened since I saw you."

She directed him upstairs and had him sit at the table. She grabbed two mugs and set them on the table, pouring tea into them. She set the pitcher down and sat next to him, joyful. "Tell me, how has life treated you?"

Qwaser, drawn to her openness and genuine feelings, something elves rarely showed, found himself telling her all that had happened in the last three years. He told her all of it. Even if he did not know her well, he felt comfortable talking to her.

As his story progressed, her face grew sad and her merry eyes darkened. She laid a hand on his, comforting him with a soft caress. When he mentioned war, she shivered and a tear ran down her cheek.

Finished with his story, Qwaser took a deep drink of his tea, trying to wash away all thoughts of Brytaya. Even though he was unsuccessful, he did manage to sooth his dry throat from so much talking.

"Qwaser, I am so sorry. I wish I had known that things were that bad in your land. I must say, though, that attacks have been happening here, too. The King has sent out soldiers to guard the towns and villages. It's helped, but it's not enough to save everyone." She paused, taking a sip of her tea. "If you can reach Jariran, you should try to find the Princess Janevra. She will help you. Her father won't. He does not believe in elves."

"How do you know the Princess does?"

"Janevra is that way. I know I don't know her, but she is the heir so word spreads. She always seemed to me to be a person who would believe in things others do not."

Qwaser nodded. "I will remember that."

Cadinyss set her tea down. "What can I do to help you, Qwaser?"

Qwaser smiled at her. "I have nothing with which to pay you."

Cadinyss waved a hand. "Do not worry. In times such as these, we must be as giving as we can to those who need our help."

"I could use a horse and some money."

Cadinyss nodded, biting her lip. "Yes, we have a horse I can give you, a few extra chips to get you to Jariran and some food. Will that be enough?"

Nodding, he grasped her hand. "Thank you, my friend. I do not know how I will repay you." He thought for a moment and then slipped his black crystal necklace off his neck. "Here, take this. It's a good luck charm. It will protect you in times of war." He laid the necklace on the table. "If the need of money ever arises, this black crystal will be able to get you a decent amount."

Cadinyss touched the necklace. "It's beautiful but won't you need it? You will be fighting much more than I."

Qwaser shook his head. "No, I've had luck my whole life. It is time for someone else to have it."

Cadinyss clasped the necklace around her neck, smiling at it. She reached into her pocket and pulled out four gold coins. Handing them to Qwaser, she stood, hurried over to a cupboard and took out a loaf of bread and a wedge of cheese. She thrust them into a bag and tossed them to Qwaser. After a moment of thought, she faced him and said, "Follow me."

Qwaser got up and followed her back down the stairs and out into a yard with a barn at the far end. She unlocked the door and motioned him in. She escorted him to a stall that housed a large gray stallion.

"I'm sorry we don't have a saddle."

"Don't worry. The horse itself will do fine," Qwaser said, stepping into the stall and grasping the horse's reins. The horse nickered quietly and allowed Qwaser to lead it from the stall and into the streets of Zarana.

Qwaser swung onto the horse's back. He looked down at Cadinyss and thanked her one last time.

"I don't suppose we will see each other again," she said.

"No, I suppose not," Qwaser said. "Promise me, if things go bad here, you will go to the Lost Mountains. That necklace will buy you safe passage, even if you are human. No elf can send off a carrier of the black crystal."

Cadinyss's eyes grew bright. "Is there a legend behind the black crystal?"

"Yes, but I have no time to tell it to you. Just promise me, you will leave if things go bad, so your child will have a life with a mother."

"I promise," she said. "As I promise to name my child Brytaya if the child is a girl."

Qwaser felt tears spring to his eyes. "Thank you," he said hoarsely. Qwaser wheeled his horse, kicked it in the sides and galloped down the street, heading southeast to Jariran.

He left the town behind him, the horse's hooves clicking on the dirt packed road. The sun began to set behind him, casting his shadow far out in front of him. The sky turned a dark blue, stars popping up to twinkle down upon him. The two moons rose in the east, shedding light onto the countryside, allowing Qwaser to see even more clearly than before. His eyes had the special ability, like all elves, to see in the dark. They could not see clearly but were able to see shapes and figures in the dark, making them fearful fighters during the night.

By the time the moons were near their peak, Qwaser slowed the horse and guided it off the road. He slept for a few hours before leading his horse back onto the road and beginning the journey once more.

For six days his pattern was riding, sleeping for five hours and then getting back on the horse and riding some more.

Nearing Jariran, Qwaser slowed his horse, the amount of people using the road forcing him to slow. Wagons crept down the road and people on horses trotted by. Qwaser made sure the hood of his cloak was up to hide his ears. He did not want unnecessary attention.

Veering past an old man driving a wagon, Qwaser looked up and gaped. Huge obsidian walls towered above him. Men patrolled the walls and the large gates were open, travelers streaming in and out of them. Steering his horse through the gates and into the city, Qwaser felt his heart soar. The city of Jariran reminded him of the elven city where the King resided. Everything, the buildings, the people, even the streets spoke of beauty. No wonder humans called it the City of Jewels. The city almost surpassed the elven cities and that would have been a feat. Rising in front of him, at the end of the street, he could see the fabled Tower of the Light as it rose above the Four Towers and the heights of the palace.

Qwaser jumped off his horse and found directions to a stable. Glad that it was close, he hurried to it, stabled his horse, paid the owner of the stable two gold chips and got back on to the main road that lead to the palace.

Moving down the street, his awe of the city settled and by the time he reached the Central Plaza, he felt almost at home.

Qwaser walked through the plaza, only knowing its name from a sign at the corner of the street. He stopped at the fountain in the center, and dipped his hands in it to wash his face. Clean and dripping, he wiped his face and hands on his cloak, careful not to remove the cloak.

"Caya, you cheated!" a young voice bellowed from outside an inn.

"I did not! I won because you can't play this game very well!"

Qwaser smiled. *Maybe those girls can help me.* Moving over to them, he took in their appearance. The girl named Caya had a long pointed nose, which, at the moment, she was staring down at her friend.

The other girl's clothes were wrinkled but were once of top quality, as were the other girl's. At the moment her thin lips were pressed in a thin line, as she glared at her companion.

"I hate it when you cheat, Caya!" the girl said, pulling out a stack of cards and glaring at her friend.

"I told you, I did not cheat, Lousai. I play fair unlike you!"

"You think *I* cheated?" Lousai's eyes narrowed.

Qwaser cleared his throat and both girls jerked, staring up at him. "May I sit?" he asked.

The girls glanced at one another then nodded.

Pulling out a chair, Qwaser sat, breathing in the deep scent of flowers that hung from above. He laid his last two gold chips on the table. Both girls perked up and raised eyebrows in question.

"I need your help," he said. "For the right information, you can have those chips."

"What do you need, sir?" the girl named Lousai asked, slapping her friend's hand away as she tried to reach for the coins. "Wait, Caya. You're being rude."

Caya rubbed her hand. "I didn't cheat," she muttered. She then brightened suddenly and turned to Qwaser, smiling broadly. "What can we do?"

"I'm looking for someone who can help. If you know of someone, please tell me where I can find them."

"Janevra will help you. She helps everyone. When she took in Mat after—" Caya began before Lousai kicked her under the table.

"Before we send you to anyone, we need to know your intentions," Lousai said.

Qwaser sighed. "I'm an elf." He pulled back his hood to show them his ears before quickly hiding it again. "My people need help. We have been isolated from the world for so long, we cannot rejoin it without help. There is also the problem of our villages being attacked. We have the power to fight them, but our Prophecies say we must look for help outside or meet our doom."

The girls gawked at him. Caya's mouth hung open and Lousai blinked rapidly.

"The Princess Janevra will help you. She lives in the palace. Her room is on the seventh floor and has large ivory doors," Lousai said, recovering before her friend. "I promise she will help you."

Qwaser, relieved that they had said the same thing as Cadinyss, thanked them. He pushed his chair in and hurried out of the plaza. Knowing the guards would not let him in to see the Princess, he left the main road and zigzagged until he came to a sidewall that divided the palace from the rest of the town.

Now the problem of how to get over the wall arose. He could not climb it. He did not have the proper equipment and more than likely, someone would see him and raise the alarm.

His eyes settled on a small door at the end of the wall by one of the

Four Towers. Grinning, Qwaser pulled an arrow from under his cloak and snapped it in half. He moved to the door and examined the lock. Perfect. He slid the broken arrow shaft into the lock and twisted until it clicked open.

Pushing the door open, he glided in, and shut it gently behind him. Qwaser found himself in the lush gardens of the palace.

Moving like a shadow, he ran through them, and into the palace where he sprinted through the hall and up seven flights of stairs, barely becoming winded in the process. He looked down the hallway, glad to find no one in sight. At the end of one hallway was a pair of large ivory doors.

Chapter 10
An Elven Stranger

ALD 3919 SD May

Janevra sat in one of the balcony chairs, reading one of the magical books of Light. She was trying to learn as much as possible about the theory of magic but so far had not learned much outside what the priest had told her when she and Mat had taken their Test of the Robe.

The sun was high above her, sending its rays down onto her back. It was a cloudless day and birds sung as they flew. It was so quiet the breath of the city itself could be heard.

A knock sounded in her room. She frowned and briefly wondered who it could be. Not Mat. Mat had gone into the city to buy some books. And it certainly wasn't Teaa. Teaa was busy with palace chores and had no time to stop.

Janevra walked through the anteroom, setting her book on a table and opened the door leading to the hallway.

Her eyebrows rose when she saw a man standing in the doorway. His face was shadowed in the hood over his head. A bow was slung over his back. His clothes were very strange. They seemed to be made of some sort of silk and leather sewn together to form a rough seeming material. He had a sword belted to his waist. She briefly wondered how he had made his way through the palace without an escort and without someone removing his sword.

The man bowed low. "Princess Janevra, I am Qwaser." And that was it. He didn't add a last name or anything and he spoke with an accent as strange as his clothes.

Janevra bit her lip. "Yes?"

The man straightened. "May I come in?"

Janevra nodded and stood aside. It was only after she had let him in did she stop to think that that wasn't smart. She shrugged to herself. *Oh well, it's not like I'm defenseless.*

Qwaser sat down on one of the anteroom chairs. He had pulled his hood back but not enough to see his ears. His eyes were a bright brilliant green and his light brown hair was short.

Janevra sat down opposite him. "How may I help you?"

Qwaser smiled grimly. "I was told by a young women that you might be able to help me. I must say I had my doubts but when I ran into two little girls who said you might help, I took them for their word." He paused then pulled down his hood.

Janevra gasped. His ears did not stop at rounded tops but continued up into elegant points. Sitting in front of her was an elf. Instantly questions popped up into her mind. *Why are you here? What happened to your immortality?* She remained silent, however, watching him.

When she didn't respond, Qwaser continued. "I'm sorry to surprise you, but I need your help. My people were attacked by rogui two weeks ago. We know the attacks will continue. Since we are spread out among the Lost Mountains, it was decided we needed the help of Men. Help that we will need with the coming of the Fifth Battle. So I was sent. I found you."

Janevra quickly swallowed her surprise and secret triumph in always believing elves were real and coming out to be right. "I will do whatever I can to help you but—"

Qwaser cut her off. "Someone is coming."

Obviously his ears, aside from being tipped, were better too. Deciding not to take the risk of Qwaser being seen, she ushered him onto the balcony and closed the door slightly.

"Wait here."

She picked up the book she had set on her table and sat down in her chair to read.

❧   ⌒   ⁊

Mat found Janevra in her rooms, looking at the magical books of the Light. He set two books on the anteroom table, their soft leather covers tingling against his skin. He had never owned his own books before.

Mat and Janevra had gone through all four of the books of the Light. Their powers grew daily and both were soon bored with the simple teachings of the books and had begun to explore things outside of what the books showed them.

Mat smiled at Janevra. She was wearing a gray dress today, and he thought it looked good on her.

Two weeks had gone by since the Festival of the Stars, and she had revealed her plans of how to escape marriage.

"Janevra, I have a something to tell you," he said, startling her.

"What is it, Mat?" she asked setting the book on the glass table.

"The King is holding a meeting in the War Room."

"The War Room. Why?" Janevra asked alarmed.

"To discuss party favors," Mat said sarcastically.

Janevra shot him a look before hopping out of her chair and hurrying out of the room. Mat followed close behind.

Mat missed his parents sorely, but there was nothing he could do about their death. He had stayed in contact with Jordan and Breon, occasionally sending them money Janevra gave him. His life was not the same. He was neither a lord nor a servant. He lived in the palace now, a friend to the Princess, trusted and cared for. But he had no place in the world, which was beginning to change from the place he once knew to something darker.

Every day Ravften came to Janevra's room, calling for an audience with her and everyday she refused him, while Mat burned in anger each time the man insisted upon seeing her. Janevra had once come to the door and punched Ravften full in the face before he had asked for an audience. Mat secretly despised the man, and wished him gone from their lives. However, much to Mat and Janevra's sorrow, the King had made the final declaration of Janevra's marriage to Ravften, all that was needed was a signing of papers to prove Ravften the legal heir as long as he married Janevra. When Janevra heard the news, she had been furious and had stormed up to her father, screaming in a deadly rage. "How dare you, Father! You have brought the glory of this nation down upon us! Ravften will annihilate everything we love and care for with his evil powers! He will see this nation turn to the Dark Lord like Angarat so long ago! How dare you!" she had shouted. The King and Queen had not responded to her anger, only saying that in time she would come to accept this new change in her life. By then Janevra was much too angered to say anything and had used her magic out of anger. She blew up one of the rooms in the palace, scorching it with fire. Her parents, astounded she could use magic, stared at her while Janevra calmly left the room. Mat remembered himself smiling at the King and Queen before shutting the doors behind them.

Janevra, who had stopped in front of large oak doors, brought him out of his thoughts. Pushing through them, she walked into a room hot with argument.

"Father, what is going on?" she demanded in surprise and anger, halting any conversation that once occupied the room.

Mat hung back, as a good servant should, barely even entering the large room.

The King smoothed down his mustache and cleared his throat. A nervous habit Mat assumed. "My daughter," the King said. "This is not something you should worry about." The King was sitting at the end of a large wooden table. Lords of all ranks surrounded him. But what made Janevra's blood boil, Mat knew, was that next to him was Ravften, her to be husband, the man she hated.

"Father, no matter what you say I am going to be here and help. If Lord Ravften can, then I can. Now tell me, what is the meaning of this talk of war?" Janevra said, her voice harsh and cold.

The King ran his eyes around the room. "You see, daughter, rumors are that forces are massing in the south. A letter from the King of Selkare said he is very worried of attack, and hopes we can help him fend off this enemy. That is all," the King said, standing up.

"Father, I know you too well. You're not telling me everything. What's the problem?" Janevra said.

"You're too smart," the King muttered under his breath. "Rumor has it that the Dragons are coming. The Priests of the Light are searching for them vigorously. If they are not found soon, our world will descend into darkness. An army is accumulating in the southern islands and it does not carry the flag of any known country. Rogui have been raiding the country-side for weeks and deaths are mounting. People are afraid. This meeting is meant to decide what Caendor should do."

"Father, it's simple. You gather together the people of the Cyrain Plains and the Forgotten people. You make alliance with Selkare, Istra, Taymyr, LTana, Riyad, Zayen, and Caroa. You get everything ready for the Dragons." Janevra tapped her foot on the floor, her arms folded.

"Daughter, I wish it were that simple. Each country has its own problems and will not do anything until the Dragons are found. Now do you see?"

"No, I don't. You haven't even tried to make an alliance with any nation. You must try if you want this nation to survive the coming war. Please, Father. Listen to me. I know what is coming."

"Janevra," the King said, "I know your mother trained you to rule. I never supported her in giving you this education because by Caendorian law, you will never rule without a king. Yet I let her and now I am regret-ting giving your mother the control of your education. It is a good thing Ravften is a strong man and can keep you under his wing. I trust you will not cause any trouble for him when he becomes King."

"If you continue on this track, Father, Caendor will fall. Ravften will destroy this nation. He will kill our people. If you think that I am not fit to rule, if you are tied so by such old traditions of forbidding a woman to rule, then maybe Caendor deserves to fall."

The lords in the room gasped at her blasphemy. The King stiffened but Ravften shot Janevra a dark look, black murder in his eyes.

The King stood. "I will not tolerate your insubordination. This War Council does not concern women. Leave."

"Yet is it a woman that only sees what you must do," Janevra said. She stabbed a finger at Ravften. "Beware of him, Father. He has powers you do not know of and will try to take this country by any means possible. And it will not be through his marriage to me. I will never rule at his side. I would die before I did." She looked at the lords. "Watch Lord Ravften. He is a dangerous man."

"Janevra, you are dismissed," the King said.

Janevra nodded, her jaw clenching. "Good-bye, Father." Janevra swept out of the room. Mat turned and bowed to the King. He followed in her wake. She slammed the doors behind them.

"Mat, go to the kitchen and get as much food as you can carry. Don't ask questions now. I will tell you all later. Meet me in my rooms."

Mat went down to the kitchen, asking the cook for as much food as she had that was available. She gave him four loaves of bread, apples, two canteens of water, cheese and hard cake.

"Mat, keep the Princess safe for me, will you?"

Mat nodded in response. Servants had a habit of knowing everything. As he hurried back up to Janevra's rooms, he pondered Janevra's lack of arguing further with her father. In the weeks he had grown to know her, she was not one to back down easily. It made him nervous.

By the time he got back, he had had several strange looks. Opening the door, he saw Janevra talking to Teaa.

"...you still need to stay here. But I'm leaving. You mustn't tell anybody, except your sisters. I can't tell you why I'm leaving, but I will need your sisters to keep in touch with me by carrier pigeon. All they need to do is get the information on what the King is planning from you and send it to me written. I'll of course pay you, four hundred gold chips, for I am asking you to risk your life even more than before. Will you do this for me?" Janevra begged, clasping Teaa's hands in her own.

"Princess, I love you as a friend, admire your courage and would follow you into the abyss if you went there. I will do this for you and Mat." Teaa kissed Janevra on the cheek and then went to the door to speak to Mat.

"Mat, promise me to keep her safe? She is going to be in a lot of danger."

"I will, you don't need to tell me this," Mat said, smiling a goodbye smile. "However I have the most unmistakable feeling she will be watching after me."

"Goodbye, Mat." Teaa hugged him and left, shutting the door quietly behind her.

"Janevra, what is going on?" Mat insisted, as he sat down in front of her on the soft velvet chair, "and who are the Forgotten People?" He raised his eyebrows in question.

"Mat, listen. You know of the Lost Mountains, right?" At his nod, she continued. "A people live in these mountains, Mat. They are elves, the people of folklore and legend. They are the people who were the first to join the First Dragons more than five hundred years ago. And they are in need of help. It wasn't what I was planning, but it will work."

"How do you know this?" Mat asked.

"One of them told me. Qwaser."

From the balcony came a young man, wearing a leather tunic and leggings, with short brown hair and bright green eyes. He was tall and lean with a bow and arrow thrown over his back. A sword was around his waist. His ears were what Mat noticed first. They were long and slender, ending in elegant tips.

"Mat, this is Qwaser. He arrived here a few hours ago. He has traveled over a hundred miles to come here, to plead for help. His village was attacked by rogui," Janevra said.

Mat stood up, flabbergasted, his mouth hanging open.

"Wait. Listen before you say anything," Qwaser said. "Rogui have been looting this country side for the last month, burning houses. They killed my friend and I hate them for it."

"Qwaser has asked us for help. I asked my father, but as you know, he refused. So I have decided to go there myself," Janevra said, standing up. "I would take us there with my magic, but Qwaser has insisted that we cannot. He says elves already distrust humans and his friends, who are warning the Elven King of our arrival, need many days to cross the mountains and speak with the King. So we will be riding there."

"Janevra, we can't do anything."

"Have you forgotten your ability to summon magic?" Mat shook his head. "Good, that is what we will use."

"Janevra, I trust you, but we are only two. Even with our magic, it would be hard. We can't possibly—"

Qwaser interrupted him. "You do not have to come. But let me tell you of my life. Two weeks ago my village was attacked by rogui and as I told you, my best friend was killed. Her last words to me were, "I hope you find the Dragons," and I remembered those words as the four of us that survived buried the dead. I took it upon myself to get help from the outside, while the others went to the King to report the news. I went through a land that had never seen or heard of an elf. I was seen as strange, as if a legend was walking, so I hid my face. During those days of travel, I saw some strange things. I have come to you for help because I believe that you can help my people. They may not trust you at first, but when they see what I see, they will."

Mat scratched his head. Life was so complicated. He looked at Janevra. She stared right back at him, cool and trusting his decision.

One more try, he thought. "Janevra, what about your obligation to your people? If you leave, aren't you abandoning them?"

Janevra gave him a furious glare that made him step back in alarm. "I am not leaving my people forever, Mat Trakall. I am helping another people. I do not foresee my parents dying any time soon, therefore I deem it safe to leave for a month or so. Are you with me or not?"

"I will go, but," he said, finally setting down the bag of provisions and looking at Qwaser. "I ask one question. Why did you come to us?"

Qwaser shrugged. "I think fate and destiny had something to do with it. Our Prophecies say the Dragon of the Coming Storm will unite our people and bring us out into the world again. One of us needs to bring the Dragon to our land in order for this to become true. Maybe I am him and you were meant to help me find the Dragon of the Coming Storm."

"It's strange how different the Prophecies appear to others," Mat pointed out. "Well, I suppose we leave tonight?"

"Yes."

∛   ∛   ∛

Caya gazed out the window as she listened to Teaa, sitting on her bed at the inn. Why couldn't they ever go on an adventure?

Caya focused her attention back on Teaa.

"…Janevra said that she wants you two to keep doing what you're doing. She said that you could still help her. She needs to know what is going on in the city. Once a week she wants you to send a pigeon to her. She wants you to write a report on what rumors are going on and what her parents are doing. You'll get that information from me. It'll be dangerous, of course.

Caya's face lit up at this news. *Danger? Danger is good. Very good, I'll do it.*

"I don't know…I want to help her but I don't really want to either," Lousai said.

"Lousai, it'll be fun…and dangerous." Caya begged her sister.

"But how do we get this message to her if we don't know where she's going?"

Teaa handed over a script. "She told me to give this to you. She said it will help you find her by pigeon." Teaa bit her lip. "Janevra told me I'm not supposed to know what it is."

Teaa walked out of the room, leaving Lousai and Caya alone. She was probably going to meet her new sweetheart, Dhamom. Their parents were out, trading, and Jarin was preparing for his wedding.

Caya moved over behind Lousai, waiting for her sister to open it.

Lousai unrolled the script. On its borders were symbols unknown to the untrained eye. In a flowing hand was written…

"Dear Caya and Lousai,
I cannot thank you more for helping me these past weeks. I owe you. But I still need your help. I need you to send me a message every week on the news going around the city. Teaa has already told you this. Now, I know you are wondering how this bird will find me. All you have to do is mutter the words 'Yilkusa Qoweut'. These words you say to the bird before you let him go. It will find me. Do not worry. Do not tell anyone of the spell. Caya, Lousai, hard times are coming and you must fulfill your job to the fullest. I trust you. Go with the Light, always.
Your Royal Princess and loyal friend,
Janevra

"We had better start getting our first letter ready," Lousai said.

Chapter 11
The Second Prophecies

"Shhhh," Qwaser said as Janevra sneezed, the sound echoing in the empty and dark hallway.

Qwaser scurried across the hallway, his back bent, his dark clothes blending in. All he carried with him was the clothes on his back and his bow and arrows slung across his shoulders. Brytaya's sword was positioned on his hip.

He waited quietly as Janevra and Mat followed, reflecting on the past.

Mat came up beside him wearing a green tunic and black breeches, clothes that were meant for travel. He carried the bag of food and some clothes that would allow them to travel far enough to get away from the city without stopping. A sword stolen out of the armory hung at his sides. A sword he couldn't use.

Janevra came up behind him. Her hair was pulled back and she wore dark blue breeches and a black shirt. She carried a bag that contained some food and a good portion of the money. It was slung over her back, gently clicking every time she moved. One or two knives were hanging at her waist.

They crept downstairs and through halls, not making a sound. If they were caught, they would be more than dead.

Qwaser breathed a sigh of relief as they entered the Palace grounds. Sweet smells met their noses, washing over them. The two moons, full and glowing, hung in the sky, watching their progress.

Now the problem of getting past the gates arose. How to get past the guards was more like it.

Janevra went right by Qwaser where he had stopped behind a large bush.

"Where are you going?" he whispered, trying to grab her arm but failing.

"Just follow me, and don't say anything."

Qwaser frowned at Mat, who shrugged his shoulders.

They walked down a side path leading to the gate. Upon reaching the gate, they were dismayed to discover it was heavily guarded, but Janevra did not falter. She walked briskly up to the guards.

"Sir, if you may let us out, I would be highly grateful," Janevra said, surprising the guards.

"What? Oh, miss…may I ask who you are?" inquired a young man wearing silver armor. He peered at the two men behind her.

"Why, I'm…Nyera, a maid working for the Princess. And these two behind me are Garet and Rave, my escorts. Might I ask why we need to be questioned in order to be let out?" She smiled sweetly at the guard, crossing her fingers behind her back.

Qwaser barely contained his smile. Charm could get you anything...
sometimes.

The guard paused for a moment, looking flustered, before saying, "You
may leave. But we only question because if anything were to happen, we
would have a record of who has entered and left the Palace."

The red haired man stepped aside, opening the gate.

Janevra swept out, quickly followed by Mat and Qwaser.

Qwaser suddenly understood why the guards hadn't noticed Janevra.
As the Princess, she had no reason to leave so late, so they didn't connect
her face to that of the Princess's.

Once they reached the Grand Plaza, they all let out the breath they had
been holding for a while.

"Should we buy horses?" Mat asked.

"Of course," Qwaser said.

They went down most of West Street before turning south towards a
stable.

Qwaser walked into the barn, his attention being directed to a soft
snore in the corner.

He gently woke the boy on duty and asked for two of their best horses,
handing him more than enough silver chips. Qwaser made sure the boy
brought out the gray stallion he had stabled there a day ago.

The lad brought out the horses, which were all very fine looking and
with an appearance that they could travel a far distance.

"Thank you," Qwaser said, as the boy grinned up at him, showing a
black tooth.

Qwaser left the stables, buying three saddles on the way.

He found Janevra and Mat sitting under a tree next to a shop.

"Shall we go?" he said getting up onto his gray stallion.

"We ride," Mat said, settling on the bay.

"You both know how to ride?" Janevra asked, sitting on her brown
horse with ease.

"Twice," Mat said, looking uncomfortable. "On the farm when I was a
boy."

"My parents were rich enough to afford the luxury of endless riding
lessons when I was living at the palace in the Lost Mountains. It's also how
I got here," Qwaser said.

They rode through the city gate with no problem, as a person leaving in
the dead of night was not a rare occurrence.

Once they had ridden out of the outskirts of the city, they fell into a
slow trot.

They rode on the well-packed road past cottages and small villages all
night.

Once the sun was near rising, flooding the land in light, they stopped at
a small inn to eat and rest their horses.

"The Dancing Clover? What kind of name is that?" asked Mat as he got down from his horse.

"It probably has something behind it," Qwaser said. "But the name doesn't matter, I'm hungry." His stomach growled to reinforce his words.

They quickly paid a boy to watch their horses and entered the inn, their eyes adjusting to the diffuse light. Mat rubbed his backside. "I swear my bottom has taken on the shape of a saddle."

The fireplace had no fire in it and most of the tables were empty. It was still too early in the morning to be drinking.

They sat down at a window table as a skinny man with humped shoulders came over. He glanced at Qwaser who had a cloak on to hide his ears.

"May I help you my Lords and Lady?" the man asked in a hoarse whisper.

"Yes, we would all like your special," Janevra said.

The man nodded and scuttled away.

"Do you think they have noticed we're gone?" Janevra whispered.

"Not yet. Not until noon will they begin to worry." Mat ran a hand through his hair. "Or at least I hope not."

They sat in silence, awaiting the innkeeper as he brought a hot mushroom soup.

They ate, talking about their past lives.

"I was born in the Fourth Age during the Second Battle." Qwaser stirred his soup. *I've lived a long time compared to these humans. And yet I feel as if they have lived more than I.*

Mat choked on his soup. "That would make you almost a thousand years old!"

Qwaser smiled. "I've lived nine hundred years. I don't remember much of the Fourth Age. I was too young. By the time the Third Battle came along I was too young to fight but old enough to remember the fires that raged across the land. And since elves didn't fight in the Fourth Battle, the only time I've ever had battle experience was over fourteen days ago."

"What was it like, fighting in a battle?" Mat asked, watching Qwaser closely. Mat put a spoon of soup in his mouth, wincing at the taste.

"It was… something I want to forget. You're full of fear, but you keep killing. I saw people I knew die in front of me. I don't want to fight ever again, but I know I must, to support the Dragons. And I must live to see the Last Battle." Qwaser's eyes lit with a fervor that quickly died out. "What of you, Mat?"

"I never had an easy life," Mat said with a far away look in his hazel eyes. "I always wanted to be somebody. I wanted to fight. But I couldn't because of the farm. My parents wanted me to be a farmer… I never wanted to be a farmer, but I had to work for every meal, and every day was a fight of survival. I can't say I like the way things have changed. I don't have much control over my life any more and I miss that."

Janevra put her elbows on the table.

"I like being a princess, I want to help the people but the people are always telling me how perfect I look. Girls only want to be my friend, because I'm a princess. People always tell me to listen to my father, saying he knows what is right for me. I didn't like it, so..."

Yelling drifted to Qwaser's ears. He put a finger to his lips. Janevra closed her mouth, her eyes wide.

All three pushed back their chairs. One hit the ground. Qwaser looked outside and saw palace guards.

A voice yelled above the noise outside. "We are looking for Princess Janevra. She was taken prisoner by two men, one her own servant. One hundred gold chips will be given to the person with information."

"Prisoner? What are they thinking? This was *your* idea!" Mat said, frowning at Janevra.

Janevra shrugged.

"Come on, out the back!" Qwaser said. He did not take more than four steps before the inn door was smashed open.

"Halt!" A voice rang out. Men filed into the room.

The three companions stopped, their hands going near weapons, whether they could use them or not. Qwaser motioned to them not to draw their weapons.

"Princess, thank Tghil that we have found you. Now if you would please move away from these men," the Captain said, his blonde head nodding in their direction.

"No, sir, I will not."

The captain blinked. "What?"

"I am not a captive, I came here on my own. I made these two come with me. Please step aside and let us pass."

The captain shook his head. "I'm sorry, Princess. I cannot. Lord Ravften's orders were to bring you back."

"Lord Ravften? These are not my father's orders?"

"No, the King told Lord Ravften that if he is to be King after him, he can take control now. We are under Lord Ravften's rule."

"Then you had better move, because Lord Ravften will never be king while I'm alive."

"I'm sorry, Princess, but your to-be-husband needs you back to become king. Arrest them," the captain said to his men.

"Don't come near us, or I'll set you on fire!" Janevra yelled, flinging her hands at them, palms facing the guards.

The captain guffawed. "How, may I ask?"

"By magic," Mat answered.

Qwaser pulled out his sword, metal sliding against leather.

"Get them," the captain spat. Guards rushed forward, smiling wickedly.

"Janevra, do something!" Qwaser spread his feet, trying to remember the stance he had been taught so long ago.

Qwaser watched as Janevra focused, her eyes darting to the empty fireplace.

Flames.

Fire formed from her hands, the glowing balls not burning her skin.

Mat followed suit.

What was told came to be.

Fire burst from their hands, shooting through the air and burning the surprised men. Flame caught on the tables sending the inn up in flames.

The captain screamed in rage and fear. He ran outside, fire chasing him.

Janevra, Mat and Qwaser sprinted out the door. They untied their horses, and put them into a gallop. They raced to the front of the burning building.

"Oops," Mat said sheepishly, watching the smoke bubble up.

Screams followed in their wake. Black smoke rose up darkening the sky. Qwaser looked back, not caring who was killed. He would never shed a tear for those who betrayed good. Never.

Ω   Ω   ‚

In the midnight skies that night, words in blood were written out. Everyone turned their heads up to see, but what they saw chilled their bones and sent shivers down their spines. The world was ending.

"The power has been used to shed Evil man's blood. The future is now in their hands, the hands of the Dragons, Rising Sun and Coming Storm.

Evil shall rise, the leader a Warlord. Things from the abyss will crawl from their caves and kill to drink the Blood. The Forgotten people will be united by a bolt of lightning, Dragon of the Coming Storm. The Ile people by a burning sun, Dragon of the Rising Sun. The Trench has been made, splitting the East Sea and opening the abyss to the World. Sylai and Rogui have entered the world. The Dragons will be found on a morning's dawn. A storm will reach the Northern Kingdom and sweep through it, binding the people to its leader, with a black skull on Warlord's arm.

The Fifth Battle will rage all over the land from now till the Death of those prophesized.

People will die in the war, people will die in the battles that come, and people will die from things yet not of this world.

The Age of Peace will come to an end under the rule of the Dragons and the Age of War will begin. The Seventh Age called by most.

No one shall not lose a loved one, everyone shall lose something. This blood in the sky is those who will die and those who bleed. To live in the Day of the Dragons is a great honor but an unlucky throw of the Dice of Life.

Six people will be born on the Day of Dragon Birth. They are
people with power of the shoi. Each has their own ability and
together make one. Powerful they are. They bind themselves to
the Dragons and follow forever, through generations. One of Fire
born of Fire, one of Water born of Water, one of Earth born of
Earth, one of Air born of Air, one of Life born of Life, one of Death
born of Death, but follows Warlord. True to the Dragons, calling
themselves the Phoenixes, they spread the Legend of the Dragons.
Together four will rule at the side under the Dragons. They are
but normal people under the spell of Light and out of Darkness.
They are paragons of humanity.

The Dragons, maid and youth, love is strong, a tie that cannot
be broken by a power on this world. The Thysia's Son will rule.
Love will conquer all but leave a path of death.

The Warlord divides the world in half, Good and Evil. He is a
lost star. He is the son of the King of Darkness, a person with the
power of hate. People throw up their hands in defeat under his
shadow. The Dragons show no fear. But fear lurks in the lightest
of corners.

The people who will destroy the World are only children. The
Dragons and the Warlord. Two men, one woman. Secrets unfold,
secrets from the Ages.

Cities will burn, towns destroyed, villages wiped out in the
heat of battle. Sorrow. Tears. Love. Hate. Life. Death.

Blood will be the color of the seas and the taste of water on
the Day of the Fifth Battle. Clouds will boil across the skies,
black. Great powers will be used.

The gods of old will hand over the world to their children
who fought long ago, the gods of the Thysians finally parting. A
new goddess will be chosen from the ashes of the war and she will
take her place until the day comes when the gods of old reclaim
their thrones.

The Prophecy stayed in the sky for hours and then was washed away
as if water was washing over the bloody words. The rain came. It was the
color of blood and people cried.

Chapter 12
The Warlord

ALD 3919 SD May

"Stupid cows," Raxsen muttered, as he leaned against a tree, watching
his father's herd of cows. He idly ran his fingers along a knife blade, a gift
from his parents for his birthday.

Raxsen was born on the Day of Dragon Birth, one of the few who were, and refused to herd cows one more year. He knew he was meant for bigger and better things than cows. The moment he turned twenty, he was gone. Never would he spend his life guarding cattle.

He lived in a small village off the coast of Nurita on the island of Atay, not far from the city of Barra. His father was a cow herder. Raxsen hated cows. They stunk and always made noise. *I will never be a cow herder,* Raxsen thought. *I am going to be a general and wipe out large armies with amazing battle plans.* Raxsen was a genius when it came to battles. He loved war and he knew he could be a grand general. All he needed was the chance to leave Atay and make a name for himself as the greatest war leader of all time.

Raxsen not only knew how to command war, but he had learned how to fight using every weapon conceivable. He had made the weapons by hand and had taught himself how to use them. Far from anywhere, he was a lost star. The closest he had been to a battle was when he read about battles in books he had borrowed. In those battles where men became heroes, Raxsen wished more than anything that he could have been there, fighting. The men who did become heroes always followed the Light. Raxsen did not follow the Light, or the Dark for that matter. He was neutral. Whichever one would give him the chance to be a general first, too bad for the other side.

A bird burst from the shelter of the trees. Raxsen, without taking time to aim, threw his knife. The bird let out a squawk and dropped to the ground several feet from Raxsen.

Ripping his knife out, Raxsen sheathed the blade after wiping the blood on the bird's rumpled feathers.

Deciding that the cows were safe, Raxsen headed back to the house, his stomach rumbling for food.

His home was small, only three rooms large. It sat at the edge of a small forest, surrounded by wavering fields of golden grass. An old stone fence encircled the fields. Inside the fence, cows grazed. Smoke came from the chimney of Raxsen's house and the smell of bread drifted in the air. A barn sat by the house, a horse and pigs inside.

Raxsen pushed the front door open, gave a polite smile to his mother, and sat down at the table.

His mother laid down a plate covered in buttered bread and vegetables. Raxsen ate slowly, not savoring the taste but trying to delay the moment when he would have to head back to the fields.

"Raxsen, what are you doing in here?" his father said as he walked into the room. "You should be watching the cows. What if they are stolen?"

Raxsen rolled his eyes. "Don't hurt yourself worrying, father. No one's going to steal those cows." Raxsen bit into a hunk of bread, washing it down with of glass of milk.

Raxsen looked down at his food, wondering what to eat next when a dead bird was dropped onto his plate. Raxsen looked up, his father standing next him, and glared defiantly at his father.

"Son, what have I told you about killing animals for sport? I told you to stop killing them. This is the third animal today! Why must you kill things? Do you take pleasure in it?"

Raxsen smiled. "Assume that I do."

His father sat down heavily in a chair. "Raxsen, this road you are going down is a dangerous one. You cannot kill things for pleasure. It will not lead you anywhere good in life. Your mother and I are worried for you, son."

Raxsen pushed the plate away from him. "You have never been worried before. You only started to worry about me when colors danced in the sky. Before then, I could do whatever I wanted. Now, once the Dragons have met and prophecy has come true, do you begin to worry. Are you afraid that I will join the Dark? Is that it? I will join whichever side offers me more."

His mother laid her hand on Raxsen's shoulder. "My son, we have tried to raise you to follow Tghil. We have tried to put good into your heart. We know it's there."

Raxsen stood up, sneering at his parents. "Good? There has never been good in me! There is no reason for it to be! Ever since I can remember, you have always feared me and never meddled in my doings! You never told me what was good and bad. You kept your distance out of fear. When I was younger, I resented that. Now I crave it. I can see the fear in your eyes even now. What are you hiding from me? What do you know that I do not that affects my future?"

His mother's face tightened and she went back into the kitchen. His father watched her go. "Raxsen, you tread on perilous ground."

"Is that a threat, Father?" Raxsen spat, turning on his heel and walking out the door, slamming it shut.

What do they see in me that makes them fear me? What power do I have that they fear? It is neither my magic nor my talents in weapons. They encouraged those two hobbies in my life, Raxen thought as he ran through the woods, trying to calm his anger and frustration. *When I brought that first magical book home and tested myself, my mother was proud that I "was of power with the Dragons" as the book had told me. My father even helped me craft some of the weapons with which I practiced. What is it they fear?*

Raxsen slowed to a walk as he saw the ocean rolling in front of him. The trees thinned and Raxsen stepped out into the open, the wind and spray from the ocean blowing over his skin.

Raxsen sat down on a large gray fungi rock. His short dirty blonde hair was blown from his face by a cold north wind. The ocean in front of him was dark, mirroring the overhanging clouds. His tanned face was tilted up to the sky, his arms wrapped around his legs. He closed his ice blue eyes. The smell of salt reached his nose. He concentrated, ignoring everything around him, trying to reach into the plane of magic. Annoyance bubbled up in him. He felt like he was trying to grasp the wind. Opening his eyes, he shook his head and stood up.

For some reason, the magic would not come to him. Never before had the magic not come to him. Today was the first day and he was worried.

The wind embraced him as he stood up, the cold soaking his clothes.

Raxsen watched the sky turn black, lightning shattering the clouds.

Raxsen looked down at the sea. It was a dark blue now, with waves the size of boulders rolling into the beach.

Suddenly a loud crack filled the air, lightning hitting the water. Raxsen was dazed by the brightness and thrown to his knees as a vision filled his eyes.

He saw himself leading armies, thousands strong into battle. Broken spears and swords covered the ground and smoke choked the air. Men and women, clutched by death's cold grip stared up at the sky. Shouts and songs filled his ears and blood stained everything. He saw victory. He saw blood on his hands, blood of people he had never met. He saw himself become famous and feared. He saw war. Two beautiful faces appeared in front of him, his enemies and how he hated them. He then heard the words that made him shiver. He heard the words of a god... *"Bring fear and hate into the world, conquer it and begin again the Age of Darkness. Lead your armies through the land, destroy it and kill the people who do not follow. Kill the Dragons, rampage the land with the Creatures of the Abyss. Drink the blood of your enemies. Imprint the sword and the flame into followers' skin to prevent betrayal. Death to all those who do not follow you, Prince of Darkness. May the shadows guide you, Warlord."* A face appeared with the words. It was the face of the Dark Lord and along with the face came more faces and knowledge of people he could use in his conquering of the world, people who already worked for the Dark.

Raxsen gulped air as the vision released him. His head hurt. No, it pounded. The magic he had been trying to reach flooded into him, and he quickly cut the bond to the magical plane, falling to his knees as the massive amounts of magic swept from his body.

He knew what he had to do. The vision had told him. He would make an army out of poor farmers, soldiers and creatures from the abyss. He would be the general he wanted to be, for the Dark side. His time had finally come and the Light would rue the day they forgot him.

Raxsen jumped off the rock and ran across cold, brown ground to his home, jumping rocks and dead trees.

The sky above rolled and heaved as it turned noon into night. Lightning flashed, illuminating the sky with jagged lights of power.

Out of the corner of his eyes, he saw creatures jump up out of the ground. He knew they wouldn't hurt him. They followed him. The living things joined him, running just footsteps behind. Soon an army of over five hundred was pounding the hard earth with running feet.

When he reached his house, he flung the door open.

His mother looked up. His father jumped from his chair.

"Son, what is the matter?" his mother asked bewildered.

"Nothing."

"Raxsen, you're all wet. Come here," his mother demanded.

"No."

"Raxen!" His mother's lips compressed.

"Goodbye."

"What?" his parents echoed.

"I have an army, the Dark Lord's army. My war has finally come."

"Raxsen?" his mother smiled uneasily. She flinched as she looked at his eyes. They were so cold.

"If I kill you now, you won't have to live in this world of war."

A scratching sound came from behind Raxsen.

His parents screamed as creatures walked past their son and slit their throats.

"The first victims of the Warlord," one hissed as it drank the dark, warm blood.

Raxsen smiled at his parents' body. "I was being kind. Be thankful for that was my last act of kindness. As my parents you deserved that much." Raxsen turned and left the house.

Behind him the blood of his parents spread slowly across wood floor, staining the ground red.

The Warlord the Prophecies had warned against walked the earth.

Raxsen stood in front of his house, surveying the sylai and rogui. All wore black armor and carried wickedly curved and freshly sharpened weapons. "We march to Barra," Raxsen shouted, raising his fist in the air. A thunderous roar tore from the throats of the rogui and sylai. *Destiny has finally come,* Raxsen thought. *I will lead the hordes of Darkness through the Northern Kingdom and claim the land as my own. My armies will cover the land and nothing will stand in my way. My power will be absolute. As the Lord of the Dark said, I will bring fear and hate into the world, and the Age of Darkness will have its king!*

Raxsen exchanged his clothes for ones a sylai handed him, a black shirt and trousers. Pulling black boots onto his feet, Raxsen curled his toes, working out the tough leather. A beautifully made sword was handed to Raxsen as was a belt and sheath. Sheathing the sword, Raxsen, his cold blue eyes sharp with sudden power, let out a scream of pure exhilaration. His blood ran hot and battle blazed in his eyes. Nothing would stand against the might of the Warlord!

Raxsen ran through woods once more, the rogui and sylai behind him. The God of Dark aided them as they ran, taking away their weariness and giving them strength. The magic of the god flowed around them.

They reached Barra at dusk.

Before entering the city, Raxsen turned to his horde. "You are to follow me and obey my command. You must not attack until I say so and once I do it will only be for killing and pillaging, not burning the buildings. I will need those."

At the head of the horde, Raxsen marched into the small city. The gates opened, unknowing of the Evil they invited within their walls. The men and women in the street cowered along the buildings, fear and horror in their eyes as they watched a young man lead five hundred sylai and rogui into their peaceful city.

Reaching the market place, a large crowd awaited Raxsen, the mayor at the front. Unused to war, the people of Barra did not know that Raxsen was invading and they were making his conquering of Barra easy.

Raxsen held out his hand and a rogui slipped a knife into it. With an accuracy only seen in seasoned warriors, Raxsen threw the knife. The knife sprouted from the mayor's chest like a thorn. Without a sound, the mayor toppled to the ground. A moment of sheer silence filled the city, before the citizens started to scream and flee in terror. Raxsen shouted orders to his army, telling his horde to keep the citizens in the market place and round up all the others.

As his army carried out his orders, Raxsen sauntered over to the dead mayor and pulled the knife from his chest. He wiped the blood on the mayor's blue vest before turning in one swift movement and sticking the captain of the city guard through the middle. The captain gurgled and collapsed on the ground, dead. The other city guards stayed back, knowing they were defeated.

Raxsen, the knife still clutched in his hand, crossed his arms and waited for the market to fill with citizens. When a rogui told him the entire city, except a few dead who had resisted, were in the market, Raxsen summoned his magic and lifted himself several feet above the ground so all could see their conqueror.

"Men of Barra," Raxsen said, excluding the women, believing they were not worth his attention, "I am the Warlord, the Prince of Darkness and the new ruler of your city. My orders are simple, but they will be obeyed. Three fourths of the male population will join my army. Any who resist this order will be hung from the walls and left to rot. This town, once I leave, will then begin building siege weapons and ships for me and when the day comes, I will call for everything you have made. All of the men will be branded with a sword, a magical tattoo that will keep them from ever betraying me. If you do and you wear my sign, death will greet you. Even the women will be marked as will every child. I promise you, it will be painful." Raxsen lowed himself to the ground, smiling at their fear.

Raxsen moved among the men, women and children, three sylai with him to protect him from a stab in the back. He laid his hand upon their left shoulders, branding the sword into their skin, weaving another curse into the tattoo. At midnight, he finished and smiled when a man tried to attack him with a knife but stumbled and died before reaching Raxsen. "Loot," Raxsen told his horde.

Howling and screaming, they charged into the city. Raxsen was left with the citizens, none daring to challenge him. "You have one day to find any weapons or forge new ones. On the second day, I leave with my army and those who remain will work. Fifty sylai and rogui each will stay behind to make sure you fulfill your orders." Raxsen watched them, knowing his charismatic allure was working its way into the hearts of the people even though they resented it. He let his magic go reluctantly.

Heads hung in shame, the shocked citizens of Barra slowly made their way home. Children cried into their mother's skirts, the pain of the tattoo hurting them. Men, once home, brought out weapons they had never used, heirlooms of their family for most. Women, putting up a brave front, hugged their husbands and wished them safety in this darkening world.

Raxsen watched them leave, sneering at them. His blue eyes seemed almost to glow with coldness and many citizens shivered under his gaze.

One young man remained in the market and he approached Raxsen. The young man, who had vivid green eyes, dark brown hair and the shadow of a beard on his chin, bowed before Raxsen. "Warlord, my name is David Pierce. I was in training as a city guard. I know my way around a sword. I have the Talent and wish to offer you my complete services, if you give me a high rank." A hint of smugness was in his voice.

Raxsen raised an eyebrow. "Your services are already mine. Why should I?" Raxsen asked, finding it hard to not like the young man because of his bravery at confronting Raxsen and his cockiness, qualities Raxsen himself displayed.

"You need people who are second or third in command to carry out the more trivial matters of war."

Raxsen smirked. "I know this. I will give you the position of second general. The position of first general goes to a man named John Andrews, a man much longer in the business of working for the Dark. I believe he is your town drunk."

Pierce stared. "How do you know that, Warlord?" All trace of his previous smugness was gone.

"The Lord of the Dark watches over me. I know many things." Raxsen looked the man up and down, noticing he carried a sword. "Find John Andrews for me, tell him of his new position and that I want him to round up the men who will come with me to Xs tomorrow at noon."

Noon the next day found Raxsen at the head of his army, sitting on a horse in front of the city gates, the road to Xs running out in front of him. General Pierce and Andrews sat on horses next to him. Raxsen gave the orders for fifty sylai and rogui to stay behind and keep watch over the citizens of Barra.

Raxsen nudged his horse and began the two-day march to Xs.

"Warlord," Peirce asked, casting a dark look at General Andrews as the man drowned himself in a flask of wine. "Once we capture Xs, how will we cross the water to Nutria?"

"We will use the ships and fishing boats of course," Raxsen said, annoyed. "The city will not take long to conquer. Several scores of sylai have tunneled under the city and have found a way to the surface. They are waiting for my order to attack. The battle will not be long. Nutrians do not know of me yet, so my arrival cannot be foreseen and victory will be quick."

Pierce frowned. "How did you know they were under the city?"

Raxsen laughed. "The abyss was opened in the East Sea with the meeting of the Dragons. Sylai have been running through the countryside of the Northern Kingdom for over a month now. The Lord of the Dark knew where I would attack first, so he laid the foundations for my plans. He will make sure my victories are swift in Atay and Nutria. The mainland is the real prize and I have no intention of losing too many warriors before stepping foot in Angarat."

Talk stopped from there and Raxsen was left to plotting and planning the downfall of the Northern Kingdom.

Raxsen did not stop his army when night fell but summoned his magic and lit their way with globes of light that hovered along the side of the marching army. In this way, they would reach Xs at noon that next day. *I must maintain the element of surprise for as long as possible. The longer I can do so, the quicker I can control these island nations and move on to larger game,* Raxsen thought, his horse plodding steadily along.

The city of Xs was larger than Barra but did not have walls protecting it. Temples to the Light were the only major buildings. Most of the homes were made from mud and brick and the other buildings cut from plain stone. The city was dreary with the smell of dead fish and salt hanging over it like a cloud. The people wore dark clothing, apparently unable to afford or find dyes. Winding through the city, dirt roads were filled with sewage thrown from windows above and were dotted with stepping-stones, so travelers would not have to wade through the muck of human waste and rotting food. Xs was the pitfall of southern civilization.

Raxsen reined his horse outside the city, watching the people with a cruel smile. Pierce reined up next to him, his vivid green eyes sweeping the city.

"Warlord," Pierce said, "Xs has very few guards. The city can be taken easily."

"I didn't think it could be taken any other way," Raxsen said. He signaled for his rogui and sylai to attack the city, killing all who resisted and herding the rest to the docks, where Raxsen would lay out his orders.

With a roar like a thunderclap, the sylai and rogui raced to the city, weapons raised and black armor glinting in the sun.

Raxsen wheeled his horse, facing the men from Barra. "Join the sylai and rogui. Your battle experience begins now."

The men, knowing if they resisted they would be killed, ran after the sylai and rogui with enthusiasm. They knew the riches that awaited them. The Warlord promised a pick of the spoils and all were intent on getting chests of gold and silver. Xs may be a poor city, but it was a port city and carried many valuables.

Raxsen, with Pierce at his heels, rode into the city. He was satisfied when he saw a dozen bodies in the street. The men of Xs would be a welcome addition to his army. They had the spirits of warriors.

The docks of Xs were the only thing of which the people could be proud. Over twenty docks, each with ships docked on their sides, made up the port. Many of the ships were large, stopping for a day on land, before they continued on to Tes or Carim. The number of ships played perfectly into Raxsen's plans.

Raxsen surveyed the gathering of people, noticing that several supported bruises. Rogui and sylai had made a perimeter around the docks, preventing anyone from escaping. The number of sylai had greatly increased from those that had hidden under the city.

Summoning his magic, Raxsen pushed the people apart, creating a walkway for himself and motioning for Pierce to stay behind. Raxsen walked through the throng of frightened and shocked people, his face as emotional as a wall.

Upon reaching the center of the crowd, Raxsen climbed off the back of his horse and onto a crate, viewing those standing below him with contempt. "Conquered of Xs," Raxsen shouted, trying to restrain the hint of sudden laughter that rose in his throat. *If this is as hard as it's going to get, then I will be Warlord and King of the Northern Kingdom by winter! Fools they all are!* "Atay has succumbed to the powers of the Warlord and soon Nutria will feel my power!" The people stared at him, silent as death. Many knew the prophecy. It had been in the sky two nights ago and they knew who he was. The name, the fabled name from the Age of Darkness, told it all. Warlord. He would stop at nothing to achieve his goal of power. "Three fourths of the men will join my army before I leave for Nutria. Those that remain will work for me, as will the women." Raxsen held out his right hand, waves of magic rippling from it. The waves of magic washed over the crowd of people, binding them to him as a sword was burned into their skin, forever marking them as spawn of the Warlord. The people dropped to their knees in agony.

Raxsen brought his hand down, his eyes winter ice. "You are bound to me and if you try to betray me, death will come," Raxsen warned.

Jumping off the crate, Raxsen smiled coldly. "Get to work," he spat. "There are many things that need to be done and if you have nothing to do, I'm sure one of my sylai can help you."

The people scrambled away from him, hurrying out of the docking area. The sylai, rogui and men of Barra reluctantly let them leave and go about their business.

"Keep an eye on them," Raxsen ordered. "Make sure none try to flee. We leave in two days for the coast of Nutria. Until then, amuse yourselves." Raxsen turned and walked down one of the docks, stopping once he reached the ship tied to it. A sailor slid down a rope, landing in front of Raxsen. Raxsen, startled, drew his sword.

"Nay, Warlord, I've no want of crossing swords with ye," the sailor said. He flourished a bow. "How can I be of service to ye?"

"How many men can this ship hold?"

The sailor rubbed his left arm where the tattoo had been branded in his skin. "About hundred men, Warlord. Ye will have't consider the ten sailors it takes to master her, though," he said, indicating the ship. "So, ye can fit 'bout ninety of your men."

Raxsen turned as Pierce came up behind him. "Pierce, since you insisted those who are in second command could deal with trivial matters, I want you to find out how many men can fit on each ship, how long the voyage will take to Nutria and the amount of food and horses we can carry. When that's done, you are to order them to sail to Tes after they leave us on Nutria. Their ships will be some of the ships that take us to the mainland."

Pierce bowed. "Yes, Warlord," he said, trying to conceal a hint of anger.

Raxsen smiled tightly, turned and walked back down the dock, his boats thunking on the wood. *Once the ships reach Cunai, our docking city, my armies will start the conquering of Nurtia. Next I will attack the capitol of Nutria, Lauot. When that city is destroyed, Melo is next and then Tes where I will have boats built to carry my army across the East Sea,* Raxsen thought, musing over his battle plans. *I shall take the city of Cunai with nothing but my magic so they all can see the power I wield.* Raxsen laughed. *Yes, the citizens of Cunai will be binded to me before they know what has happened and their temples will be burnt to ashes before they even see me. Lord of the Dark, you have chosen well. The Northern Kingdom will be mine and the world soon after. Glorious power! Darkness will blanket the land and all will bow at my feet! Nothing can stand in my way, not even the Dragons, those pitiful fools who don't even know who and what they are! My victory will be easy, my power will be clenched and ultimate rule will be mine before they know their place in life! God of Dark, you have blessed them with blindness. Keep it so!*

Raxsen walked down the city streets, winter wind in his wake. As he walked by, the people shuddered in cold. The Warlord had conquered them and they were now slaves to a cause they hated. They would betray him, but betrayal was death, and death was feared even more than the Warlord. In death, anyone could claim your soul.

Chapter 13
Dagau

Deivenada's mouth hung open. The city of the Daaguwh was amazing.

Tall pillars of limestone topped the city's walls. Buildings of granite towered over the wall. The city's houses were made of limestone and sandstone. Hanging gardens grew from the walls, and fountains sprouted fresh water. Temples to the four gods of the Ile climbed above the city, the statues of the gods glittering in the sun. Several tombs, their domes painted blue, blended in with the sky. The tombs housed the great leaders of the Daaguwh, forever making them immortal in the minds of the people. They were the Djed in times of need, during wars and starvations, who managed to bring their people back into the glory they once knew.

Since they had left the city of the Edieata, they had not seen any standing city. All were burned or destroyed. It was reassuring to see a place that might offer protection and peace.

Dei breathed in deeply. It was good to be alive but she had seen too many deaths in her young life.

A bitter tear crept down Dei's check. Zenerax walked over and hugged her, enfolding her in his arms, his bare chest warm. The tattoo on his arm shone gently in the sun and informed the people around him he was a Tarten.

Their clothes were dusty and travel worn. Dei's leather pants were ripped to the knees and her shirt barely hung on. Zenerax wasn't much better. His pants were in need of repair, but they were wearable. Their high leather shoes that went up halfway to the knee were the only new clothing they had been able to purchase.

The city of the Daaguwh, called Dagau, was two miles by two miles, a perfect square. The City Council lived behind palace walls at the center of the city. They controlled the on goings of the city and the rest of the Daaguwh Nation. It was made up of a village representative from seven villages, eleven towns and two small cities.

The Daaguwh were the most powerful Ile nation and had managed to stay the most powerful for centuries. This was due to the territory they owned, the size and location of their country, and their leadership.

Daaguwh was centered at the heart of all the Ile nations. Rich grassland covered most of the Daaguwh land. On the north eastern side of the country was a large lake. The lake provided access to the ocean and trade routes to other nations established along the lake and its river. Abundance of fishing added to the grain and fruit supplies farmed and gathered from the grasslands. Large mountains located in the middle of the Daaguwh lands were rich in obsidian, iron, copper and gold. These precious metals permitted the Ile to produce high tech weapons of perfect quality. These types of sophisticated weapons allowed the Daaguwh Ile to protect their nation against any form of invaders and were sold at markets for very high prices. Large cedar forests, which the Ile used to build merchant trading ships that sailed up and down the rivers, also covered parts of Daaguwh. The large cedar trees were also cut down for the use of making wooden handles and beams to support buildings. It was a rich land owned by a rich people.

Dei held her hand up to her face, blocking the blistering sun and the shimmering heat waves coming off the buildings. She breathed in the scents of cooking meat, wine, tanned animal skins, linen and wet clay.

Dei and Zenerax were representing the Edieata. Kayzi had stayed behind with the remaining Edieata near the outskirts of the city.

They made their way through throngs of people. During the time it took to travel from their home to here, roughly two weeks, the people had elected Dei, Zenerax and Kayzi as their leaders. They were the new Djed.

"Do you think they will accept us?" Dei asked.

"They had better," Zenerax said as he pushed past a group of people gathering around a wizened storyteller.

"Ages ago, when the Ile lived in the West," the storyteller began, "The race of men ruled the land in timeless peace…" His voice was slowly drowned out by the noise of the city as Dei and Zenerax moved away.

When they reached the palace gates, a guard stopped them. "State your name, business and where you're from," the guard said, his *khrieth* leveled at their throats.

"I'm Dei, this is Zenerax, and we are here to confront the Council about the destruction of the Edieata tribe," Dei said, her gray eyes looking deep into the guard's blue. "Our land was attacked by sylai and no one but those at your gates survived. We ask for shelter."

The guard frowned at this news but nodded and called for a servant. When the servant came, the guard moved to the side and let them pass.

The Daaguwh were the only Ile to own slaves. They called them *sehetem*, which literally meant 'the One Who Serves' and were usually prisoners of war or men and women captured from the Great Desert east of the Cyrain Plains. In Daaguwh eyes they were barbarians.

Behind the gates the guard protected were large houses, the richer Daaguwh Ile living area. The houses were at least two stories and white washed. Vines crawled up the white houses. Children in white linen played games in the shadows while dogs barked playfully at them. Some adults talked by trees, enjoying the shade. Many of the adults carried their *khrieths*.

The *sehetem* leading them, whose name was Leama, brought them past the houses to a large pond. On the other side of the pond was a magnificent palace. Large arched windows reflected the sunlight. Ebony doors with old Ile writing on them shone in the light. A stone bridge led to the doors.

"The Council is debating now. You can go in after," Leama said, giving her gray-red hair a twist.

Daaguwh Council members were twenty strong and made up of ten of each gender. Two males and one female were Yria'ti.

Dei and Zenerax followed Leama over the bridge and into the palace. Leama directed them to some chairs in the large anteroom. Other *sehetem* were cleaning, but they kept their heads down as Leama passed.

The anteroom was large. Paintings of past battles were on the ceiling and pictures of famous Ile stood on the wall. The room was the first room when you entered the palace and used as an anteroom for every room.

A short *sehetem* walked up to them and set down a basin of water and a white cloth on a table nearby.

After they had washed their faces, Leama met them again. She was not dressed in the *sehetem's* gray robes. Instead she wore a long puffy light purple skirt and white blouse. Her gray-red hair was in a braid and pulled over her shoulder. The gray in it was hardly visible. Her oval shaped face was smiling, but concern showed around the edges of her eyes.

"Deivenada, Zenerax, I am Leama, the Djed of the Daaguwh. Please follow me."

Dei and Zenerax followed, both briefly wondering why the Djed had dressed as a slave. They passed large statues of men and women, painted glass windows and indoor fountains. Finally they approached a pair of bronze doors. Leama pushed them open.

Inside was a round table. Nineteen elderly men and women sat around it talking quietly between themselves. The room had a window on the north and south side and trees could be seen from there as well as the whole city. A few candles were lit but because of the windows, candlelight was not needed. As soon as the men and women caught sight of Leama, they closed their mouths and turned towards her, standing up. The men bowed to Leama and then sat down again. Each of the women, wearing a multitude of different colors, bowed to Leama in turn, sitting themselves down once the proper greetings were carried out. One of the women, her blonde hair in a braid just like Leama's, walked over to Dei and Zenerax. She was much younger then Leama, but her hair did have some streaks of gray, her skinny face bore no scars and her gray eyes twinkled.

"Greetings, children of the Edieata, I'm Vena, a Yria'ti. Our other two Yria'ti to serve on the Council of the Djed are… Biolak! Gangu!" Vena snapped.

Two men, several years older then Vena, jumped up. Both had red gold hair, sprinkled with gray and morning blue eyes. Twins. They sat down again, smiling at each other.

"We can help you, children. We will need you to tell your whole story of why you are here. Leave nothing out, dear children," Vena continued, taking her seat.

Leama sat down at the head of the table. "We will help you. We do know something horrible is going on in the west and south. We have had reports of attacks from some of our villages."

Dei told the story from beginning to end with the help of Zenerax. She told of the massacre of their village and their run to save the other villages. She cried when she talked about Aska and the others who died, sobbing into Zenerax's shoulder until she could control her sorrow. Mentioning the names of those who had sacrificed themselves for others' survival, Dei finally recounted their journey into the Daaguwh lands. When she was done, the Council sat still, faces frozen in shock. Biolak or Gangu, Dei couldn't tell which, reached over and swallowed three glasses of wine. Leama had misty eyes and Vena was crying outright, as were most of the Council members.

"Djed, Yria'ti, I'm so sorry if I have disturbed you. I—"

"You do not understand! You are but children!" Vena stood up, her eyes red rimmed. "The Dragons are here. With the coming of the sylai this means the Ile must find the Dragons or face destruction at the Warlord's hands. We are not ready for this! The Ile are not ready to be united. We still fight amongst ourselves. We fight for the best lands, the ones best for farming and richest in metals and minerals. The world is not ready. I never wanted to be alive when this happened. I had hoped to be..." Vena sat down and buried her face in her hands.

Dei and Zenerax gaped at Vena. "The Dragons have been found?" they echoed, hope rising in their hearts for the first time in days.

Leama stood up. "Dei, Zenerax, I had a dream two nights ago that you would come. I foresee the future as every Daaguwh Djed can, as I will until I die. I saw that you would come and tell your tale. You have lost many people in your young lives, people that you grew to love, but you will lose so many more once the Dragons are discovered. Life will never be easy now that we see colors in the sky at night.

"In my dream I saw you and your one thousand Edieata travel to Dagau. I saw you lose little Aska. I saw the sylai join the Warlord. I saw the Warlord come to power over the weak nation Atay. I watch as every day more join his Evil and as one of the Tar-ten betray the Ile. I saw Vena taking you and Zenerax to a place near the Lost Mountains to get the Dragon of the Rising Sun. You made a promise to a Princess, Deivenada, that you would never betray the Dragon of the Rising Sun. I saw you leave today, carrying our hope with you. I watched you bring the Dragon back, and send him to the Temple to get his sign." Leama walked over to stare out one of the windows. "I would like to quote a saying from our Prophecies. *"He shall be brought to the land of the Ile, the Dragon of the Rising Sun. He will be brought by the Tar-ten and led by the Tar-ten. He will unite the Ile, symbolizing a new beginning. She, the Dragon of the Coming Storm, will symbolize the hard times to come and the war the world must yet fight."* Leama turned around and faced the silence of the room. "We need the Dragons if we are to survive these dark times. The Evil that is coming is stronger than ever before and the hate is pulsing. I need you, Deivenada. I need you and Zenerax to go and find the Dragon of the Rising Sun. Vena has said she would go with you to help you carry out this quest. Will you go?"

Dei nodded. "I will go for the Tar-ten."

Zenerax stepped closer to the table. "I will go, yet I need a promise from you first, Djed. You must promise that our people will be treated with respect and you must take us to Kayzi so we can tell him and our people."

Vena walked over to Zenerax. "Zenerax, we are leaders. We know how you feel about your people. You will not be gone long, child. They will be safe. Nevertheless, I will take you there." She laid her hands on Zenerax and Dei.

Dei felt as if the ground had turned upside down and then back again. Suddenly she was standing in the middle of the Edieata camp right next to her brother.

Kayzi's eyes bulged and he toppled backwards. Scrambling back up, he managed a strained, "how did you get here?"

"The Yria'ti brought us here," Dei said, laughing.

"I'm Vena, Kayzi. Gather your people around, child, all of them." Vena ordered.

It took only a few short minutes for every Edieata present to gather around the four leaders.

"Only a couple can see us and they won't be able to hear me," Dei said to Vena.

"I can fix that, child." Vena murmured a few words and Dei was lifted five feet off the ground.

"Thank…" Dei stopped. Her voice had been magnified double.

Vena smiled. "Magic."

"People of the Edieata, listen to me carefully. Zenerax and I are going far from here. We are going to the Lost Mountains to bring back the Lord Dragon. You will be safe here with our Daaguwh friends. From now on, consider them one of your own."

Most people accepted this news. After all, the Daaguwh were friends of old and Ile. They dispersed, going back to their duties that had been assigned them.

Vena lowered Dei to the ground and grasped the hands of Zenerax and Dei.

"You expect me to control all these people?" Kayzi said.

"We will only be gone a couple of hours. You'll be fine. The council is watching you," Zenerax said before he blinked out of sight from Vena's magic.

Kayzi cursed after his sister and Zenerax disappeared. This was not good. He kicked his feet in the dust.

Walking back to his campsite, he picked up his arrows, running the red fletching through his fingers. *Why do they always leave me? I am a Djed, too. Why can't I go?* Kayzi thought, sliding his arrows back into the quiver and slinging the quiver over his back. Picking up his bow, he called to another Ile. "I'll be gone for a while. If anything happens, you're in charge."

"Where are you going, Djed?" the Ile asked.

"Hunting," Kayzi said over his shoulder as he left the camp, heading towards the Plains of the Daaguwh.

Chapter 14
How Cities Fall

Raxsen smiled coldly as one of his captains told him that the city of Tes was well guarded, the positions of the city's guards and the plan to kill Raxsen.

The word of Raxsen's rule in Atay had not spread. Everyone who lived in Barra or Xs was branded to him for life. They could never escape him nor betray him. Those that did leave were spies and loyal to him. Fear of a hideous death was a powerful ally.

Raxsen had changed from the day on the cliff tops. His eyes were cold and had no humor or joy, only ice. He was nineteen and he had an army. His army was not just sylai and rogui, but also made up of over two thousand humans. He had already taken the small cities of Cunai, Melo and the capitol of Nutria, Lauot, adding another one thousand to his army. In the few battles fought, his tactics were so grand that he had lost only ten men in five battles. His plans were nothing compared to what he was developing next.

"We will attack in two hours using the battle plans I have given. Dismissed." Raxsen waved a hand as the captain bowed and left.

Once he captured Tes, he would move on to Angarat and then the battle with the Dragons, whoever they may be, would start and the world would meet death.

Raxsen leaned back in his fur chair. It was cold outside, but not as cold as the hating fire that burned within him. Raxsen did not know what caused him to hate so much, but he bathed in its sweet revenge.

Raxsen scowled. Attacking the city of Tes was much too easy. It was like walking up to a sleeping child and taking away his toy. Raxsen needed a chance to really prove himself. Perhaps Angarat would prove to do this and he would show the world his military genius.

The flap to his tent was knocked aside and David Pierce entered. He nodded to Raxsen. "Warlord, I received the news that the ships you sent to Tes arrived a few days back. In order for us to make the crossing, you will only need fifty boats."

Like Raxsen, Pierce had also changed from the young man who had first confronted Raxsen in Barra to a battle wise, loyal and powerful man. Pierce wore a light chain mail that had been burned black. His dark brown hair was short and spiky at the top making him look like a berserker when he charged into battle, fighting with a mixture of magic and steel.

"Pierce, I have a job for you once Tes is captured. There are men throughout the Northern Kingdom who are loyal to the Lord of the Dark and myself. I want you to contact these men. They are to search for anyone in their city who has a strong Talent. I want them to kill those with the strong Talent or make them join me. The Phoenixes as the Prophecies say, will join with the Dragons and "rule under their side". You must keep this from happening. I cannot have men and women strong in the Talent running around the land furthering the cause of the Dragons." Raxsen thought a moment. "I know the Phoenix of Death will join me. It is only right, but I want you to make sure that the men join me more than the women. I do not want useless women in my army."

"Yes, Warlord. Why do you despise women so?" Pierce asked. He himself had had several women in his bed after conquering the cities of Nutria.

Raxsen glared at his general. "They are the weaker of the two. They have no use but to give men pleasure and have babies. They are always under foot and those of them who are beautiful corrupt men into thinking differently."

Pierce laughed. "Why have you decided to let women join your army once we capture Tes?"

"They can entertain the men and they can be useful fighters," Raxsen said, always trying to find a way to make a seemingly useless thing into something helpful. "Once we reach the mainland, many of the women of Angarat will join us. Those women are known for their skills in battle like the women in Istra are known for their beauty. Besides, like I said, my men need diversions from dying. If they fall in love with a woman of my army, they will fight harder to protect her."

Pierce smirked. "Tricky, Warlord."

Raxsen rubbed his chin. "Not tricky, smart." He checked his sword in his belt and made sure his clothing was in order. "The battle will begin soon."

Grinning, Pierce left the tent, orders issuing from his mouth quickly and snapping like a whip.

Raxsen stretched, a yawn cracking his jaw. *Today is the day my empire of the Islands of the Northern Kingdom begins. Today is the day I begin my plans for the mainland and it is today that Darkness will truly begin to reign.*

A horn sounded from outside.

Raxsen stood up. After conquering Tes he would then control the whole East Sea. He walked out of the tent and into a field of more tents. Raxsen slept the same way everyone else in his camp slept, on the ground. It was too much of a burden to carry a bed. At this point in his plans it worked out well. He wanted his men to feel some connection to him other than seeing him only as the Warlord.

It was just before dawn and fog was rolling everywhere. The smell of smoke mixed in with the noise of weapons and armor being fixed and cleaned. Men raced all over, trying to fulfill duties left to the last minute. Two men were polishing horns that looked like a half circle with a bowl at the end. Before Raxsen attacked, he had those two young men blow the horns. It was an eerie sound. It sounded like a screaming animal but with more fullness and strength. He knew people would come to fear the sound, but he loved it.

A sylai ran up to him carrying a bunch of scrolls in its claws.

"Warlord, I have the maps you asked for," it whispered, its voice like dead leaves crawling over bare ground.

"Store the maps on the pack horses. I'll need them once we reach the mainland. When we capture Tes, you may have the pick of the spoils," Raxsen said.

The sylai bowed and scurried off.

"Time to kill," Raxsen said, and the fog lifted, showing the city its enemy.

The clanking of armor could be heard as men hurried into their ranks. Men on horses galloped into position. Sylai thumped their spears on the ground and the rogui began a low chant. The rough words of their language blended with the thumping spears. Steadily the chant grew louder and louder until it seemed as if the whole army was screaming the ghostly chant.

Raxsen slid onto his black steed.

The city of Tes stared down onto the boiling masses of the Warlord's army.

Before Raxsen could give the command to attack, a white flag was lifted above the battlements. The doors of the city gate opened and an old man came out on horseback. He rode up to Raxsen. The man was all wrinkles and his hair was a shocking white.

"I am the mayor of Tes, my Lord. Please, we surrender. I have men that will join you freely. We do not want to fight," the man said getting off his horse.

Raxsen snorted. "Do you have boats that could bring all of us to the mainland?"

"Yes. We can also build more."

"If you surrender, my men get the choice of anything in your city. I want three fourths of your able bodied men. Women may join if they choose. You are to build ships for my army, also, and provide us with food for the crossing. If you betray this in any way, you will know what it means to die."

"Yes, my lord. Come with me into the city."

Raxsen was no fool. "Old man, do you really believe I would walk in there by myself and be ambushed?"

The man went white and his eyes slid away from Raxsen's face for a moment before returning.

Raxsen motioned for his fifteen bodyguards, the best men in his army, other than himself, to surround the mayor of Tes. "Sir, life is short. Do not lie, and life can be easier. Call all your men off up on the wall."

The white haired man held up a hand and the archers on the wall put down their arrows.

"And don't forget the swordsmen by the wall, and the pot of oil above the gates."

The old man looked shaken and raised his other hand. Fifty swordsmen came out of the bush and threw down their swords.

"Next time you lie be careful of who you lie to. They just might know
the truth. If you are not careful, life could find you killed." In one swift
move Raxsen pulled the knife out of the man's belt and pushed it into the old
man's belly. Warm blood drenched his hands. He let the corpse drop to the
ground, at the feet of his bodyguards.

"Mayor!" Raxsen yelled. "I want the real mayor!"

A middle-aged man came out, wearing purple robes and also on
horseback. He rode out to the Warlord.

"Mayor, I want you to surrender three fourths of your men to my army,
and some women, boats to cross the East Sea in one month, the best
weapons made by your weapons smiths, your city's riches, most of your
stored food and in return you get life." Raxsen's voice was full of anger at
what they had attempted. He had known what these fools were going to try.
But to carry it out after seeing his forces...

The mayor paled, but nodded. "Your request shall be done, my lord."

Raxsen turned around and addressed his army. "Men, we have won!
Each of you gets your normal spoils, and what did I tell you? You are
richer than you were in the past." Raxsen turned back to the city and rode
in, followed by over two thousand men and over one thousand sylai and
rogui.

Victory was his.

Tes was a rich city due to its location. Being a port city had its advan-
tages.

Inside the gates people came out of their wood and stone houses to see
him and his army. Some cheered, others were silent. No one frowned or
grumbled. They knew that the person next to them could be a spy for the
Warlord. And if they were caught, life would get worse.

Raxsen stopped at the courthouse, a large stone building with a circular
garden at its front. He mounted the steps and held up his hands so all the
people of Tes knew who ruled.

"People of Tes, if you do not want to join me, you will die." Not a foot
stirred. No one spoke. The only sound was of gulls flying overhead.
"Three fourths of the men are to enlist in my army. If more want to, so be
it. Life is better. Ask my men. They are richer than they ever were.
Women will also enlist. I need twenty boats to be made in one month and
enough weapons for every new member to have three. War is here. The
Fifth Battle is on its way. The Dragons have not been found. They have no
army. I do, the Warlord. In the Prophecies, it says the Dragons will create a
new world. I will make a better one. If you are on the side of the one who
is strong, you will live!"

People cheered at his speech. He gave the same speech every time. He
knew people feared the Dragons and the Warlord. But the Dragons were

still legend. He was real, and people believed what they saw. It was no
strange power of the Dark Lord. It was all Raxsen's power. He could give
people what they wanted even if they never believed in the Dark before.
He made them believe. Once he binded them to him, he made them
worship.

Chapter 15
<u>Dragons</u>

Janevra awoke to Mat leaning over her holding a wooden plate of
bread and cold meat.

"Wake up. We need to leave soon."

Janevra grumbled as she sat. Life was getting better than what it was
in the first part of their journey to the Lost Mountains. She had never slept
outside before and she had never gone hungry. Janevra heaved a sigh. It
was good for her to face hardships. She ate her food half-heartedly.

"We'll reach the Lost Mountains in three days and the City in five
more," Qwaser said.

"Do you think they will accept us? We are of a different race and not
trustworthy," Mat said. "They've never seen humans before and Janevra
and I have only seen one elf. It's not a very good start and trust is hard to
get."

"You are trustworthy to me. Before I left I had word brought to the
King of what happened to my village and where I was going. They will
trust you or at least accept you."

Janevra rubbed her eyes after she pulled herself onto her horse. "Let's
go. We have another long day ahead of us."

They had camped on the side of the road, off in the brush. The sun was
just peeking over the top of the trees. Birds filled the air with their songs.

Before entering the opening, they stopped and looked around. It was
clear. They rode out singing and began a steady trot down the road.

It was well past noon when all three were knocked from their horses by
a blast of air.

Janevra sat up, a spell coming to mind. Mat and Qwaser got to their
feet and hurried over to Janevra. Their horses rolled their eyes in fright and
ran into a nearby field.

Three people were standing in front of them. The older of the two
females had blonde hair streaked with gray. Her poise held a commanding
charm and she looked at Mat and Janevra with curiosity. The younger
woman had her red hair pulled back in many braids. She held a spear with
a long blade in her hand and watched the three with hope and weariness.
The male had dark hair, a tattoo of a sun brandished on his upper arm and
his spear strapped to his back.

The older woman approached them. "I am Vena, the Yria'ti of the
Daaguwh Ile and I have come for the Dragon of the Rising Sun."

Janevra and Mat exchanged puzzled looks. Qwaser frowned. "Ma'am, I think you are mistaken. Those two behind me are not the Dragons. They already know their Talent and it is not that of the Dragons. I am sorry."

The woman shook her head. "I am not mistaken, child." Janevra frowned slightly at Qwaser being called a child. He was hundreds of years older than this woman. "These two are the Dragons, the ones meant to save the world from Darkness."

The dark haired young man and the other woman walked forward. The older woman indicated them with a tilt of her head. "This is Deivenada, and Zenerax. They have come with me on this journey to help the Dragon of the Rising Sun know his place." Vena faced Janevra. "Lady Dragon, have you and the Lord Dragon ever wondered why magic came so easy to you and why sometimes you knew things would happen and you couldn't explain it?"

"This cannot be. Janevra and I cannot be the Dragons," Mat said, watching the three warily. "We learned we could use magic only a few weeks ago. What makes you think we're the Dragons?"

"The Djed of the Daaguwh can see the future. You are the Dragons, child. Did you know that the day you both used your magic together was the night the Second Prophecies were in the sky?" Vena asked.

Janevra shook her head. "We can't be. As Mat said, we were already tested. I'm sorry but you're wrong. We're only greens."

Vena grasped Janevra's hand in her own. "Child, have you thought that perhaps you tested as greens because the world was not ready, that per-chance the gods stepped in to make sure you were not found in order for the events of the prophecy to come true?"

Janevra pulled her hand away from Vena and stepped back, moving closer to Mat. The words of the strange woman were beginning to disturb her.

Qwaser rubbed his palm across the pommel of his sword. "If they are the Dragons, it would explain the First Prophecy. I, by chance, went to Jariran and asked for someone who could help me. I was shown to the Princess. She said she would help my people and me. In the First Proph-ecy it said in times of need the Lost People would be found." Qwaser stared at Janevra and Mat. "My Lord and Lady Dragon!"

Vena looked at Mat. "We need the young man. He is the one to fulfill the Prophecy of the Ile and she the one of the Forgotten people. Child, we will not harm you. The world needs you. The Warlord has come and in one month will be crossing the East Sea." Vena spoke calmly as if she was speaking of the sun rising.

Janevra took Mat's arm. "Please excuse us for a moment." She dragged Mat several yards away. "The Dragons!" she squeaked. "How could *we* be the Dragons?" Janevra looked at Mat with a "did you know about this" expression.

Mat glanced at Vena as she talked with Qwaser. "I don't know. Do you remember that first night we got the spell book? We went through a whole book in four hours. The priest said that we were powerful."

"The priest said that we were greens," Janevra pointed out. "He said nothing about being the Dragons."

"I know, but the world did not need us yet and the Light changed it," Mat argued.

"Mat...I don't know...I...this does feel right...that we need to do this and that the world needs us," Janevra said, taking a step closer to Mat. "If it's true, I..."

"We'll be in it together. And if we are what they say we are then we can meet whenever and wherever we want."

Janevra groaned. "Why can't we go together?"

"Janevra," Mat said. "You know the prophecy."

Janevra looked over at Vena, Deivenada and Zenerax. "The prophecy did say one was to unite the Ile. I guess that's you." Janevra paused. "Don't get yourself killed. I don't know if I trust them completely. It's not everyday that people pop out of midair and tell you that you're the Dragons."

Mat smiled and gave her a quick hug. "We need to tell them."

They walked back to the strange group of four and told them of their decision. Vena smiled and her face seemed to lose it's years.

"Janevra," Deivenada said, "do not worry. I promise to keep Mat safe from any harm that might befall him."

"Thank you, Deivenada. I know it's a lot to ask of someone I don't know but will you promise me that you will not leave him, never betray him?"

Deivenada laughed. "I am Ile, Princess, I will never betray the Djed of all Djeds. His life is my life, his blood is my blood. If he falls, I will avenge him. My promise to you is that I will never betray him."

"Janevra," Mat said, "why are you so suspicious of them?"

Janevra cast him a glare. "I am a Princess, Mat. I know what people are capable of when it comes to power. Deceit is a powerful enemy."

"She speaks wisely, Dragon of the Rising Sun," Zenerax said. "Trust none but those who you know are your enemies for it is only them that you can count on to try to trick or ruin you. Everyone else you can only wonder at their intentions."

Mat's brow creased at this bit of information but he accepted it.

Janevra hugged the young Ile woman in thanks and stepped back.

"Mat, step over here with us, child. We travel by magic," Vena said, motioning with her finger for Mat to stand by her.

Mat hugged Janevra and nodded at Qwaser. "Take care of her," he said, standing next to Vena.

"I will, but if she is what she is, she will be taking care of me." Qwaser smiled.

Janevra waved to Mat as the air shimmered around him, Vena,

Deivenada and Zenerax. They disappeared.

"Come, Janevra, we still have eight days travel ahead of us," Qwaser said, bringing the horses back. He slid into the saddle with elven grace, a grace no human could master.

"Qwaser, do you believe me to be the Lady Dragon?" Janevra asked.

Qwaser looked down at her. "I do, Princess," he whispered.

Janevra pulled herself up onto her brown horse. The horse whickered slightly at the weight. She reined her horse into a gallop. As she rode, she felt the beginning stress of her new place in life. The Lady Dragon. Janevra shivered. It was a name she would prefer not to have, a name that brought much power and responsibility, a name she did not know she could live up to.

Janevra's bottom was so sore after that day of travel she knew she could not sit in a chair without wincing. She and Qwaser had ridden at a dead gallop all day after Mat left, changing horses on the way. When they had finally stopped at an inn, Janevra swore her backside had taken the shape of a saddle.

They did the same thing the next day.

When they finally caught sight of the Lost Mountains, they had a five-hour ride ahead of them still.

"Qwaser, may we please stop and rest?" Janevra begged. She was still not used to riding all day.

"Princess, if we must, then yes, but we do not need to, so we ride." Qwaser had explained as if to a child.

So they rode.

And when they reached the base of the mountains, Janevra was awe struck.

In the dying light the mountains had a purplish tint to them. Their jagged peaks tore through the sky and their snowed capped summits sparkled against the darkening night.

"They're so…lost," Janevra said, feeling ridiculous at not being able to better describe the beauty and majesty of the mountains.

"Lost. That is why we call them that. Most days their tops are swathed in the clouds. You are fortunate to see the Lost Mountains," Qwaser said. "Come, we must hurry. There is a village slightly to the north. We can stay there tonight."

It might have only been a few minutes, but being travel worn, it felt like an eternity.

Janevra's first glance at an elven village was the twinkling lights. She could not see much without light but she could feel the beauty of an ancient race surround her.

Qwaser led her down the street to an inn with light streaming out of the windows and voices inside.

They slid off their horses and handed them to a young stable boy, who stared at Janevra. He had never before seen a human woman.

Qwaser opened the door to the inn and walked in. Janevra followed him. She stopped in the doorway, suddenly conscious she was the outsider.

When the door opened, every activity in the inn had come to a halt. Visitors were rare. They stared at Qwaser then their eyes glided to Janevra and they gasped.

The innkeeper came forward. He was a thin elf with large round eyes. His ears were elegantly pointed like Qwaser's but his blonde hair had streaks of gray in it. He was elderly, perhaps two thousand years old.

"You cannot bring the likes of her into this kingdom, or this inn," the innkeeper said, his voice soft but menacing. He spoke in Janevra's tongue intentionally.

Qwaser glanced around coolly. "This woman who you see in front of you is the Lady Dragon, the Dragon of the Coming Storm."

Silence greeted his words then someone giggled and the inn burst into laughter.

Janevra moved and stood next to Qwaser. She held her head high, watching them with fierce green eyes.

When the laughter had died away Qwaser continued in elvish. *"I am not lying; she is indeed the Lady Dragon. When she struck down the first man, she used her power and that is why blood appeared in the sky. You all saw it. You all know the prophecy."*

The innkeeper scoffed. *"Coincidence."*

"It is not—"

The inn door burst open and a young elf was brought in, blood was dripping down his tunic and landing in small puddles on the floor.

"Move aside! Clear a table!" one of the elves carrying the younger one shouted.

A table was quickly cleared and the boy was laid on it. His face was ashen and his hands clutched at his stomach, trying to hold in his innards.

"What happened?" someone asked.

"Rogui attack on the Goldenleaf farm. His family was all killed. We got there just when they were about to finish him off. We killed all of them." The speaker paused, *"Much good it did though. He's dying."*

Janevra looked over the heads of the elves. *"Uth es goth minv mestho,"* (I can help him) she said in perfect elvish.

They all turned and stared at her, even Qwaser. Stunned that she could understand their language, they stepped aside.

Janevra moved up and stood beside the young elf. Her hands became sweaty. She did not know if she could summon enough magic to heal him. But something had made her speak, so she would try.

Janevra laid her hands on the elf's forehead. He gave a shudder as pain ripped through him. Blood bubbled at his lips.

She drew on her magic. She went far beyond the ability she ever thought she would be able to control.

A bright glow appeared around her hands. Surprisingly, not a drop of sweat stood out on her brow.

She concentrated hard, trying to remember something that was not a memory.

He must live. She must find it! She must find the words! The words would make the spell stronger and the boy would be completely healed. It was hard to beat death.

Her heart gave a jolt as the words came to her mind. She spoke the eerie words of magic. *"Unia dieath ack newleva!"*

The elves gasped. The wound started to close, slowly, but it was closing. Color was returning to the boy's face.

When Janevra finished, a scar was not even left. The boy seemed to be sleeping peacefully.

Janevra collapsed on the floor. She was not tired from using the magic. She had transferred some of the boy's pain into her own body, weakening herself.

Qwaser picked her up and took her up to a room.

No one stopped them.

It seemed as if the Lady Dragon had indeed come. Again.

෭   ෬   ෫

The elven city was much like Jariran and Janevra felt a pang of homesickness as she gazed down upon it from the slopes of a mountain.

A large plaza, the tiles in the design of a sun, lay in the middle of the city. The towers of the city glinted blue in the daylight. A clear river split the city in half and a hundred fishing boats glided across the water. Thousands of gardens, the plants blooming in the spring sunlight, sprouted everywhere. The Elven palace rose above the other buildings of the city, its gray stone was flecked with blue, which made it look like a massive cloud hovering close to the ground. Domes, covered in yellow, blue and red tiles dotted the city like ornaments. Traveling through the paved streets, the populace of the city moved about with timeless patience and grace.

Janevra, tearing her eyes away from the beauty of the city, took a moment to glance at Qwaser. His bright green eyes were filled with joy and sorrow as he looked down into his home city. Clenching his hands into fists, he took a deep breath and began his way down the slope, heading towards the city gates.

Hurrying after him and sliding on the loose soil, Janevra was careful not to disturb any rocks least she cause a rockslide.

It had taken Janevra and Qwaser five days, as Qwaser had predicted, to cross the mountains. The journey had been uneventful as they traveled through the snow peaked mountains and the vast forests that covered them. An escort of elves had followed them from the town where Janevra had healed the boy to the pass, adamant on protecting the Lady Dragon.

Approaching the large white gates of the Elven City, Qwaser said a few whispered words to the guard who jerked visibly and looked up at Janevra with awe. The guard opened a side door, holding it open for Janevra and Qwaser to enter and closing in quietly behind them.

Inside the Elven City, Qwaser guided Janevra through the metropolis. It was near noon and the streets were full. Many of the elves gave Janevra odd looks. Her face was far different from the ones they usually saw.

"Qwaser!" two voices called out.

Qwaser swiveled around only to be bombarded by two young elves, both ecstatic to see him. His own face spread into a pleased smile and he returned the hugs warmly.

One of the elves who greeted Qwaser was extraordinarily skinny even for an elf. He had dark brown hair, much like Mat's, Janevra noticed, that frizzed around his head. He went by the name Tasawer, if that was the right name Janevra picked out from their chatter. The other, named Danlk had blue eyes as bright as Qwaser's green. He held himself with the stance of one who knew battle and fear. Even in a moment of joy, he did not seem to let his guard down.

"Tasawer, Danlk, I want you to meet Janevra, the Princess of Caendor, the Dragon of the Coming Storm, the Lady Dragon," Qwaser said, directing the attention of both young elves to Janevra. "She is the one who is to unite us with the world."

Janevra smiled as both elves stared at her in astonishment. They dropped into deep elegant bows, both too stunned to speak.

Qwaser nudged Danlk. "Tell me, what is the news?"

Danlk smiled. "Kalioa has managed to convince the King to see whoever you brought back." Danlk eyed Janevra. "Although, I don't think he's prepared for this."

"Come," Tasawer said, grasping Janevra's arm, "we will take you to the palace. Once we introduce you to the King, if he accepts you, he will tell you all you must do in order to be proven the Lady Dragon."

Led through the streets by three elves, Janevra was hustled to the palace. The eagerness of Danlk and Tasawer for her to meet the King made her nervous and she began to worry about what might happen if he did not accept her.

They lead her up the stairs leading to the palace. Above the doors of the palace was engraved into the wood the elven words "*Soeth zioalez otxth nurmljs hmutijs xyqtia avytia eyath.*" Qwaser opened the doors of the palace, ushering them up a grand marble staircase, into what she could only call the Throne Room.

An elven woman greeted them by the doors, a wide smile growing on her face when she saw Qwaser. A sword was sheathed at her waist and a pendant of a sword hung from her neck. "Qwaser, I'm so glad you came back!" She kissed Qwaser on the cheek and Janevra had to stifle a laugh when Qwaser blushed.

The doors to the Throne Room were thrown open and the five proceeded into a room filled with courtiers dressed in simple yet attractive gowns and robes. The hush that descended onto the throne room after their entrance was almost enough to make Janevra turn and flee, but she held her head high and followed the four elves to stand before the King. She was a princess after all.

Sitting upon a jade colored throne, the Elven King was everything the stories said about elves. He was lean and graceful. A golden circlet was wrapped around his head and it glinted in the light of the room. Holding a certain ageless charm, he made all those around him look at him with awe. The King smiled when he saw Qwaser and stepped down from the dais to shake Qwaser's hand, after Qwaser bowed.

"Qwaser, your parents will be glad to see you. After your friends told us what happened at Andaon, they have been ever so fretful. Once you have finished with your tale, you must go to them and ease their worried hearts. They would be here at Court but considering the stress they've been under, I let them pass this day to rest."

Qwaser bowed. "I did not mean to worry them, my lord."

"Think nothing of it, Qwaser. Your friend Hasaxta has been comforting them through the days. He knows that you of all people could survive a trek through human lands."

"Mentioning the race of humans, my lord, you must meet someone." Qwaser motioned Janevra forward.

Janevra moved up beside her friend, feeling the eyes of all the elves in the room upon her back, calculating and deciding. *I will be strong. They will not see my unease,* Janevra thought. *They will not see my fear of whom I might be.*

"This is Princess Janevra of Caendor, the Dragon of the Coming Storm, the Lady Dragon," Qwaser said. Janevra curtsied before the Elven King.

The intake of breath from the courtiers was loud and the babble of voices rose in exclamation.

The King ran his eyes around the room and lowered his voice so only those very close could hear and spoke in elven. "Do you speak the truth, Qwaser? Is this human woman the Lady Dragon?"

"What reason would I have to lie to you, my lord?" Qwaser replied in elven.

The King watched Qwaser through narrowed eyes before accepting his response at face value. He could not resist one more question however. "What makes you certain she is what you claim her to be?"

Qwaser lifted his eyes and stared into the face of the King. "An Ile woman from the Cyrain Plains came to us on the winds of magic, asking for the Lord Dragon, a close friend of the Princess. She explained to us who Janevra and Mat were. Apparently their leader has the gift of foresight."

The King tapped his fingers on his lips, musing. "Say she is not the Lady Dragon and she undergoes the test. Does she know the price?"

Qwaser shook his head. "She does not. Her Prophecies do not talk of a test they must take to prove themselves. It is only in our and the Ile Prophecies that they do. She would not know that death calls to those who believe they are something they are not."

"Are you willing to risk her life?"

Janevra, deciding she was tired of being talked about over her head, stepped forward. "I am willing to take the test and prove who I am even if the outcome is death, my lord. For some time now I have been aware of the growing Darkness and I want to stop it."

The King gazed at Janevra, surprise at her well-spoken elven mingling in his eyes. "I will let you take the test, Princess of Caendor. Kalioa has been warning me that someone was coming who would help. You are very lucky that Qwaser was smart enough to send a warning else I might not have accepted this news." The King motioned to a cleric standing in front of the courtiers. "It takes a month for preparation before you can enter the World of Things Yet To Come and Things That Have Passed. The clerics will prepare you for this while furthering your knowledge of magic. Are you willing to wait?"

"If that is what it takes." *I will do anything to save my people and yours. Anything. Darkness will not conquer this land,* Janevra resolved. She mentally noted to ask Qwaser about the World of Things Yet To Come and Things That Have Passed.

The King clapped his hands, calling for the attention of the courtiers. "The Princess Janevra of Caendor will be staying in the palace as an honored guest. There are those among us who believe her to be the Lady Dragon. If this proves true, she is the one who will unite us with the world. I hope you accept her and let her know the great hospitality of the elven people. For if she is the Lady Dragon, our fate lies within her hands, and if she fails, so will we."

Once more hush cascaded upon the Throne Room, the silence echoing in the high dome of the ceiling.

Janevra cleared her throat and spoke, trying to ease the fear of the elves. "I know that accepting a human is a hard accomplishment. We have not always been the most trustworthy of races, but for the sake of the Light, please allow me to live here for a month. If it is proven that I am the Lady Dragon, I will do all I can to unite you with the world. If not, I will leave and not utter another word about your people unless your wishes are otherwise said. I know more about your ways than any human could possibly know. I will not offend you or your customs, I promise. *Soeth zioalez otxth nurmljs hmutijs xyqtia avytia eyath.*"

The elves stared at her. The Princess stood before them, one who knew their culture and their language, who was almost one of them. They began to see her as acceptable in their eyes. She had already proven her knowledge of their kind by speaking their language and promising to keep the knowledge of their existence a secret unless otherwise told. She had spoken not down to them nor insulted them with her human ways but had stayed composed and refined in the presences of so many. To many of them it did not matter if she was human.

The King, smiling at Janevra after her speech, dismissed the courtiers with a nod. They left the Throne room, gossiping, Janevra's name much among their lips.

Besides Janevra, Qwaser, the King, Danlk, Tasawer and Kalioa, another elf remained. He wore a sword at his side and on the breast of his coat was the insignia of a tree. From her knowledge of elves, Janevra knew that the young elf was the General of the Elven Armies. There was only one more position above that when it came to the military and that was the Head General of all the Elven Armies.

The young general bowed to the King. "My lord, since Qwaser has returned with such great hope, I deem it only right that you allow his sentence to be terminated. Surely he cannot go back into exile now."

The King laughed. "You are right, Hasaxta. It would be foolish to do so." The King turned to Qwaser. "Qwaser, you are hereby free of your sentence."

Qwaser and Hasaxta exchanged a rough hug, clearly long time friends, laughing and pounding each other on the backs.

"Thank you, my lord," Qwaser said.

The King smiled. "It seemed only right, especially since your father has declared that the moment you return, his place as Head General will go to his oldest son."

Qwaser's jaw dropped. "What?" he croaked.

"I suggest you talk to your father," the King said, bowing to Janevra and walking towards the doors of the Throne room where a cleric waited for him. The doors to the room closed, leaving the six alone.

"Janevra, this is Hasaxta, a long time friend," Qwaser said.

Hasaxta bowed deeply to Janevra, his long blonde hair almost touching the floor. "Lady Dragon, it is my pleasure to meet you."

Janevra bowed back. "I am too pleased to meet the General of the Elven Armies."

Hasaxta let out a deep laugh. "I forget how much you know of our ways, Princess of Caendor. I must say, I am impressed." He turned to Qwaser. "It is true what the King said. Your father is going to hand over his title to you. I know he is preparing a feast for you as am I."

Qwaser thanked his friend. "Where are my parents?"

"I will find them for you. It will not take long. I will tell them you are in the Garden Room." Hasaxta left the room at a brisk walk, his sword swinging at his hip.

Danlk and Tasawer also decided to leave, mentioning plans about a bodyguard needed for the Lady Dragon and new Head General.

Qwaser, Kalioa and Janevra were left in the Throne Room, standing on the stairs of the dais.

Kalioa was oddly interested in Janevra, Janevra noticed. A glint came into her eyes every time she looked at Janevra. Janevra fidgeted uncomfortably under her dark, curious gaze. In return, however, Janevra could not keep from staring at the pendant of the sword that hung around Kalioa's neck. For some reason, the sign gave her a feeling of something Evil and dangerous.

Qwaser, unaware of the tension between the two, stepped off the dais. "Hasaxta said I was to meet my parents in the Garden Room. I had better start there. Would either of you like to come?"

Janevra and Kalioa nodded and followed Qwaser out of the Throne Room. They walked down the decorated hallways, silent, until Janevra remembered something she wanted to ask Qwaser.

"Qwaser, what is this test that I must take to prove that I am the Lady Dragon?" she asked, suddenly fearful.

It was Kalioa who answered first. "Did you see the door at the far end of the Throne Room?"

Janevra squinted, trying to remember what was behind the jade colored throne. If her memory was right, behind the throne was a wooden door painted to look like part of the mural that adorned the walls of the Throne Room. "I saw the door," Janevra said.

"That is where you will take your test, to prove if you are the Lady Dragon," Kalioa said, twisting her pendant.

Qwaser cringed. "They say those that enter who are not Dragons, die, at least, most do. I've heard that it's a horrible death, too."

"That's so reassuring," Janevra said dryly.

Kalioa laughed hollowly and nudged Qwaser with an elbow. "He can be like that sometimes." She lowered her voice and whispered fiercely to Qwaser. "Do not be so somber! She's doing something for us that may cost her her life. You can at least be helpful and not say such things!"

"I'm sorry, Janevra. I'm afraid Kalioa's right. I do see the dark side of things much too often."

Janevra shrugged. "I think we all do. Can you tell me more about this place I must go?"

"There are only three places in the world where the World of Things Yet To Come and Things That Have Passed can be accessed," Qwaser said. "One is in the Cyrain Plains and the other is in the land of Angarat in the city of Carim. The only other remaining one is here. It is said that once you enter the World of Things Yet To Come and Things That Have Passed, you enter the world of the gods where they judge you for your merit. If you pass, they say, you are destined to be a great leader, a Dragon or a person of much power in the world. In the Fourth Age, the Warlords would enter this world to be judged by the God of Dark to see if they were worthy of leading the hordes of Evil."

They rounded a corner and came to a room filled with sunlight and plants. A joyful cry sounded from the other end of the corridor and Qwaser's mother ran to him, her dress fanning out behind her. His father, younger brother and Hasaxta were not far behind.

As Qwaser reunited with his family, Janevra noticed that Kalioa had vanished. She was about to mention this when Hasaxta grabbed her arm and steered her down another hallway.

"Let them reunite without us watching them. Qwaser has been gone for a long time," Hasaxta said. "His parents have been frantic since Kalioa and her friends reported to the King what happened at Andaon."

"Where are we going?" Janevra asked, suspicious.

Hasaxta looked down at her, a bemused smile on his lips. "Do not be suspicious of me, Princess of Caendor. I am not someone you should fear. Qwaser and I have been friends for Ages. We both are loyal to the Light." They started down a flight of steps.

"Who should I suspect then?"

"A wise question. Who do you think?"

"Kalioa," Janevra said bluntly.

"Why? What has she done?" Hasaxta asked but not as someone wanting the answer, as someone already knowing it.

"She has done nothing, but her pendant..." Janevra trailed off.

Hasaxta nodded approvingly. "You've noticed the Evil that it carries, I see. I noticed too when I first met her. Sadly, Qwaser has not. I am not asking you to distrust Kalioa, but to be wary of her. Dark secrets linger in her eyes."

"Eyes can tell much, Hasaxta," Janevra replied.

"Yes and that is why I think you are the Lady Dragon, Janevra," he said, turning them down another hallway. "Your eyes hold power, strength, wit, and the gaze of someone who knows the inner person of people the moment you've met them. You don't waver from stares or challenges, you face them."

"You know that from my eyes?"

"I am like you, Princess of Caendor. I can read people very well."

There is something you are not telling me, Hasaxta, Janevra thought but said, "What do you think Kalioa will do?"

"I do not know, I cannot read minds. I only know she carries a dark secret and that pendant around her neck symbolizes something that we, as believers in the Light and the Goddess Tghil, do not follow."

Janevra cocked her head, watching the young general. "What is it that makes you so caring for Qwaser and his family? What did you do?"

Hasaxta laughed. "Do you see? You truly know people." He paused. "His brother and I were responsible for sending him to Andaon. After he had spoken to a human, at that time it was illegal, we brought it to his parents who brought the matter to the King who sentenced him to a five years in exile. I suppose," Hasaxta said, his mouth twisting, "that it was meant to happen so he could find you."

Janevra rubbed her arm, trying to smooth down hairs that had risen in fear. "I think the gods have been dealing in such matters lately. Too much has been coincidence."

"I think you are right." Hasaxta stopped in front of a pair of oaken doors branded with gold. He smiled down at her and pushed the door open.

Sitting around a small table were two clerics, one of them Janevra recognized from the Throne Room. The one she recognized stood, his green robes falling around him.

"Princess of Caendor, this is the High Cleric, Cleric of the Order of the Light," Hasaxta said, bowing slightly. Janevra curtsied. "The other is the Healer of the Order of the Light. He's powerful in the Talent. They will be teaching you the ways of magic since you have had no teaching."

Janevra frowned. "How did you know I have never been taught?"

"I didn't but the High Cleric did," Hasaxta said.

"Lady Dragon," the High Cleric said, his voice heavy with age, "please sit." He placed a hand on a chair. Janevra sat, curious of what was going on.

Hasaxta bowed to her. "I will see you later, Princess of Caendor, when the matters of the army and the state attract your interests. I know the King and I are at your disposal should you wish to ask us questions." Hasaxta closed the door behind him.

Janevra turned to the High Cleric, waiting, eyebrows lifted in question. *This will be interesting,* she thought, wondering how someone of such lesser Talent could teach her.

The High Cleric took his seat. "Today, Lady Dragon, and onward for a month, you shall be taught all the proper and most useful ways to use magic."

The other cleric smiled. "First, we teach you how to feel when others of less power summon their magic."

Chapter 16
Fighting with the Staff

Dei closed her eyes and listened, a smile spreading across her features. She could hear Mat's painful yowl as Vena taught him how to catch things on fire... obviously it worked well. Perhaps too well.

Mat had been living in the Ile Plains for a week. She enjoyed his company; he was such an interesting person.

Dei had become Mat's instructor in the Ile ways. She had noticed right away that he knew nothing of the Ile past or lifestyles. He did not know that the *sehetem* were only kept by the Daaguwh Ile and not looked upon as servants but as slaves. He did not know what to say when he wanted someone to do something. He did not know anything about their people, nothing at all, and she took it upon herself to teach him.

Dei had found it interesting that Mat was especially fascinated with their beliefs. He questioned her endlessly about them.

"Why do the Ile believe in four gods instead of the Goddess Tghil?"

Mat had asked one day.

"We believe in the Light, but as you give the whole meaning of good and greatness to one being, we give it to four. Our gods..." Dei searched for the right words. "Our gods have specialties. When you want one thing, you pray to one, instead of all four. We believe the gods will hear you when you single them out instead of grouping them into a whole."

"Who are your gods?"

Dei smiled and traced four symbols in the air. "Aystarte is the goddess of war and luck, Mayita is the goddess of truth, Mandoulis is the god of the sun and Reshef-sia is the god of divine knowledge of all things."

"You have two gods and two goddesses," Mat had pointed out.

"We do. Ile believe in the complete equality of women and men. Some cultures place one above the other but we do not. It is only right that the equality of men and women is found in our gods."

Mat listened to her when she talked, but he was always practicing that magic of his or talking to Zenerax about Ile warfare and learning the sword. And he was learning very quickly. He almost rivaled her with the sword and she was good. He had an inborn talent for fighting. Once Mat beat Zenerax at the sword or spear, she knew he could beat anyone.

Tugging at a braid, she curled it around her finger, thinking of Zenerax. *When will he ask me to marry him? I know he wants to wait until peace has come, but what if it never comes? Will we never be married? I don't even care if he doesn't go through all the rituals; I just want to marry him. Maybe I could ask him?* she pondered. *Many women ask men to marry them. No, I won't ask him. I know he always wanted to be the one to ask. But if that man doesn't ask me soon, I might turn to someone else!* That was a lie, Dei knew, but she wanted so much to call Zenerax her own that sometimes it drove her crazy.

Dei smiled again as she heard Mat's yelp. He was learning. When he first came here Vena had told him that he could only "light a candle stick with a torch." Now his ability had taken an amazing turn.

Dei lay in one of the Palace's many courtyards. This particular one was right below an empty bedroom where Vena was teaching Mat.

The soft cool grass lay underneath her half bare back. Her clothes, usual for Ile in war, were dark brown leather. The top of it was a band around her chest with straps holding it together. The bottom was a soft deerskin pant, allowing her easy movement. Her boots went up to her calf, criss-cross ties clasping them to her ankle. Her long red hair was bound up into many braids, cascading down her back. The tattoo on her arm glittered today. It had been doing that recently, ever since she had met Mat. Maybe even a little before.

Dei pushed up off the ground, standing up. Her gray eyes reflected the sky, turning misty gray. She walked around the courtyard, admiring the lush trees.

A bird spoke somewhere, its song echoing faintly in the tree. Another answered it not too far from Dei. Its' melody was sweet and soft.

Dei watched as a little boy chased a young girl through the courtyard, their laughter ringing. Having a moment of envy, she sighed. She had never had much of a childhood. Most of it was spent helping her mother, getting food or cooking. She used her spare moments to learn how to fight with Kayzi or her cousin, her only friend. Her village had always been on the watch for Nekid warriors and time for fun and games had come only rarely. It did not help that food in the area had become scarce before the Nekid attack that had killed her parents. Dei had spent much time in those last few years hunting and gathering.

Dei walked out of the courtyard and turned towards a door leading inside. She walked towards the room Mat and Vena were in.

Hearing first a yell and then a curse, she saw Mat storming out of the room, cradling his hand in his right arm. It looked slightly blackened.

Dei held back a smile.

"Mat?"

Mat looked up, the frustration quickly disappearing. "Oh...hello, Dei," Mat said.

Dei bit her lip to keep back the smile. "How come you're not practicing your magic anymore?"

Mat glared at her. "Vena is a..." his mouth opened and closed, before finally snapping shut.

Vena came stalking out of the room, her hands folded under her bosom. Strays of gray-blonde hair escaped from her braid and her eyes were slits.

Mat gulped.

"Mat, what did you do?"

"Ah... I set the, um," he swallowed again. "I accidentally set the furniture on fire."

"Mat!" Vena screeched.

Mat turned and fled, with Vena hot on his tail.

"Gods, woman! *Accidentally! Did not mean to!*" he said, jumping as Vena shot a spark of fire at him.

"Run! She'll kill you if she catches you!" Dei called after him, smiling. Mat turned around a corner and she heard his continuous apologies dwindle away.

Dei jumped into a run and hurried up a flight of stairs. On the next floor, she ran down the hall until she came to the training room. She opened the door. It was dark, except for one torch at the far end. The stonewalls were silent, even the torch made no sound.

Dei smiled inwardly. Zenerax was somewhere out there, waiting for his moment to attack. They used only wooden staffs but the blows still left nasty bruises and welts.

Dei stopped and controlled her breathing; it was now above a faint whisper.

She knew her love was somewhere, but exactly where was the question. *One day I'll beat him at this game,* she thought. *Maybe today.*

Grabbing a staff that lay by the door, she felt along the edges for any faults or cracks. Finding none, she closed the door behind her and became engulfed in darkness.

She let her eyes adjust before she took a step forward.

If she knew Zenerax well, and she did, he would be towards the end in the lightest corner, the one least suspected.

She moved forward slowly, the torch sending shadows where there should be none.

Think, she told herself, think like Zenerax would.

Dei stopped moving forward. If she were Zenerax, she would be eight feet off to the left of the torch. Thankfully he couldn't see her, not with one torch lighting the room.

She had the advantage. She was not waiting. As the huntress, she knew where her prey was. Her prey would not know where she was until it was too late.

Dei moved to the left, out of the direct line of the torches light. She moved over until she touched cold stone with her hand.

"Zen, where are you?" she whispered, her words quieter than a single breath.

She moved along the wall, her heart beating and blood thudding in her temples. It was only a game but when it came to real life, it was much more than a simple game. If she found him first she would gain the upper hand. If that happened it would be easier for her to take down her bigger and in some ways better foe.

Dei froze, her ears catching the sound of quiet breathing. One foot in front of her was Zenerax.

If she attacked now she would probably win. He was looking towards the torch and its flickering heat.

Dei carefully moved her staff into an attacking position. The figure she thought was in front of her didn't move.

Her suspicion quickly arose. Zenerax had good hearing. Gods, he was a warrior and trained in such matters of improving the body. But so was she.

Dei listened again, even more carefully this time. Oh, someone was near her, that was for sure. But how close? And where?

Dei stepped back, away from the form.

And as if from some second thought, she ducked.

She felt the rush of cool air breeze harmlessly over her head.

Dei stuck her foot out, tripping her attacker. She heard her foe land heavily on his back and the air whoosh out of his lungs. She hopped away but wasn't fast enough as a hand snaked out and caught her ankle.

She fell to the floor, biting her lip. The iron taste of blood flowed into her mouth, staining her teeth red. She spat, hearing the splatter as the blood and spit hit the stone floor.

Dei turned her head and saw the grayish form of her attacker. It was Zenerax all right. She smiled. The smile did not reach her eyes. She would get him back for that.

Dei rolled away and got up, her staff out in front of her and pointing in the general direction of Zen.

"Come on, little birdie," Zenerax whispered, his voice behind her. "Catch me."

Dei swung her legs up and into the air, twisting backwards. Her body was totally suspended in the air as she felt her booted feet hit the hard pans of Zenerax's stomach. She fell to the ground. Her momentum was lost once she hit her objective. Dei swung her staff out before her, smacking it against Zenerax's. She pushed against his staff, but he was too strong. He forced her onto her knees. Sweat rolled down her back.

Zenerax pushed his face near hers and kissed her mouth.

Enraged that he would kiss her when they were fighting, she somehow found the energy to push back.

Her burst of strength was so strong a surprised Zenerax lost his balance and toppled, his staff flying out from his fingers.

But his second of surprise was short lived. He kicked up a leg, sending Dei's own staff whirling off into the inky darkness.

Dei groaned. Hand to hand fighting she was good at until her attacker used sheer strength to overtake her. She touched the blood on her chin, smearing it on her fingers.

Dei brought up her leg and smacked Zenerax in the chest with her foot. Zenerax dropped back, catching her foot with a hand.

Balancing on one foot, Dei swung her hips around, getting free and tripping Zenerax in the same breath. It looked like she was winning.

Zenerax swept his leg along the floor and caught Dei's calf, dropping her to the ground.

Her breath knocked out of her, Dei got shakily to her feet.

She was thrown against the wall as Zenerax's body slammed into her. Her breath was forced out of her lungs, making her head whirl for a second.

She shook her head and glared at where she thought Zenerax was. Her hand formed a fist and she threw it at Zenerax's face. If she lost at least he would walk away with a sore nose.

She felt something warm and liquidly seep onto her fingers as she drew her hand away.

The torches around the room flickered into a magical life, chasing away the darkness.

Zenerax's nose was bleeding and her own lip had blood trickling down.

"Sorry, Zen," she said rubbing her chest to slowly get the air to return to her lungs.

"It's all right, my little lioness," he said, pulling her into a hug. "You're getting better everyday, love," he murmured into her hair.

"Thanks."

"What next?" Dei asked, turning her head to look up at Zenerax.

"We teach Mat how to use a staff." He grinned, and they turned around as the door to the practice room opened and Mat entered.

Waving briefly to them, Mat focused his attention on the staffs leaned against the wall and studied them before picking one up and attempting to swing it.

"Oh, this'll be fun." She snickered evilly.

"And when we're done, the rest of the day will be for the two of us," Zenerax said, his own roguish grin rising forth.

Dei blushed and moved away to find her staff. Zenerax went over to Mat and helped him select a good staff. Dei laughed when he handed Mat the shortest staff in the bunch.

Mat threw up his hands. "Stop laughing you two. I have a meeting with the Daaguwh Council members in an hour. They won't hand command over to me until I've taken the test. Before that happens, I have history lessons. I need to learn about your people and how to rule this land, so let's make this lesson quick."

Zenerax slid his staff through his hands. "No one can learn anything quickly. It takes practice." He got into a fighting stance. "You will first learn how to fight with the smallest staff. Since the one you are holding is smaller then mine you must be very careful."

"How so?" Mat asked.

"Mine is a full seven inches longer. I can reach you where you cannot reach me. In this lesson you will learn agility and how to block." Zenerax brought his staff down on top of Mat's. "Dei will watch from the side, instructing you."

Mat looked over at Dei. She smiled at him. "Spread your feet apart like Zenerax has done." Mat mimicked Zenerax's stance.

Zenerax grinned. "Let's dance."

Zenerax flowed into move after move. It was all Mat could do to keep Zenerax from smacking him with his staff. Dei called advice from the sidelines, shouting instructions. Mat followed her orders fairly well, if a little shabbily. Zenerax did manage to hit him several times, welts growing on Mat's skin every time staff and skin made contact.

"Careful on him, Zenerax. You don't want him looking like a target for archery practice!" Dei called as Zenerax's staff whacked Mat smartly on the thigh. "I don't think Leama would be too pleased with that!"

Not too soon after they had started, Zenerax pulled back. "Enough Mat. I was wrong. You learn very quickly. We work on the sword tomorrow."

"Thank you. I must be going now anyhow. The council is waiting." Mat put his staff back along with all the others and left the practice room.

Zenerax and Dei put their own staffs back. Hand in hand they exited the training room and made their way up to their rooms. Zenerax bent down and whispered something into Dei's ear. Dei looked at him with astonishment and blushed.

"Zenerax! How dare you!" Dei said, shocked, her face flaming hot. "Do not say things like that to me here!"

Zenerax laughed. "Why not here, if not anywhere else, love?"

"It's not like we're married, Zen."

Casting her a mischievous glance, Zenerax took her hand in his own and pulled her down the hallway; his long strides making Dei run to keep up. "Where are we going?" she asked.

"It should be ready," was all he said.

He took her out of the palace, over the bridge that led to the palace, through the gates protected by the guard and into the city.

Stopping in front of a metallurgy shop, Zenerax turned to her, kissing her lightly on the tip of her nose. "Wait here for me." He vanished into the store.

Dei felt her stomach lurch. *Is he finally going to ask me? Is he getting the wedding bands now?* Closing her eyes, Dei said a silent prayer. *Please, gods, please let this be what I'm hoping it is!* She could already imagine herself wearing the golden armband, Zenerax wearing an identical one, as they walked down the street together, people congratulating them on their wedding.

Finding a bench to sit on, Dei stretched her legs out, watching the people as they hurried by her. Many wore the white linen usually worn by Ile when not in battle but their *khrieths* were still strapped to their waists or backs. An Ile was never far from their weapon. At the moment, Dei felt naked without hers, having forgotten it in her rooms. At least she wasn't weaponless, she thought, brushing her fingers against the knife in her belt.

The door to the store opened, and Dei saw Zenerax's back, hurriedly speaking thanks to the storekeeper. Turning around, she saw that he held a long and well crafted spear in his hand. The blade at the end was black and curved as in the style of the Ile. The long shaft of the spear was beautifully crafted, an art that could only be done by a master. Zenerax handed her the spear.

Dei gasped, taking the spear carefully into her hands. "What is this for?" she asked, too stunned to care that she was being rude.

Zenerax smiled. "A gift for the woman I love. I had the blade imported from the lands of the Lost Tribe. It cost me much, but it was worth it to see the look on your face."

Dei felt tears slip down her cheeks. The Lost Tribe was a nation of golden skinned warriors who stained their weapons to show they were masters of the sword. They called themselves Thysians and isolated themselves from the Ile. The Thysians were an odd race, who held Ile in contempt and refused to trade with them. Of course, there were always a few who wanted trade and would trade the metal to the Ile for high prices. Dei did not doubt the trouble Zenerax had to go through to get this blade and then find a metallurgist with enough talent to fix a shaft onto the blade.

Zenerax brushed her tears away with a finger. "Do not cry, love. It is my gift to you, to show you how much you mean to me."

"I didn't get you anything," she said, running her hand along the black blade. To the Thysians, black was the ultimate goal, the highest honor bestowed upon a warrior.

Zenerax drew her near, oblivious of the spear, and kissed her forehead. "I do not need anything, only your love."

"You have it. You have always had it," Dei whispered.

"Yes, but I wanted to make sure before..." he stopped suddenly.

"Before what?" Dei pressed.

Zenerax smiled at her. "You will know soon enough. Now, let's see how good you are with this new weapon."

They started back towards the palace. In one hand Dei held her new spear, in the other she held Zenerax's hand.

Chapter 17
Hunting

Qwaser watched Kalioa draw her bow and take aim.

The deer was sitting there, its eight-point rack standing on its head like a crown. It was a beautiful deer, the one most hunters dream of shooting.

Her bow aimed and the muscles on her arm rippling, she let the arrow fly.

It thudded into the deer.

The deer fell over, with the arrow protruding from its chest. Many holes covered its wooden body. It was a practice deer, one hunters shot at before they went out hunting. They had hauled it here for some practice and quiet time together.

"Nice shot," Qwaser muttered as Kalioa plucked the arrow from the deer's breast.

"Too bad it wasn't real," Kalioa said. "What a prize it would be."

Qwaser's eyes widened. Elven people never killed animals for sport or to show off to friends. They only killed animals for food.

Kalioa tossed the arrow into her quiver.

Her honey hair was pulled back into a ponytail. Some wisps had escaped, sending golden curls about her head and dancing over her long elegant ears. Her blue eyes sparkled and her lips were in a smile. She wore her normal clothes, russet breeches, and a gray shirt. A strange pendant encircled her neck. Upon it was a sword. Why she wore it, Qwaser did not know.

Qwaser on the other hand had on brown pants and a green tunic, his hunting clothes. His bright green eyes were smiling at the moment but something behind them told of a hard past. His smooth cheeks, which would never grow any facial hair, were a rosy pink from warmth of the day.

The meadow they were standing in was filled with flowers and new grass. The trees that outlined it were tall evergreens, their branches reaching up to the sky. Birds flocked everywhere, some landing in the pond at the center of the meadow others hopping from tree branch to tree branch.

"She's only been here a week and yet people seem to trust her. Why?" Kalioa asked, startling him with the question.

Even though she had not said Janevra's name, he knew whom she was talking about. Qwaser shook his head. "I don't know. Before I met her I was afraid and I wasn't sure I would trust her. After she spoke to me, I felt as if all my... distrust had disappeared and been replaced with awe. It was strange," he frowned. "The same thing happened with Mat. I seemed to accept that they were going to change the world, that in the end it would be okay. I've never met anyone who had the power to wash away all mistrust and doubt." Qwaser looked at Kalioa, calculating. *What is she thinking?* he wondered.

"I don't trust her. She's been here a week. A week! And the elven people don't care she's a human, a mortal."

"We are not immortals," Qwaser said coldly.

"A four thousand year life, near enough. But still, she's a...a..."

"Kalioa," Qwaser said, warning in his tone. *I don't understand why you don't like Janevra, Kalioa. Everyone else thinks of her as just another elf, another person. Maybe you don't because Janevra is only nineteen, but even then the people seem to see past her young age to something that she shows within, an ancient wisdom that shines from her eyes. Why don't you accept her?*

Kalioa glared at him, her eyes blue daggers. Qwaser twisted his face, trying to hide his smile. She was so adorable when she was angry.

Her eyes became slits as she saw the mirth behind his eyes and her foot started to tap.

Qwaser let out a bark of laughter.

"What?" Kalioa asked, her mouth a thin line.

Qwaser masked his face. "What?"

"Why are you laughing?"

The sun was at noon and shining down into the meadow, sending a feeling of warmth through the body.

"Nothing."

"Oh." Kalioa raised an eyebrow and her eyes took on the appearance of boredom. Her lips dipped down, hiding her grin.

Suddenly all the laughter and joy left her face. "Qwaser, how long do you think it will take Janevra to get as strong as the Prophecies say?"

Qwaser was taken back at her sudden seriousness. "I don't know. She has a lot to learn, and no one to teach her except people whose ability is far below her own. Why?" he inquired.

"Just curious."

Qwaser shrugged. If she didn't want to share her thoughts it was fine by him.

"Do you think the Warlord will win?"

A shiver went up his spine at that. "If the Warlord wins, Tghil protect us, we are in for a short life of fear and hate." Qwaser thought for a moment. "He won't win, I'm sure."

"Are you sure?" Kalioa whispered just below Qwaser's hearing.

"What?"

"I hope you're right," she said.

Qwaser stared at her. She seemed different than when he had first met her, as if a change had occurred overnight.

Kalioa grinned seductively. "Do you want to go for a swim?"

Qwaser cocked his head sideways, was that thrumming he heard? It was very distant but definitely thrumming.

"Qwaser?"

"Shhhh," he whispered harshly, straining his ears to trace the direction of the sound. He frowned. It seemed to be coming from the ground. He bent down, putting his ear to the ground. The sound increased. It was as if something was hitting a drum, deep down within the soil. Leaves crinkled under his weight and he stilled, listening for the sound. "Do you hear that?"

"No."

Qwaser reached up and pulled Kalioa down. "Put your ear to the ground and tell me what you hear." Qwaser waited as Kalioa did as he asked.

"A thrumming. I hear a thrumming," she said, pulling away, a leaf getting stuck in her hair.

Qwaser pulled it out of her hair, his fingers gently brushing her cheek.

"What is it?" Kalioa asked, standing up and combing off the dirt and leaves on her clothes.

Qwaser stood up with her, brushing off his pants. "Something that deep in the earth could not be elf or human."

"Do you think it's…" Kalioa trailed off, biting her lip.

Qwaser shook his head furiously. "It couldn't be."

"But what if the legends are true? What if it is the…" Kalioa paused as if fearing that the name would rain fire down upon her head. She swallowed hard. "What if it is the Htowi?" she whispered.

The Htowi was a legendary snake that had lived thousands of years before the time of the Light and the Dark. It was said to be as long as a river and as wide as a mountain. It lived underground sleeping for thousands of years and then it would wreak havoc on the countryside, eating people and animals, destroying villages and towns for ten years. It was whispered in the darkest corners of taverns that when Htowi was awaking, it made a thrumming noise, and that it would only do so when the Dark tried to take the world again.

"It can't be," Qwaser said, his face becoming pale. It couldn't be.

"Why not?"

Qwaser shook his head, saying he was not talking about the Htowi.

"It's not that. Look." He pointed to the horizon where the trees met mountains and jagged peaks joined the sky. Qwaser's eyes had a strange look in them, one mixed with fear and yet tinted with excitement.

Smoke was rising above the mountains, dark, murky smoke.

"That thrumming we heard was not the Htowi. It was the pain of the forest burning." Qwaser closed his eyes, a tear leaking out. "Magic is at work."

They both stared at the smoke rising above the mountains.

"Do you think we can help?" Qwaser asked.

Kalioa's look became flat. "No."

Qwaser stared at her.

"We can't help them. It's on the other side of the mountain range, and because of that, it's a *human* civilization. We would never reach it in time."

"True," Qwaser rolled his shoulders as if waving off a bad dream.

"Let's go before that smoke reaches the meadow and we can't breathe."

Qwaser nodded, but did not turn his back before taking one last look. "I wonder why it's burning."

Kalioa pulled him away.

They walked across the meadow, their footsteps nearly unheard.

Qwaser wrapped an arm around her waist and pulled her close as they entered the still forest.

The smoke had silenced even the birds.

"Qwaser, you trust me, right?"

Qwaser leaned over and kissed her. "Of course I do. Why wouldn't I?"

Kalioa shrugged.

Qwaser did not see Kalioa smile and trace a finger around the pendant with the sword.

They made their way back to the city, Qwaser carrying the wooden deer. They walked through the dense woods that lay on the outskirts of the city, both enjoying each other's company and the feel of the living forest.

They reached the walls of the city after an hour of walking through the forest. Qwaser gave the elf on guard their names and they were allowed entrance. He dropped off the wooden deer in a small storage shed near the gatehouse.

He and Kalioa strolled down the streets of the elven city, savoring the beauty of their home. Trees grew on every block, massive, green trees, that turned fiery in fall. The homes of the elves were made of white stone that winked in the sunlight. Large, gorgeously decorated plazas were the streets in which the elven people walked. Fountains sprung clear water that shone like diamonds. Flowers grew in the thousands of gardens filling the city, flowers of every color. The people living there moved about as if in a dream, slowly and with liquid grace. They wore the colors of the world around them, blue, green, yellow, black, white, red, turquoise. The grace of the people gave the land in which they walked an unworldly beauty. They moved with such love of the world and understanding, your breath would catch in your throat and tears would fall from your eyes. This was the world in which Qwaser and Kalioa lived. This was the world that was now threatened by war and the Prophecies of old coming to life. This was the world they would protect.

Qwaser and Kalioa reached the stairs to the Elven King's palace. Surrounding the palace were gardens rich in exotic plants and flowers. Trees blossomed and fountains put music in the air. The double doors that led to the inside of the palace were a polished gold. Imprinted above these doors were the elven words *Soeth zioalez otxth nurmljs hmutijs xyqtia avytia es eyath.*

They entered the doors and walked into a large room lined with tan marble pillars. The floor was a mosaic of tan marble with swirls of gray and gold. At the end of this room, on the far wall, hung a huge painting of trees and flowers with elven children playing in a small pool of water. A grand marble staircase started on either side of the painting, directing people to different parts of the palace.

Qwaser and Kalioa took one of the staircases and walked down a hallway covered in more paintings. This took them to their rooms where they both changed into clothes more fitting for a day in the palace. After getting dressed they left their rooms and went to the King's Council Room.

Qwaser paused with his hand on the doorknob. He glanced at Kalioa. She nodded at him and he opened the door.

They came upon Janevra, the King, Hasaxta, and another noble unknown in name to Qwaser. They all sat around an oak table.

Janevra was saying, "... my lord, I know I am not yet proclaimed the Dragon of the Coming Storm, the Lady Dragon, but if you could just—"

The King stood up from where he was sitting. "Janevra, I will give you control of my lands as long as I remain King."

The noble unknown to Qwaser jumped up, his cheeks hot with anger. "My lord, you cannot do that! She is a human! Our people learned long ago that they are not to be trusted."

The King faced the noble. "My Lord Dimsenlos, I never said I was handing over my kingdom. I simply said she had control over it. She rules this kingdom when it comes to anything that affects the outside. I still rule this land itself. I have foreseen that she is the Dragon of the Coming Storm and I must trust her with all my power. If I do not, the elven world we love will be destroyed."

The Lord Dimsenlos nodded tightly and sat back down.

The King nodded at Qwaser and Kalioa to take a seat and he turned his attention back to Janevra. "My Lady Dragon, the elven people are behind you. We are ready to be united with the world."

Hasaxta stood up and put his hands on the table. "My Lady Dragon, as a second general I have the power to say that the elven military is behind you. I know Qwaser supports my decision in this."

Janevra bowed her head in thanks. "I am glad for your support, Hasaxta. I had a feeling you would give me your loyalty today, so I have some detailed orders I want you to carry out." Janevra was suddenly holding a piece of paper she had attained from somewhere. "After I take my test to see if I am the Dragon, I will probably be leaving very soon after. Qwaser will be with me. I want you to stay here and not only train and gather new recruits but start preparing this land for war."

Hasaxta frowned. "I assumed Qwaser would be coming with you but war?"

"Yes. I pray to the Light that the Fifth Battle will not be carried this far to the west but I still want you to prepare. Caendor has fallen. It will not defend you. I want the elvish lands and its beauty protected."

Hasaxta took the paper Janevra handed him. "I will start now, my Lady Dragon." Hasaxta bowed and left the room, nodding to Qwaser on the way out.

Janevra turned her attention to the Lord Dimsenlos. "My Lord, I know you do not support me but I will still ask this from you. The Elven people need someone who they know, who can deal with the other countries, as a foreign affairs adviser."

Lord Dimsenlos looked flattered. Janevra had just bestowed upon him a very great honor. "What is it that you will have me do?"

"I want to you handle treaties that come in from other countries, wanting to make an alliance with me. I want you to send treaties out to other countries. I want you to talk to the elven people and find out their ideas about foreigners. I want to you become an expert in foreign affairs."

"Why, my Lady Dragon, do you want such a thing?"

"I want such a thing so that when I come back I will have someone who is completely up to date and understands how his people want things and how other nations would like them," Janevra said.

Lord Dimsenlos got up from his chair, his face filled with pride. He bowed low to the King and lower to Janevra. "I will start right away." The lord left the room, gently closing the doors behind him.

The King smiled at Janevra. "That's one way to get rid of those who resist you, give them something so important to accomplish they'll forget they opposed you."

Janevra laughed. "Yes, my father used to do that. It always worked well for him."

The King looked outside at the position of the sun. "I think you had better go. The High Cleric won't wait for you forever, Janevra. You need to learn."

Janevra followed the King's gaze outside and nodded. "Thank you for the meeting, Your Majesty." Janevra quit the room, the door swinging shut behind her.

"My Lord," Qwaser said. "You mentioned you wanted to visit the barracks today, did you not?"

The King stood up, adjusting the gold circlet upon his head. "Yes, I did. Lead the way, General."

They walked out of the room.

"My King, I thought I should mention something that Kalioa and I saw. When we were out we glimpsed smoke on the other side of the mountains. The forest was burning."

The King's face became grave. "I know. Janevra told us to expect an attack from rogui in one month's time."

Qwaser was taken back. "How did she know?"

The King shrugged. "Even though she has not taken the test, she *is* the Dragon of the Coming Storm and very powerful in the art of magic. This I know, I can feel it."

Kalioa glared at the Elven King and Qwaser behind their backs as they made their way to the barracks. She touched the pendant hanging from her neck. In one month the Dragon of the Coming Storm would be dead and her army defeated.

Chapter 18
The East Sea

ALD 3919 SD June

Raxsen breathed in the heavy salt air.

It had taken one month to build fifteen ships with the help of magic. He had acted furious when they did not fulfill his orders. He increased taxes, and the price of food. He had done it on purpose to show that he was the leader. He even had several men hanged because he needed to put the blame on someone.

He had left no one in charge of Atay or Nurita. Instead he planned to use the extra land as a gift to the new Queen-to-be of Angarat to win her loyalty.

Raxsen smiled as the ship crested the wave. It was a stormy day, with a little rain, but it was hard to see far and that was what he wanted. Cover was a big thing when it came to attacking a seashore city.

Raxsen watched a wave wash over his high black boots.

His army had increased by six hundred. He now had women who wanted to fight. One of his captains was overseeing their training now. Women in his army would be a bonus, one, because they usually turn out to be good fighters and two, they could prove much needed entertainment for his men. But over all rogui and sylai out numbered the men four to one. He couldn't remember when the rogui had joined.

Raxsen turned his head and bellowed, "General Andrews!" into the wind.

A middle age man approached, his clothes whipping about him. John Andrews had traveled the world as a young man, and had even fought in some civil wars. He knew everything concerning the current nations, from what the princess liked to eat to war plans. It was a gift the Dark Lord had given him as a boy if he would follow the Warlord. Whenever he slept he would "see" what had happened in every nation. Andrews' one blue eye, the other had been hurt in a skirmish and had a patch over it, held a lust for battle. He was a strong man and scars criss-crossed his arms and face.

"Yes, my lord?" Andrews answered, his mustache fluttering about his upper lip.

"Come with me into my cabin," Raxsen said, wrapping his black cloak around his body. Raxsen jumped off the rail where he had been standing, holding onto a rope, watching the churning sea.

Across the deck of the ship the men called *My Lady*, were tents that Raxsen's men had pitched to keep off the cold. Most of his men were at the bottom of the boat sharpening weapons or entertaining themselves in some way or form, but the ones who were up on the deck were either helping steer the boat or fixing a large crossbow the Warlord had had them make while waiting for the boats to be made.

Raxsen opened the door to his cabin. It was nicely furnished, with a bed, two chairs and a table, all made out of ebony. A mirror hanging on one side of the cabin watched the two men enter.

"Sit down, general," Raxsen motioned to one of the chairs.

As the general sat down Raxsen poured two glasses of Tes's finest wine. "Tell me of the nations we are about to destroy," Raxsen asked, sitting down and pretending to sip at his wine.

"Well," Andrews said, gulping down a portion of his wine, "the princesses of all the countries are beautiful. The most beautiful would be the one of Istra, a beauty she be. My Dark Lord! She is…prettier than the Purple Sea during sunset."

"Purple Sea?" Raxsen asked, already bored. *Come, General, drink up.*

"Ah…yes, my lord, you have't heard of some of these places?"

"I have heard of most of them but not this one."

"The Purple Sea is next to Caendor and it earned its name for when the sun sets it turns the water there purple." Andrews swallowed the rest of his wine and stood up. "My lord, may I?" he asked pointing to the carafe of wine, his eye patch giving off a dull shine.

Raxsen waved his hand

"The princess of Istra is a catch. She is twenty and not yet married." Andrews frowned and sat back down. "Alas, I think she might be engaged."

"What are the other princesses like?" Raxsen asked. *I don't care about the princess, fool. Perhaps if you were brighter, you would stop drinking. It's a good thing I want you dead. You're utterly useless as it is.*

"The princess of Angarat, Princess Syilvia, holds a dark beauty but she has a mean streak and loves power. She'll stab you in the back if you're not careful."

Raxsen nodded. He would remember that.

Andrews gulped down the last of his wine, and poured himself another. "The Princesses of Riyad and Zayen are close friends, as their fathers were before they became the kings. They are always together, planning for something. It's strange because they seem to know something I don't when I spy upon them, a secret that they conceal so well. Of course Angarat, Selkare, Zayen, and Riyad, all have a prince to succeed the throne. Caroa has only one prince, but LTana has five princesses and five princes. I see a future civil war for that country. Taymyr has also one prince as Istra has only one princess, and their fathers hope to get them to marry and join their two nations together. Caendor has a princess to succeed the throne and a very good queen she will be, but she seems to have disappeared and a man named Ravften has taken the throne after he killed the King and Queen. It is rumored that he is a shoi, and a powerful one, too. So far, Caendor is still the most powerful nation. But now that you..." Andrews trailed off and slumped to the floor.

Raxsen whispered, "fool" as Andrews became unconscious.

Raxsen stood up and moved over to Andrews, checking to make sure he was out.

"Idiot, why do you think I wasn't drinking the wine? I drugged it," Raxsen said, squatting next to the general.

"Works every time, Andrews, a magical potion meant to knock one out but obey whatever I say. You did not tell me everything. You know some things I need to know. What are the Princesses of Riyad and Zayen really planning on doing?"

Andrews's showed the whites of his eyes. "They are planning to gather an army."

"Why?"

"They want to have their two nations ready for when the Dragons come. So far, no one has volunteered to join their army."

"Who are the Dragons, Andrews?"

"The male Dragon to unite the Ile under the golden sun, the female Dragon to unite the Lost People under a lightning bolt."

"Andrews, who are they?"

"The male Dragon is a farmer's son named Mat Trakall. The female Dragon is a princess named Janevra, daughter of the Tower of the Light in Caendor."

"Tell me, where have the Dragons gone?"

"One has gone to the Lost Mountains and the other to the Cyrain Plains."

"Do they know any magic yet?"

"Everyday they excel and within a month they will surpass the strongest shoi."

"Thank you, Andrews."

Raxsen pulled a knife out of his belt and slit Andrews's throat, the blood spilling to the floor and soaking through the floorboards.

"Dark Lord, you wanted someone to watch me. Well I found him and I killed him. Try again," Raxsen muttered as he opened a round window. It was just big enough for the General's body to fit through.

Raxsen smiled as he heard the body hit the sea. The Dark Lord had made a mistake making Raxsen the Warlord. Raxsen was becoming stronger than the Dark Lord himself. *One day I will even take his place as the God of the Dark.*

Closing the window, Raxsen left the cabin. Soon the ships were going to land near Carim and the city would fall under his might.

The city of Carim had nothing that would help it if an army attacked its port. There were no towers stationed by the docks where archers could rain arrows down upon the attackers or natural intrusions that might hinder the progress of an invading army like dangerous rocks or sandbars. There was a nice fog covering the land, preventing the city from seeing his fleet and Raxsen planned to use this to his advantage. The only threat that might delay his invasion of the city was the city guard and barracks located near the docks. Lately, the King of Angarat had been building an army and one hundred of those men were currently in Angarat. Raxsen expected to be attacked by them. Even though Angarat held a hidden desire for dark power, they also liked their independence from all others save their King and Queen.

"Warlord?" a voice at his shoulder asked.

Raxsen's eyes slanted, glancing at Pierce. "What?"

Pierce, his vivid green eyes peering from under the depth of long black lashes, looked eager for battle. His face was unshaven and prickles stood out on his chin and cheeks. He looked like he had been at sea for weeks. "I've been meaning to speak to General Andrews about how you want us to position the large crossbow. I know you ordered us to use it from the ship, yet I can't help but think that it would be better to use from the shore, Warlord."

Raxsen lifted one eyebrow. "Do you know where Andrews is?"

"No, Warlord."

The corner of Raxsen's lip curled upward. "I killed him."

"Why, Warlord?" Pierce croaked, a thin sheen of sweat shining on his nose and forehead.

"He wasn't on my side."

"Whose side was he on?"

"The Lord of the Dark's. Andrews was a spy for the God of Darkness, making sure I kept my place. Look how it turned out for him. You don't want to end up like Andrews, do you?"

"No, Warlord."

Raxsen touched Pierce's left arm where the tattoo of a sword was branded into his skin. "You would never think of betraying me, would you?" Raxsen's ice blue eyes drilled into Pierce's spring green ones.

"Never, Warlord. My place is with you."

Raxsen felt spray from the ocean caress his face. He ignored it, intent on Pierce. "Make sure you don't follow in the footsteps of Andrews, Pierce. It's a dangerous road. Since he is gone, you are my first general. If you ever have a problem with my command you can speak to me away from the ears of my men. If you fail to obey that, a knife will find its way into your back."

Pierce nodded stiffly. Bowing low, he turned, sweat dripping between his shoulder blades.

"Pierce," Raxsen said. Pierce glanced over his shoulder. "Move the crossbow to the shore before you fire it. I think it will be more useful there."

Swaying to the movement of the ship, Raxsen walked to the bow of the ship. Placing his hands on the rail, he waited, the mist covering him like a damp blanket.

The side of the ship scraped along the dock, the sailors trying to steady her as they tied ropes to the dock. It edged closer to the dock until it was unable to go any further. Other ships began pulling in along side *My Lady*, the grating of wood against wood filling the air, as the pier of Carim was crammed with the ships of the Warlord.

"Wait for me to enter the barracks. Once you cannot see me, attack," Raxsen ordered, touching his sword to make sure it was secure in the sheath. "Kill any who stand against me." *I don't care who they kill. Once I capture Carim, then the rest of Angarat will follow. Those who die here do not matter.* "Make sure no one leaves the city, I don't want our attack to go beyond the city limits."

Shouts ran up and down the line of ships and the sound of metal sliding out of leather and voices lowered in anticipation clung to the air.

Raxsen summoned his magic and jumped over the side of the ship. His boots landed on the dock with a thump. He paused for a moment, casting a quick spell.

Glancing up at the ship, he saw Pierce overseeing the loading of the crossbow onto a small safety boat, which would lower it to the dock. *He will serve me well,* Raxsen thought before walking down the dock and setting foot on the cobblestone street that ran along the length of the docks.

The port of Carim was spread out before him, empty of life. No one dared to sail the seas on days such as these, only the very reckless did. Even the sea gulls were quiet, perched on posts or lounging in the water.

Lights from the city were dimmed from the dark mist, as was the sound of voices.

Raxsen's eyes flittered over the city, searching for the barracks. Spotting it near the far end of the pier, he headed towards it.

Voices raised in loud talk and the occasional crash of arms drifted from the soldiers' barracks.

Bracing his hand on the door, Raxsen threw it open and the noise wavered, dying into silence. The door slammed shut behind him.

"Where is your captain?" Raxsen demanded, his blue eyes bright as winter.

"'E's not here," a man said, beer making his voice slurred.

"Then where is he?" Raxsen said, barely able to contain his disgust. These men did not know who he was, and they should. Word would have reached this land by now of a Warlord that had conquered the island nations.

"Who wants to know?" another man said, his hand resting on his sword. "You don't look like a very nice fellow. Why should we inform you?"

Raxsen threw back his head and laughed evilly, a deep sound coming from his chest and vibrating in his throat. He cut the laugh short, his eyes blazing with the power of magic and war. "I am the Warlord."

The men of the barracks drew their swords and others grabbed shields imprinted with the iron hand of Angarat.

"You cannot have our land!" someone shouted.

Raxsen chuckled and drew his sword. "I already do." He kicked the door open and stepped out of the barracks. His army filled the streets. Rogui and sylai screamed in their barbaric tongue, weapons bloodied and gore splattered on their black armor. The men of his army fought with a new skill, taught to them during the month awaiting the building of the ships in Tes. Bolts of fire rained overhead, the combination of Pierce's magic and the large crossbow spears. One missile hit a large stone building. The building exploded into fire, stone raining down.

Keeping his back to the doings of his army, Raxsen smiled coldly at the men of the barracks, the soldiers of Carim. "You see," he said, "the city will be mine come night fall."

The soldiers tore out of the open door, staring at the chaos, mouths agape with horror.

"You have two choices, join me or die."

"We will never serve you, Warlord!" a man spat.

Raxsen pointed his finger at the man. "That was a grave mistake." A line of red shot from Raxsen's finger and sprouted into red flame on the chest of the man who had spoken. With a cry he fell to the ground, blood seeping from his mouth.

"Any more?" Raxsen drew his sword. "Do you wish to test the might of the Warlord against your puny blades?"

Three men came at him. One died from a blast of fire bursting from Raxsen's hand, the other died with a knife in his throat.

Crossing blades with the sole remaining man, Raxsen pressed down, his strength thrusting the man to his knees. "Die or join," Raxsen whispered.

The man, seeing he was bested, dropped his eyes and lowered his sword. Raxsen laid a hand on his shoulder, and tattooed a sword into his skin. The man screamed and collapsed to the ground, withering. "Now you are mine until death releases you."

Tears rolling down his cheeks, the man scurried to his feet.

"Find your captain and bring him to me," Raxsen ordered.

The man hurried off.

"The rest of you, die or join."

The men dropped their swords to the ground and Raxsen bound everyone of them to him. They were his, for now and forever, until death and maybe even after. Souls were not hard to triumph over.

"This city will be mine by nightfall," Raxsen hissed. "Pick up your swords and conquer it for me!"

The men snatched their swords, hesitated and then ran into the chaos, fighting men who had been friends to them yesterday.

Raxsen followed them into battle, dancing with death on his blade, watching men fall as they tried to stand against him. Blood drenched his hands and splashed his clothing. It ran down his face and into his mouth and dried.

His sword was slick with blood and his fingers crackled with the power of magic as he fought. The air was smothered with smoke and the cries of women and children pierced his senses. Sweet victory. Raxsen breathed in deep, the smoke, the smell of death and fear swelling his lungs with power.

Crashing his fist into a man who attacked him with a knife, Raxsen felt the man's nose break. Using the flat of his blade, he knocked the man down.

He rammed his blade into the stomach of another before slicing his sword across the neck of a fat man fighting with an axe.

A wild, crazed grin crossed Raxsen's face as he fought, speaking words of magic under his breath and killing men before they even saw him.

Fighting with a double bladed sword black with blood, a woman made her way to him. Raxsen turned towards her, eyebrows cocked quizzically.

"A woman challenges the Warlord," Raxsen said, amused.

"Yes," she said, "and I will win."

Raxsen could not keep from laughing. "A woman has never beaten me in my life, and one never will. Your sex is too weak."

She spat, the spittle landing on his boots.

"Charming," Raxsen said, wiping it off on a dead man.

"Fight me, or are you afraid?" the woman sneered.

Raxsen smirked back at her. "You should be."

Tossing the blade back and forth between her hands, she advanced. Raxsen held his sword in front of him.

With a cry resonating deep within her throat, she ran at him, blood lust in her eyes. Their swords meet with a clang of steel and sparks.

"I could use you," Raxsen whispered in her ear, their swords straining against each other. "I need strong women in my army to… entertain my men."

"You bastard," she screeched and pushed away from him only to come back with her sword aiming at his heart.

Raxsen stepped aside and trapped her sword beneath his. "You're not too ugly. I'm sure some man would take you." He laid his hand on her arm. A burst of fire seared her skin as he bound her.

Breathless with pain, she dropped her sword, clutching her arm, tears bright in her eyes.

"Warlord!"

Raxsen turned, his sword in front of him. He lowered it when he saw Pierce. Pierce had blood and dirt smeared across his face. His sword was at his hip, but Raxsen could feel the magic in the young man. "What is it, Pierce?" he asked.

"We have the mayor. Several of your men have him locked in a room in his mansion."

"Take me there."

Raxsen pushed his sword into his scabbard, moving to go.

"Warlord!" the woman hollered. She picked up her sword and charged towards him. Half way there she suddenly convulsed and let forth a scream that tore through the hearts of any who heard it, except Raxsen. He smiled, watching her as the penalties for betrayal took their toll on her body. Boils sprung up on her face and arms and blood dripped from her eyes. Coughing in agony, blood poured from her mouth and her skin began to dry, the water misting up from it.

"Shall we?" Raxsen said as the woman died from loss of blood and dehydration.

"Done with your fun?" Pierce said, unconsciously rubbing his shoulder.

"For now."

Thrusting their way through the fighting and fighting themselves, Raxsen and Pierce came to a large white house. Plants hung from the windows and a large fountain gurgled in the courtyard. A horse with a rider galloped past them, a piece of parchment grasped in the rider's hand. Raxsen frowned at the rider, wondering where the man was going.

Pierce pushed the iron gate open and walked into the courtyard. Several men shouted to Raxsen, proclaiming the city his. Raxsen ignored them and sprinted up the steps. "Bring the mayor to me!" Raxsen snapped at a man.

The man, eyes wide in fright, ran off.

"What's with you?" Pierce asked, leaning up against a white pillar.

Raxsen shot his general a dark glare. "Nothing," he said, rage burning in his eyes.

In an unexpected show of anger, Raxsen threw out his hand and a ball of black blasted from it to land on a nearby building. The building, in a flash of light, exploded, sending shock waves across the city.

"Careful, we still need most of the city intact," Pierce said, dark amusement in his eyes. "Why the mood?" he inquired again.

"The rider," Raxsen said. *The rider!* he screamed at himself. *Fool! Idiot! How could you let him get away?! Now all of Angarat will know we're here!*

Three men came around the corner. The man in the middle was old, his hair receding from his head and his teeth a deep yellow. Behind the man was a young woman and three children, escorted by five more soldiers from Raxsen's army.

"The old man is sure doing well," Pierce muttered, eyeing the young woman whose large brown eyes held fear. He smiled at her. The woman lowered her eyes, a flush spreading across her cheeks.

"Pierce," Raxsen said.

Pierce shrugged and leaned back against the pillar, watching the young woman.

"Where was the rider going?" Raxsen growled, his sword out of the scabbard and digging into the man's neck.

The old man lifted his chin but did not speak.

"Tell me," Raxsen said, "or your wife dies."

Pierce, moving with the swiftness of an attacking cat, pulled a knife from his belt, grabbed the woman's arm, twisted it behind her back and held the dagger to her throat. "Don't move," he whispered, pressing the blade deeper, a trickle of blood springing from the wound and dribbling down into her bodice.

The woman whimpered, pressing against Pierce in her haste to inch away from the knife.

"Where did the rider go?" Raxsen pressed the sword tip deeper.

"He... he w-went to Rawuki," the man stuttered.

Raxsen bared his teeth in a smile and pressed the sword through the old man's neck. Ripping his sword back out, Raxsen wiped the dirtied blade on the body. He kicked the body down the stairs, watching it tumble lifelessly until it stopped at the base of the stairs.

Small cries drew Raxsen's attention down to the three children huddling together, shaking in horror. "How old are they?"

The young woman's lip quivered. "The boys are nigh twelve and the girl nine."

"Make the two boys pages. They can care for horses." Two of the men hoisted up the boys and carried them down the stairs and out through the iron gate. Raxsen motioned for the guards to let the little girl go. The girl ran to her mother, burying her face in the folds of the mother's skirts.

"You, woman, will help me win the lords of this city by hosting parties for me. You will make them accept me and work for me. If you do this, the girl will live."

The woman nodded tightly, the knife still pressed against her throat. Raxsen moved next to her, laying his hand on her fleshy deltoid muscle. He engraved a sword into her skin. "Never lie to me, never betray me, or you won't be around to protect your little girl."

Tears leaked from the woman's eyes. "Yes, Warlord," she murmured.

Raxsen glanced at Pierce. Pierce pulled his knife back, sheathing it in his belt. The woman, free, scooped up her child, hugging her fiercely.

"Don't get too attached. You can still fail me," Raxsen warned.

The woman stepped back from Raxsen, pressing her back against a wall. "I will never serve you," she cursed.

Raxsen smiled thinly at her. "You will, if you want your child to see another day. Guards," Raxsen said, addressing the men who had guarded the woman and her children. "Find horses and take the road to Rawuki. Bring down that rider. It is too soon yet for Angarat to know I'm here."

The guards flexed their muscles and hurried down the stairs, shouting for horses.

Raxsen turned his attention to Pierce. "Make sure all is under control. I will begin branding people tomorrow. Any who stand against me hang from the walls."

Pierce nodded, cast one last look at the young woman and left.

"Now," Raxsen said, "you will show me around this mansion and help me find a way into the World of the Gods." The young woman nodded, holding her daughter closer.

Chapter 20

A Past

ALD 3919 SD June

Dear Janevra,

We are very sorry to have to tell you of the death of your parents at the hands of one of your most hated enemies, Lord Ravften. Ravften killed your parents at dawn yesterday and proclaimed himself the new King of Caendor. Our family has decided to leave the city. Ravften has increased taxes, food prices and lowered pay. Most can barely survive, but thanks to your pay we have been able to feed ourselves and those we care about. But we still must leave. We are moving to Regigan, and hopefully life will be better. In the last letter you sent, it said that you would be taking a test that would tell you if you and Mat are the Dragons, and if not you will die. We wish you luck on this and we hope you know that no one else could do the job better.

Your friends,
Caya and Lousai

Janevra sat on the cool stone floor in the Palace of the Elves watching the night sky turn to light, tears trickling down her cheek, the pigeon by her side cooing softly.

She had been living with the elves for one month now. During that time she had expanded her ability to cast spells from a beginner to a white robe and had learned a great deal of the past from the records of the elven people. She had also learned much about the elven kingdom. They worshipped life and would fight for the Dragons. She knew they were united already, but they needed to be united with mankind, the other Forgotten people and with the Plains people. It was hard trying to get them to trust her with their lands and people.

The Elves had learned long ago not to trust humans. This distrust had begun before the First Battle, before the time of Darkness and Light but when gods became true.

଼   ଌ   ಔ

It was in the Age of Magic and happened during a time when there were many different races living in the world. Humans lived alongside elves, goblins, ogres, dwarfs, and the little peoples. They showed that they were united with a blue lightning bolt of power and a golden sun. The end to the reign of peace came in the War of the Races.

Darkness arose in the heart of a young boy, a boy of the age of fifteen. He had the idea that to have a good life one must be powerful, rich and in control of all other beings. The boy had the power to be the most powerful shoi in all of the Nations. His power passed the High Shoi by ten fold.

The young boy, known as Kard, rose to power over the Nation of Humans. He made them fear him. He made their nation strong and rich, but only by breaking the Holy Peace Bonds of The Six Nations. Kard created an army, an army of humans, something that no other nation had done before, because it was not needed. Peace was forever, war not even a word. Kard had the armies of his humans attack the goblin and ogre kingdoms. He beat them all, and he joined goblins and ogres in his army. He became known as the Destroyer, the Prince of Death, and the Boy of Darkness.

The other remaining Nations heard of this Evil boy who lived to kill. They feared his attack and built their own armies and weapons.

One human girl, the same age as Kard, ran away from her home nation five years before his rise in power and went to the Elven Nation. There she stayed until she was fifteen, learning magic, and leaving the year Kard took over three nations. Her name was Tghil and growing up with elves, she learned that good was supreme and that she alone had the power to match Kard.

In fear of Kard's rise to power, she secretly gathered together an army of volunteer elves, dwarves and little peoples. But by the time her army was enough to challenge Kard's trusted few and destroy Kard, the rest of the nations had made their own armies and formed a pact of peace with each other. After the pact, the dwarves were destroyed by Kard and the remaining few joined Tghil.

With only two remaining free nations, the Elves and the Little People, they went to war. Tghil warned them not to go to war, as they would destroy themselves. The leaders of each nation paid her no heed. On the day of battle, called the Battle for Freedom and Goodness, both armies clashed on a barren plain by the River Ijan near the city of now-a-day Jariran. Neither side won. The day after that a small battle erupted between the humans and ogres. All but three ogres were killed. The three ogres were said to be cursed in the last battle. In it their beauty was taken away. Ashamed of their hideousness, they traveled to an island off the coast of Atay where they live in dying peace. The remaining elves escaped to the Lost Mountains, only resurfacing to fight in the Battles between the Light and Dark. The Little People sailed across the Jayapur Ocean to the Lone Islands, where they lived away from mankind. The Dwarves retreated into their ancient homeland, an underground city. The goblins, it was said, fled to the lower Gangga Mountains where they were killed by creatures of the Dark Lord's creation, rogui and sylai.

Kard never was near the Battle for Freedom and Goodness. He and his most trusted humans met Tghil and her followers where present day Jariran is now. They fought until the only two standing were Kard and Tghil. They both stopped channeling their magic and walked over to meet each other.

"You succeeded. You killed off the Six Nations and made trust a rare thing," Tghil said.

"Aaah, but so did you. You made it possible for us to become gods," Kard said.

"How?"

"It was written long ago that when a man and a woman fight against each other for the cause of Good and Evil, they will become the Darkness and the Light." Kard smiled, his thin lips turning upward. "They would become the new gods and the old would prepare to step aside."

"What? Are you saying we are immortal because we—you destroyed the Six Nations and I fought you for peace?"

"That is correct, my love, forever together."

Before Tghil could utter another word, a beam of pure white light tore through the dark sky and struck the pair standing in the middle of a field of blood.

Kard and Tghil felt their feet leave the ground.

From far away a young elf, one of Tghil's followers, watched in amazement as the two disappeared into the sky. He would spread the word to others of his kind that the two humans, one fighting for Light, one fighting for Darkness, became the Light and Dark.

There was one rumor behind the story, which no one knew if it was true. Tghil and Kard were lovers, and before the Battle of Freedom and Goodness, she had given birth to two babies. She had handed the children over to a young woman and told her to keep one and the other give to another human family far away from hers. Tghil said to the young woman, "They are brother and sister. Make sure their descendants never meet until the Second Dragons. Your family has the duty of making sure of that. In return I give your family land in A'unat and I give the other family land in the old ogre city of Ruakis." The woman had asked Tghil how she could give her land and Tghil had replied, "The world is changing. Gods walk the earth."

No one save one young elf, the same who saw Tghil and Kard become gods, knew of the two children Tghil had birthed. He reported this to his people. They had felt betrayed by Tghil, she who fought against Evil, had lain with a man who was the cause of all Evil. Even though she was now their goddess and above human mistakes, they viewed her wrongdoing as a common human trait and swore on the graves of their ancestors they would never trust a human again unless a greater power said they had to in order to survive.

08   08   80

The elves trust was just beginning, but once she took the test they would have to trust or face destruction.

Janevra wiped the tears off her face. Her parents had not always been the best but she still loved them and would get revenge.

Today she had to take the test to see if she was one of the Dragons, beginning at dawn. It would last all day. She didn't know what would happen, no one did, but she would do it, because she somehow knew she would live through it.

A clear knock rocked her from her sorrows and Qwaser entered the room with Kalioa. Janevra and Qwaser had become close friends in past weeks.

With Qwaser's return from being an outcast and bringing back the woman meant to save the elven kind, Qwasers's family had held a grand feast in his honor and his father resigned the position of the Head of the Army and gave it to Qwaser. Qwaser was now the Head General of all the Elven Armies. His friend Hasaxta, the General of the Armies, just one seat below Qwaser, held another feast in Qwasers's honor. The most powerful elf next to the King was Qwaser.

During that time, young elves, with the help of Danlk and Tasawer, the other two survivors of the village, gathered together a group of people loyal to Qwaser, Kalioa and Janevra. The group called themselves the Jynnyqh, or the Followers in common speech and had become the bodyguards for the three and the other Dragon. Janevra was grateful for their belief in her but she thought bodyguards a little too much.

Kalioa sat down next to Janevra. She had a small scar above her eye from the battle she had fought. Around her neck hung a medallion of a sword. Janevra did not know what it symbolized but she feared it.

"Janevra, it's time," Kalioa said softly.

"Good luck, Queen of Caendor," Qwaser said.

Janevra looked up at him.

"Word travels fast. A Lord Ravften killed your parents and may have taken the throne. But you are the heir."

Janevra stood up. "Thank you, Qwaser and Kalioa. I'll be right there. I have something to do first."

The two nodded and left the room.

Janevra said a word and the ink and pen floated over to her from a desk. Taking them out of the air she wrote a quick letter.

Dear Lousai and Caya,

Thank you for telling me about my parents. I will get revenge on Ravften. I will see him dead. I am about to take my test to see if I'm the Dragon. If I die, tell Mat for me. May the Goddess of Light favor you.

The Princess-Queen of Caendor,
Janevra

Janevra sealed the letter with magic and handed it to the bird that took it in its beak and flew out the open window.

Janevra met Qwaser and Kalioa. They walked down the marble floored hall in silence, until they came to the Throne Room where they all assembled, waiting for the King.

The Elven King entered the Throne Room. He bowed low to Janevra. "Janevra, are you ready?" the King asked in a deep voice.

Janevra nodded, afraid. She had a feeling that her life was not in her hands anymore. *When has it ever been?* she thought sardonically.

"Walk into that room beyond and lay your hands on the globe. It will bring you into the World of Things Yet to Come and Things That Have Passed. May the Light and all powers of Time and Fate be with you."

Janevra nodded again, and step-by-step she walked into the room.

Sweat slid down her face and her heart thumped loudly. She jumped as the doors slammed shut behind her.

The room she was in was made of crystal and marble. Her attention was on the clear ball in front of her, hovering in mid air. She walked over to it, remembering laying her hand on a similar ball in Jariran with Mat. She put her hands on the ball.

Chapter 21
A New People

Mat was out on a balcony in the Cyrain Plains, waiting like Janevra for the sun to rise. Like her, today was the day he would take the Test of the Dragons.

The scorching sun of the plains had darkened Mat's skin and he felt more like an Ile than he had when he had first arrived. He had struggled to learn their ways and their orders from Vena, Deivenada, Zenerax and Kayzi in the one month he had been here.

Mat knew how the Ile and the Tar-ten came to be.

ж ђ Ѫ

After the fight between Tghil and Kard, humans were the only ones who had not left and isolated themselves from the world. It was up to them to form new nations, nations of humans. First they had to clean up the mess left by Kard. It was carried out in peace, the people thankful they were alive. Following the clean up of the land came the selecting of leaders for the groups into which the people had divided themselves. This was easy. Next they had to divide the land up into portions for each group. This passed with little difficulty. Everyone got what they wanted.

The leaders became known as Kings and Queens and peace and prosperity returned to the land like in the old days. After thirty years of peace, new kings and queens took the throne, the sons and daughters of the past kings and queens. They had forgotten the peace and had forgotten the war between Kard and Tghil. Only in thirty years did they forget that Kard and Tghil were humans fighting against each other. The people had forgotten peace, once more.

War broke out between the fifteen nations that were once strong and when peace came again, only eleven nations survived. The eleven nations made a peace bond and swore an oath that no more war would break out.

The people of the nations who had lost their land fled to the Gangga Mountains and into the Cyrain Plains. Over the years the people started to call themselves the Ile, and they specialized in the art of war. Among themselves they formed their own nations and their own ideas of the past. They became the Daaguwh, Edieata, Latyre, Siatue, Ryaji, Jaara and Nekid.

The rest of the people living on the other side of the Gangga Mountains fought among themselves, forgetting their peace bonds after a new king took the throne.

All stories are changed as time goes by and in the case of the Ile, the full truth was soon lost just as it was lost in the west. They do not know the real past. Over the years, the Ile did hold true to one thing. They did remember one sign from the past, and that was a golden sun and white lightning bolt of being united. They feared the symbol themselves. A hidden power lurked behind it, they said, and they refused to use it in battle. Too many men and women, they said, died under the symbol. Too many.

ж ђ Ѫ

Mat walked off the balcony as the sun was about to rise, out of his room and down one of the long halls of the Daaguwh City Palace to a circular room with five people in it.

Leama moved away from the group of people to speak to him first.

"Mat, you are the Dragon. I know you will bring the world together," Leama said.

Mat nodded and moved on to Vena.

"Lord Dragon, I wish you well, and the Lady Dragon, wherever she may be." Vena bowed to Mat.

Mat nodded, his heart beating faster for fear of Janevra getting hurt.

"Mat, I don't know what to say. If Tghil is willing, you'll come back to us as the Dragon of the Rising Sun," Kayzi said, shaking Mat's hand. The tattoo of the sun on Kayzi's arm looked like it was glowing.

Mat nodded his thanks.

"Janevra will be okay," Zenerax said, his tattoo also appearing to Mat as if it was glowing. Zenerax was the only one who knew how Mat felt about Janevra.

Dei came over and hugged him. She didn't need to say anything.

Mat turned his back on his five friends. He knew what to do once he got inside the room. Leama had told him yesterday.

"Remember, Mat, your future lies in there. Expect nothing, ask for nothing, keep nothing. It is in there the gods will judge you. When you lay your hands on that glass ball, you will leave this world. I do not know if pain will come to you, but expect it, always expect it. Everything will come easier if you expect it.

Mat walked into the room, his feet feeling like stone.

His heart stopped as the door slammed shut, dimming the lights.

Mat looked across the room and at the clear globe floating in mid air. He walked over to it and laid his hands on the ball.

ଔ   ଊ   ଠ

At the same time, both Janevra and Mat felt their world turn underneath their feet. Their bodies and souls seemed to shimmer in time and they felt as if all they knew was being torn from them. Pain raged through them like fire. Stars wheeled overhead and the sun rose and fell. Countless days or years, maybe even centuries seemed to pass, or did they? Eternity swallowed them, showing them sights no ordinary man or woman could or would wish to see.

It all stopped, the spinning, twirling and even the pain to leave them in cool mist.

Chapter 22
To Meet Gods

Mat stood up, the mist swirling around his feet. His head hurt from the fall like he had drunk too much wine. He heard a noise behind and turned around.

There was Janevra, her back towards him, shaking her head.

"Janevra?" Mat asked, uncertain.

Janevra twirled around, her face showing hope.

"Mat?"

"Hello."

Janevra ran towards him and threw her arms around his neck. "You have no idea how much I missed you."

"I missed you too," Mat said, taking her hands off the back of his neck. "Where are we?"

Janevra looked around. "The Elven King told me it was the World of Things Yet To Come and Things That Have Passed."

All around them was a gray, cool mist. There was no way of telling which way was up or down. Not a sound pierced the fog.

Mat glanced down at Janevra. She was wearing a white dress made out of what appeared to be the mist itself. It was almost translucent. "Janevra, what type of clothes do they wear in the Lost Mountains?"

"Why?" Janevra asked frowning. "It is nothing vastly different from what we would normally wear in Caendor."

"Take a look at what you're wearing." Mat looked Janevra up and down. *Too bad it isn't completely transparent.*

Janevra looked down at herself, and gasped.

"Don't look!" she snapped at Mat. Mat turned around, a grin splitting his face.

Janevra picked at the dress. "This must change."

Her clothes immediately changed to a dress that started white at the top and slowly changed to a dark blue. It went down to her thighs and then on one end continued down to her ankle. Her hair also changed and went from down, up into a braid.

Janevra smiled, turning around and admiring it.

Mat looked at his clothes and found himself to be wearing the same white color. He issued a silent curse, and his clothes went to a dark purple shirt and baggy black trousers with a belt of diamonds. He faced Janevra again.

"This is interesting. The World of Things Yet to Come and Things That Have Passed, you called it?" Mat asked. He shook his head at the belt. *Who would wear a belt of diamonds? An Emperor, perhaps?*

"Yes. Do you have any idea what we are supposed to do here?"

Before Mat could answer a serration appeared in the mist.

Mat cocked an eyebrow at it. "Should we go in?"

"Everyone dies sometime."

"Yes, but I don't think I want it to be now." Mat scratched his head. "I have a feeling that we don't have a choice, do we?"

"You first," Janevra said.

Mat smiled at her with sarcastic politeness. He stepped into the portal, Janevra close behind.

They found themselves on a ship. The ship was heading east, across the Jayapur Ocean. A young woman was in front of them, her purple eyes focusing on something. The boat gave a violent shake and screams could be heard from somewhere.

The image in front of them faded and was replaced by the image of a young man with the lightest brown eyes that when seen in the right light looked red. He was watching a flame flicker on a wick. It was dark outside and in, except for the flame. Suddenly the door banged open and the city guard entered, letting in the storm outside. The boy dove under the table as thunder sounded.

The image moved again and they were standing in a forest watching a young man touch a rock. The earth moved by simple commands from his mouth or a wave of his hand. He was suddenly thrown back as lightning struck a tree. A storm was brewing.

The picture melted in front of them again and focused on a young woman feeding the birds in a courtyard. The birds would walk right up to her and land on her shoulders and feed right out of her hands. There was a slight breeze and the birds flew off. The girl stood up, her dress fanning out behind her, her whitish-blonde hair flying. Clouds started to gather in the sky. Dark clouds.

The image disappeared and a young woman was seen twirling a flower. Around her neck was a necklace of flowers eight years old but looking as if she had just picked them. Her eyes were gray and reflected the darkening sky. She screamed as a flash of light hit the ground by her. The storm got darker still, but her scream carried over the noise.

The image shifted and a young man with thin lips, and coal dark eyes lifted his face to the dark sky. His eyes were open and he stared at the sky as if he controlled it but fear also stormed in the corner of those dark eyes. The boy toppled over when the wall next to him crashed to the ground. He scrambled back up, blood seeping out of his mouth, hate in his eyes.

Janevra and Mat found themselves, again, in the mist, stunned.

Mat's hand reached up and touched his lip. There was blood on it where he had bitten his lip.

The mist parted and a man and a woman appeared in front of Mat and Janevra.

The man had coal dark eyes, black hair, thin lips and was very handsome. The woman was the same height with brown hair, gray eyes, red lips and was stunningly beautiful. Both had no lines on their face. They had pure skin, not a mark touching their ageless faces.

The woman was wearing a white dress and when Mat looked at it he felt as if he was staring into the universe. The man wore black trousers and a black shirt so dark he felt as if the abyss was staring down at him. The clothing of both was strange and simple, carrying with it an ancient, deadly past. Neither wore any jewelry expect for the woman who wore a silver chain with a pink pearl hanging down around her elegant neck.

"Janevra, Mat," the woman said, her voice like a song.

The man only nodded.

"We are what you humans call the Light and the Dark, your gods."

Mat frowned, a feeling of unease sinking into his stomach. Janevra's mouth dropped open.

In the shocked silence that followed a figure dropped from the "sky".

It quickly stood up and turned around, bringing it to the attention of all four. The thing was a young man, Janevra and Mat's age. He had ice blue eyes and dirty blonde hair. Standing as tall as Mat, he was obviously strong. The sword at his waist proved a talent in weaponry. It was his eyes that caught Mat's interest. His eyes were like winter's freeze.

The Dark Lord smiled. "Mat, Janevra, meet Raxsen, the Warlord, as you are the Dragons." The Dark Lord gave a cool smile at the three mortals.

Janevra looked at Raxsen.

Mat glared at him.

Raxsen smiled back, aware of Janevra's staring.

"How did you get here?" Mat asked.

Already hatred had formed between them.

"In Carim they have a room in their mayor's mansion with a clear glass globe in it. It was meant for the Warlord. Me. The one who will take over the world," Raxsen said, his eyes blazing at the vision of his future glory.

"Warlord, we'll still beat you in the Fifth Battle and the world will live in peace," Mat said, his lips bared across his teeth.

Raxsen's face went taunt. "We shall see."

Janevra move to stand in front of Raxsen. "We *will* beat you."

"Women are weak, and because of this *I* will win." Raxsen smiled coldly.

Janevra grinded her teeth together. "A woman will then be your downfall."

They were interrupted by a laugh, a sound like crinkling paper. "Children, how they love to fight," the Dark Lord said, rubbing his hands together.

"Kard, be quiet," the Lady of Light snapped. "You three have been picked to battle for Good... and Evil. As we did long ago, and will do again, in this war."

Janevra stared at the Lady. "You're Tghil, aren't you? And he's Kard."

Tghil nodded smiling, her teeth perfect. Janevra's eyebrows rose all the way up to her hairline and her eyes were wide.

"You fought each other in the War of the Races, ending the Age of Magic, the First Age. You, Tghil, gave birth to two babies. It was only a rumor, and you told the woman helping you that the babies must be separated and never meet till the Second Dragons. You became the Light, he the Dark. You were lovers and still are." It was hard for her, Mat noticed, not to keep the betrayal out of her voice.

Kard smiled at Janevra, showing sharp, white teeth.

Tghil smiled. "Yes, we love each other. I do not know how you know that but yes, we were and are lovers. If the young elf had told of our love, our people would have felt betrayed. In name, worst enemies, in reality, lovers. That was how we lived our life. Only eight people knew of our secret, and they never told a soul."

"But the elves always knew, in the end. They're the only reason I know the truth," Janevra said. "How could you?"

Tghil gave a little shrug. "Love is a strange thing."

For a split second the tightness of the Dark Lord's face eased up and he and the Lady of the Light shared a look that no one had ever seen before, a look of love and trust. A look of true love.

Raxsen interrupted the moment. "How can a Lord so Evil, love a woman so pure? And she love him when he is threatened by a simple cow herder boy now a Warlord?"

Kard glared at Raxsen. "My young Warlord, you think you can beat me, you think you can out think me and you think I'm not as immortal as people believe. You do not know anything. I have been living for almost two thousand years. I've lived since the Second Age and I will live through the Seventh Age, the Age of the Second Dragons and the Fifth Battle. I have seen ages and times that you could never dream of. I have seen peoples you could in no way imagine, things that have been lost in the past. I have seen the Little People, the Goblins, the Ogres, the Dwarves, and the Elves. I made the humans betray their Peace Bond. I took the Harp of Song and broke it. I saw the First Kings of the current Nations rise to power and die. I watched you in your mother's womb. I watched you, Mat and Janevra grow as I watched Ake, Ryen Dael, Eside Thron, Kiera Aade, Riak Tghil, and Dorl Kard, grow into young men and women. I saw all this. And I will see it again."

"Kard, love, calm down. Children, rip off the sleeves on your right shoulder," Tghil said, her musical voice commanding them to obey.

All three ripped off their sleeves.

Tghil walked over to Mat and touched his bicep. Mat cried out in pain as a golden sun was melted into his skin. The pain seemed to lance through his very blood, burning his soul. The sun glowed, pulsing with power.

The Lady of the Light moved next to Janevra and touched her upper right arm. Tears spilled out of Janevra's eyes and she whimpered as a white lightning bolt was forced into her skin. The lightning bolt danced like all lightning did.

The sun and the lightning glowed, both hot.

Kard went over to Raxsen and touched his arm. Raxsen yelled as a black skull was stuck into his skin. The skull was cold and blood seeped around the edges of the skull.

"Once you return to your world, six will be called and on the wings of magic they will fly to you," Tghil said. "Bring good into the World, Dragons." Her song like voice carried a tremendous power.

"Bring death into the world, Warlord," Kard whispered, their voices intertwining.

Cʒ   Cʁ   ʚ

Tghil looked at Kard as the three disappeared. "I think you made a mistake in picking Raxsen."

"I did not."

"Why do you say that?"

Kard glared at Tghil, a full wine glass appearing in his hands. "I chose him for a reason. He was made to be the Warlord. Raxsen may be the smartest strategist ever, but he has no heart. He does not care for his men, and he does not care for women most of all, and that will be his downfall as Janevra said. To Raxsen women are like tools. They are there to make life easier but when he's done with them, he'll let them rust or he'll sell them."

"Perhaps you are right. Raxsen did seem to look down upon Janevra and I," Tghil said, her clothes changing to a clear blue, showing off her slender form.

Kard smiled. "Raxsen does not even know this world's true history."

Tghil walked over to Kard and took a sip of his wine. "Janevra and Mat seem to be a good pick for the Dragons, do you agree?"

"Yes, but like last time, I think we should have taken the place of the Dragons." Kard wrinkled his nose.

"You hated being the Dragons. You hated seeing your empire of Evil come to an end." Tghil caressed Kard's face with a long smooth finger.

"Ah, I might have, but I got to be with you, did I not?" Kard arched an eyebrow, his hand resting on Tghil's hip. "Besides, their ancestry will not allow it. The Dragons ruled once, they will rule again whether through Good or Evil. At least we can watch and decide the future of the world together."

"I would say the best part is that we get to watch our very own great grand children, Riak and Dorl," Tghil said, taking another sip of the wine, her fingers wrapping around Kard's.

"They are the few people who can trace their families all the way back to the First Age. It's a pity they don't know," Kard said, pulling his wine out of Tghil's hand. He set the wine down, the glass disappearing into thin air.

Kard took his other hand and caressed Tghil's back.

"Love, what a strange word," Tghil said against Kard's lips.

True love could be no purer than theirs. A love so pure, death could not claim it.

Chapter 23
An Assassin

Saviak Diqrama rubbed her nose…waiting was always a problem.

It was gloomy out, the stars dully gleaming through the thin veil of clouds.

Saviak's golden eyes glowed, her black hair shining in the moonlight. Her form blended into her dark surroundings.

Nothing moved in the plaza below her, no wind stirred.

Saviak pulled a knife out of her belt and a small vial of liquid. The liquid was a form of poison.

Living as a thief and a professional assassin was not easy. It did not help that she was a female and held in low regard for jobs by customers. That was something that irked Saviak more than anything, the putting of women below men. She had always believed they were equal. It was a belief her mother had passed down to her when Saviak was young. Her mother was dead now, killed by an assassin. It was a male assassin, someone her mother had worked with. It was a man who had been overlooked for a big job because of Saviak's mother's known talent in killing. Later Saviak had killed the man.

They had called her mother the Cat and it was a nickname Saviak had gained not long ago, proud she could follow in her mother's footsteps.

She had earned her name five years ago when she was fifteen, robbing a merchant wagon coming into Debon. Everyone with her was killed, but somehow she managed to get away. That day, the merchants had come into town. They told of what had happened, how a group of thieves had tried to rob their caravan, but were fought off by the guards. They told of a young woman with golden eyes who had escaped. They said she moved like a black cat.

Saviak's gold eyes jerked out of the past as a shadow moved down below her. A smile tainted her lips.

Her hands moved quickly. She put a drop of the liquid from the vial on her knife and placed the vial back in her shirt.

The shadow moved into the moonlight and the Cat struck. Her knife flew straight and true, as it should have for she had the fastest and most centered throw of all.

The shadow was down before it could blink.

Her job done, Saviak hurried across rooftops, reaching an inn within seconds of her kill.

Walking into the inn, the sounds of gambling and drinking washed over her as she sat down at a corner table. She asked for a drink of purple wine that came from the far wine harvesting city of Aryta.

The heat from the fire warmed her cheeks and gave her the appearance that she was drunk. Her gold eyes brightened, watching the people around her, possible victims.

The drink came fairly fast, but she did not drink from her mug. She waited.

An hour later, after the inn had started to empty, a black-cloaked figure entered.

The figure came over to her table, not sitting down.

"Is it done?"

She nodded.

The black-cloaked figure pulled out a sack of money and tossed it to her. She grabbed the money out of the air, the bag of coins clinking.

"Very good," it whispered. "We all change the balance of life in some way, our kind more than others. But I wonder how much you will change it. There is something odd about you, Diqrama, something very odd indeed. Perhaps it would be best if you were not around anymore."

It left the inn, disappearing into the night's dark shadow.

Saviak sat, clutching her money. *Not around any more? What is that supposed to mean? I have no place in society, no importance. I affect the changing of life as much as a grain of sand affects a mountain!* She shrugged. Sometimes her employers were a little odd themselves. Deciding to forget what he said, she jumped out of her chair and casually pushed it in. She dashed up to her room two floors above the main level and quickly lit three candles. Her room was small, with a bed, a rickety washstand, a small cracked mirror and a trunk containing her clothes. The innkeeper let her stay up here as long as she paid five copper chips a week. It was cold in the winter, but in the summer it was always cool with the southeast breeze in the afternoon.

She spilled the contents of the bag out on the floor, squealing in delight when she saw the money glinting back at her. One hundred gold chips, two hundred silver ones and fifty copper chips. She was rich!

With this much money she could just lay around for months! She could buy her own house! She could...

Saviak stopped, frowning. Why so much money for one kill? The man in the black cloak, come to think of it, had the accent of a noble. But commoners could copy it and make it believable. Still...maybe she should hide the money and only take out a little at a time.

Saviak ruffled her short hair in frustration. Getting rich fast in Debon was not always good. Debon was a rich town thanks to its new mayor, but folks were still superstitious of people getting too rich too fast. It was a place where half of it was made up of thieves, assassins, murders and such. People who got rich fast and lived in the "right" part of town were alleged to be thieves or assassins. If the rumor reached the ears of one of the nobles or the mayor, the one suspected would be put on trial and if found guilty, hanged.

Saviak had watched a hanging before. The man hanged was one of her fellow thieves. He had suddenly become richer than the mayor and all the arrogant nobles. He was found guilty and hanged. Unlucky for Saviak, he was the Leader of the Thieves Guild and she had been very close to him. With his death she was thrown out of the Guild. Most of the thieves thought her to be his downfall.

Sighing, she stared at the money. She would hide the money and take out a little everyday. Or she could just move.

Shouts from below brought Saviak out of her brooding. Getting up she walked over to her window. Down below her was a mob of people. The ones she could make out had torches in their hands. There was something funny about them as they set a tree on fire, illuminating parts of their faces.

Saviak moved away from the window and quickly put all of her money and few belongings in a bag. She made sure she brought with her the precious bottles of poison she owned, her climbing gloves and a magic wrought rope.

She climbed out of her window with ease built of practice. Once on the rooftop she jumped the space between the inn and the next building.

As soon as she did the inn exploded into fire, the warmth licking her back. She looked behind her at the flames, the heat burning her eyes. Saviak set her bag down and crawled to the edge of the building. She peered over the side.

"By the Dark Lord," she whispered. Down below her the people had taken off their cloak hoods. She knew every single one of them. They were trained assassins, all of them. She had trained with a few of them. It was said that when assassins got together there was going to be another war between Good and Evil. That was only myth but it sent the hairs on Saviak's arm standing up. What scared her the most about them was their leader was the man who had given her the money for her kill. She recognized his body and the way he moved his head when he spoke.

Saviak gasped. That man! She had learned never to trust them, but this time she did and she had to pay for it.

Saviak's eyes grew wider when she thought of the money he gave her. She hastily pulled the money out of her bag and dumped it out. Picking up a gold chip, she scratched the top. The gold came off under her fingernail. She almost screamed. She picked up a copper piece and rubbed the top, it too peeled off. She ground her teeth together.

Saviak stood up, careful not to come into view of the people below. She left her moneybag and jumped the space between the buildings and the next. When she finally came down, she was five blocks away from the burning inn.

Running among the shadows, her baggy gray pants and black shirt blending into the buildings, the light of the two moons guided her. She was leaving Debon; things had gone strange, stranger than usual. She would go to Calahar, the home of the ruling family of Selkare. There she would find her friend and ask him a question that was most important. Which side are you on? She hated knowing too much and getting involved with too many things that could so easily fly out of her hands. But she had to know. She knew now that her spot in life was much more important than she had ever thought. The attempt on her life proved that much more clearly than she would have ever liked.

Saviak paused in a shadow as a group of horseman galloped by. She was about to move again when she saw the slightest movement out of the corner of her eye. Turning her head ever so slightly, she got a good view of a form.

It was a person following her.

Saviak pulled a knife out of her shirtsleeve.

The figure was level with her now.

"Stop."

It stopped.

"Why are you following me?" she said, her hand drawing back to throw her knife.

"Saviak?"

"Who are you?"

The figure came closer.

"A friend of yours," he said.

"I don't have any—"

Saviak jumped out of the way as the man lunged at her with a knife he had produced from somewhere. Her hand darted out and quickly went up against his throat. "What do you want?" she said, her knife pressing deeper into his skin.

"Please don't kill me," the man whimpered, his eyes fearful.

Saviak tightened the knife against his throat until a small trickle of blood ran down his neck.

"I—I was sent here to… to kill you," he said, his hair in his eyes.

"By who?"

"The—" Saviak leaped out of the way as the assassin's eyes turned red and blood poured out of his mouth. The man was still standing but his ears were bleeding now and his skin turned white.

Saviak watched as some invisible force broke the back of the man and fell to the ground. She had killed people and seen some gruesome death but never in her life had she seen such a kill.

She turned around and threw up.

Wiping her mouth with her sleeve, she took one last look at the body and started to run as fast. *Why am I suddenly a target?* She didn't know why he wanted to kill her. She didn't owe anybody, and most all she had no real place in society. *So,* Saviak thought, *that means it has something to do with the future. But what is so important that in the future I will harm it? What is my part in life that demands I be killed?*

Chapter 24
The Phoenix of Water

"Wine! More wine!" a man bellowed.

"Quiet! Don't fret yourself, I'm coming," Ake shouted back, carrying a tray of wine glasses. She set one down in front of him. She held out her hand for the coins.

The man looked up at her sheepishly. "Errr...I don't have 'nymore."

Ake whisked the glass from his clutching hands. "No coin, no wine."

Ake was young, only nineteen, with her hair cut short, purple eyes, dark skin, as all islanders had, and she had reached the height of five feet, eleven inches. Breathtakingly attractive, her clothes were that of an Islander, a purple tank top with a V-neck that tied together above her stomach. She had on a dark red skirt that had two slits on the sides going up to her thigh, which allowed movement. A small crystal was on her left nostril, glinting in the sunlight. From her ears hung a star inside a crescent moon. Around her neck was a silver chain with a blue stone at the end, treasures given to her by her mother. Even though it was unseemly, she wore the jewelry while she worked, fearing to take them off and risk them getting stolen.

She worked at a small tavern called the Island Tree Inn for half the day. With the pay she earned from serving she bought spell books in order to further her Talent. During the latter part of the day and whenever she could vanish for a time, she worked at her other job. She rarely slept, maybe three hours a day. The rest was spent studying and working.

Moving behind the counter, Ake picked up an empty tankard and began to wash it, eying the customers in the inn, making sure a brawl did not suddenly let loose.

As a child Ake had always been different. Others had never accepted her. Her family was on the border of poor and rich and continuously fell in and out of both stations. That had never helped her situation. At the Shoi School, everyone, even the teachers, disliked her, because she had so much Talent. At home it was a different matter. Her father made money by gambling, her mother by working at a rich merchant's house down the street, and her older brother worked as a dockhand and fisherman.

When her mother was with child and died giving birth, Ake had to tend her new baby sister, study and work.

Her father was of no help. All he did was get drunk and lose their money gambling. Her brother's income helped but he used most of the money to buy himself a small fishing boat and a small house by the docks.

Her brother had moved out and married by the time her father died from a broken neck in a drunken fray.

Ake and her baby sister moved in with their brother and his wife. The baby did not survive the next year. An epidemic struck the island and killed over one-fourth of the population.

Ake knew her brother didn't want her living there. In order to accommodate him and his growing family, she had left, buying a place of her own. She had quit her schooling as a shoi and instead learned on her own, knowing there was little the teachers could teach her.

Setting down the tankard, she threw the dirty rag over her shoulder, glancing up as a shadow filled the doorway. The shadow advanced into the room, sitting at a chair pulled up next to the counter. He was a large man, rolls of fat spreading from his neck down. The strong smell of body odor steamed off him, causing several men near him to get up and sit on the other end of the room. The man paid them no heed except to give them a lazily almost bored look. "Water," the man said, waving with his hand at Ake.

Eyebrows rising at this odd request, she brought him a pitcher of water and a small glass, holding her breath as she neared him. He laid down a gold coin. Ake scooped up the coin and slipped it into her pocket. *Either you are a very rich man or in desperate need of water,* she thought, watching him.

The man poured himself a glass of water and swallowed it in a gulp. He smacked his lips together contentedly. "Nice water," he said. "Where do you find water this good on an island?" His speech labeled him a mainlander.

"You don't find it that good on the island. I made it." A reason why the innkeeper paid Ake so much was that she used her magic to give the inn a constant supply of cool, fresh water.

Ake loved the water. She loved anything to do with water. Perhaps it was when she was five and the shoi of Zinder Island found that she had a knack for water magic, a very rare gift, that she began to love it. She had studied the Art of Water magic ever since.

The fat man eyed her, his face trying to hide a smirk. "You're a shoi," he said with contempt.

"Not yet, although I could be," Ake said, cleaning a plate in a bucket of hot water. "I have not received my *lapis lazuli.* My betters," she spat the word, "don't think I'm ready." *I am, though,* she thought. *I have more Talent than all of them. They cannot deny much longer that I am stronger than all of them in the Art. If they don't like me teaching myself, too bad. I'm not going to stop. I'll find a way to get those* lapis lazuli.

The man relaxed slightly. "It was the best thing that happened to this land, the downfall of the shoi. They were greedy little bastards."

Ake ignored the man's insult. "We will return to our glory when the Dragons are found."

"You believe that they will come?" His tone implied that he did not.

"Yes, I do." Ake faced him, her hands on her hips. "The Warlord is on the mainland. It will be soon for the coming of the Dragons."

"Futile. I don't believe they will come. I don't believe in the battles between Good and Evil. It's all mendacious, I say. There is only one type of power. Power of the Great God of Darkness."

Ake quenched her anger, her cheeks turning red. "If you are not going to order any more food or drink, sir," she said stiffly, "I suggest you leave."

The man slapped another coin down on the table. "For your information then."

Ake picked up the coin, holding it between her fingers. It was pure gold, very rare. The coin had a small face stamped upon it with strange words beneath it. She had seen a chest full of these coins once before, when her ship had raided a small but very rich island settlement. Unfortunately, the gold coins were melted and made into other trinkets. Few of the coins had been saved and used for barter.

"What information?" She watched him through narrowed eyes. It was unsafe to trust a man who believed in the powers of the dark no matter how much money he had.

"Tell me, where can I find a girl by the name of Ake? My employer has a message for her."

Ake summoned her magic, setting the coin back on the table. "You will get no such information from me," she said.

The man picked up the coin, examining it in the light. "My employer said she was a beautiful young woman with purple eyes and three piercings, one in her nose and the others in her ears. He said I could find her at an inn or at the docks. If I did not find her, he said, I was to wait for her ship to return from its raiding. She's a pirate, you see."

Taking the dirty cloth from her shoulder and setting in on the counter, she leaned against the bar. "What do you want?"

The man ran a hand over his fat face. "Nothing much. It's only a trivial matter."

"What trivial matter is this?"

"Your life," he said, springing from his chair with speed unknown to a man of his bulk and yanking a knife from his belt. The knife whizzed towards Ake.

Throwing her hands in front of her, water sprayed from them. The knife clattered to the ground.

The huge man gawked at her, then a slow smile spread across his face. "I was warned you'd be hard to kill." He reached for another knife.

Ake pointed a finger at him. "Don't move."

The other men in the inn remained standing, watching the proceedings with suspicion. Many had drawn their knives or cutlasses, watching the fat man.

The fat man raised his hands but Ake pinned them together with a flow of water, making sure it was tight.

"Who are you?" Ake demanded.

"Do you really want to know?"

Ake tightened the flow of magic. "Tell me."

The fat man sneered at her. "I'm the man who killed your father. He owed my employer a debt and his death did not pay for it."

Ake cut off the flow of her magic, keeping the man's hands clasped together. "Your employer, who is he?"

The fat man clamped his mouth shut.

Ake shrugged. "I'm sure these men will have fun with you then," she said, nodding her head at the men standing behind the fat man. "I'm rather well loved, you see. I give them water when the shipment of fresh water is late. If I die, so will they. If I die the water that keeps these barrels from going dry will disappear." She tapped a barrel near her hip.

The man remained silent. "Then kill me. I needed to collect what was owed to my employer. He said if I failed, he would kill me. I would rather die by your hand then his."

Ake cocked her head at him. "With your life I will avenge my father's death."

The man looked shocked. "You wouldn't kill me, would you?" Apparently he had not expected Ake to carry out his killing.

"No, but these men will make sure you never leave prison." Ake nodded to the men behind the fat man. They sheathed their weapons and grabbed the fat man roughly by his arms, dragging him from the inn.

A young woman squished through the door, edging past the men. "You certainly know how ta clear a place out," she said.

"Have fun, Sicquia," Ake called at her replacement as she walked through the inn door and into the bright sunlight of the day. Digging her hand into her pocket, it came out with several gold, silver and copper coins. She plopped all but the copper chips back into her pocket and set off to the market.

Buying a few vegetables from a vender, she slung the sack containing her food over her shoulder and hurried off to the docks. She had an hour before the her ship set sail, enough time to take a dip in the ocean and say goodbye to her brother.

ଔ   ଔ   ଞ

Rinsing the salt from her hair, Ake watched as Zinder Island disappeared in the distance.

She was traveling from Wakee, Zinder Island to Brinya, Caendor. This time her ship had taken on several passengers, men and women heading for the mainland.

The life of a serving maid had never been enough for Ake. It was only her cover, a job to hide her real profession, piracy and smuggling. Practicing smuggling for this trip, Ake's captain had set a course for Brinya where they were to unload the rich Wakeean wine that was illegal on the mainland in exchange for rare silks not available under the current government of Wakee.

Ake turned away from the vanishing island, the wind ruffling her black hair. She leaned against the rail, spray droplets landing on her face. The Warlord had control of lower Angarat and the Dragons were somewhere, planning. With the thought of war suddenly on her mind, Ake knew that with a war, her business would either take a hard hit or flourish, depending on goods they smuggled or what settlements they terrorized.

Not a sailor on the ship, but a barterer, Ake was a very important asset to the business for another reason. Her magic and power in the element of water was used frequently for the ship to escape unwanted trouble or to approach a port under the cover of a dense mist. She occasionally helped arranging the where and what of the deals but tended to be the one who finalized the amounts and whether the profit was worth the risk. It was also she who picked the settlements they were to raid.

Ake turned her face north as a gust of wind blew across the ship. Wind from the north? That was odd. The wind usually came from the east or the south, sometimes the west. Never the north.

Ake looked around her. It was a fairly nice sized ship, with a large cabin area for passengers and a large hold for cargo. Dark skinned sailors rushed about, trying to adjust to the new wind. Other passengers came out on deck, feeling the change beneath their feet.

Ake looked again to the north. There were clouds there, dark clouds. And lightning.

Waves started crashing into the boat, throwing Ake against the rail. Rain pelted her face like drops of fire. She heard people retching over the edge of the ship.

Ake looked up, into the black sky, shielding her eyes with her hands. Above was a swirling black cloud. The cloud had moved fast, unnaturally fast to reach them so quickly.

Lightning struck the water and the mast at the same time. The mast cracked off, falling into the waves, leaving the rest of it burning.

As if in a dream, Ake stood up and moved to the front of the ship. Sailors tried to pull her away, but she shook them off.

Her purple eyes focused on the ocean waves. She watched them, bringing in the power of water to her soul. She turned her face up to the clouds, the rain like tiny swords.

The ship gave a violent shake and Ake heard screams from somewhere, but she was too lost in her magic to notice the screaming or the giant wave looming over the craft.

Ake's hands moved, forming an intricate pattern. It formed a pattern of Water Magic, a symbol of waves and crystals. Except the designs she made stayed in the air, glowing an uncanny light blue.

Just when the giant wave was about to hit the ship, just when more water was going to flood the cargo hold, just when the rain was going to rip the canvas off the mast, it all stopped.

The dark cloud was still present, but without the rain and waves. The people on deck fell to their knees as the ship gave a massive lurch. The ship started moving in the direction of Brinya, without the help of the sails and the sailors.

Lightning struck here and there, and the clouds swirled above their heads, but the water was not a menace anymore.

Ake dropped to the ground, exhausted. That cloud had drained her strength. There had been something in that cloud, something bizarre.

People rushed over to her side. They knew she had saved them. They had watched the symbols in the air. They had watched them glow.

Two sailors picked her up and carried her into the captain's cabin. She was laid on a soft bed, concerned faces leaning over her. One of the faces she recognized, and she smiled weakly at him before falling into a faint.

Pulling herself from the darkness, Ake tried to focus on the timbers above. When they did not come into focus, she closed her eyes.

Ake's hair was plastered to her skull, and her face was pale under her dark skin. One sailor put a cool cloth on her forehead as she opened her eyes, a painful headache pounding in her temples.

"Ye saved our life, missy," the sailor said. "My name's Bilor."

"Ake," Ake whispered, her head pounding. She looked up into the eyes of the sailor. They glinted with a keen stare. His hair was wet and dripping onto the blanket covering her. *I've never seen you before,* she thought.

"Come from Wakee?" he asked, his voice deep and masculine.

"How did you know?"

"Your accent. Wakeean's sound just a little different than mainland folk and you have that crystal nose ring. Only Wakeean's have it."

Ake pulled the blanket closer around her.

"Where you be going?" Bilor inquired.

"I'm not going anywhere. I work on this ship," Ake answered, her body regaining some strength.

Bilor frowned. "What do you do?"

"I can't tell you that," Ake said. "You should know what I do if you work on this ship. Are you only a one time sailor for the captain?"

Bilor looked at her with puzzled eyes. "Why…yes. Yes, I am. But what were ye doing like that, standing up right afore the wave hit? You lookin' to get killed?"

It was Ake's turn to frown. Bilor kept switching his accent. It went from mainland to an island sailor. And if he was indeed an islander, he would not have needed to ask her if she was an islander.

"No, I was saving the ship." Ake flickered a look at him, suddenly aware of the pounding on the other side of the door that she had mistaken for a headache. She looked around the room and screamed when she saw the body of a sailor on the floor.

"Who are you?" she said, edging away from him, letting go of the blanket.

"A man sent here to kill you," he said, his lip curling upwards.

Ake's eyes grew big. "What have I done?" *Why is everyone after me?*

she thought, recalling the fat man at the inn.

The man smiled. "It's not what you've done. It's what you could and will do," he said, pulling a wickedly curved dagger from his belt.

Ake crawled off the bed, her body weak. She landed on the floor with a painful crunch.

Bilor moved in front of her, blocking her escape to the door.

"And Ake dies, the first of the Phoenixes to do so at the hands of the Warlord." Bilor grabbed her hair and yanked her head back.

"You...*teraw hsalp*!" Ake said, using up the last of her energy.

Bilor flew back as Ake's hands sprouted water and pushed him against the wall, and knocked him breathless.

Ake crawled over to the door, slowly, and unlocked it.

A sailor looked in, his eyes taking in the unconscious man and the corpse.

"Are you alright?" he asked, helping Ake stand up.

She nodded. "He tried to kill me," she said, looking at Bilor.

"We'll deal with him. You might want to change, Ake. We're almost to Brinya," he said carrying her out of the room.

"How?" Ake asked. How could they almost be to Brinya? It was a four-day sail with favorable winds.

"Well," the man looked down at her, "we have you to thank for that."

"Oh," Ake sighed, dropping into unconsciousness.

The sailor took Ake to her room and laid her on her bed.

He stood in the doorway. "Ake, learn not to trust many." He closed the door behind him.

Ake murmured in her sleep, her lips forming spells.

In a matter of seconds her hair was dry and clean as were her clothes and skin. In Shoi School she had not only studied Water Magic.

Her dreams were strange. An evil face seemed to work its way into her thoughts and an equally good face seemed to chase it off. She dreamed of battles where thousands died and thousands more hated. Always during the battle, magic cracked around the edges, sending its sharp sparks towards unknown targets. Over one battle was a golden sun and blue lightning bolt.

Ake woke up not shortly after that.

She sat up in bed, her head hammering. She needed to go to the Lost Mountains and had to get there within two days. Urgency gripped her, causing a mild stomachache and an even worse headache. No time, a voice whispered to her. You have no time, Phoenix of Water. Hurry. Forget everything else, it said. You are needed. Go, fast. All will be well. Hurry!

Throwing aside the blankets, she sprinted out of the cabin and onto the deck, her head aching. She looked around, the smells of dry land filling her nose. They had reached Brinya.

Brinya was a moderate sized town with large jagged mountain peaks in the distance. The docks were crowded with merchant ships loaded down with foreign goods. White sails blew gently in the wind and gulls flocked around, adding their call to the loud murmur of human voices. People from many different lands walked the wooden docks. Women wearing turbans with gold and silver jewelry walked the streets flaunting their full bodies. Men wearing brightly colored pants with scimitars lashed onto their wide leather belts swaggered around with a look of importance. Dockhands ran to do the biddings of captains, and merchants thrust merchandise under the noses of buyers. The smell of salt and water hung heavily in the air, adding to the humid heat of the day.

Swaggering over to the captain's cabin, her sea legs still on her, Ake pounded on the door.

"Yes? Come in," a high-pitched voice called.

Ake nudged the door open, coughing as a billow of smoke wafted over her, the smell of tobacco strong in the air. "Captain, I—"

The captain jumped out of his chair, his arms spread wide. "Ake! My dear, how are you feeling? I heard that you saved the ship! Well done, my girl! That man who tried to kill you, he'll be hanged, of course," the captain reassured her.

Ake took a deep breath, ignoring the smoke that suddenly clogged her lungs. "Captain, I came to tell you that I cann…"

The captain began rummaging through a pile of papers. "I believe we're picking up silk this time, my dear. I don't think I got those last numbers from you. I can't remember if the amount we were getting was worth it or not." He scratched his head. "Once we leave Brinya, the men wanted to go after one of those Caendorian ships that are still loyal to the Princess of Caendor. They've heard rumors about the ships being loaded with gold and silver."

"Captain, I won't be coming back with you." Ake felt a sharp pang in her stomach. *I wish I could go on one last raid.*

The captain jerked as if he had been slapped. "What?"

"I won't be coming back. My days as a smuggler and pirate are over. I'm going east, towards the Lost Mountains."

The captain puffed out a ring of smoke. "Does your brother know?"

"He doesn't even know that I'm a smuggler and pirate in my free time," Ake said wryly.

"Ah," the captain said. "I see. Well, my dear, we will miss you. Your magic that is."

Ake laughed. "I'm sure you will." She had pulled them out of a many tight spots before. "Thank you, captain, for understanding."

The captain shrugged offhandedly. "We all have our callings. I'm just disappointed that yours is not along the lines of smuggling and piracy, my dear." He bent down to the papers, murmuring to himself.

Dismissed, Ake shut the door to the cabin behind her and walked down the plank holding the ship to the dock. The wind whipped water off the ocean waves and sprinkled it on her hair. Ake sighed. *A new life in a matter of moments with almost no money to help create it.*

Moving off the docks, she noticed she fit in perfectly with her nose ring and dangling earrings. Her dark red skirt with the slits drew men's eyes but her rough appearance warned them of danger.

Ake walked around the main street. She was looking for a place to buy maps. Since she had never been to the Lost Mountains she could not transport herself there. But where would she find a place to buy a map?

She traveled farther down the street. When she didn't find anything, she went into a tavern and asked for directions. When she came back out she turned left, back towards the docks and continued on until she came to a small alley way. Turning down the alley, she spotted a store at the end.

The alley was dark and quiet compared to the sunny streets and many people. Water was dripping from somewhere, echoing off the damp wooden walls.

As her eyes looked above her for any possible trap, she missed the rope that was thrown out of the dark and pulled her hands tightly to her sides.

A voice followed the rope. "It seems as if we caught a rich girl, boys." Guffaws sounded from the dark corners of the alley way.

The man who had spoken stepped out of the shadows and grinned at Ake. He was short and slim. He only came up to her shoulder and the middle finger on his left hand was missing.

The man came over and walked around her, talking aloud as he did. "Fine clothes, well cut, will come for a good price. Earrings silver-iron, an odd and rare thing. Found only in Wakee and expensive. Nose ring crystal, not worth much. The necklace," he picked it up off her chest, "not crystal but it will fetch a wonderful price." He dropped it back down her shirt. "All in all you will bring me and my boys much money on the slave market." The man reached up and caressed her face. "But perhaps I will have you first."

Ake spat in his face.

Laughter again rang from the shadowed corners, high pitched and crackling.

The man stepped back, rubbing his hand over his face. "That will cost you." He reached for a knife hidden in his belt.

"If you knew who you were dealing with you would untie me."

The man threw back his head and wheezed in laughter. "There is not a thing you can do to me."

Ake whispered one word in magic and the rope fell away.

The man studied her. "How did you do that? No matter. I do not care."

Ake drew in the full power of her magic, waiting.

The man sheathed his knife. "Men!" he roared into the shadow corners. "Pin her for me."

Five men leapt from the shadows of the alley. They ran towards Ake, but when she did not turn to run, they slowed their attack.

"Afraid?" Ake said smugly. She let the dam on her magic go. Water flowed from her fingers.

The five men stared as ropes of water tied them together. They were too shocked to fight back.

Ake shot her other hand at the first man as he ran for the open streets of Brinya. He too was quickly bonded in ropes of water. Ake pulled the one man and put him in with his fellows and lashed the water bindings tighter.

She glared at them. "You should never attack a woman even if she looks armed or not. For most of us have hidden powers." That was a lie, most people did not study magic.

She let go of the flow of magic.

They dropped to the ground with a crunch. There was a few seconds of scrambling before they all sprinted to the main street, running from the strange young woman with magical powers.

Ake giggled. It was not every day you beat off half a dozen armed men.

Glancing back at the store she shrugged. If someone in there wanted to hurt her, they would get the full blast of her magic.

She opened the door to the store and peered inside.

The only light source was a fire at the back of the room. Bookshelves filled the room and scrolls loaded them. A chair sat facing the fire.

"The map right next to you, little one, is the one you seek. But be gone, it is dangerous to travel the alley ways once dusk sets, no matter what power you have."

Ake looked down on the floor. Sure enough there was a map. The large letters printed on the front said Caendor. Just what she needed.

She bent down and picked up the map. When she turned to go, the person in the chair spoke. "Fly carefully, Phoenix of Water."

Shivers worked their way up Ake's back as she closed the door behind her.

It was a bizarre world in which she lived, a bizarre world indeed.

Chapter 25
The Phoenix of Fire

A creature bounced on his bed, laughing shrilly. "Wake up, wake up!" it shouted in his ear. "You're late to get Cobrau! The sun is up and you're not! Up! Up!"

Eside Thron sat up abruptly, nearly knocking his sister off his bed. Throwing the covers off, he shot out of bed, pulling on a pair of black pants and a shirt, clothes that would soon be dirty from hauling barrels off the ships that set anchor in Sunda. He rubbed his ear where the small crystal-gold earring stud was. In his deep sleep it had dug into his skin and left a sore spot.

"You're late!" his sister shouted again.

"Lana, yes, I heard," he said, clamping a hand over her mouth. She spit on his hand.

"You little monster!" Eside grabbed her and rubbed her face in the hand she had spit on. Screaming even louder, near enough to break Eside's ears, he let go, laughing. "Has Father left?"

"Before the sun rose," she said. "He was supposed to get you up, lazy."

Eside shot her a good-natured glare. "I think he did, but I fell back to sleep."

Lana jumped lightly on the bed. "Hurry, Cobrau's gonna be mad, lazy."

Running out of his room, he grabbed a slice of bread and shot out the front door, speaking a quick word of good morning to his mother on the way out.

Once in the busy street of Sunda, he weaved his way through the crowd for one block until he reached a small run down house. He thumped on the door.

A young woman threw open the door, blue eyes sharpening when she saw who it was. "You're late, Eside," she said, closing the door and joining him in the street.

"I slept in."

"So I thought but there's no time to waste." She burst into a run, pushing past the crowds of people. Surprised by her want to get to work, a job she hated, Eside watched her for a moment before running after her.

Wheezing from the exertion and hot day, Eside quickly dropped further behind his friend.

"Cobrau! Wait!" Eside yelled.

The young woman turned and tapped her fingers on her hips. She had red hair cut to her scalp with a sun shaped scar on her right cheek. Her clothes, green pants with white strips and a small white shirt, were grimy. A necklace with a seashell hung around her neck. At the moment her body language spoke of annoyance and a twinge of amusement.

Eside caught up at last, panting. He was relatively tall for his nineteen years. His own short red hair was drenched in sweat and his breathing was heavy. Running had never been an aptitude for him.

"Thank...you... for...waiting," Eside said between breaths.

Cobrau snorted. "You need to learn how to run."

Eside put his hands on his knees, trying to regain his breath.

"Come on. We're late and the boss is gonna kill us if we don't arrive at the dock before the first ship opens her haul." Eside straightened and followed Cobrau at a slow trot.

They finally reached the docks and Eside was more winded than he had ever been. The hot morning sun beat down on his neck already giving his fair skin a light sunburn.

The ships had not put down anchor yet and most were still coming into the bay. The white sails of the ships glistened, rippling with the moving of the ship. Sea gulls wheeled overhead, screeching. Men cleared the docks and merchants waited, hoping to get the best of the ship's supplies.

"Where have you two been?" a deep voice bellowed out.

Eside flinched and Cobrau stepped closer to him.

A large porky man came into view. His face was sunburned and his bald head was running with sweat. He stood in front of them, his stench washing over them.

Eside breathed through his mouth, gagging even so.

The man looked down at them. "Well?"

Cobrau stepped forward. "The ships haven't set anchor yet. We're on time."

"I said to get here by the time they enter the bay, not before anchor," the porky man said.

Cobrau lifted her lip. "Oh, shut it. You know we're on time." She pushed past the porky man and Eside followed her, murmuring a quick apology to their boss.

When they reached their work part of the docks, Eside threw off his shirt and began to unload the ship that had just set anchor.

Before long his back was sweaty. Next to him Cobrau wiped her hand across her brow.

"You know," Cobrau said as they carried a large barrel off the ship, "I'm leaving Sunda."

Eside almost dropped the barrel. Cobrau was his best friend. She was more than a friend. As little children they had been together day and night. She had given him his first kiss. He had always thought they would end up getting married.

"Eside?" Cobrau said, drawing Eside out of his past.

"What?"

"I'm leaving Sunda."

They set the barrel down and walked back to the ship to heave out another one.

"Where do you think you'll go?" Eside asked, forcing the words out.

"Wherever the winds take me. South, I think."

Eside grunted as they picked up another barrel. "To the lands of the Warlord?"

She ignored his question. "I know this is hard for you, Eside," Cobrau said, her blue eyes truly sorry. "I know we always thought we would grow old together and have grandchildren play at our house during Summer's Eve. But I don't feel complete. I need to go somewhere. Something calls," she uttered as an after thought.

They lowered the barrel to the ground.

"I'll wait for you," Eside said.

Cobrau smiled and pulled Eside over to the side, clasping his hands. "I might never come back."

Eside fought against the rising panic. Of course she wouldn't come back. "What are you going to do?" he asked, swallowing.

"I'll let fate decide that."

"When are you leaving?"

"After the third shift of dock hands today."

Eside clenched his jaw.

Cobrau put his hands around her waist and leaned her head on his shoulder.

"Perhaps, one day we will meet again."

Eside held her closer.

"I told you two not to smooch when on duty," their boss yelled.

Cobrau faced their boss, her temper flaming, "And I told you to shut it." Their boss went purple in the face but he turned around and walked away. Cobrau turned back to Eside and snuggled closer. "One day, I promise you, we'll meet again."

They hugged for a moment longer before getting back to work. It was an effort for Eside not to have his eyes water with tears.

When their shift ended, Cobrau pulled Eside behind a large crate.

"Before I go," she said, "I need something from you."

Eside pulled her close. "What?" he said sadly.

"A kiss."

Eside smiled and bent his head as her arms encircled his neck. Her lips met his and he moved his hands to her waist. She pressed closer to him.

Somehow, Eside thought, *this doesn't feel right. As much as I love her, we've never been this close.*

"I'm going to miss you," he said, breaking their kiss.

She looked up at him, her blue eyes bright. "Keep a place for me in your heart."

Cobrau stepped back and slipped off her seashell necklace. She hung it around Eside's neck.

"I will never forget what we had," she whispered, wrapping her arms around him one more time.

"Then why must you leave?" Eside murmured into her red hair.

"Because I'm called."

Eside kissed her one last time.

She turned to go.

Eside grabbed her arm. "Wait, I have something for you." Eside summoned his magic and created a pair of earrings. They were small round balls but inside was flaming fire.

He hung them in her ears. "Remember."

Cobrau kissed him one more time on the lips with soft passion. "Good-bye." She turned and left.

Eside pounded his fist into the crate. Life wasn't fair.

"Hey, kid!" his employer roared. "Get back to work! We have another ship coming in at noon with full cargo! Move it!"

Eside scowled, wishing he had Cobrau's talent at making people listen to him. Rubbing his sore muscles, he stepped back onto the gangplank and hurried up. Inside the cool cargo hold and away from the beady eyes of his boss, Eside leaned against a barrel.

She's gone, he thought, his heart beating painfully in his chest. *Why did she leave? And to the lands of the Warlord? What is she doing? Is life not good enough for her here? She has a good family, friends, a well paying job and me. I know she said she was called but who is calling her? Gods, why can't she stay?* Eside pleaded, trying hold back his tears.

Knowing it was fruitless, this crying and pleading with the gods, Eside wiped his cheeks with the back of his hand, took a deep breath and picked up the barrel.

Tottering down the gangplank under the weight of the barrel, he set it down among the others, the heat of the day once more making sweat break out across his forehead.

A bell tolled, announcing a quick break for the laborers. Eside joined a group of men standing by the barrels, passing around a large tankard of ale. He meant to get stinking drunk, but he could never stomach more than a cup full of the stuff. Even the smell of ale made him sick. When the tankard was handed to him, he shook his head and left to sit alone, deciding to take his misery as it came and not dampen the pain.

Ringing once more, the bell ended break and with a groan meant for someone of advanced years, Eside heaved himself to his feet and went back to work, every moment of it thinking of Cobrau.

Cß   Cℛ   ßʊ

"Aseik means Lord of Magic in the Old Tongue. In past days it meant Bringer of Death. Before the time of the First Dragons, being a shoi was the most honored thing, and armies were made up of only Lauke Aseik, Warrior Shoi," the head shoi of the Shoi School of Sunda said, rolling his quill between two fingers. "When two Lauke Aseik armies joined on the field of battle, it was said that it was lucky if more than ten were still alive. It was a slaughter. Days after the shoi war people living in the vicinity would report of strange happenings and sudden disappearances. So much magic had been used it continued to affect the surrounding area for years after the battle."

Sitting in a classroom with six other students, Eside cracked a yawn. It was near midnight and his daily lesson in magic always dragged on near the end. *It's time to bring out the fun.*

"Sir," Eside said respectfully, noticing the class was beginning to daydream, their eyes turning glassy, "I was wondering whether there were any places in the Northern Kingdom which still have unstable magic surrounding them."

The class perked up, interested.

The instructor frowned pensively. "There is only one that comes to memory. It is the Gangga Pass where the First Dragons fought their last battle. So much magic was used there that the magical plane actually merged with this world for a few seconds and created total chaos."

"Like this?" Eside summoned his magic and set the instructors quill on fire. With a yelp the instructor threw it on the floor and stamped out the fire. The class erupted into laughs and the instructor spent several hectic minutes calming everyone down.

"No, Eside Thron, I do not believe it was like that. I highly doubt they found it amusing." The instructor smoothed out his shirt, flickering off ash. "As much as your classmates enjoy your shenanigans, I do not, and I would appreciate it if you did not attempt another one."

Eside shrugged. "Why not, sir? This is a shoi school, after all. Aren't we supposed to be learning magic?"

"History, Eside, is part of learning magic. In order to understand something you must know its past."

Eside screwed up his face. "Really, sir? I understand you but I don't know your past."

The instructor let out an exasperated sigh. "Everyday we go through this, Eside, everyday. I want you to keep your mouth shut, you little fiend. I will never finish the lesson if you don't." The instructor's tone was annoyed but held a hint of affection.

Slouching in his chair, Eside clamped his mouth shut, watching the instructor. Talking about war and magic, the head shoi carried on in a dull tone, boring his subjects.

"Tell me," the teacher said, "when did the last Aseik shoi die?"

The class stared at the instructor, dumbfounded. Eside's lips quirked in a smile, but he kept them closed, pressing them together.

Rolling his eyes, the instructor waved at Eside. "Answer the question, Eside. You're the only one who can."

Eside smiled. "In the Fifth Age after hiding the Dragon's Rings somewhere in the Northern Kingdom."

The instructor nodded and went to describe the slow decline of shoi and how those gifted in the Art were slowly rebuilding their status in society.

Eside's mind drifted. *Yes, I know,* he thought, impatiently. *I've known this forever. Just let me get my ring and I won't ever disrupt your class again. I'm better than you, you know. Fire is my Talent and I'm stronger than all of you in it. I know the other Talents too, and I'm almost as good. Why won't you let me pass? I'll be stuck here forever!*

"Class dismissed," the instructor said.

Groaning as he massaged the cramps out of his legs, Eside left the Shoi School, hurrying down the dark street towards home.

Summoning his magic, he lit a flame on his palm to light his way. It was a damp night, the smell of rain thick in the air. His boots slid on the wet cobblestones but he managed to keep his balance all the way home.

Squeezing the door open and slipping in, he lit a small candle on the table, and extinguished the one on his palm. Exhausted, he collapsed on a chair, laying his head on the table, staring at the flame as it flickered.

He loved flame, how it mesmerized the eyes, and looked into the soul. His light brown eyes looked red as they reflected the fire, looking like small flames in the night.

The flame seemed to conquer the soul. It captured the mind and let it see into the depth of fire and its wonderful secrets. The lone flickering flame just sat there casting shadows on the wall and radiating a magic that filled Eside's blood with its power. The power of that single flame was enough to spellbind Eside. His eyes drank in its glowing heat and his face felt its gentle touch of magic.

But right now he was not thinking of the flame. His mind was on Cobrau and their last meeting. His dark mood crackled with the storm outside. He was angered about Cobrau's sudden departure.

Eside jumped as the storm outside got worse, the thunder screaming at the dark.

His parents and sister were asleep down the hall. *It's a wonder they can sleep in this racket,* Eside thought.

Eside's father was a fisherman and sold his catch everyday at the market, where he made little over ten copper chips. There were so many fishermen in the city that people could afford to be picky. His mother was a seamstress at one of the local stores. She made enough money to spend on clothes for her own family and to buy food. His sister was only twelve and went to school where she studied to become an artist. She was very good, Eside admitted, but painting was a poor job when it came to pay, but then again, so was being a shoi.

Eside jolted upright as a sudden thought jumped into his head. It was whispered that the Dragons were found and that one was in the Lost Mountains and the other in the Cyrain Plains. *The Dragons need me.* Eside shook his head. *No, I'm not needed. The Dragons do not need me. Don't be absurd. I'm just a common dockhand. Who studies magic,* a voice added. But the thought would not leave him alone. He kept feeling a tug to leave, a voice saying he was the Phoenix of the Fire, one of the six Phoenixes. *Is this what Cobrau felt, this tug, that feeling of need?*

Eside looked up as yelling voices could be heard outside over the din. They were probably the city guards going after Ole Clenny. Ole Clenny always refused to pay taxes. The guards came by once a month to get the money.

Leaping when the front door banged open, Eside gave a startled exclamation of surprise. Rain and wind swept in and the city guard entered.

Eside dove under the table as thunder sounded. The city guard's torches lit up the room. Eside's candle had blown out and fallen on the floor, plastering hot wax over the wood.

His parents came into the room, followed by his sister, holding a moth eaten stuffed rabbit. His sister looked a lot like him. Only her eyes were different.

"What do you want? We paid our taxes yesterday, as asked," his father said, his baldhead showing beads of sweat even though it was cold outside. His father was a tall, stocky man with a round ruby face and a square jaw. He constantly smelled of fish and ocean.

His mother was a short and round woman with a pointed chin. She had long delicate fingers that were meant for needlework, which clung to her husband's arm.

"We are not here to collect taxes, peasant," the Captain of the Guard said.

Eside's father knew he was poor but it was something else to say it to his face. He was a man of much pride. His father's face grew cherry red and his eyes popped out. "We are not peasants," he said in a strained voice, the veins in his neck sticking out. He took a menacing step forward.

The city guard pulled out his sword and ran his father through.

Eside choked, but shut up, knowing the city guard did not know he was there. His eyes filled with hot tears. His sister shrieked.

Screaming, his mother took a step to his fallen father, but the city guard shook his head. "You don't want to make your children parentless do you?"

His mother stepped back. "Who are you? What do you want?"

The city guard smiled coldly. "Your son."

"Why? What has he done?" his mother said, holding his sister closer.

"He is one of the Phoenixes meant to rule at the side under the Dragons. And by the Warlord's order, to be killed," he said. "Where is he?"

"You cannot have him."

The guard sneered. He took his already bloody sword and slashed his sword into her stomach. He smiled wickedly.

His mother's eyes dimmed and she dropped to the floor, dead.

Eside swallowed his scream one more time. Guilt rose up but he pushed it down.

"Burn the house. The boy is here. I know it. Set up a perimeter and make sure no one escapes." The captain left, followed by the other guards, the door slamming shut behind them.

Eside crawled out from under the table.

His sister was crying, kneeling at her mother's side. The blood had pooled around his sister and soaked into the bottom of her nightdress. Her fingers clutched her mother's and she whispered words that fell on deaf ears.

Eside went over to her and pulled her off the floor. "Lana, there is no time to mourn now. You must be strong," Eside said, feeling the loss of his parents sink down into him, a scar forever unhealed and unseen. He quickly kissed his fingers and pressed them on his mother and father's foreheads. In Sunda, it was a sign of blessing the souls in the Light.

"They're going to burn the house," Lana said, still crying.

"Don't worry."

Lana nodded.

"Fire can't burn me, Lana. I have a special power and it can't burn you as long as you hold my hand." Eside felt as his sister's small hand wrapped around his own and clung to it tightly.

Outside the rain and the wind continued, and over the noise Eside heard the order for their house to burn.

"Take my hand, be quiet and follow me."

Eside moved to their back door and waited.

"Eside..." his sister whimpered.

"Shhhh."

Eside watched as a torch was thrown through the window and landed on the wooden table. It sprang up into flame.

Two more were thrown in on the other side of the house and Eside heard more break the windows down the hall.

"It won't burn you. You'll just feel uncomfortable," Eside said pulling his sister to his side.

"You don't look uncomfortable." She watched, sweating, as the fire crept up the wall, the ceiling above them burning.

"I won't be. Burns and heat have never affected my body. Now, when I say three, we kick this wall, and it'll fall down. Then we run."

Lana dropped her stuffed rabbit, the flame consuming it intently. "Won't they see us?"

"No. I put an invisibility spell on us but it'll only last a few minutes. One...Two."

The wall in front of them went up in flame, as did all the other walls.

"Three!"

They both kicked the wall with all their might, and to Eside's surprise it fell over.

"Run," Eside whispered, the wind pushing them along.

They ran past the guards standing watch, without a glance in their direction.

"Hurry, we must get to the stables."

"Stables?" Lana asked, looking up at Eside.

"Quiet."

They ran down the street, splashing through puddles. The rain matted their hair to their heads and the water ran down their faces. Their clothes were wet and Lana's bare feet smacked against the cobblestones. The rain washed away the blood from their clothes and skin, leaving them clean.

They stopped by an old looking barn that showed the signs of rotting wood.

"Wait here. In the shadows," Eside said, the wind carrying his words to Lana's ears.

Eside crept into the building; the smell of wet hay and horse clogging his nose.

The stable was old. Rafters that supported the ceiling had large cracks in them and occasionally creaked when the wind blew too hard. Pigeons cooed from above and flapped their short wings, sending feathers floating down. Water dripped from the roof and fell to the ground to land in muddy pools. Wet yellow hay littered the floor.

He hurried over to a stall holding two horses. He quickly untied them and pulled them out into the storm, muttering a spell.

Lana was nearby waiting for him when he rushed out.

"Horses? We can't ride!" she said. "Why can't you transport us with your magic?"

"I've never been there before. I would get us lost in the magical plane if I tried to use my magic to get us there." Eside came over and picked Lana up. She was much smaller than him. He hoisted her up on the horse.

"I put a fire net spell on them. You can't fall off," he said, getting onto his own horse.

"Where are we going?"

"The Cyrain Plains," Eside said, kicking his horse into a gallop, Lana doing the same. They had seen enough nobles ride that they knew the main idea.

Lana's hands hugged the neck of her horse. "Why?"

Eside didn't answer. They rode in silence until they got out of the city and into open fields and treeless hills, the two moons shining behind the gliding clouds.

"Because I'm the Phoenix of Fire," Eside said. "And the Lord Dragon is there."

"Can I cry now?" Lana said softly.

"Yes."

Eside looked at his sister, silver tears were rolling down her face, her cheeks wet.

Eside didn't cry, he would not cry, not again. To cry was to show weakness and to show a weakness was to die. He could not keep his mind off his parents however and he thought over their murder. They had died trying to protect him. They had sacrificed themselves for someone they loved. He would never forget what they did. Just as he would never forget Cobrau.

He knew war was coming, he could feel it in his bones and they shivered with fear. But the fear was laced with anticipation.

Chapter 26
The Phoenix of Earth

The wet clay molded under his deft touch, slowly shaping into a bowl. Using his magic to keep the clay from falling into itself, Ryen applied the last touches, admiring his work as he set it into the kiln.

Washing his hands in water and drying them on his pants, Ryen tore another hunk of clay from the much larger pile. This time he did not dirty his hands but summoned his magic once more and sculpted the clay into a beautifully wrought vase. Taking three more pieces of clay, he crafted them into another vase, a large bowl and a plate. Setting them in the kiln, he washed his hands once more.

"Anything else you would like me to do, sir?" Ryen asked the man who owned the pottery shop, the man who employed Ryen for his Talent in earth magic.

The potter looked up from a pot he was painting, his spectacles perched on his nose. "Did you finish all twelve of the ones I asked you to do? Several of those pieces are being picked up tomorrow."

"Yes, sir. I finished all of them," Ryen said.

"Well and good, Ryen." The potter reached into his pocket and pulled out a small bag of money. "Here's today's pay and I expect to see you tomorrow. Business is always good when people know you've been working. They particularly like the spell you put on the pots to keep them from breaking." The potter looked at Ryen, tapping his fingers on the clay he was molding. "I really should pay you more. You keep my customers coming back for the quality of work."

Ryen shook his head. "That won't be necessary, sir. The money you give me is more than enough." Ryen did not add that it was all that kept him alive when his parents declined to feed him. "It's not like I asked you to pay me in the first place. I enjoy making pots. You were the one who decided to give me the money, sir."

"Until later then," the potter replied, turning back to his work at hand.

Ryen left the shop and walked out into the streets of Manel, enjoying the warm sun that shone down.

Ryen Dael, born of the Day of Dragon Birth, was nineteen. He was thin from the occasional lack of food, his ribs and collar bone showing through. His skin was tanned and spotted with moles and freckles. His short hair was the color of dirt, dark and rich, his eyes the color of a forest of bloom-ing trees.

Coming from a home that had money to spend, many people new to the city wondered why Ryen worked for the potter. They thought that question was answered when they hit their first bankruptcy. Living in Manel, money could come and go as fast as the clouds in the sky swept by. But they were wrong. His family was one of the few that knew how to keep the money flowing in and that was why Ryen did not work for the money. He worked to get away from his family.

He lived in a nice house, with his two sisters and younger brother, and his parents. Ryen hated his parents. His mother always insulted him, and said he was not good enough; his father beat him. Ryen spent as much time away as he could. He had a scar on his back where his father had hit him with a whip. It had put a five inch long, bloody slash down his backside.

His parents wouldn't take care of it so he had spent a whole month at a neighbor's, who cleaned the wounds and cared for him. When he got back his father had beat him, for "scaring them and disappearing." His sisters, mainly the older one, were not of any help. All they did was tattle on him and get him into more trouble. His brother looked up to him, but his parents saw it was fear instead of awe, and it gave his father more reasons to beat him.

Ryen had found out he had magical talents when he was twelve. It was ironic that it was through his father Ryen found his only joy in life.

༼ ༼ ༽

His father had just finished beating him. It was supper time and the family was around the table, everyone except his brother. He was still in his mother's womb. His mother served his sisters as much as they wanted, and his father heaping piles. His mother missed him.

Ryen had looked at his mother and said, "Don't I get any?"

His mother looked back at him and scowled. "What have you done today to deserve dinner?"

"I washed the clothes, tended the garden and went to the market to buy food, just as you asked," Ryen had said.

His father, who had remained quiet, burst in. "I don't care what you have done, and for all I care you are a slave, a thing meant to fulfill our needs. You have no place in society. You are scum! We are disgraced to have one such as you in the family." His father had yelled at him, screaming his rage.

He had learned long ago never to yell at his father but sometimes all you learn is forgotten. Ryen exploded, his temper cold. "You have treated me like I was nothing since I was born. I have done nothing to you. I have made this place a better home by cleaning it. I helped you create a new drink for your customers at your inn that brought in more money. I bought all the food that sits on this table. I have done nothing but help, and all you do is beat me, starve me, and make me sleep in the attic! You—"

His father had slammed his meaty hand down on the table, the dishes rattling. "Shut up!" he bellowed, standing up, his chair hitting the floor. "You must learn not to talk back. A beating for you, boy!"

His father grabbed Ryen by the hair.

Ryen snapped. Something within boiled, as if fuel had been added on to flame.

Ryen felt a power come into him. It swept him up, binding him to its sweetness.

Without knowing it, Ryen caused an earthquake. It only had lasted a second, and it was small.

His father stopped then continued his advance.

"Stop! Or I'll hurt you," Ryen had yelled.

His father guffawed, a snort blowing out his moustache.

Ryen felt the power inside him, and he used it this time. He made the ground roll with waves, like an ocean during a storm. This time he caused damage. All across the small city of Manel, buildings collapsed and houses caught on fire when they fell. From the nearby mountains rocks had fallen, damming streams and flattening homes.

His father fell on his face with a most satisfying crunch.

CR   CR   RO

Ryen shook his head, clearing his mind of that bittersweet memory. That day Ryen knew he had powerful magical abilities. He had gone to the small magic school down the street, to find out if it were true. They had tested him and said he was a shoi of Earth Magic, a rare thing for one to be so powerful in an element.

Never going to Shoi School, Ryen had instead taught himself the ways of earth magic and had learned more than he could ever learn from an instructor or so he hoped.

Smiling to an old couple walking past him down the street, Ryen opened his moneybag and jingled out several coins. Ducking under a doorway, the smell of bread surrounded him.

"Ah, Ryen, how nice it is to see you," a young woman said as she kneaded bread on a table. A smear of flour was across her forehead. She dusted her hands off, pushing back a loose strand of hair. "What can I do for you today?"

"Hello, Lyrina. I'll have two of your loaves today," he said. "How's your uncle doing?"

Lyrina waved a hand as she wrapped one of his loaves in brown paper. "You know how that old grouch is," she said with affection. "He's been uptight lately with the news of war in the south, says the war is going to put him out of business. Don't know where he got that. I tried to tell him that a baker will never go out of business unless everyone else dies. People gotta eat, you know." She handed him the loaves, smiling. "He doesn't listen to me."

Ryen laughed. "I don't see why not." He thanked her and ducked back out the door, continuing along his route home.

Moving down the street, saying greetings to some of the people he knew, Ryen came to small house on the edge of town. He knocked on the door and waited patiently.

The door creaked opened and a pair of blue eyes peered out. When they spotted Ryen, the door swung open and a middle-aged woman with a child on her hip smiled warmly at Ryen.

Ryen handed her the loaves. "These are for you, ma'am."

"Ryen, my dear, you shouldn't. I-I can manage on my own," the woman said. "Every day after work you come here and give us bread. You should not."

Ryen shoved the loaves into her hands. "Think of your children, ma'am. You don't want them to go hungry."

She nodded, and blinked a few times, clearing her eyes of the tears. "You're so good to us, Ryen. With my husband leaving…what would I do without you?"

"It's the best I can do, ma'am, and I'm proud to do it," he said. "If I could spare all my money, I'd give it to you."

The woman patted his arm. "I'm glad you don't, dear. You need it for yourself. Mind me, leave your father's house as soon as possible. I don't want him finally killing you with those beatings of his. Save up your money, dear, and buy a house far from here where they cannot find you."

"Don't worry, ma'am, I will in just time. I almost have enough."

"That's good to hear, dear. Now, send your brother over later to play with my children. They do love it when he comes over to play, especially when he brings that candy those sisters of yours make."

"I'll tell him, ma'am," Ryen said, giving her a low bow and closing the door to the rickety house.

Hopping off the steps to the house, Ryen jogged down the road towards home, a feeling of immense dislike wallowing up in him when he saw the large white house in the distance, the stone wall surrounding the house reminding him of a prison.

Ryen stopped before reaching the house, and bent down, shifting the dirt with his magic to uncover a small chest. Unlocking the chest, he dumped all, save three of the coins, into it and buried it once more.

He hid his money in the chest and underground for fear of his sisters finding it if he kept it in his room and giving all his hard earned money to their father.

Reaching the walls that protected the mansion, Ryen slipped in a small side door and made his way across the grounds to the servant's quarters, a place where he was safe until dinner came around and he was forced to eat with his family.

A young servant boy caught his arm as Ryen walked into the kitchen. "Ryen," the voice said, high and frightened. "They're looking for ye."

Ryen did not need to ask who "they" were. His parents no doubt had a chore for him, as they always did.

"Where are they?"

The boy smiled a gaped tooth smile. "I told them ye were in the root cellar. They're heading there now, ye might want to go before they come back. I heard ye father say somethin' about a whippin'."

Ryen cursed. *Damn them*, he thought furiously. *Why can't they ever leave me alone? I did all they asked of me this morning. I cleaned the gutters and the walkways, I fixed that hole in the roof and I cleaned the library. What do they want?* Ryen's eyes widened. *Damn it to hell! I forgot to clean that dining room! Damn it! Now I'm really in for it.*

Ryen thanked the servant boy and handed him the coins. "Keep one for yourself and give the others to the cook. I believe it's her turn." Ryen had made it a habit to pay the servants extra in turns since his father paid the bare minimum for the amount of work they did.

Standing in the shadow of the doorway, Ryen looked over the grounds, searching for his parents. Not finding them, he let out a sigh of relief, stepped from the doorway and walked quickly across the grounds and towards the gates. His heart was in his throat, fear of a beating first on his mind.

Running the last few feet to the gate, he unlocked it and slipped out. *I have to get to the forest. It's the only place they won't go to get me.*

Sprinting down the road for all he was worth, he charged head long into the woods, branches snapping against his face.

Ryen flew through the forest, jumping rocks and dodging downed trees. Out of breath and breathing heavily, he stopped next to a large boulder. He leaned up against it, his chest constricting in pain. Gulping down air he slid down to the forest floor.

He had not had a beating for several days and the many welts on his back were almost gone. The scars on his back he would carry for the rest of his life, the markings of the father he resented.

I hate them! Ryen screamed in his mind. *I hate them! Why do they hate me? What have I done? I will leave one day and never come back. I will go so far, they will not be able to find me!* The thoughts in his mind jumbled together in pain and hate, rolling over each other and giving him a headache.

His breath recovered, Ryen pushed himself to his feet and laid his hand on the gray rock he had been leaning against.

Ryen felt the power underneath his hands as he moved them along the rock's surface. The earth magic was everywhere in a forest, beneath him, above him, next to him, everywhere. The power was a sweet thing, like honey and flowers with sugar, a taste so sweet it surpassed even the sweetest of candies.

Ryen looked up at the tree canopy, dark clouds could be seen above. Dark rolling clouds and lightning.

If Ryen had taken a step forward at that time, he would have been killed. A lightning bolt whizzed down and struck the tree nearest to him.

Ryen flew backwards and hit the ground, knocking the breath out of his lungs. His vision swam for several moments.

When he finally got up, his hair was standing on end. The tree that had been hit was gone; nothing remained but a black spot on the ground.

"Close, uh?" a voice said.

Ryen whirled around. Standing a few feet away was a man who held himself in such a manner that made Ryen feel threatened. "Who are you?" Ryen asked.

"The name's Cor. I was sent here to get you," Cor said, his voice light, giving away nothing but hinting at something.

"Me? Why?" Ryen asked cagily.

Cor took a step forward and sat on a nearby rock, his gray cloak swimming around his feet. "I was sent here by his Lord, the Warlord Raxsen."

Ryen was taken back. The Warlord was Evil. What the hell would the Warlord want with a despised son of a rich merchant who worked with a potter to make extra money and keep himself from starving to death?

"You never answered why," Ryen said, a deep loathing bubbling up from somewhere.

Cor smiled. "Ryen, hard times are coming. The Dragons have been found and so have three of the Phoenixes. One of them is you." Ryen was stunned. "You are the Phoenix of Earth, the other two of Fire and Water. They have already chosen to join the Dragons. Now it is your turn to choose, Good or Evil, Light or Dark. Choose wisely." The man clenched his fist, his eyes clouding over.

"Tell me, what does a person such as yourself do?" Ryen asked. There was no way he would join the side of the Warlord, but he would get as much information as possible.

"We have many different jobs. Mostly it's assassination that we excel in, that and getting men to join the Warlord. We rate just below sylai and rogui, which is a grand thing, for they are of the Dark Lord's own blood and we are of the Warlord's creation."

Ryen had heard of sylai, those strange seemingly human like beasts. The legends of the past told of them and how they conquered the world for the Dark Lord in the Second Age.

Cor suddenly became cold. "Decide. Which side are you on?"

Ryen grabbed at the magic deep within him. "Not yours."

"Then I shall kill you." Cor pulled a dirk from within his cloak.

Before Cor could react Ryen threw a ball of molten earth at him. Cor's skin sizzled, blisters expanding and popping. Cor died there, his body nothing but ash.

Ryen stood there, frozen. He had killed a man; one filled with malice but still a man, someone who breathed, who had a life.

As Ryen stood staring at the corpse, a sudden spontaneous thought entered his mind. He was needed, in the Cyrain Plains, with the Lord Dragon. It was a need so imposing Ryen felt his feet moving before he could stop them.

He ran as fast as he could, all the way back to his home. He pushed aside anything in his way, including trees. The forest looked like a huge beast had run through it by the time he reached the road to his house.

He opened the gate to his house and was immediately confronted by his father. His father stalked towards Ryen and barked, "Boy! Where do you think you are going? Stop! You have chores to do, boy! Stop or I will beat you!"

Ryen ignored him and raced into the barn. He pushed down the stable boy who tried to stop him. Throwing open the doors, he jumped onto a big gray. He did not need a saddle. Bare back was good enough. Kicking the gray in its sides, the horse knocked down the stable doors and bolted from the stable.

His father blocked Ryen's way out of the courtyard. Ryen reined his horse to a stop. "Put that horse back! Now!" his father screamed, spittle flying from his mouth.

"I'm leaving," Ryen said coldly. He moved his stunned father aside with magic, lifting him up in the air and setting him none too gently on the ground. "I am done with this family and I will not come back. If I do, it won't be because I want to."

Ryen threw his horse into a gallop. He had two days to get from Manel to the Pass between the Gangga Mountains and to the city of the Daaguwh.

He made his horse go faster.

He was not certain of his future anymore. He had once thought that he would have his own little farm, far away from his parents when he saved up enough money to buy his own place. He would marry and have children and live to an old age. He would tell stories to his grandchildren and sit by the warm fire on a rainy day covered in blankets. When he died only his children and grandchildren would remember him. He would be forgotten but his life would have been filled with love.

Now the future was a misty haze that floated over a valley, obscuring the cliff not far from where he was standing. Oh how cruel the gods could be of cheating a man from his life and giving him certain death.

Ryen stopped once as he left his father's house, and that was to pick up the chest filled with his money. He did not stop as he rode his horse southeast towards the Gangga Pass, flying across the hilly land.

The Gangga Mountains, their peaks dappled with snow, watched him as he rode, his horse given speed and endurance from the gods to let him accomplish his journey to the Cyrain Plains and Dagau, the land of the Daaguwh Ile.

His horse gave out even with the power of the gods behind it as he galloped through Saar.

Ryen tumbled across the cobblestone, skin ripping from his hands and knees as he tried to slow his rolling.

Bleeding and sore, he ignored the pain and left his dead horse in the street. He found his way to the stables and handed the grooms several gold chips for the best horse. Once more in the saddle, he pushed his horse east along the Gangga River.

Ryen had been riding a day when the ground began to incline upwards. He slowed his horse to a trot, all his senses alert. Aware of the rumors of the Gangga Pass and the dangers that dwelled there, he was careful not to make too much noise as he crossed the pass.

As he neared the pass, a spear sprung out of the ground in front of his horse. His horse reared and Ryen fought to control the spooked beast. Calming the horse, Ryen sat in the saddle. "Who's there?" he called, the hair prickling along the back of his neck.

"What are you doing crossing into the land of the Ile?" a voice called from one of the rocks.

Ryen searched the rocks for a person but to no avail. "I was called by the Lord Dragon."

A woman and a man, one on either side of Ryen, stood up on the rocks. Both had weapons adorning their bodies so that they reminded Ryen of a moving armory. The woman had her bow notched and pointed at Ryen, a gleam of suspicion in her eyes. The man, his arms covered in strange tattoos, held a spear with a curved blade in his hands.

"The Lord Dragon, you say?" the woman said, her voice accented. "Are you a Phoenix?"

Ryen nodded. "I am the Phoenix of Earth."

The woman lowered her bow. "Cross the pass carefully, Phoenix of Earth. The Nekid are joining for battle. The Lord Dragon would not be pleased if one of them killed you."

Ryen nudged his horse on, his back itching, as he knew the Ile warriors watched him from above.

Reaching the pass, Ryen was surprised to find that the land of the Ile was not far below, only a few hundred feet. On the other side of the pass he had had to climb thousands of feet up to reach the pass. His decent would be easy.

Guiding his horse down, Ryen felt destiny suddenly weigh down his shoulders, the lives of thousands a burden he now had to carry until his dying day.

Leaving the dangers of the pass, Ryen forced his horse into a gallop across the Cyrain Plains, heading towards the Lord Dragon, the Dragon of the Rising Sun.

Chapter 27
The Phoenix of Air

The music carried over the low babble of voices, filling the ballroom with its sweet and delicate melody. Adding richness to the surroundings, the music carried on, pleasing to the ears and eyes as it controlled the movement of the dancers on the ballroom floor.

Kiera Aade watched them sullenly. The Prince of Zayen, a handsome man in his middle twenties danced with one of the court beauties, a girl whose family was low in court and held no sway with the King much unlike Kiera's family.

Her family was next in line to succeed the throne. If for any reason the prince, the current heir, should fall ill and die before he had any children, Kiera's father would be crowned prince and heir to the throne. Once the

King died her father would then be King and she would be the Princess, heir
to the throne. She lavished in the possibility of becoming a princess. To her
a princess was what every girl strived to be. Kiera knew that if she ever
became the Princess of Zayen, she would be considered the most beautiful
woman in the country. Of course she thought she was already beautiful so it
did not matter much, one way or the other.

Kiera was not beautiful. She was plain and could even be considered
ugly, but she believed she was the most gorgeous of all ladies. She was
nineteen, of medium height, and very slim. She had long white-blonde hair
that shone in the sunlight, probably the most intriguing thing regarding her
appearance. Her blue eyes were normal and her pointed chin made her full
lips seem barely above standard. From her ears hung silver earrings
encrusted with blue jewels and around her throat was a silver necklace with
a large black stone at the end, which matched the lace garnishing her gown.
Her dress didn't help her appearance. It was a dark blue with long sleeves
and a very low neck, so low it brought jealous looks from the other women
in the room and appraising looks from the men. The dress puffed out
enough to make her look like an over grown pumpkin. It was the style at
Court and Kiera was always in style, never wanting to be thought of less
because of the gowns she wore. In commoner terms she was considered a
snotty brat.

The only other interesting thing about Kiera was the fact that she
studied the art of magic. Not just plain magic but air magic. She proved
this by wearing a silver chain necklace with a *lapis lazuli* dangling from the
end. Or she usually wore it, she had taken off the necklace for the ball.

Fanning her face with a lavish fan, she glared at the beauty the prince
danced with. The young woman caught Kiera's gaze and faltered.

Kiera smirked. *Get your hands off my prince*! she thought. *He's mine
and you cannot take him from me!*

Never having talked intimately with the prince, she only knew him
from the few moments they had talked together and those moments were
spent exchanging juicy bits of gossip.

"How dare he," she muttered, sipping at her wine, her pale blue eyes
staring at the pair with malevolence.

Glancing around the room, she noticed a man dressed in well cut black
clothes finer than those of the prince, watching her from a distance, his face
masked of any thought. He saw her glance and his lips quirked in a smile.
Pushing through the crowd of people, he moved up beside her.

Handsome was not a strong enough word to describe the face and body
of the man. His green eyes were vivid and carried a look of power Kiera
had only seen in Kings. Clean-shaven as his face was, a dark appearance of
a beard showed, matching the dark brown of his hair. His high cheekbones
gave his eyes a slanted look and made the admirer notice the secrets hidden
behind them. Body lean and powerful in such a way that caused Kiera to
think of him as a warrior, the man moved with a feline grace and certain

swagger to his walk. His clothes were black as pitch but a silver belt bejeweled his waist and a large ring with a blue diamond clasped to it encircled his middle finger.

Standing near to him, Kiera felt her breath squeeze from her lungs and her heart fluttered in her breast. "Milord," she said, demurely, "I see you were entranced by my appearance, if that is what made you stare so."

The man, no more than twenty five, gave her an approving glance with his vivid green eyes. "My lady, surely you know your appearance draws the eyes of all."

Kiera laid a hand on his arm, facing him and letting him get a good look at her bosom. "Do you think so? You honor me, milord."

The man, keeping his eyes locked at her face, did not flush. Instead he held out his arm. "Dance with me," he commanded.

She obeyed, letting him walk her to the center of the dance floor. As they spun around the dance floor, she watched him under the long lashes, fascinated by him.

"Do you dapple in the Art?" he asked suddenly, smiling down at her with such charm she felt as if her heart had stopped beating.

"I am a shoi, if that is what you mean, my lord. I received my *lapis lazuli* a year ago. Why do you ask?"

"You had the look of a woman who knew magic, my lady," he said.

"Why thank you, milord," Kiera said cordially. "Not many notice my Talent. What of yourself, milord? Do you study the Art?"

He laughed, a deep rich sound that Kiera felt drawn to. "I have studied with some of the most powerful shoi, my lady."

"Really? Who might that be, milord?" she murmured huskily. "Any whom I would know?"

He cocked an eyebrow at her. "Perhaps."

She frowned up at him, giving him her practiced pouting look. "Won't you tell me, milord? I'm sure I know of whom you speak."

"I'm sure you do," he said, gracefully changing dances as the music switched.

When he refused to answer her about who he had studied under and would not be persuaded by any of her tricks to get men to do what she wanted, she heaved a sigh, exaggerating it in her bosom. She smiled with triumph when she saw his eyes travel down to her cleavage. She had him where she wanted him. He was caught nicely in her snare.

"Milord, I am growing weary of this dancing. May we sit and talk, perhaps?"

He nodded and twirled her off the dance floor to a pair of chairs. Fanning herself, Kiera sat, the strange lord sitting next to her.

"You have not told me your name yet, milord," she said, turning to him and bending over slightly to fix her gown, knowing his eyes traveled elsewhere.

"I did not give it."

She held out her hand. "I am Kiera Aade, milord."

He brought her gloved hand to his lips and brushed them against her hand. "A pleasure, my lady." His green eyes twinkled with a dark light.

Fanning herself vigorously, Kiera turned to him and said, "I'm growing hot, would you accompany me outside for some fresh air, milord?" *I will get answers from you, strange man, and maybe I will be able to use you to elevate my own standing with the prince,* she thought.

Giving her a bemused glance, he stood, laid her arm on his and escorted her outside. Once the fresh air enveloped them, Kiera clipped her fan shut and hung it around her wrist, letting it dangle there.

They walked along one of the paths twisting throughout the gardens, the glow of the two moons bathing everything in a soft white light.

"Where are you from, milord?" Kiera asked, moving close enough so their arms brushed as they walked.

The man chuckled. "A land you know nothing about."

"Where?" she insisted. "I'm sure I know of it."

"I am from Atay," he said.

"Atay? But I know of it! It is the land of the Warlord," Kiera said, intrigued by the handsome stranger. "Why are you here?" she asked, pressing closer to him, dying for answers and letting her body get them for her.

The man shook himself free. "As much as you think you have seduced me, my lady, you have not."

Kiera gaped at him, an angry red creeping across her cheeks. "How dare you accuse me of—"

"Seduction?" he laughed darkly. "My lady, I am not accusing you of it. It is simply your style just as my style is to confront my target head on."

"Target?" Kiera said weakly, a feeling of dread descending upon her.

"I've been watching you for a while, Kiera. My lord would be pleased to know that you fit his needs well. It is only a matter of time before I get what I want of you." He grasped her shoulders. "As of now, however, I suggest that you get home. A storm is coming."

Kiera wrenched herself from his grasp and fled, running through the ballroom and across the hall, down a flight of steps and out the main door, issuing orders to have her carriage brought around.

Quicker than she expected, the carriage came and the door opened for her. Kiera jumped in, saying, "Take me home."

Pulling into the courtyard, Kiera got out, sighing in relief, knowing she was a safe distance from the strange man and his strange master.

The carriage pulled away and Kiera, not wanting to face her parents over why she had left the ball so early, sat down on a small stone bench. Picking up a bag of bird seed she had laid there earlier, she poured it out and flung it across the ground, amazed as birds suddenly flocked to the ground, nibbling the ground for the seeds.

She held out her hand filled with seed and waited for a bird to come and eat. Kiera smiled as a blue bird nibbled at the seeds in her hand. She loved birds.

Trees lined the walls of the courtyard and two fountains sprouted water. About ten yards away was her younger brother playing a game of Fox's with three friends, oblivious to her return. Another ten yards stood her house. It was a grand house, the biggest in all of Mauke, Zayen, not including the palace. Her family was second when it came to money in Mauke, the palace only beating them because of taxes.

A bird jumped into her hand.

A slight breeze blew by and the birds she was feeding flew off. Kiera stood up, her whitish-blonde hair flying out behind her. Clouds had started to gather in the sky.

Kiera looked up at the sky, worry twisting her face. *He said there would be a storm.*

Shivering with sudden cold, she hurried towards the house, sidestepping as her brother shot a rock at her.

Kiera was the oldest in the family. Her other sister was four years younger and her brother eight. Being the oldest she got spoiled, a little bit too much she admitted, but so what? She would inherit the family estates and place in court as the representative to the King as the next family in line for the throne.

By the time she got inside and to the antechamber, the wind had picked up speed and the rain pelted the windows. Kiera shivered. She hated storms.

"You..."

Kiera looked around, startled, but she was alone. There were no guests standing in the room, chatting. No parents softly scolding her brother. The two sofas and four chairs were empty. The window seat sat vacant and the fire crackled, dying embers creating a shadow. She was alone.

Kiera shook her head and sat down on a large cream sofa. She picked up a book lying on the table in front of her and began to read by candle-light.

"*You should...not...be...alone,*" a voice said like the wind murmuring over water.

Kiera looked up from her book. Her hand reached up to grab the necklace encircling her throat.

"*Whisper...to...me,*" it said.

Kiera closed her book, the noise echoing like a horn in the mist.

"Hello? Who's there?" Kiera whispered, frightened. The candles blew out.

"*Ahhh...to whisper...*"

Kiera froze as a breeze drifted by her ear.

"*I...seek...the...one...who...is...the...Phoenix of Air.*"

Kiera's eyes widened and she pulled her knees up to her chest.

"*In...danger...you...are, Kiera,*" the voice sighed.

A door banged shut somewhere.

Kiera screamed. The sound fell into silence, her heart racing.

"To...scream...is...to...do...nothing...Do not...fear."

Kiera scrambled over to the fire, throwing log after log onto it, until it was blazing. The heat seared her face.

Kiera pushed back up against a wall covered with paintings.

"You... cannot... hide...from...me," the thing said, its voice becoming a low hum.

"Who are you?" Kiera said, her face pale.

"A...messenger."

"From who?"

"I... was...sent...on...wings...of...Air. I'm... a... spirit... of... Air. I... was...told...to warn...you ...you...are...the...Phoenix of Air. Tried...to... warn others...too... late." The voice grew dimmer.

Suddenly a gust of wind shot down the chimney and the fire went out, leaving Kiera in utter blackness.

"Warlord...knew...you... would...be... easiest...to...win...to...his ...side. Riches...power...could... win...you ...over." The voice became lower then a whisper, *"I...must...go. Beware."*

Kiera felt a presence leave the room, and emptiness settled.

"Hello, Kiera," a deep voice said.

Kiera jumped. She pressed herself up closer to the wall as she saw a figure enter the room.

"Don't pretend I don't know where you are. I know everything." Light flooded the room as four candles were suddenly lit.

Kiera stared at the man in front of her. He was the man she had danced with at the ball, the one who had worn clothes more expensive than the prince, the one who had warned her about the storm, the man from Atay.

He smiled at her. She almost fainted his smile was so stunning.

"I'm David Peirce, First General in the Warlord's Army." He smiled again, and Kiera had to push herself against the wall to stay standing. She had become dizzy when he smiled.

"What do you want, milord?"

"A decision," he said. "It won't hurt you. All I need is for you to make a choice. Not that it really matters. It seems as if the others did not manage to get the other Phoenixes. So why get one when you need them all?"

"What must I decide?" Kiera said, moving off the wall.

"You must decide the side you want to be on, between Dragon and Warlord."

"You promise you won't kill me?"

"Of course, the Warlord said that you are least powerful, so I could do as I wished. He said it didn't matter since the other fools didn't finish their jobs," Pierce said, his deep voice like a curse.

Kiera moved behind the couch. Now there were two objects between them.

"My little sweet, if I wanted to hurt you, I would. You will owe me now for my kindness," he said, proving his words by forming a ball of fire in his hands.

"I... want to be on... the Dragons' side. I am the Phoenix of Air, am I not?"

Kiera jumped as he suddenly roared with laughter.

"So, she did get to you first. It was pointless to come," Pierce said shrugging, his smile dimming. "I thought perhaps our little rendezvous at the ball would help you decide."

Kiera watched him as he murmured a spell.

"Ah well," he bit his lip in sarcastic pity. "Now you are a parentless child. Your parents have forgotten of you."

Kiera felt her heart give a jerk. He had cast a very powerful spell, one that could cause people to forget everything, even that they had a daughter. She had no family, she wasn't an heir nor in line for the throne. "No!" she cried, fear clutching her heart and tearing up her insides.

Kiera started to move further away, but he stopped her. "No, my little one." She felt herself being picked up by powers of air and moved forward until she was face to face with her captor.

She couldn't use her magic. He had put a bind on it and if she reached for the power within her being, he would kill her.

"You see, I decided to leave my mark on you," Pierce whispered in her ear, his breath warm against her neck.

Kiera pulled away. She was quickly stopped as Pierce used more magic and froze her movements.

Pierce put his forefinger and middle finger together. "This will only hurt a little." He pulled back her hair with his other hand. He put his two fingers to her neck, digging the nails into her skin.

Kiera whimpered as she felt the skin on her neck sizzle.

If she could have looked, she would have seen a black skull with glowing red eyes, and blood around the edges.

Pierce dropped her hair. "The Warlord's Mark, my love. You can never escape it. It has sealed your fate to him."

And he disappeared.

Kiera dropped onto the floor, tears leaking out of her eyes. She laid there, breathing hard, her eyes half closed.

She pushed herself up, her neck aching in unbearable pain.

As she put her hand on her skin to feel the pain, she felt the urge to leave. She knew her parents had forgotten she was even born. She believed Pierce. The need to leave grew stronger. She needed to go to the Lost Mountains. For the Lady Dragon. For the Light and all that was good in the world.

Kiera ran out of the house, the storm outside thrashing at her clothes, the trees bending like toys in the wind. Lightning crackled in the sky and the rain felt like bee stings. She ran to the stables and saddled her horse.

She took one last look at her house as she rode through the courtyard and into the street. No more a princess. Her dreams died there in the rain. Now her way of life depended solely on others.

Two days to get from Mauke to the Lost Mountains. She couldn't afford to stop. Wishing she could transport herself there, but knowing she could not, she pushed her horse to go faster.

The pain in her neck was now a dull throb. That skull on her neck had a purpose, she knew. The purpose eluded her, however. She knew, as Pierce had said, that it sealed her fate to that of the Warlord, but she did not know what else it did.

The skull's eyes burned red as she rode through the city in the rain, blood trickling down her back and staining her dress.

Chapter 28
The Phoenix of Life

Riak Tghil bit into a slice of bread, chewing thoughtfully as she looked out the window, watching the sky slowly change into daylight. Her gray and black cat lay curled in her lap, its orange eyes slits of pleasure.

The flower near the windowsill of the kitchen was wilted. Summoning her magic for a brief moment, she breathed life into the small plant, smiling to herself when the flower turned a dazzling red and its once brown leaves a lush green.

The cook of the manor walked briskly into the room, a movement odd for one of her weight. She threw a log onto the fire and stirred the large pot boiling above it. "Ye'd better hurry it up, Riak dear. The Lady Rachelas will be up soon," the cook said.

Riak waved her piece of bread. "The Lady won't be up for a while. She has a picnic planned with Lord Styade and wants her beauty rest."

The cook nodded and turned back to her stirring, adding in spices every now and then.

Riak got up, finishing off her morning meal. The cat dropped to the ground and immediately began meowing to be picked up. Riak picked up the cat, plopping it around her shoulders. The cat snuggled into her neck, its tail curling under her chin.

Shorter than average height, Riak had a round figure. She had a little more weight than most, but she did not mind. She was a firm believer in beauty coming from the soul. Her long brown hair tinted with blonde was pulled back in a loose ponytail. Her gray eyes were always filled with a passion in everything she did. Her natural red lips were luscious and held a ready smile. The clothes she was wearing did nothing for her figure. A dark blue skirt and white blouse were clean, as was required if you were a maid. Even though the high neck of her clothes hid it, a unique necklace was around her neck. Encircled around her throat was a small wreath of flowers, eight years old but looking as if they had just been picked.

Riak had been a student at the Shoi School since she was three. After the death of her parents at age fourteen she had dropped out, needing to take care of herself. Her teacher had told her she was beyond comparison unless one included the Dragons. She used her magic occasionally, usually for chores or getting simple things done quickly. When she worked at the temples in Atii on her days off, she used her magic to heal the sick or wounded. It was a pastime of hers. She was not one to put aside a chance to help someone else.

Bounding up the stairs of the manor, she paused at the top, a hand pressed over her chest as she regained her breath. Smoothing down her clothes to look presentable, she pushed open the door to Lady Rachelas' room.

A lump lay sprawled in the middle of the large bed, a small snoring issuing from it. Resisting the urge to jump on the lump, Riak walked across the large room and thrust aside the curtains, shedding bright sunlight into the bedroom. Her cat bounded off her shoulders into a pool of sunlight where he set about the task of cleaning himself from tail to head.

"Go away, Riak. I want to sleep," the lump on the bed mumbled.

"That won't do, Lady Rachelas." Riak ripped away the sheets and blankets covering the young woman. "It's time to get up."

"You're so mean to me. I'm going to tell father and get you replaced," Lady Rachelas said, sitting up in bed and rubbing a hand across her eyes, blinking in the light. The Lady's father was the Head of the King's Council in Atii and held great power having such a direct access to the King.

Riak opened the closet doors, frowning thoughtfully as she looked for the dress the Lady was to wear. "The threat would be more threatening if you didn't say it every morning, Lady." Selecting a rosewood colored gown meant for riding, Riak laid it on the bed along with the Lady's undergarments.

Lady Rachelas moved over to a chair, scrutinizing her appearance in the mirror. "Am I beautiful, Riak?" she said, touching her face.

Picking up a brush, Riak ran it through the Lady's long ginger colored hair until the hair shone like threads of silk. "You are beautiful, Lady. Certainly Lord Styade thinks so or else he wouldn't be so infatuated with you."

Lady Rachelas laughed. "You are right, Riak." She patted her face in content and let Riak dab on some beauty cream.

"How old are you, Riak?" the Lady asked, clipping on a pair of earrings as Riak hooked a red pearl necklace around the Lady's neck.

"I'm nineteen, Lady. A year older than you."

"If you weren't as round as you are, you would look your age. As it is you look younger than me," the lady said. "Get my dress." Once fully awake, the Lady could be nasty.

Riak, holding back an ugly remark regarding the Lady's real beauty, held up the dress and the undergarments as the Lady changed into them. Once clothed, Riak fixed the Lady's hair up into a neat cascade of ginger hair.

"Why is that cat in here?" Rachelas said, staring down her nose at the creature.

"Lady, you know Curly keeps the mice away."

"We don't have mice. This is a mansion, not a hovel. Why do you call him Curly, Riak? It's a horrible name."

Curly lifted his head and cast the Lady a piercing stare as if he knew the Lady had insulted him.

Riak was very tempted to hit the Lady on the head with the brush. "I named him Curly," she said tightly, "because his whiskers curl, Lady."

"They don't anymore," Rachelas pointed out, patting at her hair and heading for the door.

"Riak, clean up my room," said the Lady, flouncing out of the room and heading to break her fast.

Growling under her breath, Riak made the bed. *I hope Lord Styade pushes her into a pond. That would serve her right,* Riak thought, snickering at the thought. *At least her father pays me enough to be her maid or else I wouldn't be caught dead taking care of her!*

Throwing the pillows onto the finished bed, she hurried around the room opening the other curtains and picking up the Lady's sleeping attire.

Cracking the window open, Riak leaned out, breathing in deeply as a gentle wind brushed by carrying with it the scents of spring. The fresh breeze wafted into the room, cleaning out the bad smell of the Lady's breath as she had slept.

Invigorated and for the moment, content, Riak left the window opened, checked the room one last time for any mishaps, grabbed the Lady's riding cloak and left, closing the door behind her. Curly slipped out the door before she closed it, walking at her heels.

Voices drifted up from the front door. Riak crept over to the edge, looking down. Lord Styade was waiting by the door, his gloved hands clasped in front of him.

Riak started down the stairs, the riding cloak clutched in her hands. She had met Lord Styade once before, at a party the Lady's father had thrown. Riak had found him to be a polite man, even to the servants, none too handsome with a wide mouth and long nose that hooked at the end. The only flaw she could find was that he was shallow, only calling on women who he designed to be pretty who would in turn return his affections.

Waiting on the last stair for the Lady to come out of her dining room, Riak watched the Lord out of the corner of her eyes, Curly sitting at her feet.

"My lord," she said, "perhaps you would like to wait in the anteroom?"

Lord Styade waved a hand. "That will not be required. The Lady Rachelas will be along soon."

Riak shrugged. *You apparently don't know her too well, then, do you?* The Lady Rachelas had a special talent for timing. She knew, somehow, exactly when to make an appearance. In the case of suitors like Lord Styade, she had been known to wait up to an hour before coming out of the dining room. The Lady had once told Riak, "The longer you make some of them wait, the more they're looking forward to seeing you. Once you have that, there's nothing they won't do for you." Riak had found this bit of advice lacking but it seemed to work for the Lady.

The Lord Styade shifted and Riak had no doubt his legs were getting tired of standing.

"You are the Lady Rachelas's personal maid?" Lord Styade inquired.

"Yes, my lord."

"Could you tell me what the Lady Rachelas is wearing? I was hoping to match her today."

"She is wearing a rosewood dress. The dress is red at top and fades to black at the bottom through streaking." Riak eyed the Lord's blue coat and black trousers. White lace hung from the sleeves and poured from the neck. "I could tell her of your wish, my lord. The Lady might be willing to change."

"I do not wish to inconvenience the Lady. No, I will change." And he did. As fast as Riak could blink, his clothes changed to a dark red coat with white lace and black trousers tucked into black boots.

Riak gasped. "My lord, you're a shoi!"

A smile quirked around Lord Styade's mouth. "Indeed, I am. You do not seemed put off by this. Most people I meet are either hateful of my kind or fearful."

"I studied at the Shoi School for many years, my Lord." Riak felt the boundaries of rank suddenly evaporate.

"Indeed? Why did you not continue?"

"My parents died and I needed to take care of myself. I did not have the time to continue my studies."

"I am sorry for your loss," he said, looking genuinely sorry.

Curly purred, drawing the attention of the Lord. "Is this your cat?"

"Yes, I've had him ever since my parents left me."

"He is your familiar!" Lord Styade said, shocked. "That is very rare. Most shoi never have familiars. How intriguing!"

"Riak, there you are!" Lady Rachelas said, coming out of the dining room, her face alight with pleasure at seeing Lord Styade.

Riak handed her the riding cloak and the couple left the house.

Heaving a sigh of relief that her duties for the day were over, Riak turned on her heel, moved swiftly through the mansion and headed out the back door, Curly at her feet.

Outside, she climbed the nearby hill, the long grasses waving in the breeze. Close to the top, she lay down, disappearing from view and letting the warmth of the sun soak into her bones. Curly went back to cleaning himself, his pink tongue washing vigorously.

The blue sky above glowed with a warm spring day. Riak lazily watched a bee land on a pink flower. There was a small breeze that ruffled the tall grass that Riak lay in and disrupted the bee. It flew angrily for a few seconds and then landed on a yellow flower further down the hill.

"Riak, get down here now!" a harsh voice yelled down below.

Riak sighed. *Why can't they ever give me peace? All I am paid for is to take care of the Lady, nothing else!*

"What?" Riak yelled down the hill. Her face lit with laughter as the housekeeper stomped her foot in rage.

"Lady Rachelas wants you!" the housekeeper bellowed over the coming wind. "She says she needs her hair done up!"

Bloody hell, Riak thought, rolling her eyes. "The Lady left. She went riding with Lord Styade."

The housekeeper scowled and walked away. She was always attempting to get Riak to clean the house when all she was paid to do was watch Rachelas and make sure the Lady got what she wanted. Riak secretly believed the housekeeper did not like her because Riak was lucky enough to spend most of her day doing whatever she wanted.

Riak laid down again and frowned. The sky had clouded over. Dark, boiling clouds with flickers of lightning rolled over the once blue skies. The weather never changed that fast in Istra, nor anywhere else that Riak was aware for that matter.

She brushed her hand along her arm where the hairs were standing up. She plucked a near-by flower, twirling it in her hands. As long as she said a small spell, the flower would never die.

Curly meowed and she looked down at him. His hair was standing on end from the electricity in the air.

Riak looked up just as a lightning bolted snaked down and struck the ground near her. She screamed, the sound carrying over the clamor of the storm. Lights flashed in her eyes, obscuring her vision. She lay in the grass stunned.

Trying to get up again, she saw a young woman walking up the hill towards her. Riak crouched lower in the long grass, fearful of the woman.

The woman walked up to her.

"Riak, stand up," the woman said, her green eyes smiling.

Riak stood up, unsure. Curly peered at the strange woman from behind Riak's legs.

The woman was taller than Riak by several inches with freckles on her face. She had long, streaming auburn hair filled with tints of gold and red. She was strikingly beautiful with full red lips, curved eyebrows and a straight nose. Eyes a green Riak had never seen in nature before, gave her a commanding presence. She appeared to be Riak's age, as if to the day. *If this woman is not a royal, I don't know what is,* Riak thought.

"Who are you?" Riak asked, drawing on her magic just in case.

"There is no need for you to summon your magic, Riak, I will not hurt you," the young woman said.

Riak let the magic go, bewildered. *How did the woman know I had drawn on my magic? Is she a shoi of the Green Robes?*

"What do you want with me?" Riak demanded, putting her hands on her hips and giving the young woman a challenging stare.

"I want you to leave everything you know behind. I want you to risk your life with death. I want you to see your own past, and I want you to follow in the Light. I want you to join the Dragons and become what you were destined to be, a Phoenix," the woman said, her gaze bright.

"You think I'm a Phoenix, one of the ones meant to "rule at the side under the Dragons"?" Riak said, giggling. *Oh, Light! Is that a joke!*

Anger flashed in the green eyes of the woman. "Riak, you are the Phoenix of Life. You are Riak Tghil, who can trace her family all the way back to the Age of Magic. I know everything about you, things you don't even know. I know your mother's name was the same as yours and your family is rumored to be descendants from the gods."

Riak felt her skin prickle. *This woman is scaring me!* Even with the fright, the strange woman had managed to gain Riak's trust. The woman seemed to demand the trust.

"I'll go with you, and I'll become the Phoenix of Life. First you must tell me who you are."

"You can't become the Phoenix, you are the Phoenix of Life," the woman said, sniffing. "I am Janevra, the Lady Dragon, the Dragon of the Coming Storm."

Riak's mouth dropped open, and she blinked several times before she could say something.

"Prove it. Show me the lightning bolt on your arm."

The woman pushed up her elbow length sleeves. On her shoulder was a lightning bolt, a real one too. It was bright and seemed to glow with an eerie white light. The lightning bolt danced across her deltoid muscle, twisting and withering like the ones that had shot from the sky during the storm.

"So you are the Dragon of the Coming Storm." Riak swallowed. *Oh, gods.*

"You should not to be scared of me, Riak. I won't ever hurt you. I need you to come with me to the Lost Mountains."

"My Lady Dragon," Riak began.

"Janevra."

"Janevra, how do I know if you're telling the truth?"

Janevra raised her eyebrows. "You don't."

Riak bit her lip, her eyes looking at the ground. Her head came back up, her eyes agreeable. "I'll go with you, but if I want to leave at any time you must promise you'll let me."

"Agreed," Janevra said. "You don't need to say goodbye?" she said, cocking an eyebrow in question.

"No."

Janevra smiled sadly. "Summon your magic, please."

Riak did as she was bid and she felt her magic being…used. Janevra had somehow taken her magic and wrapped it into her own, allowing her to…

Riak never finished that thought as the ground underneath went side ways and she was suddenly standing on a cool stone floor in a richly furnished room. Curly screeched in shock and she quickly picked him up, setting him on her shoulders.

She felt the connection to Janevra disappear, the only connection that had allowed the Lady Dragon to transport Riak here without touching her.

"Welcome to the City of the Stars," Janevra said, walking over to a table holding a pitcher filled with water, and pouring herself a cup.

"Drink?" Janevra asked.

"No, thanks. Where are we?" Riak asked.

"Feel lost?" Janevra suggested. She swallowed a glass of water, her eyes bright over the rim of the glass.

Riak frowned, rolling her shoulders. "As if I've been so for millennium."

Janevra moved over to the window.

"You are in the Lost Mountains, the home of the Elves. I'm sure you read about them? Or heard legends of the Elves? Anyhow, when they named these mountains the Lost Mountains, they meant it."

Riak followed her gaze and gasped as she looked down at the city below her.

In every direction the eye looked, mountains surrounded the city, mountains so high that mist swathed the tops. Buildings of white marble and limestone gently glinted in the sun. A large plaza was at the center of the city, creating the design of a sun. Fountains birthed clear water and people moved slowly as if they had all the time in the world. Tall, spiraled towers glowed in the setting sun. A river split the city in half. Barges moved up and down. Fishing boats pulling up nets of silvery fish, floated on the water. Bridges crossed the river every two hundred feet. Trees were everywhere, large beautiful trees. Trees so massive that ten people could link arms around the trunk and still not touch. Thousands of gardens covered the city. Birds swooped in the air and added their pretty songs to the city's hum.

"What is the name of that river?" Riak said, admiring the beautiful city.

"Cupicjs yjia Viogijs. It means the River of Peace."

"You speak elvish?" Riak said, bewildered.

"I've been living here for a month. I've learned a lot. But I learned elvish back home," Janevra said, turning away from the window.

"Janevra, what of the other Phoenixes?"

"I could not reach the other two. Ake was already sailing towards Brinya and Kiera would not listen to the spirit that I sent to warn her. Ake is safe and so is Kiera." Janevra paused, tapping her lips in thought. "Riak, watch out for Kiera. Something happened to her the night I told her to come to me. I cannot tell you what because mistrust of someone you have never met is no way to start a friendship," Janevra said.

"What about the other three Phoenixes?" Riak asked.

"Two are headed for the Lord Dragon, but the other is the Phoenix of Death and will meet the Warlord."

"Oh," Riak said, leaving the subject alone.

"Are you going to introduce us, Janevra?" a male voice said.

Riak turned around and her eyes widened. Standing before her was an elf, a good-looking one at that. He had brown hair with shocking green eyes. Elven grace flowed about him as he moved. His left arm had scars on it from shooting arrows, or so she guessed.

"Riak, this is Qwaser. He's the one who brought me here. He is the Head General of the Army. And behind him is Kalioa, his right hand," Janevra said her eyes twinkling with some inner amusement.

Kalioa stepped out from behind Qwaser, fiddling with a pendant that hung around her neck. She was plain to look at, except that her short hair was a striking honey-blonde and her blue eyes filled with some guarded secret. Both of them had long elegant ears and thin frames.

"I'm pleased to meet both of you," Riak said as suddenly Kalioa bubbled with laughter.

"Riak, that's your name, right? Forget the sweet noble greetings. We're warriors. Introductions and the sort are a waste of time." Kalioa gurgled with pleasure but kept a wary eye on Curly.

Riak watched as small darts of anger filled Janevra's eyes. "Kalioa, please."

"Sorry, Janevra, my mistake. Do you know that you need to smile a little bit more?" Kalioa said, pressing her lips together matter-a-fact-ly. "This war will be over soon, maybe then you can laugh and smile."

Sadness swept into Janevra's green eyes. "You don't have the world in your hands. I don't think I can ever laugh or smile about serious matters anymore."

Riak suddenly felt sympathy for this young woman, this Dragon of a Coming Storm who was not even twenty, her age too young to take the world on her shoulders. She watched Janevra, deciding she liked this woman whom she had just met. *She has a strange aurora surrounding her that makes her seem to carry a particular hope. Janevra is different from any woman I've ever met. She knows her responsibilities, and she doesn't hide from them.* Riak noticed hardness in Janevra's eyes, a determination, but sadness was there too. *She makes you feel as if you are different than everyone else.*

Qwaser smiled at Riak. It was just an upturn of his lips but it told her that he knew her feelings.

"Come, Kalioa, we need to run a few drills for the new recruits." Qwaser turned and walked out of the room, muttering a quick goodbye.

Kalioa nodded and walked out of the room, shutting the door.

"Shall I show you to your room? It's not far from here. You won't get lost if you need me for some reason," Janevra said, linking arms with Riak.

Riak felt her heart go out to Janevra, who had so much responsibility and no matter the pressures, would always manage to smile. It seemed as if Riak had made her first friend. *Aside from Curly,* she quickly amended.

Chapter 29
The Phoenix of Death

"Where is that spell?" Dorl Kard muttered to himself, shifting through the papers and scrolls piled around him. He summoned his magic and created a glow of light, the light emitting from the candles scattered about the room not sufficient enough.

Kard's finger's brushed against a scroll and a jolt of pain shot through him. He had found it.

Slowly and carefully he began writing down the words of the scroll into a large book, his book of spells that he was working on memorizing. His Talent was great, but not great enough to wield these spells without uttering their words.

The candles burning low, Kard laid down the quill, massaging his left hand and forcing out the cramps. He snapped the book shut, locking it with his magic and blew out the candles. He opened the trap door, and slithered down the ladder.

His parents, not supportive of him dabbling in the Art, had given him the attic to keep all of his scrolls and spell books, not wanting guests to see the clutter.

"Kard, love," his mother called. "We have visitors coming soon. I would like it if you cleaned up."

"Oh, shut up, Mother," he mumbled, heading towards his bedroom.

Opening the door to his room, he was surprised to find his sister and brother sitting on his bed playing with a magical charm he had bought off a street vender.

"Give me that!" He snatched it from their grasp, glowering. "I've told you a thousand times, don't come into my room, you little urchins!"

His sister blinked her round black eyes that were so much like his at him. "But, Dorl, Mother told us to make sure you got ready."

"Ready for what?" Kard snarled, placing the charm away from their reach.

"For the luncheon with the…" she trailed off. "Who's eating here?"

"Don't know," Kard's brother replied.

"Yes you do!"

"Do not!"

"Tell me," his sister whispered darkly, "or I'll put something nasty in your bed."

Kard's brother shrugged his little shoulders. "A woman with a girl."

Kard had only been listening with half an ear, making sure everything else in the room was where he had left it. When his brother mentioned "girl", he had sprung off the floor and had moved in front of his siblings, staring down at them. "What girl did Mother invite?"

"A girl whose father isn't as highly placed as ours. Don't worry about it, Dorl. I think her father is a lesser noble. He owns some lands outside of Carim."

"Mother said the girl is a possible wife for you, Dorl," the little boy piped in.

Kard rubbed his forehead. His mother was always trying to find him a bride, something he did not want. He wished adamantly that his mother was more like his father, never caring and leaving him alone.

Furious that she was at it again, it was the third time this week, Kard dashed out of the room, down the hall and stairs where he threw open the drawing room doors, only to find his mother chatting with an older woman and her daughter.

"Damn it," Kard cursed.

"Oh, Dorl, love, come here," his mother said, patting the couch. "Do chat with us. I'm sure Susyana would love your company."

The girl sitting across from his mother blushed and looked down at the floor. Kard lifted his lip. *Disgusting, she can't even look me in the eye.* He sat down next to his mother, rigid with anger.

"Oh, he's so handsome," Susyana's mother said, reaching over and pinching Kard's cheek. Kard drew back, slouching in the pillows, glaring at the company.

"Isn't he?" his mother sighed and pinched his other cheek. Kard pulled away from her.

Droning on like this, Kard ignored their conversation, his eyes settling on the girl. She was not his type; he knew that from looking at her. She had a dull face that could easily be forgotten, a pretty little mouth and probably had never done a day of work in her life. Her face was round and did not fit her skinny body.

"Kard, love, I'm going to show Susyana's mother the house. Do entertain Susyana for us, love," his mother said, sweeping out the door with Susyana's mother in tow.

Kard flickered a glance at the girl and frowned when he saw her looking at him. "What?"

"I've never seen anyone so pale," she said, awed.

"I don't go outside much."

"Me neither," the girl said cheerily. "Well, at least since the Warlord claimed the city. Mother says I shouldn't go out or the Warlord's men might kill or..." she stopped, her fingers twisting in her lap.

"Might rape you?" Kard said causally, staring up at the ceiling. He brought his eyes down to meet hers.

Susyana gave a squeak. "Errr...yes."

"Are you afraid of the Warlord, Susyana?"

"Aren't you, Dorl?"

Kard jumped off the couch and pushed his face close to Susyana's. "Don't ever call me Dorl, do you hear?" Susyana whimpered, cringing back in fear.

Straightening, Kard moved in front of the bay window. "I do not fear the Warlord."

Joining him at the window, Susyana stared at him. "Why not? He is the most evil man that has ever walked the earth. How can you not fear him?"

Kard smiled coldly and traced Susyana's jaw. She flinched from his touch but did not step back. "Because," he breathed, "I've used the same dark Art that the Warlord does and I do not fear it. Why should I fear a man who uses the same power as myself?"

"You're a shoi?" Susyana took a step back, pressing her back against the windowpane.

"I'm a very powerful one, Susyana. Very powerful. Enough so I could rival the Warlord if I tried. What? Are you afraid?"

"My mother told me shoi are bad, that they eat your soul."

Kard threw back his head and cackled with laughter. "That is the most entertaining thought I've heard in a long time. Some shoi, the particularly evil ones, would take your soul. I might," Kard said, flashing her his teeth.

Susyana let out a muffled shriek, Kard's hand clapping over her mouth. "Don't scream," he whispered in her ear. "I'm not going to hurt you. You're not worth it." He pulled his hand off her mouth.

Running from the room, screaming at the top of her lungs, Susyana burst out the door and into the crowded street still screaming.

Kard's mother found him laughing on the couch, tears streaming from his eyes. She stamped her foot when she saw him, an unattractive flush in her cheeks. Her eyes were narrowed to nothing but slits and her nose flared dangerously.

"Dorl, what did you do this time?"

"I corrected her misunderstandings about shoi and magic," he laughed.

"How am I ever going to find you a wife if you kept chasing all the good ones away?" she asked.

Kard sobered, casting his mother a dark look. "Have you ever considered that I don't want to get married, Mother dear?" He stood up and walked out of the drawing room, temper burning inside. Stalking out the door and into the hub of the city, he pushed his way past a group of rogui and sylai, earning curses from the creatures in their dark tongues.

Won't she get it? he thought, still moving down the street. *I don't want marriage. I was meant for better things, bigger things, than having a family and taking over father's job at the city council. I don't want children, I don't want a normal life! I want power and to be able to use my Talent to its greatest abilities! If she won't see, then I will show her!*

Kard was instantly jarred from thought when he ran into a young
woman. The woman had her red hair cropped short and a small circular
scar on her cheek. A sword hung from her waist and a tattoo of a sword
was on her left arm. She was a warrior for the Warlord.

"Hey! Watch it!" she snapped, giving him a blue daggered glare.

"Watch yourself!" Kard shouted back, his black eyes narrowed.

The woman drew herself up. "I am a captain in the Warlord's army,
rich boy. Do not mock or anger me! You wouldn't be able to live to regret
it!"

"Same goes to you."

"Oh, really now? Does it?" she said, raising an eyebrow and running
her eyes over his body, searching for a weapon.

"I'm a shoi," Kard said, saving her the worry when she did not find any
observable weapon on his body.

"A shoi, huh? I would be careful then, if I were you, rich boy. The
Warlord is looking for shoi and only those who will join him in the Darkness." With a dark giggle, she pushed past him. "Watch your back, rich
boy. If the Warlord decides you're a threat, it will be my blade in your
back," she said over her shoulder, vanishing into the crowd.

Almost feeling the knife blade sinking into his back, Kard glided out of
the crowds and walked down an alley.

"You're in our dominion, lordy," said a voice scornfully. "Do you
know what happens when you enter it uninvited?"

Kard glanced around, searching for the owner of the voice. "My name
is Dorl Kard. If you do any harm to me, my father's wrath will be swift."

"He's a Kard!" another voice whispered.

"Do you know how rich they are?"

"Very, or so I hear."

"Let's get him. I'm sure he's got some chips on him."

A fist came out of nowhere and smashed into Kard's face, another
pounding into his side. He dropped to the ground amid howls of laughter
while several fists rammed into his body.

Kard wiped the blood off his chin, smearing it on his hand. He lifted
his eyes to see five boys standing in front of him, the beginning of the
alleyway seeming miles away.

Kard stood up, his body aching where punches had landed. He was
skinny and weak compared to the other boys nor was he one to fight back
using bodily strength since he didn't have it. Magic was his only safeguard.

"Come on, Kard, fight back!" one of the boys yelled.

Kard shook his head, the cut on his thin lips bleeding again.

"Are you a girl, Kard, afraid to fight back?" a blonde haired youth
asked, rousing evil snickers from the other boys.

Kard's coal colored eyes flashed. "I don't want to hurt you." This
brought even more laughter from the group. The fools.

One of the youths, a freckled face redhead with large ears, came up and put his hand on Kard's shoulder.

"Kard, look, you're very rich, we're poor. We'll stop if you give us some chips, or else we'll just have to hurt you again." He grinned, showing crooked teeth.

"I won't give you money."

The red haired boy brought his fist up and hit Kard in the nose. Kard's nose started to fountain with dark red blood. He fell down on the hard pavement, the blood from his nose spraying on to his black shirt and black trousers. His pale face was paler than usual and his black hair clung with blood. At nineteen one would think he would be able to defend himself.

Kard got up again. A silver chain slipped out of the confinement of his shirt.

"What's this?" one of the boys spat, yanking the chain off and the lapis lazuli attached.

"Ha! He thinks he's a shoi!" the boy crackled with laughter. The other boys followed suit and laughed with him.

Kard clenched his hands. Fools they were to mess with someone of such high powers.

"What could *he* possibly be good at?"

All common sense fled as Kard's temper cracked. He pulled on the dark weaves of magic. Let them see what he could do.

The boys stopped laughing as the sky above got darker.

"Ah, it's going to rain," one said.

"Let's go."

"No. You will not be going anywhere," Kard said coolly.

The five boys turned around.

"Shut up," one of the blonde ones said.

Kard thrust his hands outwards and the boy flew against the building, his head hitting the wall. His body slid down, a trail of blood staining the stone, and slumped at the bottom. All life was gone from his pale blue eyes.

The red haired boy ran over to the body, and felt for a pulse.

He turned around, anger and fear filling his eyes. "You killed him!" he screeched.

"That was my idea," Kard said.

One of them turned and ran, his footsteps echoing on the walls.

The sky above got darker.

"Who are you? A minion for the Warlord?" the redhead asked, his eyes accusing.

The Warlord had not moved his army out of the city yet. Every day more men and women, whose seeds of Evil grew with the promise of money, became filled with greed and joined the Warlord. Every day his army grew. Every day the patrols of sylai and rogui shoved more people out of their homes and into streets making them decide if they would work for the Warlord. Angarat was known for its past in accepting the Dark Lord and many people now were doing just that. For each one who did not accept, twenty did. Those who went willingly were paid. Those who were forced became footmen or worse. They became slaves. But some of them were killed. Their bodies could be seen hanging from the walls surrounding Carim, their faces purple, their bodies rotting. Crows feasted on the corpses. Flies buzzed around and the smell of the dead covered the city like a blanket. Every day the Warlord became more powerful and every day more people began to lose hope.

"No. I work for no one," Kard said, smiling. His black eyes remained impassive. "Living in Carim, a city under the influence of the Warlord, one would think that all people would work for him. Am I not right?" Kard pressed his thin lips together.

"We don't, we are free," one of the boys said. "Free and not tainted by Evil."

Kard grinned, a small uplift of his lips.

The boy who spoke coughed and blood came out of his mouth. He coughed harder as if he was choking on something.

"One should learn to hold one's tongue," Kard said, killing the youth with a flicker of his eyes.

"Two left. Do you want to die, or leave and not speak of what has happened?"

In answer the two youths fled, their footsteps disappearing.

Kard followed them, picking up the silver chain and hanging it around his neck. He walked out of the alley. The street in front of him was empty. The people had gone in because of the storm.

Kard turned his face to the dark sky. The rain stung his face. His eyes were open and he stared at the sky. He challenged it. He was not afraid of it like he had been in the past. He controlled it. Lightning crashed across the sky. The clouds became an alarming black.

Kard toppled over as the wall next to him crashed to the ground. He got up, blood seeping out of his mouth. He spat it out, the irony taste slowly mixing in with his spit. He would ignore the pain.

Kard looked up. A sudden instinct told him he was being watched. Up ahead of him was a man cloaked in black leaning against the side of a squat building.

Kard pretended not to notice him. He kept his eyes staring past the figure.

The figure's face was hidden by the shadows of his cloak.

He was across from the cloaked man when the man spoke.

"Dorl Kard," was what he whispered.

Kard turned his head and looked at the man, his eyes meeting what he hoped were the man's eyes. "What?" Kard said, suspicion hanging on the one word. The man was taller than Kard even when he was slouching.

The man pushed himself off the building, standing upright.

"I have been watching you," he said, stepping closer to Kard.

Kard's eyes became slits. He caught the magic in his mind, coming up with a quick spell in case the stranger tried something.

"Let go of your magic."

Kard released the magic as if he had been struck. A tingle of fear twisted through him. *How did he know?*

The man lowered his hood, revealing short dirty blonde hair and ice-cold blue eyes. Kard felt as if he had seen the man somewhere. He just couldn't place where.

"I have a question to ask you, Kard. It's a very simple question. Once you answer it, I will tell you who I am, and what I want from you," the man said, his voice low.

The storm above lightened a little and a slow drizzle began.

The man didn't wait for Kard to respond.

"Are you for the Light or the Dark?" the man said, his cold eyes boring into Kard's black ones.

"I...I'm on Dark." Kard didn't know what made him say it. Mayhap it was because he dealt in the darker arts of magic or because he had never followed the Light too willingly.

"An answer I expected," the man said.

"Tell me who you are," Kard demanded.

The man smirked. He rolled up his sleeve on his right arm. Upon his skin was a black skull. Blood oozed around the edges. The mouth of the skull was split by a grin, and its eyes were darker than blood red.

"My lord," Kard said, his eyes widening. He started to bow.

"Shut up! I don't want people to know I'm here and what I'm doing," the Warlord hissed.

The Warlord was composed in a second and it would have been hard to believe that a moment ago he looked as if he was going to strangle Kard.

"You, Kard, are the Phoenix of Death," the Warlord said simply.

Kard wasn't surprised. Long ago he expected something was different about his magical ability. When magic came to you so easily, you got beyond suspicion.

"And what do you want with me?" Kard asked.

"I want you to train other people in the Art. I want you to make an army of shoi, like in the old days. You will be my left hand. You will follow my orders. I will give you an army and whenever I need you, your army will come. Understood?"

Kard nodded, his head swimming with visions.

"And, Kard, I am and will ever be stronger than you," the Warlord said, his icy eyes regarding Dorl with scorn.

Kard nodded, he had known that. The man's presence sent his mind reeling with his power. "I'll do it," Kard said firmly.

"Good. Before I can create my army of shoi , my army must move on to Calahar."

Kard felt himself hit hard ground before he knew what had happened.

The Warlord had drawn on the forces of magic and transported them to the Warlord's camp, which lay spread out around the city.

Kard scrambled up, his lip bleeding again. The Warlord was already ten steps ahead and Kard hurried to catch up.

The Warlord stopped in front of a large, black tent.

A man exited and nodded to the Warlord, who, Kard noticed had somewhere dropped his cloak.

"Warlord, everyone is ready to move out. One of the captains and eight scores of men have been picked to stay behind as you ordered," the man said. He had dark brown hair and vivid green eyes. He was as tall as the Warlord and he wore a light chain mail shirt under his black tunic.

"Kard, this is David Pierce, First General in my army. His position of Second General is being given over to you," the Warlord said to Kard before turning his attention back to his General.

"My Lord, I put the Mark on the Phoenix of Air as you asked. You can watch through her eyes."

The Warlord and Pierce shared a smile that Kard could never begin to understand.

"Kard, come and stand here." The Warlord motioned him to stand in front of him.

Kard obeyed.

The Warlord pressed two fingers to the left side of Kard's shoulder. The shirt melted away under the Warlord's touch. Kard screamed as a flame was tattooed into his skin.

"Every shoi will have this mark, Kard, every shoi. It binds you to me. If you ever think of betraying me, you will die. I have done the same to every warrior under my command with the symbol of a sword."

The young redheaded woman with the scar on her cheek came out of the tent, the scar on her cheek pale against her tan. Spotting Kard, her mouth drew into a sneer. "What's rich boy doing here?"

The Warlord gave her an annoyed look. "He's the Phoenix of Death, the head of my shoi. You would do best to befriend him."

The woman laughed. "I befriend all who can stand up to me, and that rich boy did it very well when we met in the street." With another laugh, she walked off, swaying her hips like a snake sways before it strikes.

Kard followed the Warlord and the General into the tent and wondered what would happen when the Warlord's armies met the Dragon's.

Before he entered he took notice of two people standing by the tent flap. They were both cloaked in black. One had tan skin and a tattoo on his arm. As for the other the only feature he could see, beside the pendant with a sword on it hanging out of the cloak, was a long pointed ear.

Kard frowned. Pointed?

He passed the thought away as he entered the tent.

Chapter 30
Voices

Janevra drummed her fingers lightly on the windowsill.

Riak had arrived two days ago, and the other two were expected anytime. Riak had made herself comfortable as had her cat. She had taken the room in the left upper wing of the palace where the other two would also be sleeping.

Janevra had told the elves that two women would be coming, asking for entrance. She told the elves to let the two humans have access into their kingdom and guide them to the city. The elves did not give their full trust to humans yet, but Janevra hoped she could change that.

Qwaser and Kalioa had left yesterday to scout the land and make sure the maps were all updated. Janevra knew they used this time between them well. But it made her notice how lonely she felt. No one else understood. They did not understand the fact that she, a nineteen-year-old girl, had the world in her hands. They knew she did, but they didn't feel the pressure, the hate, and the fear. No one understood. They couldn't kill thousands with a simple command. They didn't have power beyond imagination. No one except Mat.

Janevra shook her head. The Warlord had already taken Angarat. In two days he had moved from Carim to the capital. Angarat had surrendered. No other nation would go down without a fight. She knew in the Cyrain Plains they had an army. They just needed to be united. As did the Forgotten People.

Janevra looked out the window watching as people far below her moved about, knowing that above their heads was the Lady Dragon, a woman meant to rip the world in half with her power and kill the Warlord with her strength. They thought of her as more than a queen. They knew she was mortal but that thought was passed from their heads when they heard of the Prophecies. They forgot she was only human. They forgot she could bleed. They only saw the Lady Dragon, ruler of all.

Janevra pulled her legs up, glad she was wearing trousers instead of a dress. Her light silk shirt felt good alongside her skin. She leaned her head against the wall, closing her eyes and trying to remember the days when she was only a princess. By the gods did those days seem far away. The days when she could curl up on her bed and read a book, when she didn't have to worry over invading armies, when Caendor was strong.

Caendor was under the control of Ravften, and it was becoming a living nightmare. Under the rule of a dark shoi, Jariran became a place were the dead lived and the living died. Several cities had begun a Civil War. They had taken themselves away from Caendor in hope that the Warlord would take control. Myra, Ryune, Tezeru, Kindero, and Luzon all closed themselves off from the capitol. Caendor's former glory was now in ruins. The city that had stood proud and strong for thousands of years had fallen to a nightmare of one man's twisted dream.

A tear leaked out of Janevra's eye.

"Where are they?"

Janevra jumped up, the voice sounding like it had come from her head.

"Who's there?" Janevra said, her voice wavering, drawing on her magic.

"This is getting very annoying! I have a meeting with the Council in one hour!"

Janevra surveyed the whole room. She was alone.

"The gods gave them two days. Two days for the Phoenixes of both Earth and Fire to get here and they are late. This is not good. The Warlord is soon to attack Selkare and they need help." And then the voice, which Janevra had decided had come from her head, added as if an after thought, *"I wonder if the other Phoenixes have reached Janevra?"*

Janevra caught her breath. This could not be! After they had left the World of Things Yet to Come and Things That Have Passed, something must have happened to them. Somehow they were telekinetic with each other.

"Mat?" Janevra whispered.

Janevra felt Mat's mind jump. She grinned. Feeling his panic and sudden fear she could not keep from laughing, having no doubt he could hear her laugh as well.

"Hello Mat. It's Janevra."

"Janevra? What?"

"Somehow after we left the World of Dreams, we can read each other's minds, even over long distances. Is this not amazing?" Janevra grew more excited. *"Mat, this is perfect. When we are far apart like we are now, we can still communicate. When we don't want someone to hear what we're saying, we can do this."*

"So?"

"Don't you get it? We will always know what is happening to the other. We don't need to speak where people can hear us. We don't need to worry about prying ears."

Janevra felt Mat abruptly understand.

"Are you saying everything I say to myself, you can hear?"

"I'm sure there is a way to guard if we must. But this way we form a perfect circle of trust. Mat, I know you understand, I can feel it."

"You can?" Janevra sensed Mat's smile.

"Yes. Please don't act stupid, Mat. I can tell that you understand this as well as I do. I know you're waiting for the Phoenixes as I am. I know you are worried about Raxsen taking all of Selkare, but he won't."

Janevra mentally heard Mat sigh. She smiled.

"I have so much to tell you...Mat?" Janevra stopped as she felt Mat's mind shift to verbal talking. She felt his laughter leaking out.

"Sorry, Janevra. So sorry. Dei and Zenerax just walked in, the leaders

*of the Edieata tribe. You should have seen their faces after I didn't answer
their question for the fifth time. They had to tap me on the shoulder before I
knew they were there."*

Janevra giggled after Mat showed her his memory of the scene.

"Mat, how did you do that?"

*"What? Show you the memory of their faces? Easy, you just have to
remember what you want to remember and I guess you can just replay it. I
need to go."*

*"Mat, don't tell anyone of our new found power. We can't trust anyone.
If anyone did find out about this new power, people would be even more
suspicious of us."* Janevra heard his hurried *"yes"* and then his leaving.

"Wait! Mat!" she called.

Janevra felt his mind swiveled back to her. *"Yes?"*

"How are things in the Cyrain Plains?"

*"The Nekid, a rebel Ile group, are marching towards the city. I fear
there will be a fight. I can't figure out who is leading them."*

"It is probably the Warlord, Mat. You know how strong he is."

*"Yes, I suppose you're right. What of the Lost Mountains? How are
things?"*

*"I've been expecting an attack from a horde of rogui that were spotted
over the mountains weeks ago. I think the battle will happen soon."*

They said their goodbyes once more and Janevra felt his presence in
her mind leave, regretting that the sudden feeling of safety she had felt
talking to Mat had disappeared.

Janevra turned away from the window and was surprised to see Riak
standing there, her cat at her feet.

"How long have you been standing there?" Janevra asked, her brows
raising in question. *I really hope she didn't see my face when I was talking
to Mat. I bet it looked funny.*

"I just got here. I came to tell you that the other two Phoenixes are
here," Riak said, her brown hair bobbing around her head.

"Are they being directed up to this room?"

"Yes."

They were standing in what the elves called a sunroom. It was a room
made out of pure glass on three sides. It let the sun in and allowed thousands of plants to grow even during winter. It never became hot in the
sunroom, just slightly above a nice, comfortable temperature. Surrounding
both young women were flowering plants. Every color conceivable was
blooming out of some plant. It made both women appear to be standing in a
sea of magic.

"I had better change then." Janevra smiled. "Kiera will be disappointed if I don't wear something beautiful."

Riak giggled.

Janevra had told Riak all about the two other Phoenixes. She had told
her that Kiera loved looking beautiful, even though she wasn't, and admired

jewels. Her greatest ambition was to be a princess and she seduced men as a hobby. She thought highly of herself.

Ake, on the other hand, was beautiful in a rustic and exotic way but did not care. She had a pierced nose and her previous occupation was piracy. She was devoted to those she grew close to and believed firmly in independence.

Janevra thought a single command and her hair was piled up on her head instead of down and her clothes became a tank-top dress that slowly faded from purple to blue. Without sleeves the silver-blue lightning bolt on her upper arm was revealed.

A knock sounded on the double ebony doors.

Janevra glanced at Riak. She hid a smile behind her hands.

Two women entered. One had short black hair, purple eyes and was just an inch taller than Janevra. From her ears hung a star inside a crescent moon and in her nose was a small crystal stud. Her clothes had no appearance of being travel worn. Obviously her magic had helped her there.

The other girl had whitish blonde hair and blue eyes. She was slim, of medium height, with a pointed chin and full lips. Her chin made her lips seem too large. Like an over grown slug.

Janevra moved to stand in front of both the women. "Ake, Kiera, I know you two are acquainted. As you have guessed, I am the Lady Dragon, the Dragon of the Coming Storm. Please call me Janevra. This is Riak Tghil, the Phoenix of Life."

Janevra gave a bemused glance at Ake as Kiera curtsied. She could tell Ake held some dislike for Kiera and suspicion about Kiera's person.

"Riak, can you take Kiera and show her to her rooms? Thank you."

Riak left with a chatting Kiera next to her and an annoyed cat at her heels, demanding attention.

Janevra turned to Ake. "Ake, I know you don't like Kiera but put up with her for now. She has lost her family. Treat her kindly and no harm will come to you from her."

Ake frowned. "What?"

"I cannot tell you now, for even I am not sure what has happened to her, but treat her kindly, or at least until we meet up with the Lord Dragon. Then she will be preoccupied with men," Janevra said, stifling a smile.

"And who will she be looking at, Janevra?" Ake asked, smiling.

"The only man she will never have a chance with. The Lord Dragon."

Ake started giggling. Janevra smiled, the other woman's joy flooding over her and becoming her own.

"Come, Ake," Janevra said, motioning with her hands, her eyes dancing with laughter. "Let me show you to your rooms."

Janevra walked alongside Ake. "Ake, let me tell you how I met Mat, the Lord Dragon. It's a rather amusing story. He was on trial for theft…"

Chapter 31
A Golden Bird

Mat waited for the two Phoenixes. He hated waiting.

He stood in the Council Room of the Daaguwh Ile, which was not in session today after he had decided to cancel it. His eyes ran around the room, taking in the long circular table with twenty chairs sitting around it and wide windows in the north and south.

Mat had just finished talking to Janevra and had found it refreshing to remember that he was not alone in this fight against the Dark. He had a very powerful woman at his side who, he believed, could do anything.

Since the day he had come out of the World of Dreams people had looked at him in fear. Even Dei and Zenerax had looked upon him with something close to fear. Vena had told him that living in the day of the Dragons, people suddenly became scared. They were not as sure of their future as they once were. War was always on the horizon.

Most of the Ile were treating him as they had before if with a little more awe and respect. But there were some who would see him dead. In all the Ile nations rebellion was rising. There were days when people would disappear and never be seen again. Mat knew they were the ones against him, the ones for the Dark Lord. Rebellion had come from every tribe, men and women disappearing and joining the Warlord. The only tribe that had not rebelled was the Edieata. They were for the Dragons. Mat could only guess why none of them feared him. Maybe because they knew three of his friends were their leaders or maybe it was that the Dark Lord's minions had almost destroyed them.

Most of the Daaguwh had stayed loyal to him but the other Ile nations that had never seen or heard of him were either rebelling or sending men and women to become part of his army. The Jaara, Ryaji, Siatue and the Latyre had sent over half of their warriors, showing full loyalty. From the Nekid no one had come. They had all demonstrated that they would take no part in the Dragons and those Prophecies. Instead they had sent men to find the Warlord and tell him that he had all the Nekid behind him. The Warlord had responded by telling the Nekid to destroy the Ile that allied with Mat. Now Mat had a full-fledged war on his hands, centered in the Ile heartlands.

The Nekid were crossing the borders of neighboring nations, destroying the outlying villages. Refugees were swarming into cities, joining the ranks of warriors. Defenses were being made. Spears, swords, arrows, bows, and staffs were fashioned. The Yria'ti were practicing spells and expanding their knowledge. Leaders of every nation and city were gathering in Daaguwh with full force.

Mat put his head in his hands, sitting down at the round table. From farmer boy wanting adventure to the Lord Dragon, accepting his responsibility but wanting his old life back.

"My Lord Dragon?"

Mat looked up.

Leama was standing in the doorway, her gray-red hair pulled back in a braid, some small wisps of hair escaping. She closed the door behind her.

Leama was a middle aged, wise and respected woman. She was the head of the Daaguwh Council, as was her place as the Djed, and now the head of the Dragon's Council, which consisted of men and women from every tribe under the Dragons. He never called the Council, it was meant for a power order only. He did not want to be overwhelmed by hundreds of Ile demanding things of him. Instead he had assigned positions to several Ile in each nation to talk to him about the things most grievances were about. It worked well. He set aside time every day to talk to those he had assigned.

"My Lord, I have bad news," Leama said, twisting her hands together.

Mat stood up. Leama was usually a very composed person.

"What?"

"Um..." Leama's hand reached up and tugged on her braid.

"Tell me," Mat said, his jaw tightening.

"The Nekid are fifty miles from the city. They have over one thousand men and women, each armed...with black knol."

In Ile customs black knol meant death, red war, white peace, and blue health. For every Ile there was a different symbol that told a warning, secret or purpose. Mat had still not learned to read the ones besides the obvious.

Mat stared at Leama until she shifted uncomfortably, his hazel eyes then going past her.

"My Lord?" Leama inquired.

Mat shook his head, running a hand through his hair. He started pacing the council room, his hands locked behind his back. "Double the men on guard. Tell everyone to prepare for battle."

Leama nodded, her steps quickly fading from hearing as she left.

Mat pounded a fist into the table, clenching his jaw.

"Damn it," he muttered.

His silent cursing was interrupted by Vena, the leading Yria'ti of the Daaguwh.

"What is it, Vena?" he said, his back to her.

She stopped, surprised.

Mat felt her draw on her magic. She was wary of him, but he accepted that. She had met him when he was nothing but a young man, now she saw him practicing the Art of Magic, making battle plans, and taking the name Dragon. And he wasn't even twenty.

"My Lord, the Phoenixes are here."

Mat turned around, a small smile lighting his face. "Finally. Bring them in."

Vena poked her head out of the door, and whispered something Mat didn't catch. She motioned with her hands and stood aside.

Two young men entered. One looked like flame, the other like earth.

"Ryen, Eside," Mat said. He had no clue how he had come up with their names.

The one called Eside stepped forward. "My Lord Dragon…" he began, his eyes uncertain.

"Call me Mat, and yes, your sister can come in."

Eside's jaw dropped, but he nodded a quick thanks.

"Lana come here," Eside called.

From behind the door came a young girl around the age of twelve, the exact image of her brother but with dark brown eyes. Her clothes were travel worn but she managed a curtsy.

Mat smiled at her.

"Vena, can you make sure Lana gets anything she wants. Dresses, toys, painting utensils…anything?"

"Yes, my lord," Vena said, bobbing her head.

Lana squealed, her delight making the gloomy room warm and joyful. She ran over and threw her arms around Mat's waist.

"Thank you, sir, thank you so much." She giggled.

Mat patted her awkwardly on the back.

She let go and took Vena's hand, pulling her out of the room, questions streaming out of her mouth.

Eside smiled. "Thanks Mat, she lost her parents two days ago and she… you can guess the rest," Eside said, his eyes covering pain.

Mat nodded sadly. But the sadness quickly was covered with hardness. "Ryen, Eside, tell me, what would you do if this city was attacked?"

Ryen frowned. "I would increase the defense and prepare people."

"Same." Eside shrugged. "But I'm not the one who has studied battle tactics. That's just common sense to me."

"Good. Whenever we are going to be attacked or going to attack, I want you to give me your opinions, even if I'm angry."

"Does this mean we're going to get attacked?" Ryen said at the same moment Eside grimaced and said, "Who's attacking us?"

"The Nekid are attacking us," Mat said, watching as the two men's faces went from curiosity to dread. "You're Phoenixes?"

Ryen bobbled his head.

"I hope, or I came here for nothing," Eside said.

Mat grinned. "Of Fire and Earth?"

"Yes."

"Wait, which one am I?" Eside said, giving Ryen a bewildered look. Ryen grinned and Mat could see the instant friendship flare up between them.

Mat directed his gaze at Ryen. "Ryen, come here. Roll up the left sleeve of your shirt."

Ryen obeyed if hesitantly.

"As you know all full fledged shoi wear rings or necklaces signifying that they are shoi. Those who are powerful in certain elements wear special rings or necklaces. Anybody can copy that and with magic disguise themselves as either one of you. But something they can't copy is if I put something into your skin."

Eside's eyes widened, appalled.

Ryen stepped back.

Mat rolled up his right shirtsleeve, reveling the golden sun.

"No one can copy this, as no one can copy something like this if it's in you, but they can make a replica of this," he said. "I will put a phoenix on your skin. For my safety, yours and anybody you care for…" Mat didn't finish.

"Where will you put it?"

"On your left arm."

Ryen stuck out his left arm, closing his eyes tightly. Mat summoned his magic and put his hand on Ryen's upper arm. Ryen gasped, as his arm suddenly glowed red, his face twisting in pain.

Mat let go and he knew that Janevra had done the same thing to the other Phoenixes. On Ake's arm encircling was a beautiful gold bird, a phoenix.

Ryen staggered back.

Wrapped around his upper arm was a stunning gold and red bird. It started at his shoulder and traveled all the way to his elbow, its feathers gleaming.

Eside rolled up his left arm sleeve.

Mat put his hand on Eside's arm. The outcome was the same.

"Mat, they all have the Phoenix," Mat felt Janevra say, and then her presence left.

Chapter 32
Causalities of War

Dei woke up, her legs entangled in white sheets. She rolled over, smiling as she found Zenerax next to her, snoring gently. How much she loved him.

She sighed. Getting out of bed she put on a pair of loose linen pants and a shirt. In the last month their love for each other had bloomed. The council members kept hinting at marriage and even Mat snickered behind his hand when Zenerax said something that caused Dei to blush. Kayzi pretended not to notice their love and Vena kept asking Zenerax if he had given Dei a potion that made her shine so when he was around. Leama, the Djed, went so far as to act as Dei's mother and give Zenerax permission to marry Dei. Dei was waiting for the day Zenerax would ask her, when he would hand her the wedding gift, the *iltqau*, something special to both of them.

For an Ile man to ask for a woman's hand in marriage he had to get permission from her mother and then for fourteen days, everyday, give a gift to her family. On the last day he would give her a golden armband, signifying his intentions. If the woman had no family, he would forego the fourteen days of gifts and only give her the golden armband. The woman, at this time, could refuse her suitor. If she did not refuse, then the mother would say whether she approved of him. If the mother approved, the man would take the hand of his beloved and they would walk to the nearest Yria'ti house, while their relatives threw flowers at their feet. Throwing the flowers meant a sign of happiness and health. Once the couple reached the Yria'ti house, the head of that house would hand the *iltqau* to the man who would hand it to the woman. If she accepted the gift they were married but if she turned her head they would not join in marriage.

In Dei's case, since she did not have a mother, the most prominent female figure in her life would have to give permission to Zenerax or Dei could give herself the permission but many frowned upon that, believing a young woman needed another woman's permission to marry.

Dei finished tying up her boots and glanced at Zenerax. He snorted in his sleep.

Dei reached over and slapped his buttock. He jumped up, falling out of bed, getting tangled in the white sheets.

He looked up at her, hurriedly standing up and wrapping the blanket about his waist.

"Good morning, Zenerax," Dei said, blushing at his bare chest.

"Hello," he mumbled, still half asleep.

Dei walked to the window. "Zen, did you know the Phoenixes are here?"

"Yah," Zenerax muttered, tugging on linen trousers.

Dei frowned, looking out into the city of the Daaguwh. They were high up and able to see the surrounding countryside. The sky seemed a little bit darker than it usually did as if smoke was in the air.

"Dei," Zenerax said, moving to stand behind her. He encircled her in his arms. She leaned against him, slightly frowning at the city. He nibbled at her ear. "Do you think we should mention the Thysians to the Lord Dragon? They are very strong fighters and would help the cause greatly."

"I don't think it's Mat's place to lead them," Dei said thoughtfully. "Janevra is the one who will unite the Forgotten Peoples. The Lost Tribe is forgotten and it will be her they seek to be brought back into the world."

"Do you know their Prophecies, Dei?"

"No. Do you?" Dei asked, enjoying the warmth of Zenerax's body.

"Yes." Zenerax began quoting part of it. "*...When deed is done, and the one with the lightning bolt on shoulder, the* teth'e'dsaer, *is found, the people of the Lost tribe, the Thysians, shall be united with the world once more. For unity to become reality a union of hands, a cross of swords, a fletching of arrow must occur with the* teth'e'dsaer *and child of the Thysia, the First Son. Then the Thysians will join the world and it's people in the Fifth Battle of Good and Evil where the* teth'e'dsaer *will lead the Thysians* *into battle."* Zenerax shifted Dei's weight slightly. "I think Janevra is the *teth'e'dsaer*," he said. "I wish I knew what that word meant."

Dei ran her fingers along Zenerax's arm, still gazing out at the city, watching the smoke. "When we see Janevra again, tell her the prophecy. It would be helpful."

Zenerax nodded and together they watched the city. Dei's frown deepened, still watching the haze. *What is it?* she thought.

Zenerax cleared his throat. "I've been meaning to ask—but I never really had the chance. Dei, will—"

"Great Gods!" she said, jumping out of his arms.

"What?" Zenerax said, startled.

"The city is burning!" she said.

"What?"

"Look!" Dei pointed to a smudge of black on the horizon.

Zenerax's eyes grew wide. He swore, naming as many curses as he knew. "Get your *khrieth!*"

Deivenada hurriedly found her battle spear, the one Zenerax had given her, meeting Zenerax at the door. They sprinted out, feet padding lightly on the cool stone floor. As they ran, Zenerax muttered prayers to Aystarte, the goddess of war and luck. "Let us live," he finished.

They ran into Mat on the second floor, Council leaders surrounding him. He looked Dei in the eyes. She shivered. What she saw was not the boy she had met a month ago, but a strange young man with cold hazel eyes. He broke eye contact, ordering three men to take four hundred warriors to the east and swing back on the fighting.

Dei and Zenerax darted through the front doors, looking up at the dark, curling smoke to the north.

They ran along deserted streets, their breathing the only noise. Once Dei saw a young girl, her face tear stained. She watched as her mother scooped her up, running away from the fighting.

As they neared the fighting it became hard to move faster, people were running, pushing to get away from the death. Dei watched as an old man fell to the ground, an arrow protruding from his back. Bile rose in her throat, acid bitter, but she swallowed.

Zenerax and Dei slowed as they reached the front.

It was chaos. The Nekid wore black knol on their faces, a color rarely used in modern Ile war. Most of the Daaguwh warriors had no paint on their faces, but their tattoos glowed with an eerie light Dei assumed was Mat's doing. War cries rang over the din. They were chilling sounds, high pitched and in the Old Tongue. Arrows flew true, hitting their targets. Men and women fell, some scrambling back up, but most unmoving and bloody. Burning buildings crashed to the ground and added deafening sounds to the battle. The flames licked at the sky, black smoke spiraling upwards.

Dei and Zenerax went back to back into the battle, their spears and knives flashing.

Dei didn't think about what she was doing as she plunged a knife into a Nekid's belly, warm blood spreading over her hands. It was best not to think when you killed people.

She felt Zenerax behind her, his muscles digging into her back. Screaming filled Dei's ears, death clogged her nose.

A piercing noise split the air. Bodies flew back where a lightning bolt hit a group of men and women.

One of the bodies landed in front of Dei. It was a Nekid, her body half burned off. Dei looked closer, and was taken back when the woman blinked. The woman sneered at her, then death slid across her eyes.

She was pushed from behind as Zenerax blocked a spear aimed at her.

She saw him fall to the ground, a spear sticking out of his leg and an arrow from his back. The arrow had a red fletching. It was not a Nekid arrow and it would be the arrow that killed him.

He grinned weakly up at her.

All the blood left her face. She screamed, the words forming in her mouth. *"A'shaing te kra de naum!"* The ancient words flew out of her mouth as a fireball whizzed down and struck a building sending splinters flying.

Dei killed the man poised above Zenerax.

She stood by Zenerax's still form, blood dripping from her face. Sweat rolled down her cheeks, smearing the smudges of black soot.

Anyone who came near her she killed. Anyone who was an enemy.

She looked up once to see three figures standing on the walls surrounding the inner city. The middle one was Mat. A white light was lancing from his palm when he mouthed a word. Every word meant ten more Nekid dead.

Soon the Daaguwh forces were pushing the Nekid back.

When the street became quiet, Dei dropped down to the ground, cradling Zenerax's head in her lap. Tears slid down her smoke streaked face.

"Don't leave me, Zen, don't," she whispered. "You can't."

He looked up at her, slowly moving a hand to clasp hers in his own.

"Dei..." he coughed, blood leaking from his lips, "I ... wanted...to ask...you...didn't get the...chance..."

"Shhhh, don't waste your strength. You'll need it later," Deivenada said, a salty-tear dropping on to his bloody face, her hair wet from sweat. He was unmoving for a moment, shivers of pain shooting through him.

"No...I need to...tell you..." he caught her gray gaze in his own blue. "Will you...be...my wife?" he asked.

Deivenada smiled, tears now flowing freely from her face. She wiped them away with a dirty hand.

"I...love...you..." were his last words, as they died from his lips. His morning blue eyes dimmed.

"I love you, Zenerax, I always will. Gods, why?" she screamed, hugging his body close. She placed a kiss on his lips, a tear trailing down into his mouth. "Gods, no," she whispered. "I love him."

Chapter 33
Artifacts and Pearls

Mat watched Deivenada from above, walking among the garden roses and trees. She had cut her red hair in mourning. He knew she had lost a great deal in her life, everything held dear to her. All she had left was her brother.

Yesterday, four hundred and fifty-three men and women had died, good and bad. He mourned every one of them.

The smoke still hung in the air and some after effects from his magic lingered. Eside and Ryen had been relatively shaken after they had used their magic to kill, but more so Eside than Ryen. Mat himself was shaken, but he would not let it be known. It would be hard, his face impassive, showing nothing.

With the Nekid destroyed, he and his army needed to be moving out, past the Gangga mountains and into Selkare. He needed to make himself known to the world and get reunited with Janevra.

Mat pulled back from the window.

Mat was in his room. It was a nice room. A large carpet covered the stone floor. An old tapestry of a Daaguwh meeting hung above the fire-place. Red chairs were placed around a dark wood table. A canopy covered bed lay in a connecting room. On the far wall were stacks of books, each dating back to the days of the First Dragons and up to the Fifth Age. Some even talked about the time before the Dragons.

Mat walked over to the pile of books and picked up one with a blue cover that had been lying on the floor away from the others.

He sat down in a chair, folding his legs. The title of the book read *Dragon Artifact*. Mat opened the book and dust gently floated from the pages. The book was old, very old and when he touched it it seemed as if it would crumble to dust. It was one of the rarest books in the world; only two copies had been made. Mat's had been in the Dagau Library and the other was in Carim, Angarat. It was only by the will of the Gods that this one had fallen into Mat's hands.

Mat began to read, his mind becoming engrossed in the pages.

"There are eight known Artifacts of the Dragons.
The first, the Moons of Iwo, increases one's magical ability by twofold. It is a small object only about four inches by four inches and glows a dark red when in use. After the Third Battle it was hidden somewhere by a woman loyal to the Dragons. It is rumored that she hid it in the Lone Islands upon a rock that looks like a sword.
The second is called Dragons' Rings made up of two. Both rings are gold and circular. The last Aseik Shoi made it in the Fifth Age. These two rings

can only be used by the Dragons and increases their power by threefold, a
very powerful ring indeed. The maker of the Rings hid them in a secret
place, which can only be found by one loyal to the Dragons. He left this
riddle to find them,
"High in sky
Not low on ground.
Mountains south.
Jagged peaks north.
Plains west.
Glint in rising sun
Shines in star light night
A place of Worship
Battles fought
Death of Dragons it is thought."
The third Artifact, the Horn of Quna'a, was used in the First Battle
between Good and Evil. It widens one's ability and does something of
which I am not aware. All I know is that it is lost in the Lost Mountains.
The Lord Dragon can only use the Fourth, the Sword of Hadar. It increases
his power by sevenfold. This sword is in the Iwo Mountains, under the
guard of someone much forgotten.
The Fifth, the White Staff of Jayapur can only be used by the Lady Dragon
and increases her power by sevenfold. This Artifact is considered lost for it
has sunk in the Jayapur. It is rumored that when the Sword and the White
Staff are put together they can control life and death, challenge the Dark
Lord, and move the stars.
The Sixth Artifact is called the Knives of Thorn. They are two beautifully
wrought daggers that are ancient artifacts used by the First Dragons.
They increase power by fourfold but their own ability is amazing. If a
person not gifted in the art of magic used these weapons, they would
suddenly gain knowledge otherwise forbidden to them. They too are
hidden in a splitting river.
The Warlord can only use the seventh, the Iron Hand on Carim. It increases his power by sevenfold. Like the Staff and the Sword, the Hand is
lost. On Caendor soil it is said to be guarded by a fiery demon of a once
powerful realm.
The Pearls of Light, the last and most desired Artifact, increases one's
power by half the fold of the Artifact it is connected to. These pearls, eight
roses in all, are lost around the Kingdom. Each Pearl is linked to an
Artifact. If one holds a Pearl, they gain half of that Artifact's power. If all
the pearls are found and brought together they can control all of the Seven
Artifacts, from any distance. The eighth Pearl is black and connected to the
Hawk, the Hand, and the Eye.
To find the other seven, one must think. Here is the riddle:
"Day sun a fiery ball, night the moons an eerie glow. In southeast, three
they be, where creatures of once beauty live in dying peace.

Right under the shadow of a dangerous jewel, in a cave where no sunlight rules. Eyes of dead rosy red.
Again we watch the colors in the sky and see people die on a field where blood was spilled, where gods became true and mortals said good-bye. Gone, they are, a treasure held dear, a place of fear, Devils here. Forgotten in time, no sacrifice.
On the plains in a forest of green, a girl, a boy find true love in A'unat, a Pearl there be veiled.
North of here lies an island, hidden and forbidden, on no map but here, under water on a long forgotten pillar of fear.
Shadow of hell, no soft ringing bell, battle now ridden of Warlord and Dragon, covered in fire, no Pearl of be hire."

Mat closed the book, his mind deep in thought. *If I could get one of those Artifacts…*

Mat opened his mind to Janevra.

"Janevra?"

"What, Mat?"

"How are things going there?"

"Not too well. We're about to get attacked by a horde of rogui. There are lots of them."

"We were just attacked by the Nekid, the group that follows the Warlord."

"Things are getting out of hand. He's moving towards Selkare soon. We're not ready, not unless we can get over five thousand men and women there in fifteen days."

"If we don't, innocent people will die. Do you want that?"

"No."

"I thought so. I'm leaving tomorrow. I'll meet you there with two thousand strong in fifteen days."

"I'll try to meet you."

"Oh, I forgot. I found this interesting book about Artifacts." Mat sent her a mind image of what he had just read.

He said his good-bye then moved his mind away from the connection.

Mat stood up and walked out of the room and into a long, vast hall.

Vena walked by, her arms piled high with dirty bloody bandages. She had just come from the hospital wing.

"Vena, do you have a moment?"

"Yes," she answered, turning around, her face questioning.

"I think that it is time for us to leave," Mat said.

"Leave?" she asked, bewildered.

"Yes."

"Where?" Vena said, motioning to a servant to take the pile of bandages from her.

Once the servant had left Mat answered. "We're going to Calahar."

"We? Why?"

"The Warlord is leaving Angarat and is shifting his attention to Selkare. We will be leaving tomorrow, with two thousand. Leama will stay behind being she is Djed. I want you to first ask for volunteers. If you don't get over two thousand men we're in trouble. Make sure we have enough chariots for half the force. The chariots will be a large asset in the battle."

"Yes." She turned to leave.

"I've been practicing, Vena, my magic."

Vena looked at his eyes, her gray one's calculating. "And what have you learned to do now, child?"

"Watch."

Mat reached for the magic, an easy thing now. He felt it flow through his veins, in his blood.

Whispering no words but just simple mind commands he felt the powers of Air. He wove a net beneath Vena, lifting her up into the air. He read her feelings, her mixed emotions and her thoughts. He sent her his own memories of his past life as a farmer.

She gasped.

Mat let her down softly, her feet slowly touching the floor.

Vena sniffed, arranging her clothes. "Very good." She whirled away, walking swiftly.

Mat frowned thoughtfully. *How is it that I scare her? She taught me everything.*

Walking down the hall until he came to Ryen's room, Mat knocked on the door.

Ryen opened it, surprised when he saw who it was. "Hello, Mat." He stepped aside to let Mat in.

Mat walked passed him and into the spacious anteroom. Eside was there, in front of him a board game.

"We're leaving tomorrow. I need you two to get ready. We're going to Selkare. The Warlord will be attacking us there," Mat said as he poured himself a glass of white wine.

Ryen sat down in a chair, and exchanged a glance with Eside.

"The Lady Dragon will be there and so will your fellow Phoenixes." Mat grinned. Both would be surprised once they knew what type of women they would be working with. Head strong and smart, beautiful and competitive.

"Mat," Eside said, "Ryen is beating me horribly in this game of Arrows. I'm assuming you know how to play it since it's an Ile game. Could you help me? Just give me a couple words of advice?"

"That's not fair," Ryen said. "You'll win."

"Perhaps," Mat said, smiling and moving over to stand in front of the table. He bent down and scrutinized the pieces. "Well, you've lowered your defenses here." Mat indicated the large castle that stood for a city. "You need to protect your castle. If you move your footmen here," Mat pointed to the circle in front of the castle, "then you force him to attack your footmen with his horsemen. After he attacks you, you are free to attack his archers with your horsemen behind."

Eside grinned at Mat. "Thanks."

Mat nodded.

Leaving the room and closing the door behind him, Mat swished the wine around in his glass. He quickly drank it, setting the empty glass on a table in one of the hallways. He hurried down two flights of stairs, and out into the garden where he found Deivenada, holding a rose in her hand.

"Dei?" he said quietly. She didn't look up. "We're leaving tomorrow." He turned away.

"I'm coming," she said.

Mat nodded, turning his head and looking out the corner of his eye. A silver tear slid down Dei's check.

He moved away, anger raging behind his eyes.

Chapter 34
Elven Battle

Janevra stood on top of the highest tower in the Elven city watching the flickering campfires of the rogui army.

It was dusk, the sun was setting in a red sky. The color streaked across the sky like blood from a fresh wound. There was a slight breeze bringing to her the scent of campfires. Above her the stars were coming out, full and bright as if the world below them was of no concern.

Not wanting to be caught out in the descending darkness the people down below her hurried, their steps swift. The outer walls of the city were seemingly deserted, but the trained eye knew better. Hidden in the battlement's shadows were archers.

Janevra's auburn hair shone in the dying light. Her dress gently fanned out behind her, the sleeveless dress showing the lightning bolt, its white light a mysterious power. A star itself was her beauty.

Ake was standing next to her, her earrings, nose stud and necklace giving her the appearance of a foreign goddess. Her outlandish clothes and short midnight hair only added to her figure. Her purple eyes were staring at the fires as if she could read the minds of those below. The phoenix on her arm looked real with its red and gold feathers.

Riak stood on the other side of Janevra, her gray eyes unreadable. Her loose brown hair streaked out behind her like a running dapple. Even though her clothes were simple, she still looked as if she was straight from a legend. Her proud posture and soft face was hidden in the lengthening shadows. As Ake, the phoenix burnished pride on her arm. Curly lay perched on her neck, purring in contentment.

Kiera was standing next to her. Her fine dress and heavy jewelry stated she was rich and noble, too proud to stick her nose into others affairs unless they directly affected her. Her white hair was loaded with little sparkling diamonds cascading down her back. Her long sleeved dress covered up the dazzling phoenix on her arm.

Kiera turned towards Janevra. "My Lady Dragon, may I leave?" she asked, her voice giving off the slight hint of dislike of being inferior to another.

"If you wish," Janevra said, hoping Kiera would try to understand what was going to happen tomorrow.

The sound of Kiera's rustling dress was the only sound on the High Tower of Stars.

The sun had set completely, the last few rays allowed little vision.

"How many do you think will die?" Janevra asked, the question hanging in the air.

Riak and Ake were silent. The unanswered question was like a curse. Janevra looked at both of them, sadness creeping into her eyes. "Then only the stars will know," Janevra said turning her gaze back out into the inky blackness, the darkness only being driven away by the glow of the city's lights.

Janevra watched as the last red left the sky. At first, duty had never been that demanding, only a tiny dot on a sheet of millions. Now her duty to the people, her duty to the world, her duty to herself was like a thousand weights added on her shoulders.

Janevra's hand trailed a crack in the stone of the Tower. "The Warlord has control of all of Angarat. His army is believed to be in the thousands and rumor has it the Phoenix of Death has joined his side and is now training men and women in the Art of Death magic.

Drumming her fingers on the tower wall, Janevra voiced her thoughts. "Jariran is turning into a nightmare under the rule of Ravften. They say that Ravften has raised the dead from the ground. The City guard is mostly made up of skeletons. The remaining people in the city are thought dead or dying. But they do not find relief in the afterlife. They become the minions of Ravften. What is the world coming to?"

"War," Ake said.

Janevra shivered. *War, war that will engulf the whole Northern Kingdom.* Janevra glowered. *It is war to the people but to history it is only another battle fought between the Light and Dark.*

"Janevra," Riak said, "what if Ravften joins the Warlord?"

"Thousands more would be added to his army and that much more land would be under his control, that many more people. If Ravften joins the Warlord, we will be even more outnumbered than before."

"But what of the other nations that have not chosen sides? What of Istra, Riyad, Zayen, LTana, Sunda, Caroa and Taymyr? What if they followed you? That would make the numbers even," Riak said.

"Yes, it would." Janevra touched the lightning bolt on her arm. "But I cannot march into their countries and demand an army. I would need to talk to the King before I could do anything. Right now there is not enough time to talk to them. The Warlord is pressing us. We must use the forces we have for the first battle between the Warlord, Mat and I."

"Is there any news from the other nations?" Ake asked.

"Istra has hinted that they will follow us but the King wants us to talk to him first. Riyad and Zayen are trying to organize an army for themselves, but I wouldn't be surprised if the Warlord attacked them before they are ready. Selkare has foolishly decided to stand up to the Warlord alone. Of the other nations I have heard nothing."

Janevra sighed. With the Warlord so organized, the forces of good seemed to have little chance. The Forgotten people were not even united, most were probably dead.

She had to meet Mat in Selkare in fifteen days. By gods did she wish she had learned how to move more than five hundred people with magic. With Mat's help they could jump a thousand, as could two of the Phoenixes together. Perhaps there was a better way to transport people. She had read in one of the books the priest had given her about a portal used long ago to carry people far distances. When she had some free time she would practice visualizing the portal so when the moment came she could use one.

Janevra looked around and found that both Ake and Riak had left. She shrugged and centered on her thinking.

She missed Mat. It was funny when she thought of it. When he was gone she felt a kind of unease as if she had no power.

Janevra thought of how far both of them had gone. From princess and peasant to Dragons, the most powerful people next to the Warlord. It was a strangely frightening step.

She had not one idea what to do as the Lady Dragon. The Prophecies were of no help and neither was anything else. When she thought of it real hard, she sent shivers down her back. If you were a middle age person or older and you looked at the Warlord and the Dragons you would swear and curse. The entire world was in the hands of children.

Janevra smiled bitterly. It was going to be miserable having power over who lived and who died. She knew in the end all the sacrifices of others that she asked them to make might save thousands. She frowned. But it was still asking someone to give up something precious. Their life. And she knew it would be hard to ask someone for this. Gods, but she would give anything for her normal life back.

Taking one last look at the burning campfires of the enemy, she left the tower. Qwaser must have known she wanted him for he was waiting for her at the base of the stairs that lead to the tower.

"Qwaser, good. I need to talk to you."

Qwaser smiled, his eyes bright. Janevra had no doubt he was anticipating the coming battle.

"After tomorrow, we need to leave."

Qwaser looked at her. "I knew we were going to leave soon but after a battle, Janevra? That's trying on the nerves."

Janevra nodded wearily. "I know, Qwaser. I have no choice. The Warlord is eyeing Calahar and Mat wants to stop him from taking it. I think it's a good idea. We've let the Warlord reign free for far too long."

Qwaser gave her an odd look. "When have you talked to Mat?"

Janevra paused. "I—"

Qwaser laughed. "Don't fret. I don't need to know. What is it that you want me to do?"

"After the battle." *If you live through it*, she thought, "I need you to ask for volunteers. I will not force anyone to come. They must all want to go. 'An unwilling army is a defeated army,'" she quoted.

"What book is that from?"

"A Lady Thysi. I was browsing through the library and came upon it. Very good reading, I would recommend you read it once this is all over."

Qwaser held out his hand, ticking off the things she wanted him to do with his fingers. "Gather an army after the battle, read a book."

Janevra punched his arm. "You are useless sometimes, Qwaser."

Qwaser's face lost its joy. "Kalioa is right, Janevra, you do need to laugh and smile more."

"I will," she said, "when it's all over."

⊂⊃   ⊂⊋   ⊱⊰

They were attacked that morning.

The sun rose up, sending its golden glow across the sky. It was a strange morning. It was cold and people's breath hung in the air. The dew on the grass and the leaves was almost frozen. Everything was still.

Horns sounded everywhere in the city and out. The battle would be fought on the slopes of Qolic Cattutr, the base of the mountain at which the city lay.

Janevra was standing on the top of the west wall, looking down into the valley where the battle would take place in two hours, when Ake found her. Ake sprinted down the battlements, her face pale underneath her dark skin.

"Janevra."

Janevra turned around, alarm growing in her ever-knowing green eyes.

"Janevra, this is horrible!" Ake panted.

"Calm down, Ake. Tell me, what's wrong?" Janevra said, grabbing Ake by the shoulders, steadying Ake's panic.

"There is rumor in the palace that someone, a close friend, is a spy!"

Janevra's face became rigid, her eyes hard.

"Who else knows of this rumor?"

"Riak, Qwaser, Kalioa, Kiera, the King, his council and everyone else." Ake pressed her lips together. "I'm also here to tell you that five-hundred elves are ready to fight. I believe that they are out in that valley now, hidden by those thick trees." Ake pointed to the south, and then to the north where the rogui were marching towards the city. She turned to leave.

"Stay here. Riak and Kiera are coming. Then we can use our magic."

Janevra watched the trees intently. She had wanted to fight alongside the elves. Qwaser, Kalioa and the King had forbade her, saying if she was killed by an arrow or sword, all hope would be lost for the future for the Lord Dragon could not carry on the fight against the Darkness alone. She understood their reasoning, but it did not keep her from wanting to go. Her fingers itched to feel a sword in her hands.

ロ   ロ   ロ

Qwaser slung his bow over his shoulder, checking his arrows one more time.

"Ready," he whispered, hearing it get passed down the tree line by birdcalls.

Along the tree line greenish shadows moved, each one equipped with over three-dozen arrows. The infantry was further back, hidden in the denser trees, their leader Kalioa.

The plan was for the archers to finish off or injure as many as they could before the approaching army reached the tree line. Once this happened the archers who could not wield other weapons would climb high in the trees and swing around to the back of the rogui army. When they reached this position they would shoot at the back of the rogui forces using extra quivers of arrows. The archers who could use other weapons would drop down once the infantry reached the tree line and fight side by side with elven soldiers. As General of the Army, it was his job to know everything that was going to happen and lead troops into battle.

He moved swiftly, as silent as a cat stalking prey, along the lines of elves, making sure all was ready.

An uncanny sound rose out across the grassland. It was a strange sound, like a dying animal's scream.

The hairs on the back of his neck rose. He shrugged a shoulder to push the feeling away. His palms began to sweat. He had not fought in a battle for over a month.

Qwaser stopped in the center of the elven archers, mouth dry and demanding water he could not give it.

The heads of the rogui came into view over the small ridge. They were marching in rows of twenty.

He heard the sounds of arrows sliding out of leather quivers. He listened as bowstrings were drawn, the scrape of wooden arrows against the thin bow cords.

"Hold," Qwaser said.

The army came closer, only a hundred yards away. He could almost see the eyes of some.

"Hold!"

They were ugly creatures with their gray skin and squatty bodies. Each rogui was covered in black armor and had spears dangling in their fleshy hands.

"Hold!"

They marched steadily closer; their creepy chants being carried to him by the wind.

Above him the sun reached two points, two hours after dawn. Birds flew above the armies, running from warfare.

"Hold!" Qwaser screamed again.

The words of the chant he could now distinguish.

> *"Bloody blood, watch it run.*
> *Bloody blood, enjoy the fun.*
> *Bloody blood, watch it spread.*
> *Bloody blood, cut the head.*
> *Bloody blood, for the dead.*
> *Bloody blood, put in bed.*
> *Bloody blood, see how red."*

Qwaser swallowed, the bile in his mouth sour.

"Aim!" This time he yelled in elven.

One hundred and twenty arrows came up.

Qwaser aimed his own bow at a greenish looking one, its mouth open and drooling.

He looked over at the two elves next to him, surprised to see Tasawer and Danlk. Qwaser smiled at them when they looked over.

Tasawer with his dark eyes and hair and Danlk with his blue eyes and brown hair, both looked ready to kill the rogui, their last battle still fresh in their minds.

Qwaser looked back at the approaching swarm of black armor. They were forty feet away.

"Fire!" the sound of his voice rang out in the trees.

The sound of twanging strings were heard in the air as was the sound of hissing arrows. All of the arrows found their marks. Many of the rogui fell, arrows sticking out of their heads or holes in their armor. Some fell shrieking, others dropped silently.

The next rally of arrows fell down upon the evil creatures, the arrows looking like deadly birds of prey in the sky.

More rogui fell.

The army was now twenty feet away, behind them the dead bodies of their fellow warriors, arrows sticking out of them like lifeless flowers.

By the time the rogui were ten feet away every archer was out of arrows, each of them hitting their marks over half the time.

"Archers drop back! Infantry forward!" Qwaser yelled.

Danlk and Tasawer dropped back taking Qwaser's bow and empty quiver with them.

Qwaser pulled out Brytaya's sword.

He heard the foot soldiers down below, their running and hard breathing quickening his own. Qwaser dropped down from the trees onto a rogui, cutting its throat with a swipe of his sword.

He found Kalioa next to him. They went back to back, swinging and lashing, sometimes getting minor wounds of their own.

He slashed at the snarling faces with the protruding yellow fangs. He hacked at the bloated fleshy bodies. A hate grew in him, one he had experienced before.

Blood flew freely. Everything seemed to be black, and red.

Bolts of white lightning flashed everywhere, hitting down foes and setting some on fire. The smell of burning flesh filled the crisp air.

Qwaser was caught up in the battle.

Fireballs from Janevra and the Phoenixes took out several rogui at a time. Screams from the end of the rogui army proved that the archers were doing their job.

He felt a sharp pain in his back leg and he fell to the ground, visions of death flashing through his head.

Kalioa stood above him.

He smiled. He was glad she was there to help him.

"Kalioa, help." His sword had fallen a foot away, just out of reach.

She looked down at him. An emotion he could not identify flittered across her face.

"Help, Kalioa," he repeated, throwing aside the wonder of why she was not getting attacked. People were fighting around them but no one attacked them. It was as if no one was paying attention.

Gods, but his leg hurt.

"No," she said, staring at him, dark amusement in her eyes.

"This is no game," Qwaser said, fear clenching in his heart. The sounds of battle seemed to die away as Qwaser focused all of his attention on Kalioa.

"I know." She smiled wickedly, a malicious expression on her face.

"Kalioa, help me. I got my leg nicked. I can't get up."

"Sorry."

Qwaser frowned. "Sorry?"

"Tell me, why should I help you?" she asked, her blade swishing back and forth between his body and hers.

"I'm your friend...well, more than that." He looked at her.

"Ah, Qwaser, so naive, so innocent, so trusting. What a pity you will die."

"What?" He shivered, his voice growing harsh. His leg hurt, but what Kalioa was hinting at hurt far worse.

"Yes, die. A pity like I said. The Warlord could use someone like you." She moved closer, her sword streaked with blood.

"You're … you're…" he couldn't finish. He had trusted her! He had asked Janevra to trust her. He could have ruined everything with his trust for her. He could have destroyed what he was trying to save. "Why?" he finally managed.

"I was offered more, better things, than freedom."

"But…"

"Yes, Qwaser, it's a pity to kill you. I enjoyed our days together. But it would have never worked out," Kalioa said, an uncaring look in her blue eyes.

"Why not?" he said coldly, using his stomach muscles to stay upright.

"Because you cherish freedom and good. I love imprisonment and evil."

Qwaser's eyes grew wide and a hate settled within them. "You… bitch!" he spat. "You used me! You used me to know everything!"

Kalioa cocked her head to one side. "That's right, love." She smiled, pure evil shining in her eyes. The moans and screams of people in the background somehow made her face seem twisted with some sort of triumph.

Qwaser glanced at his sword, just out of reach.

"Like I said, a pity to kill you." Kalioa stood at his side, her sword held high.

She plunged her sword down.

Qwaser rolled over, the sword narrowly missing his side. Pain lanced through his leg, but he put it behind him, and grabbed the sword, its blood tip gleaming.

Kalioa screamed when her sword hit earth. She looked up and found Qwaser's sword at her throat. He knocked hers out of her grasp.

She smiled. "Nice."

Qwaser's eyes became hooded. "Go to hell." He thrust his sword into her belly.

She fell to the ground, blood staining her teeth and spilling out of her mouth. "Bastard," she choked.

She died and Qwaser felt an emptiness take hold of his heart.

He looked around. The battle was over. Elves moved around, caring for wounded. All around him lay dead rogui and elves. Ravens were already feasting on the bodies of those dead and those still alive. Screams echoed around the valley walls.

Qwaser sneered up at the sunny blue sky.

Chapter 35
The Thieves Guild

Saviak craned her neck, looking up at the high walls surrounding Calahar. It had taken her five days on foot to reach her destination.

With no money, no food, and no place to stay, she needed to find her friend before she did anything else. The money, the food and the place to stay could wait.

Saviak's stomach grumbled. *Food first, then,* she thought.

Her clothes were travel worn. Her once clean pants had holes in the knees and her black shirt was dusty. Her short black hair was greasy and needed to be washed.

Saviak walked underneath the gatehouse and stopped in the middle of the road, gaping.

Calahar was huge and beautiful, as was expected of a city that lay over the ancient city of the elves, Calahadar. Magnificent buildings rose up into the pale blue sky. Colorful plazas were around twinkling fountains. Potted flowers draped from windows. Little children chased each other around the streets, their laughter rising like bells. Adults talked among themselves, some quietly, some angrily. Shops were open and the smell of bread, cooking meat, horses, flowers and rich perfumes floated on the warm air.

A richly dressed woman walked by her, closer than a hands length away. Saviak darted her hand along the edges of the woman's purse, neatly pulling it off without the slightest jerk.

Saviak walked away, no guilt on her face.

She opened the purse. A grin slid across her face as she found the purse loaded with silver and gold coins.

Time to eat.

Saviak located a tavern and walked in. She found a table in the back, next to the fireplace.

A bar maid came up.

"What ye like?" the young woman asked, her heavy accent labeling her as an eastward Angaratian.

"Soup."

The girl nodded and walked away, her attention being called elsewhere.

Saviak sat back, putting her hands behind her head.

A group of men came in laughing at some unknown joke. They sat at the table next to Saviak.

Saviak closed her golden eyes, but her ears were still alert. She listened to the men.

"Oi, guess what I heard?" one said. He didn't wait for an answer, but kept on talking. "I 'ear that an army be on the march, the Warlord's army. Said to be coming 'ere now that the Warlord bagged Angarat."

Saviak started at that but kept her eyes closed.

"Why would 'e come 'ere?" another asked.

"Dunno," the first one said.

"Miss, your food."

Saviak opened her yellow stare, and found a bowl of soup in front of her. She handed the serving woman a gold coin, feeling generous.

Saviak finished off the soup quickly. It didn't fill her stomach but she needed to find her friend.

Hurrying out of the tavern, she moved down the street. The sun was still high in the sky. There was plenty of time.

She became engrossed in thought. If the Warlord really was coming to Calahar, it would be a great chance to get a job. A lot of people would become angry and revengeful. Saviak clapped her hands in joy.

She needed to find the city's Thieves Guild before she started planning her business. That was where her friend would be and that was where she could start over again.

Being a thief herself, she knew what certain signs hanging above inns and taverns meant. She just needed to find one that directed her to the Guild.

Saviak moved on, her eyes reading the tavern and inn signs. The sky above her gradually grew darker, the sun setting behind the Iwo Mountains.

She finally found what she was looking for. It was an old run down tavern. The sign above it that read "Coins" swung gently, its hinges creaking.

Saviak walked in, tense. Who knew what she might find. She blinked several times before her eyes grew accustomed to the dark.

She found no fire in the hearth. Tables were overturned and lamps shattered across the floor. Cups and mugs were on the ground. Whatever they were holding had dried up long ago. Some plates still had food on them but maggots were growing in them, diminishing Saviak's appetite in the meantime. The door leading into the kitchen was hanging on two crooked hinges.

Saviak touched one of her knives, moving out into the middle of the tavern, feeling unseen eyes on her back.

Broken pottery crunched underneath her small feet.

Upstairs something crashed to the floor.

Saviak froze, her golden eyes glowing like a cat's in the gloom.

It was silent, so silent a pin could drop and sound like an explosion.

"A strange girl."

Saviak startled. She slowly turned around.

The speaker was in the shadows, his face unknown to her, his height medium, his body slim, and his voice sounding young.

"Who are you?" Saviak asked.

"You should not be the one asking questions."

Saviak's lips became tight. She held her head up a little bit higher.

"Why have you come here?" he asked.

"Why do you want to know?"

His shadow spread his hands. "It is my business to know everything."

Saviak paused.

She didn't trust him, but if she was to find her friend she needed to get information and in the process give some too.

Her eyes formed a golden glare.

"I'm looking for a friend."

"A friend you say? For revenge? For love? For what?"

Saviak muttered something unintelligible then said, "For a question that must be answered."

"A question? How interesting," the man murmured silkily. "What kind of question?"

"A question that involves him and me only," Saviak said darkly.

The man wangled a finger back and forth, and laughed smugly. "Girl, I advise you to answer every one of my questions."

Saviak clenched her jaw. "I need to ask him what side he is on."

"Ah, a very good question indeed." The man seemed to ponder for a moment. "What is the name of this man you are looking for?"

"His name is Taimakr."

The man jerked as if a blow had landed on him. "Taimakr? Taimakr Aedun?" he asked, disbelief in his voice.

"Yes."

"Are you Saviak?" he inquired

"Taimakr, is that you?" Saviak strained her eyes to see into the hazy gray.

The man shook his head. "No, but he said you might come."

"He's here? Where is he? I must see him!" Saviak whispered.

"He is not... here," the man said, pointing to the tavern.

"Where is he? I must know," Saviak said.

"He has left this world."

"What?" Alarm sounded in Saviak's voice.

"He's dead."

"Dead, how?" Shock reverberated through her body and a sharp pain clenched her heart.

"When he became the Thieves' Guild Leader, he planned a robbery, that if it succeeded would be the most famous and grandest theft of all. We were to rob the Palace, never before done. Twenty thieves were hand picked by Taimakr and me to help us accomplish this seemingly impossible job. We succeeded. We were rich, richer than any of us had ever dreamed. News was spreading through the city and the countryside of a grand robbery. Taimakr was named the greatest thief of all time. But someone betrayed us. They told the city guards where to find the Thieves Guild and how to get the stolen treasure back. Taimakr was killed in that battle and all but a few lucky ones who the guards thought of as dead escaped. When the guards had left, the few remaining survivors salvaged through the wreckage. We found some things of value, not much. The strongest Thieves Guild was in ruin. There were twenty-seven of us who survived and we each swore to get revenge. And we will." The man's hands formed fists, shaking them in anger.

"Are you telling me there is no Thieves Guild?" Saviak said, astonished.

"No, there is. You're standing in it. After the attack we buried our dead with the few remaining treasures. We then searched for a place to have our new headquarters. The old one had been found, and we knew the sewers were not safe anymore. So we found a run down building and made it our headquarters. They haven't found us yet, and never will."

Saviak sunk down onto the floor. Gone was her friend. Hot tears spilled out of her eyes.

"Get up." Saviak's head came up. The man was still in the shadows. She stood up, her face damp. "I need to decide what to do with you, Saviak."

Saviak shivered, her eyes hot.

"Don't worry, I won't kill you. We need all the thieves we can get." He sounded amused.

The man moved out of the shadows.

He was lean, and held himself in a way that could only be described as dangerous. His eyes were a strange light blue, the color of dawn. Dark lashes rimmed his eyes and his eyebrows were cocked in amusement. His lips were turned upward and his long fingers were running up and down a long sword. His hair was long and straight, reaching down to his collar-bone. It had been unevenly cut and dyed a midnight blue. A quiver of arrows was slung across his back in the most nonchalant manner.

"My name, Saviak, is Dashar. I'm the leader of the Thieves' Guild." As he spoke dark forms detached themselves from the walls and from underneath tables. They were all skinny, most short as a thief should be. They moved around and surrounded Saviak. Weapons of so many different sorts glinted in the moonlight coming in the window. Moonlight? How long had she been in here?

"Saviak, you have a choice. Join us or face the rest of your life in misery."

"Why must I join?"

"I told you where our hideout is and we're planning a raid soon. We need all the experienced hands we can get." Dashar smiled.

It was no choice for her. She needed money, and a home, and friends and she needed her question answered, somehow.

"I'll join."

Laughter rang out and before she knew it people were hugging her and slapping her on the back.

Dashar only watched her.

Chapter 36
Splendor Destroyed

The strongest Nation had fallen and lay in shadow.

He had turned the city into a nightmare, a dream where the living never awoke and the dead ruled.

Buildings were burned and stood in the gloom like skeletons, their rough shattered edges reaching for a black sky. Store windows were broken and the insides raided but many buildings were burned to nothing save ash. Pieces of cloth that had covered windows fluttered out but there was no breeze. Broken pottery lay where it had fallen.

The Grand Plaza was filled with rubble. The fountain in the middle spouted no water and the beautiful design that had been inlaid in the stone was scraped off. The Theater with its black granite and white marble was in ruins. Its towering pillars that had supported the stand had crashed to the ground, flinging large chunks of marble and granite into the streets. The Great Library's roof had caved in, books buried beneath sheets of gold. Once the roof had caved in, the limestone and marble walls had too. They had fallen inward, crashing down onto the fallen gold roof, hiding the precious metal and valuable books and scrolls. All of the temples in the city had been burned to ashes. Nothing remained of the temples except the bodies of the priests who had carried out their day-to-day rituals and chores. The beautiful gardens of Jariran with their green grass, blossoming trees and sparkling fountains were no more. Instead in their place stood gnarled trees, their twisted branches reaching up to the dark sky as if looking for a lost soul. The blossoms on the trees had fallen to the ground where they lay black. The fountains were but shattered piles of stone. In place of the grass was dirt. Nothing was green. The Jariran College was beyond recognition. All the walls had collapsed into the street, spitting debris into the nearby homes and gardens. The Palace was the same, except that the Tower of the Light was missing its top, as if some invisible force had ripped it off and thrown it into the streets below. The Palace was now black instead of its once shimmering white, layered in soot from the many fires.

The dead lay everywhere. The charred remains of the people lay strewn in the streets. Most seemed to have died horribly. Blood had come out of their noses, trailing down and clogging their mouths. It had leaked out of their ears and run down their necks to pool in their collarbones. Dark blood had dripped out of the corners of their eyes, looking like tears. The bodies had limbs missing, the jagged parts of bones sticking through the skin or bits of clothing. Most looked like they had been ripped off by animals. Deep gashes were across the bellies of some, the innards spilling out over the ground, staining the cobblestone streets red. Crows had pecked the eyes out of corpses. Some of the bodies were already skeletons, the bones having small amounts of flesh on them, just enough for the birds to bite off and swallow. But most of the bodies were hanging from the walls, ropes around their necks. The faces purple and the tongues black, the body bloated with maggots. The white worms wiggled around, crawling out of the eyes and nose, from the ears and open wounds filled with dried blood.

The clouds above the sky were murky and dark, as if a terrible storm was hanging over the city.

The streets were deserted except for some patrols of the dead. These were people who he killed and brought back from the graves. The patrols

were all white and yellow bone, some with missing pieces. All had swords
that they carried in a skeleton hand, and each was grinning a devilish grin,
cracked teeth showing through. These patrols killed any living thing they
found.

The people of Jariran had fled, even those in the surrounding countryside. A very few had chosen to stay with Ravften and have power and even
fewer had chosen to stay and avenge the death of the beloved King and
Queen. Hence was the reason Aivon Valynier peered out from behind an
old jewelry store, its standing stone cold against his skin.

Aivon was in his twenties with pitch-black hair and blue eyes like rain
clouds. His skin had smudges of dirt and ashes on it. He was the spy for
the Rebellion and his job was to map out the patrol routes and plan the
ambushes that they used to kill the undead. The Rebellion was over two
hundred strong, but their numbers shrank weekly with deaths and deser-
tions.

In the belt around Aivon's waist were over a dozen knives. Slung
across his shoulder was a quiver of arrows and a bow. In a sheath connected to his belt was a long knife. In his left hand he gripped a slingshot,
and with that did he have deadly aim.

It was dark out. There was no moon to shine out light, not even light
that a month ago would have streamed from windows and doors. The only
light came from the eerie glow of the magic that hung around the city like a
fog.

During the time of the late King and Queen he had been in training to
be a soldier. Thus he was skilled in weaponry and fighting.

He heard the clanking of armor. A patrol was coming.

Aivon crouched down low, disappearing into the shadows.

The only way to kill the undead was to shine light, pure sunlight, at
them or disembody the head.

Aivon watched as the undead cracked by him, their bones grinding
together and twisting without the help of muscles.

Hatred came into his eyes. The undead had killed his little sister. His
eyes blinked back tears at her memory.

She had died unlike most people. She had died not by magic but by
torture. Ravften had allowed any people related to soldiers to be tortured
by the undead if they fought against him.

He remembered her last words before they took her away.

"Fight, Aivon! Fight! For Good! Fight for me!" she had screamed as
they bore her away, never for him to see again. She had only been fourteen,
barely a young woman. She had always been smiling. In fact the last thing
he saw of her was her smile. She had smiled at him and in her eyes told
him it would be all right.

Aivon clenched his teeth together and pulled a rock out of his belt
pouch. He loaded it into his sling.

The patrol had passed him and was looking in a still standing building.

Mist swirled around their feet and their empty eyes stared around.

Aivon took aim.

"For Fanny," he whispered.

He shot the rock at the patrol leader, the one at the front of the group.

A tearing sound sounded as the rock collided with the head, throwing it off. The patrol leader fell to the ground, now another pile of bones. The other undead looked around, their sightless eyes searching, but not finding.

Aivon smiled coldly as they walked away as if nothing had happened. But one death of those things was not enough, not enough to avenge Fanny. Killing them would never be enough. His revenge would come when he killed Ravften.

His job done, he slithered along the building wall until he came to an empty street. He crossed it, his eyes darting around and searching for anything hiding in the shadows. He had several more blocks of fallen stone to go before he reached the hideout of the Rebellion. He moved among the stones and buildings like a ghost in the flesh.

It was so quiet. Aivon did not even make a sound.

Sometimes when he closed his eyes for a brief instant and opened them again, he could see the city as it was in its original splendor.

He could hear the laughter of a young girl as she splashed water at a boy. He could hear the sound of low talking and children giggling. He could hear the sound of horses whickering, the sounds of metal pounding, fire crackling and footsteps on stone. Sometimes he caught glimpses of the people, a woman washing clothes, a man selling bread, children playing cover and seek around their mothers, and the elder people talking of old days past. But they would fade as quickly as they came like water over ink. And he was left with the cold stone and the harsh future that lay ahead.

They were all dead now, the people. The formal grandeur of the city was only a memory, a ghost that taunted the remaining citizens with its past joy. Nothing living could live in the city anymore, only the dead could. It was a hell for the living. The dead walked the streets in the endless night, and good, anything good, was eliminated. Beauty was no more and dreams of the city haunted those who still lived within it. Death was the only way out and even that was a prison if the Dead King found you. The city was a dark fortress, a place of nightmares, a hell, a haven for the Evil. Aivon hated it.

Aivon had at last reached his destination. It was a strange building indeed. One would not think it to be a place where outlaws hid. It was the Theater. Most of it still stood, except the dais and the pillars. The rest of it was still standing like a dark sentry over a dark city.

What most people did not know was that underneath the Theater was a vast connection of rooms, where in the past costumes, food, scripts and the occasional furniture were stored. Most of the rooms had not been opened in many years, their insides dusty and the bolts rusty. Some rooms were open, the most important ones and this was where the Rebellion lived. It was a safe place for there was only one obvious place out and that was connected to the Theater. If you stayed under the Theater long enough you would learn that there were many more ways out that led to homes and shops.

This was where the Thieves Guild of Jariran lived. And it was these people that made up the Rebellion with a few others. Since it was a hideaway in the old days and was never found, it would be a hideaway in the new days. But something was highly to their advantage. All the locked doors were filled with treasures. And treasure was what Ravften was looking for. All he wanted was treasure and if they put some in the right spot for an ambush, they could kill the undead everyday for five years.

The Thieves Guild had been rich.

Aivon stood out in front of the Theater.

He waited.

"Password," a voice whispered.

"Hope, freedom, and trust."

The door in front of him opened.

Aivon walked in.

He stood inside a magnificent building.

He was in the process of entering the secret doorway to the underground hideaway, when a hand stopped him.

Aivon turned around and stared into the eerie sapphire eyes of a young woman.

"Aivon, something is wrong," she said.

"What?" he asked, recalling her name was Meria, the name of a shoi.

"I... feel something... different... something not quite right. The air... it seems to be... crawling."

Aivon stepped back. Her eyes had taken on a strange look, the look of one possessed.

"Aivon, help me!" she screamed suddenly, causing hidden sentries to start and stare at her.

"Shhhh, quiet, Meria," he whispered fearfully. Ravften's spies were everywhere.

"Gods no! He's in my head! He's—" she cut off and dropped to the floor, withering and screaming. Blood came out of her mouth, and slowly grew on the gray stone floor, thick and red.

She was dead.

A man came up to Aivon, who was staring at the corpse of the woman. "What happened?"

"I think she was killed by Ravften."

The man's eyes went wide, hate lurking in their corners. "How?"

"Magic. He knows we're here."

The man stared at Aivon.

Aivon stared back, his blue eyes cold. "We need to leave. Soon, or we'll all be dead," Aivon said.

The man nodded and ran away. Shouts could soon be heard. Aivon moved away from the body.

Soon the Rebellion was gone, nothing proved that they had once been there, except for a pool of warm blood and a deformed body of a woman. The Theater was empty.

But somewhere the sound of a harp rose up as if from the dreary stones itself and played a sad tune.

Somewhere a tear dropped.

Chapter 37
An Appearance Changed

Raxsen stared at the young man sitting across from him. Actually Dorl Kard was his age, but Raxsen was the one in power, therefore Kard was below him. In everything.

They were in the large tent where Raxsen held meetings with his generals, captains, lieutenants, and his scouts. There was no meeting at the moment, so the table sitting in the center was empty except for Kard, Peirce, a sylai and Raxsen himself. Raxsen wanted to see how strong he was in the art of magic, so he commanded Kard to test him.

Raxsen's ice blue eyes watched as Kard opened a tattered book with a skull on the front.

Dorl Kard was in short sleeves. The flame on his left arm was bright against his white skin. Kard's black eyes studied the book he had opened.

Raxsen glanced over at his general, David Peirce, and found him looking at Kard with something akin to hate.

Raxsen smiled, a thing he rarely did. But it went across his features so fast no one would have noticed.

"Ha! I found it," Kard said jabbing a finger down onto a page littered with strange symbols.

Kard pushed the book closer to Raxsen. "It's on the third line. Read that whole line and if it happens… you'll be the most powerful shoi, the only one equal to the power of the Dragons."

Raxsen pulled the book closer and located the third line on the first page. The writing looked like gibberish to him, but for some odd reason he knew what it meant.

Raxsen went over the words silently in his head first, then spoke the chilling words. The words that all men would soon fear.

He directed the words at the sylai sitting nearby. *"Ach neacvk deatask laciha,"* Raxsen whispered, the words harsh on his tongue.

The sylai suddenly grabbed at his throat, then howled when the blood flooding his eyes obscured his vision. He scratched at his throat, his actions frantic. He dropped to the floor, dead. He had choked on his own blood running down his throat.

Raxsen stared at the body. The spell not only caused the victim to choke on his own blood, but the body rotted from the inside out. This took serious concentration for the spell caster. It aged everything under the skin, causing it to rot. Sometimes the victim would die instantly from the dying organs in its body, or they would have a slower more painful death from choking on their own blood. The other key to the spell was that it could affect up to one hundred people at the time of the spell caster's choosing.

Pierce went over and nudged the body. It collapsed into a pile of bones and skin, the blood splattering on the floor.

Raxsen smirked, pleased.

Looking up, Raxsen found Kard staring at him. "Next, Kard," Raxsen snapped.

Kard reached over and grabbed the book. He flipped through several pages before nodding to himself and pushing the book back over to Raxsen.

"The second page, last line. If it works you should be able to bring that sylai back to life."

Peirce raised his eyebrows at that pile of bones and blood, his vivid green eyes doubtful.

Raxsen took a deep breath and held it. If he could pull this off, it would prove that he could challenge the Dark Lord, or so said the legends.

Raxsen pointed at the corpse, its stench starting to fill the room.

Kard gagged, the smell was too much for him.

"Watch this," Raxsen said. "*Esir pu morf eht htaed,*" he hissed.

The sylai stirred. Blood could be seen forming around the bones and the muscle pulling the ripped body back together. Soon the sylai was sitting again in the chair. But it looked different. It was more muscular and fiercer seeming.

"Shadow will rule the world again," Kard murmured as he closed the book.

Pierce nodded. "Shadow that will make us rich and powerful men."

"My Lord?"

Raxsen swiveled around.

Standing in the doorway was a young woman. She had red hair cropped close to her skull and blue eyes. She was the captain of all the women in the army. Her status was high. Her clothes were made of leather. She had on high leather boots, a loose-fitting shirt and baggy black silk pants. Freckles dotted her face and a small sun shaped scar was on her cheek. How she got a scar like that Raxsen could only guess. From her ears hung earrings made from globes of fire.

"What, Cobrau?" Raxsen said, sitting down and watching the woman.

"My Lord, the scouts have returned and say that we are ten miles away from crossing the border into Selkare. Tomorrow, once we break camp, we will reach Selkare within two hours," Cobrau said, her stance stiff.

"Hmmm," Raxsen said rubbing his chin.

He had taken over the capital of Angarat two days ago with minimum losses. The King had willingly surrendered, saying he surrendered because he didn't want any deaths. Raxsen doubted this. He knew in the past that Angarat had been fueled by power and Evil. Even if Angarat had not surrendered, it would still be his. To ensure this, the lasting loyalty of the country, he had killed the King and Queen and put their daughter on the throne. He remembered what Andrews had told him, that she was a back stabber. That she was greedy. He had given her power in exchange for loyalty. He had cast a spell on her that if she were to betray him, she would die. Not a real death to most but a death to her. She would become a peasant, something she despised and hated. To her this was death. She would never betray him now. Queen Syilvia was another soul bound to him for eternity.

Raxsen now had his eye fixed on Selkare. It was the next easiest nation to attack. They had foolishly not joined any alliances and left themselves open for attack. That was where he was going next, and that was where he and the Dragons would battle their first of many battles.

Raxsen waved a hand to dismiss everyone.

Kard rose and hurried out of the tent. He had shoi to train, and was late. Peirce left with Cobrau, discussing war tactics.

Raxsen sighed as they left. He needed to be alone. But before he could have his moment alone, another person entered the tent. The figure was cloaked in black and its face was hidden in shadows.

"Sir, I need to talk to you," the visitor said, a little too much command in his voice.

"You need?" Raxsen stared at the man before him, his tone icy.

The man shivered. "I want to talk to you, Warlord." His voice shook as he spoke.

Raxsen let it pass, overlooking the command in the man's voice.

"What?" he demanded.

"The Lord Dragon has left the Daaguwh capital. He is heading west, towards Selkare. His power grows daily in both magic and loyalty. The Phoenixes are with him. They are strong. The entire Ile nations have united under him except the Nekid. He left the Daaguwh capital very well defended and he instructed all the Ile leaders to be watchful. They are ready to back him up if the need arises." The man bowed low when he finished his message.

"You did well. Go back to the Lord Dragon's army. Watch. Listen. And when he reaches Calahar come back to me and report. Tell me all that he plans." Raxsen smiled but the smile was just an up turn of his lips.

The man bowed again and walked out of the tent. But before he was out of Raxsen's eyesight the cloak slipped down slightly to reveal a sun tattooed on his left arm.

Raxsen stared after the man, his eyes going to slits. The man would do well.

Raxsen departed out the back, his black cloak snapping against his sword hilt. The warm wind caressed his face. He walked towards the forest.

His army was camped along the banks of a river. A forest was off to one side of the camp, with a pool of hot springs near the river. His men were there. He could hear them and the occasional laugh of a woman. The warm water would feel good after a day of marching.

Perhaps they should stay here for another day, to boost the morale of the men.

Raxsen walked among the tall cedar trees. The smell of pine reached his nose and he was brought back to a time that seemed so long ago. A time when his parents were alive. When he was not the Warlord.

Raxsen's eyes held a distant look in them as he remembered.

"Mother, tell me a tale. I want to hear a tale of the Ancient Peoples, when there were dragons," little Raxsen said, begging his mother.

She had smiled at him, and wrapped her arms round him. Her perfume that she made herself was a pine smell, a motherly smell. Carrying him to bed and tucking him in, she smiled warmly at her young son.

"I shall tell you a tale, my love, a tale of Dragons and shoi. Legend tells of a fiery beast who ruled the Northern Kingdom before the Age of Magic.

"There were three other beasts that spouted fire and they controlled the Eastern, Southern and Western Kingdoms.

"The beasts were called Dragons and they scourged the land and wrecked havoc among the peoples of Ancient times. They had huge treasures of gold and jewels, enough to buy twenty kingdoms. They kept their treasures in their liars and killed anything that tried to steal that cursed treasure. They used beautiful human women as their consorts and took pleasure in killing men. The Dragons were proud, too proud to ever believe that the people they enslaved could rise up and rebel. When the people rebelled, the Dragons died. The Dragons were killed by an ancient power of Evil, an Evil so powerful the gods feared it. The Ancient Peoples used this power to create magics never before seen or dreamed of. They created gateways to other worlds and strange flying machines. Many believe that it was not the Ancients that created these flying machines but a much older race, a race that had enslaved the Dragons and Ancients thousands of years before. The Ancients, with their power, their Evil power, used it against the Dragons. The Dragons fought ferociously against this power, destroying village after village, city after city. Thousands died and the land was burned so badly in many places that crops could never be grown there again. People fled in terror when the trumpet of the Dragon was heard or the shadow passed over them. Many died before they could run, Dragon fear seizing their hearts and killing them where they stood. Seeing their efforts thwarted by the Dragons, the Ancients used more of the Evil power and the Dragons fell, dropping into the sea, their bodies never to be seen again. With the war against the Dragons over, the Ancient Peoples became torn by civil war. The four factions that came out on top ruled a Kingdom each. The Ancients lived in peace for many years thereafter but the Evil they had discovered to fight the Dragons would not stop haunting them. The Ancients began to crave the Evil power. Many grew to love the Evil yet they knew they had discovered something wicked, something they had to destroy no matter the consequences. If they could not destroy it, then they vowed to seal it away and make sure no one ever found it again. Once more the Ancients became divided, some wanted to destroy the Evil, others keep it. Their different wants threw the Ancients into their last war. After years of bloody fighting only the strongest remained. Turning their power against the Evil, they shut the Evil away, using the power of the elves' immortality, and hid the Books of Power, warding them with Relics. If either are ever found, pray, pray hard, pray loud to your god. If they are found, Evil will rise again and the world will be swallowed by Darkness."

Raxsen's mother bent over and kissed him on the forehead. He was her joy, her life. He meant everything to her. Yet he had been her undoing.

Raxsen snapped back to the present. The tale his mother had told him so long ago, caused him to wonder if there was this Evil hiding somewhere and what it was.

The sound of his men swimming in the water sent an idea into Raxsen's head. It was time to learn what his men thought about him.

The air around him shimmered and in the place of Raxsen was a slightly older looking man with stringy blonde hair, watery blue eyes and a robust build. His clothes were gray and of such a material the casual observer's eyes would pass over Raxsen without seeing.

Raxsen smiled to himself. No one would know who he really was. He looked different. It was the perfect way to weed out those who spoke against him but never committed an act of betrayal.

Raxsen whistled as he walked out of the forest and towards the swimming pool.

He whistled a tune.

When he arrived at the pool he found some fifty men there and several women. He held back an evil snicker. Sometimes he just felt like killing something.

Raxsen sauntered up to a man sitting at the bank of the river, cooling off his blistered feet.

He sat down and pulled off his own boots.

The man looked at him, his brown eyes curious. He held out a large meaty hand. "The name's Togjis."

Raxsen took the hand, and shook it. "Niol."

"I haven't seen you around 'ere much. New?"

Raxsen nodded.

The man nodded his head at the reply. "I've been 'ere since Carim."

"I joined up yesterday."

"What da ya think of it?"

"It's great for a war."

"Yah, I agree. The food's good, the women can be plentiful and the

Warlord, well he's fair. But the asshole that runs my section, he hates him. I don't know why, just does. Wants to rebel. Personally I don't think it's very smart to go preaching 'bout a guy you don't like who has the power," Togjis said, his face getting slightly red from anger.

Raxsen watched the man carefully. "You hate him?"

Togjis nodded.

Raxsen stood up, putting his boots back on. "Come with me."

Togjis frowned and stayed with his feet in the water until Raxsen insisted that he come along.

"It'll be worth it. Believe me."

Togjis stood. He was a tall man, and bulky, and much more muscular than the image Raxsen was appearing as.

They walked over to the pool of water where men were diving in. All around the pool lush vegetation grew and sand banks sloped down to meet the river. Men's clothes were laying on the ground, hanging on bushes or half buried in the sand.

"Which one is he?" Raxsen said, summoning his magic.

Togjis scanned the crowd, his brown eyes searching.

"There. By the large boulder." Togjis pointed.

Raxsen squared his shoulder, trying to look like a new recruit. He jumped across the small stream where the pool emptied into the river.

Raxsen watched the man, who was draped over a rock and getting severely burned.

Rolling up his sleeves, Raxsen came up to the man and pushed him off the rock.

The man gave an angry squawk as he landed on the hard ground. He got up, his anger flaming.

"Who do ya think ya are to push me around like that? I'm a captain. I can report you," the man said shocked, spittle flying from his thin lips.

Raxsen stayed quiet. This enraged the man even more.

"I'll bloody kill you!" the man screamed, pulling a knife from his belt pocket.

Raxsen folded his arms, and looked lazily at the man.

The man flew at Raxsen, and smiled triumphantly when he felt his blade sink into flesh.

Raxsen heard Togjis yell, but he just looked at the man. He pulled out his knife, no blood was on it and no blood was coming out of the wound.

The man looked at Raxsen, and he stabbed at him again, this time where a lung would be.

Still no blood. Could it be magic?

Raxsen just looked at the man.

The man took a step back, confused.

Raxsen smiled and finally spoke. "Fool."

A crowd had gathered and most drew in their breath when they heard what Raxsen said. No one called Deverd a fool. No one.

Deverd snarled, a muscle in his jaw tightening.

Deverd brought up the hand that held the knife and his eyes bulged, for the knife was no longer in his hands.

His head slowly moved sideways to look at Raxsen. Raxsen held the knife.

"How?" Deverd started.

Raxsen just commanded a simple spell and the iron knife went up in flames.

This brought gasps from the crowd. The man challenging Deverd was a shoi!

Silence whispered in the air. No one made a sound. It was quiet, even the birds were not singing.

"I heard you were saying bad things about me," Raxsen said.

Deverd looked taken back. "About you?"

"Yes, about me."

Deverd frowned, straightening his stance.

Raxsen severed the strings holding his magical image in place.

Silence was everywhere. This time it was a shocked and fearful silence. Togjis's eyes grew wide and he swallowed. The man Deverd was attacking was the Warlord! Suddenly things had grown more interesting.

Deverd's jaw dropped. His face became ashen and he trembled.

Raxsen addressed the people standing around the pool.

"I heard from someone that Deverd hated me with a passion." The crowd's attention shifted back to Deverd as he started to choke, his cough hacking.

Raxsen didn't seem to notice.

"I want you all to know the penalty for being disloyal."

Deverd's eyes showed their whites. He scratched at his skin, ripping it raw in some parts. Foam lathered at his mouth. Blood slowly trickled down his lip. His head rolled sideways and he screamed. Everyone within ten miles heard the scream. It was the sound of a man dying in something much more than pain.

When the scream sounded Kard looked up, the hair on the back of his neck rising and his students froze.

Pierce and Cobrau stopped their talk of war, fear rising in their hearts.

People all around stopped what they were doing and listened to the scream.

Everyone watching the death of Deverd stood riveted, if they moved they could die the same unpleasant death.

Raxsen just watched.

The scream cut off, and yet again the woods and river were quiet.

Before the crowd turned their attention back to Raxsen, they watched the last phase of Deverd's death. Any opening on his body, blood spurted forth. From his eyes, his nose, his ears, his mouth and the pores in his skin, blood pooled. A gruesome pop filled the air and Deverd's neck hung at an odd angle. He died then. And the awesome power of the Warlord was proven.

Raxsen spoke. "I want all of you to know that this could be you. It could be your blood I am standing in. If I ever hear or even get a vague idea of you thinking of betraying me, I will kill you. I will kill you and I promise it will be much worse than what you have just witnessed."

Raxsen paused. He felt their fear. Lavishing in it for a moment, he let the fear soak into him, revitalizing his soul.

"Togjis, come here." Raxsen cocked a finger at the bulky man.

The people standing next to Togjis moved away, afraid.

Togjis went down the slope and stood in front of Raxsen, if reluctantly. He was sweating, the beads trickling down his forehead and dropping off his chin.

"Togjis here told me of his loyalty. Even though he did not know it was I, he spoke the truth. And for this I repay him. Togjis is the Captain of the twenty sixth division."

Togjis let out a breath he had been holding and smiled.

Raxsen nodded at Togjis and then he disappeared. More magic was at play.

Raxsen laughed as he appeared back in his tent. He had sent the tongues flying. Rumors would be spreading around the camp like wildfire.

He had won fear and respect from his army and he knew that the ones who had watched the death of Deverd would never think of rebellion, not after the power they had seen him impose.

Raxsen smiled. They would leave tomorrow instead of waiting a day. He had a nation to conquer and his first battle with the Dragons to win.

Raxsen turned around as he heard someone enter.

Kard stood there, a smile twitching his lips. "Warlord."

"What is it, Kard?"

"One of my students has a book concerning the lost Artifacts."

Raxsen raised his eyebrows. "And?"

"We need to find the Pearls of Light."

Raxsen sat down in a chair, indicating Kard should tell him more about these Artifacts and Pearls.

Chapter 38
The Gangga Pass

Mat surveyed the Gangga Pass. *It could be a trap. But the Ile have always been fearful of the place.*

The last battle between the First Dragons and Warlord was fought at the Gangga Pass and many unexploded spells lay scattered around the pass. So much magic had been used on that day that the magical plane had merged with this plane creating total chaos and danger. The chaos had disappeared at the end of the battle but the danger remained to lurk and wait for more victims.

Mat jumped off his chestnut colored horse, his emerald green cloak fanning out behind him. He took in the jagged cliffs and the large boulders. He looked for possible attacks. From what, he did not know. He only knew something was there, waiting and watching, for the moment when his army would enter the pass.

Ryen came up next to him, his dirt brown hair blowing in the wind. "I don't like it here. Something is wrong."

"I know," Mat said as Eside moved on Ryen's other side.

"But what?" Eside asked.

"I don't know, but be careful and alert," Mat said closing his eyes and feeling the flood of magic in his veins.

Ryen and Eside drew on their magic as well, adding to Mat's power.

Mat's mind flew above the army of two thousand souls. His mind soared up to the clouds and looked down. What he saw was... nothing. Nothing but rocks and people. Oh, he felt a presence of something, something he could not see. This was not good.

Mat's mind came back to his body.

"Did you see anything?" Eside asked him, fear lurking in the corners of his light brown eyes.

"No." Mat shook his head, thinking.

"What is that... feeling?" Eside persisted. "I know something is there."

Mat didn't answer. He studied the gray rocks and the small amounts of green plants. The hair on the back of his neck stood up and a shiver shot down his spine.

"What is it?" Eside's eyes darted around, searching the high rocks of the pass.

"Ghosts," Mat said, his eyes sliding to lock onto Eside's and Ryen's in the same glance.

The two looked at him.

"You may choose not to believe me, but they are here. And they want revenge."

"Revenge?" Ryen glanced around uneasily.

"Yes. Hundreds of years ago, in the time of the First Dragons, this was where the Last Battle of the First Dragons was fought, and this is where it will be fought again. They died here. The ghosts that now inhabit the land hunger still for what was taken from them." Mat paused. "They are not the ghosts of dead people, they are ghosts of creatures that inhabit the magical plane. They want blood."

Eside shivered, recalling what his instructor at the Shoi School had said. Ryen drew on his magic, spells in mind.

Mat glanced at Ryen, amusement in his eyes. "We cannot do anything if they choose to attack us. The only thing we can do is wait until night falls."

Ryen's disbelief was plain on his face. "Wait until night? Isn't that when most ghosts come out?"

Mat nodded. "Yes. However, since this battle was fought during the day, day is the time when these spirits are most powerful. The sun gives them more power. They are only fearful of pure light, forged from magic and the sun itself. We will be particularly vulnerable because we are a large force. Spirits won't bother several people. But a large host is another thing, a dangerous thing."

Eside went all pale and he hugged himself. He started shivering uncontrollably, his arms wrapped around his body.

Mat frowned. "Eside?"

"Wh-what?" Eside's whispered, his teeth chattering.

"Are you okay?" Ryen said, putting his cool hand on Eside's hot forehead.

Eside shook his head. His face became as pale as snow and his red hair like a flame against it.

"Get away from him," Mat spoke suddenly. *Please, gods, don't let it be what I'm fearing! Please do not let it have him!*

Ryen looked at him but didn't move.

"Get away!" Mat shouted.

Ryen pulled away, puzzled at the alarm in Mat's voice.

Mat murmured a quick spell.

"Oh, gods," he whispered. "He's infected."

"By what?"

"A disease."

"How?"

"When the last battle between the Dragons and Warlord was fought, so many spells were used that some became unexploded. Some never happened. And they have been waiting to detonate. Eside has caught a sickness spell. Get Vena. Now. I can't be sure until she looks at him. Her Talent lies along healing." *At least a ghost has not attacked Eside. He may be the safest when we cross the Pass.*

Ryen ran down the slope towards the waiting army.

While he was gone Mat cast another spell. What he found caused his blood to freeze. *Why Eside? Why? Why could it have not been me? Why won't you take me instead of him?* Mat asked the gods silently.

The sky seemed to get darker and the wind colder.

Ryen came running back, a puffing Vena behind him.

"What is it, child?" Vena said, her cheeks red from the running and the cold.

Mat pointed to Eside. "A powerful spell has infected him. You excel in magical healing. See what it is that our friend has started to battle," Mat said.

Vena laid her hands on Eside's forehead and her lips formed words. Her eyes flew open and she scrambled away from Eside who was an almost transparent white.

"This… this cannot be true." She stared at Eside then brought her eyes up to meet Mat's.

"I wish many things weren't true," Mat said

"What can we do?" Ryen asked, her face as pale as Eside's.

Mat looked grim. "Nothing."

Ryen's head jerked up. "Nothing? How can you say that?"

Mat stared at Ryen coolly. "This is a trance spell, and it puts the victim into a deep sleep. In this sleep he will battle something of the abyss. If he does not awake in a day, he will be lost. We can do nothing for him."

Ryen sank down to his friend's side, grief written all over his face.

"Vena, make him comfortable. Put him in a wagon. We leave tonight."

Vena nodded and she quickly ran down the slope yelling commands to empty a wagon.

"Mat, why are we leaving so soon when Eside is in such a state?"

Mat's eyes seemed to become unfocused for a second and he said nothing.

Only when Ryen asked Mat again, did he respond.

"Eside is in such a deep sleep he would not notice if you cut his arm off. When we travel through this pass, he will be the safest of us all."

೮   ೮   ೮

The night was eerily quiet. No crickets chirped. No one spoke. The creaking wagons and chariots were the only sound. Even the owls were silent.

The two moons were full, their bright light raining down upon the two thousand souls. The stars twinkled above, oblivious to the tension below them.

It was cold. The wind whipped through the pass and shouted down on the army. People's breath hung in the air creating a small fog over the camp.

Everyone was tense.

Ryen and Mat were up front, chills darting down both of their backs.

Mat felt Ryen draw on his magic. "Let it go," Mat said. "We will be easier to find if you don't." Ryen let go as if he had grabbed at a poisonous snake.

At a signal from Mat, the army began to move. Hundreds of eyes darted around, glancing up at the high cliffs, fingers wrapped tightly around weapons.

They were all afraid, and the spirits knew it.

Mutterings, curses and ghostly songs arose from the thin layer of fog that covered the ground.

The horse's eyes rolled and they shivered with fear. Even the toughest warrior glanced around with feelings of vulnerability. Ile driving the wagons and chariots clenched the reins in their hands to stop from shaking in horror. Weapons were pulled out and hefted in hands. Bodies tensed.

They moved slowly, the voices of the long dead following them. Occasionally a body appeared with the voice and cried endlessly for their death to be complete.

The veterans of the army paled when a particularly hideous body floated out from under the ground and many others lost their stomachs.

They were halfway there when it started.

They were halfway there before the horror happened.

Mat was the first of them to feel the gathering of the dead souls. The dead souls that were not supposed to be there.

"Oh no," he whispered.

Ryen looked at him, his face puzzled. Then he felt it too, the feeling of his soul trying to separate. The feeling of being devoured whole.

Everything erupted in chaos.

Horses thrashed and bolted to the end of the pass, their hooves kicking up dust and old dry bones. Men and women started screaming. The wagon drivers tried controlling their steeds but some tipped and goods were spilled out on the ground.

"Run!" Mat yelled into the melee of men and horses. All of the Ile in chariots flipped the reins and raced off, gathering as many people as could fit into the chariots before they ran. The horses pulling the wagons were slightly slower, but not much so. When a fear chases an animal, exhaustion or extra weight will not stop it from running.

The majority of people were on foot. They ran, but not fast enough.

Mat jumped off his horse and threw the reins to a young woman. She slid onto the horse and galloped away.

"Ryen, go to the end, make sure everything is under control," Mat shouted, his magic gathering within his veins.

"What about you?"

"I'll be fine. Go!" Mat said, pushing his magic in Ryen's direction and shooting him forward a couple hundred feet.

Mat pulled his magic back into him again, as much as he could take. He could feel his own soul being attacked by these creatures of legend, creatures that had existed thousands of years ago.

He did not want to hurt anyone and only when the last Ile was behind him did he start fighting.

He was powerful. They knew that right away, but he was alone and therefore weak. This was their grave mistake.

Mat pulled all the magic he could hold into himself. He pulled it from the rocks, the ground, the black sky, the stars and even the ones attacking him.

Thus he entrapped them in their own prison. He trapped them within the pass. They could never leave; they were forever stuck.

Mat did not know he had only added to their strength.

They weren't caged.

He held the magic within him, defending himself by a shield the weakest shoi could create. His mind worked, quickly paging through memories. He searched for a memory that was not his. He searched for a memory of these creatures when he had fought them those thousands of years ago. But he had never fought them. Someone else had, someone who was giving him the knowledge to battle the spirits. His forefathers used their magic in battle against creatures of the dark, when the gods had destroyed their own reign of darkness. It was his ancestors that knew how to defeat the creatures of the darkness.

It came to him, a flicker of a thought.

He drew in more power, more than anyone had ever held before.

Night became day.

Somehow Mat had sped up time. He had made the five hours till dusk turn into a mere second. He made pure sunlight forged from magic.

The creatures fled before the light, their pale bloodless faces screeching in terror. They fled, their mouths agape in a silent scream of agony. They fled back into the dark caves of the underworld.

Mat let out a breath he was holding, his fear slowly disappearing. He turned and trudged towards the end.

When he came out, he walked into a deafening silence. Everyone was staring at him, even Ryen, their eyes wide.

Vena was the only one who didn't look, her concern for Eside plain on her face.

Ryen came up to him, a bit slowly, and said, "Everyone's alright." He paused as if considering something. "What did you do?" he blurted out.

"I made it day," Mat said, watching the Ile watch him.

"I know. We all felt you. You used everything. Look at the land. It's dead for miles."

Mat stared around him. Indeed the land was dead. Trees had lost their leaves, and their branches were dead, as if a fire had swept through. The ground was dry dust and animal bones could be seen lying on the arid ground.

He hadn't used that much power. Something else had happened. But Mat pushed the thought away, not wanting to dwell on the impossible.

"Plains People," he said addressing his followers. "From now on you must be on your constant guard. What I fought back there was a creature from another plane of existence. We fought and we won, but I have no doubt the Warlord will try something next. The Lord of the Dark will not be thwarted. Stay awake." Mat paused to let his words sink in. "We must move on. We have another battle to win."

Mat did not know that at the moment when he had saved the lives of all the two thousand people, that he had ensured their loyalty. He had risked his life to save others. They would now follow him to the abyss and back.

"You have an hour to gather yourselves."

Mat then hurried down to the wagon holding Eside. Eside lay pale and sweating, his body twitching in spasms of pain. Vena swiped a wet cloth across his forehead, speaking words of comfort to him.

"How is he?" Mat asked.

"Not well, I'm afraid." She glanced at him. Mat knew what she was thinking. *You speed up time; you lessoned the time he has to fight it. You might have killed him.*

"I'm sorry, Vena. I didn't think. I had to save everyone else. I..." Mat didn't finish.

Vena nodded grimly. "It's better to kill one than a thousand even if that one is more important."

Mat stayed there awhile, watching Eside sweat and tense in silent agony. Moments would pass when he would not move at all. Just as quickly he would scream and his eyes would flash open staring up at the wagon top. His hands would form fists and his body would arch up in pain. Then he went limp, more sweat pouring out of him.

Watching and praying, Mat moved away, leaving Vena to care for Eside.

"If he comes back, he'll be changed," Mat muttered. "He will be haunted forever." He looked up at the blue sky, to where the gods of Light and Dark watched. "Damn you," he spat. "Damn you!"

Chapter 39
The Abyss

Eside was standing in the dark. He didn't know where he was except that a fiery pain consumed him. He felt his soul ripped from his body.

Images shot through his mind. He saw his mother and father talking at dinner, his sister in her crib. Cobrau laughing, his sister jumping on his bed. His father teaching him how to fish, his mother singing him to sleep. He saw his parents laughing and crying and he saw them die. He saw fire and darkness. Then a burning ripped through his heart, tearing him from the world.

He flew through the stars and across blackness so deep it held no light. He slowly started to spiral downward. He fell, his mind without a body and he landed in the abyss.

Eside heaved himself up. He had a body now, not his own but nevertheless a body. Eside felt burning heat on his skin and his breath was short, not enough to keep him alive for very long. A headache soon blossomed in his brain. Eside winced, forcing the pain to the back of his mind.

He got his first glimpse of the abyss.

It was hellish. Red pillars of stone rose up to the red sky. The sun above was red itself but dimmed, the smoke in the air blocking it out. Geysers spit boiling water into the air with a sulfuric smell. Large trenches dropped away from the ground, going down into nothing but blackness. Rivers of lava flowed across the red land, heat shimmering up in forms of deadly gasses. The red ground was covered in a layer of black ash and soot. Off in the distance sat a huge mountain, its top on fire. Lava spewed from the top and slid down its steep sides. Lava bombs shot through the air and landed with loud bangs on the earth, roughly shaking the unstable ground.

The body Eside's mind inhabited started walking away from the twisted rock where he had stood. He stumbled over loose rocks and his feet sunk in the ash-covered ground.

He came upon a pool of molten rock. The heat from the pool blistered the skin on Eside's face and stole the water from his eyes and mouth. The ground crumbled under his feet. Eside screamed and fell into the fiery depths. Fire was now his enemy.

He was where he had first stood in the abyss, next to that twisted rock.

Eside took shallow breaths of air, his heart beating painfully in his chest. He ran a hand over his face, not feeling the blister. He had died and then he was back where he had started.

Eside jumped as a hand slapped onto his shoulder.

"Come on! The Lord is going to be furious if we don't get these slaves to him in time." Eside felt his head nod. He turned around and screamed. Standing in front of him was a very deformed man. His eyes were all gray and he had no nose. From his mouth protruded two black fangs. In his hand he held two whips, one he thrust at Eside.

Eside took the whip and followed the man to a small train of wagons. The wagons were pulled by some four legged fire demons. Controlling those wagons were men just like the one Eside had first seen. Inside the wagons were barrels and other boxes. But what shocked Eside the most was the train of chained men, women, and children. They were all soot smudged and their hands and feet were chained. The length of the slave line was twice the length of the wagon train. Warped men walked up and down the length of slaves whipping any who looked too bold or too strong.

Eside felt his feet take him to the slave line and to the place he was supposed to watch.

The slave train and the wagons started moving. Eside walked stiffly with the slaves, a potent stench coming from the sunken bodies.

"Sir, water, I need water," a voice called behind him. Eside whirled around, his hand unbidden, raising the whip.

The speaker was a woman. Eside could not make out her facial features, but he knew who it was.

It was his mother.

Eside tried to keep the whip from coming down and striking his mother across the face but he couldn't.

His mother screamed in pain as the pointed end of the whip lashed across her face, leaving a line of oozing blood.

The man in front of her stopped walking. "You bastard, she didn't do anything!"

Eside stared at the man. This man was his father.

Again the whip came down and again. Every time, Eside tried to stop it, but whatever was making him do this was much stronger.

A little girl started crying.

"Shut up!" Eside screamed at the little girl. He brought his whip down again and he realized he was whipping his sister. He tried, by the Light and the Darkness did he try to stop the whip but his body did not respond to his commands.

Soon his sister was laying lifeless on the ground, long marks of red appearing on her back and sides.

The whip fell from Eside's frozen fingers. He fell to the ground, staring at his sister. What had he done?

A man came running over, one of the other slave drivers. "Get up!" he shouted at Eside.

Eside didn't move.

The slaver brought down his whip but still Eside didn't move.

Eside flinched as the whip came down again and again. A hundred more times. His vision blurred and blood seeped from his mouth.

Then he was standing by that twisted rock again.

He felt iron embrace his neck, feet, and wrists, cold, black iron.

Voices sounded behind him. Eside hung his head, afraid at what was happening now.

"Shouldn't we kill him? I mean, he did run away," someone said.

"Naw, the Lord likes 'hum with a little bit o' spirit. He'll live." A hand cuffed Eside on the back of the head. "Ya 'ere that? Ya get to live. Now, move!"

Eside cried out as the tip of the whip lashed across his back. He shuffled his feet, his head bent. He joined the line of slaves walking to the fiery mountain.

His feet burned in the hot ash. His head throbbed with an unimaginable headache and his chest jolted every time he took a breath. The sky above grew a darker red, the color of fresh blood. The slavers moved up and down the slave line, beating those not moving fast enough or those complaining.

The slave train reached the fiery mountain when the sky turned the darkest red.

The unexpected exploding of the mountain lit the red sky. Fireballs rained down on the slave train. Eside tried to run but his shackled feet threw him to the ground. Little drops of lava and ash began to rain down and blisters popped on Eside's skin. Eside screamed. He flipped over on his back and his heart stopped as a huge boiling mass of ash ran down the mountain towards him.

Then he was standing next to the twisted rock again.

"Hurry up! You're 'olding up the train," a voice yelled at him.

Eside turned around and ran, surprised his heart did not burst with less oxygen. He looked down at his body and had to suppress the urge to throw up. He was one of the warped men, with the strange eyes and twisted bodies.

He hopped up onto one of the wagons, picking up his whip. He brought it down on the demon pulling the cart. The thing screeched at him but started moving.

The wagon rolled over the harsh ground at a steady pace.

They reached the mountain quicker this time.

Instead of going up the mountain, they entered a tunnel. The cool darkness enveloped Eside and he sighed.

Eside was surprised when he could see and what he saw caused his mind to reel. On either side of the eight-foot wide road, the edge dropped off. It fell some thousand or so feet before it hit hot magma. The heat came up and scorched Eside's face.

A rumbling shook the mountain and the road collapsed.

Eside fell, a high-pitched scream tearing out of his mouth.

Then he was standing next to the twisted rock again.

"My Lord, what are you doing here?" a shocked voice asked.

Eside turned around, a grin splitting his face. "I'm here to check on my merchandise. What did you think I was doing, worm?"

The warped man cringed and bowed low. "So-sorry, my Lord, I- I—"

Eside flickered his hand and the man burst into flame. He walked up to the slave train and smiled. He looked down at a little girl, her face tear stained.

"Ah, are you scared?" he asked.

The little girl whimpered, her brown eyes brimming with tears.

"Let me end it for you." Eside smacked the girl across the face, hard. The girl fell to the ground. A woman ran to her side and shook the little girl. "Baby," the woman whispered, "get back up."

"Isn't this touching," Eside said. He struck the woman too. The woman collapsed over her daughter. It was his mother.

Eside screamed inside of his head. No, this was not happening! He had not just hit his mother and sister! He hadn't! It was not real!

Eside's mind shot from the body and hurtled into space, across the inky blackness. He began falling. He fell down, down, down and landed with a thunk back into his old body.

He stirred and opened his eyes. Breath came through his lungs and filled his body with life. He focused his vision to the dark shape above him.

Vena was over him, concern in her eyes. "You're back," she whispered, for all the world like a mother.

Eside's eyes filled with tears.

Chapter 40
A Riddle

"The Sword of Steel and Power was given to the Men.
The Axe of Stone and Force was given to the Dwarves.
The Bow of Wood and Stealth was given to the Elves.
The Knife of Bronze and Swiftness was given to the Little Peoples.
The Spear of Flint and Greed was given to the Goblins.
The Staff of Redwood and Strength was given to the Ogres.
The Shield of Iron and Peace was given to all the nations for ever lasting
peace among them."

Lousai chanted this to herself as she washed the clothes by the river.
"Where did you learn that?" Caya asked.
"I don't know, I can't remember."
Lousai and Caya along with their family had fled Jariran after Ravften
had taken control. They had escaped to Regigan, a city on the eastern
border of Caendor. Their whole family had settled in a tiny house on the
outskirts of the city. Their father was gone daily trying to sell his exotic
perfumes and their mother was employed under a seamstress. Teaa was
always with their father, learning the trade that would someday be hers.
Jarin and his new wife lived separately from them, making a living off
carpentering. To Caya and Lousai was left the household chores. They
cleaned the clothes, made breakfast and dinner, made the beds, bought the
food, paid the taxes and any other chore that needed to be done.

The money from Janevra had not stopped coming but it seemed to be
less and less everyday. It wasn't that the amount of money was less; it just
wasn't enough for their needs. They barely got by. The money Janevra
sent them was used mostly for buying off the rest of the house and getting
new clothes and dishes.

Catching a glimpse of herself in the water, Lousai grimaced. She had
changed after they left Jariran. Her fourteenth birthday had come and gone,
leaving Lousai feeling as if the gods were controlling her life. Her mind
was filled with troubled thoughts and a sense of vulnerability weighed
down her heart.

Lousai wished she could be more like her sister. Caya never seemed to
show a sense of unease or discontent. She smiled at almost everything and
rarely looked depressed.

Lousai rolled up her sleeves and soaked a white shirt in the river water.
The clothes never really got clean this way but it was the only way they
could afford to wash their clothes.

"I wish things had never changed," Lousai said as she viciously
scrubbed the shirt.

"Me too," said Caya, sounding regretful yet thrilled to be on an
adventure.

They sat there awhile, letting the clothes dry, watching and listening to the river as it flowed by.

A gentle singing came to their ears. It seemed to come from the river, a beautifully calming sound. The music sent Lousai's blood dancing, a chill flowing through her very being. It called to her, called to her soul and spoke of life. The music was sung in a strange language she had never heard before. The words, though foreign, spoke of a time when all that there was, was peace. It was an endless peace that covered the whole land and brought prosperity to all. No one suffered, no one beheld misfortune and no one felt pain.

As the music stopped they both turned their heads and stared at the woman a few feet down the river from them.

She turned and looked at them, smiling. She started walking towards them, her white dress fanning out behind her.

She was stunningly beautiful. Her gray eyes were full of some inner light and wisdom. Her long brown hair shone in the sunlight and an aura of power seemed to radiate from her. She moved with a grace that no human could possibly master. The sun seemed to shine brighter and the river seemed to sparkle more as the young woman moved towards them. The woman was the one they had met before, in the common room of the Drinking Woman.

When she came within a few feet of them, a strange joy seemed to burst in Lousai's heart. Her sister wore an awed expression.

She smiled at them again. "My dear children, I hope you are fine?"

They both nodded.

"Good. I have something very important to tell you."

Lousai lit with curiosity and interest appeared in Caya's eyes.

"Children, what I am to ask of you will be no easy task. It will require all of your cunning and wisdom. It will take everything in you to succeed. But you must be willing to risk your lives for the good of mankind before I tell you anymore. Are you willing?" she asked, her voice flowing like clean water, soothing past hurts and calming the heart.

Maybe it was the aura of good surrounding the woman or the way she asked them to help mankind. Whatever the reason Lousai nodded, Caya bobbing her head along with her sister.

The woman looked at them for a few more minutes before continuing.

"I want you to go on a search for the seven Pearls of Light."

Caya scratched her head. "What?"

The woman frowned herself then she smiled, shaking her head. "The Pearls of Light will allow the holder to control any of the Seven Artifacts wherever they may be. The Dragons need these pearls if they are to succeed, assuming they cannot find the Artifacts themselves. A very Powerful Artifact they are and they *must not* travel into the hands of the Warlord. If they do, this world will have a cataclysm on its hands."

Questions erupted from Lousai and Caya burst out her own.

"Why did you pick us?"

"How will we find them?"

"To whom do we give them?"

"What is your name?"

The woman smiled at the two girls, internal amusement lighting her gray eyes. "I picked you because you have already talked with both of the Dragons and swore you would help them, even if you did it unknowingly. When you find all seven of the Pearls, you will give them to the Dragons. I will tell you a riddle that will help you locate the Seven Pearls of Light. Are you ready? You must commit this to memory." The woman looked at Lousai.

Lousai prepared herself to pay attention. If she listened carefully she could remember anything.

"It goes like this," the woman lifted her head and spoke with godlike precision.

> *"Day sun a fiery ball, night the moons an eerie glow. In southeast, three they be, where creatures of once beauty live in dying peace.*
> *Right under the shadow of a dangerous jewel, in a cave where no sunlight rules. Eyes of dead rosy red.*
> *Again we watch the colors in the sky and see people die, on a field where blood was spilled, where gods became true and mortals said good-bye.*
> *Gone, they are, a treasure held dear, a place of fear, Devils here. Forgotten in time, no sacrifice.*
> *On the plains in a forest of green, a girl, a boy find true love in A'unat, a Pearl there be veiled.*
> *North of here lies an island, hidden and forbidden, on no map but here, under water on a long forgotten pillar of fear.*
> *Shadow of hell, no soft ringing bell, battle now ridden of Warlord and Dragon, covered in fire, no Pearl of be hire."*

"That is what you must remember. You must leave within three days to where you think the riddle leads you. But be careful, the fate of the Dragons rests in your hands," the woman warned, her eyes suddenly widening.

"What of our parents?" Caya asked.

"Your parents have known from the start that you were important and connected to the Dragons some way. They will understand. Now, my children, I must leave. I wish you luck on your trip."

The woman turned to go, her hair falling like a sheet of bronze down her back.

"Wait!" Caya shouted getting up and running towards the woman. Lousai followed her.

"What is your name?"

The woman grinned. "Call me Light." She turned and disappeared.

Her voice could still be heard even though her body did not remain. "Unlikely heroes will arise and the world will lie in the hands of children."

Her voice slowly died until it was lost in the wind. The day suddenly seemed to grow dimmer.

"Light? What kind of a name is that?" Caya said.

"How did she do that?" Lousai asked, standing in the spot where the woman had vanished. It was astounding! No one could just disappear unless they knew a lot about magic and not many people did.

"Probably a shoi or something," Caya said, shrugging, still frowning over the strange name.

Lousai shouted and clapped her hands together. "Caya, this is going to be so fun. We get to go on an adventure! Let's start by going to the library and figuring out the first part of the riddle."

The girls quickly threw their laundry in a basket and hurried home to drop it off. They stopped long enough to tell their mother what had just happened. Their mother seemed to smile sadly and swept them both up into a tight hug before they left.

The Library of Regigan was not nearly as impressive as the Library of Jariran, but it fulfilled their purpose.

"Tell me the first line of the riddle," Caya said as they stood along the rows of books.

"Day sun a fiery ball, night the moons an eerie glow. In southeast, three they be, where creatures of once beauty live in dying peace."

"I'm lost," Caya said, plopping down on the cool marble floor.

Lousai repeated the riddle to herself. It really wasn't too hard, it played with words was all. "We need to look up ancient creatures," she said and started to run her fingers over the binding of the books.

"How do you know that?" Caya said, looking at the book covers.

"I don't even know if it is right. The riddle said creatures so I figured..."

The two girls stayed at the library for six hours, pouring over book after book. They found many interesting passages and Lousai read several of them out loud.

"Listen to this, "...it is called the Eastern Kingdom, it has no name other than that. I do not know much of Evil for no one of Good knows nothing of Evil and as one of Evil knows nothing of Good..." And there it ends with a Lady Thysi signed at the bottom. It seems as if part of the passage was cut out."

"Put it back. It can't help us," Caya said.

Lousai closed the book and slipped it back onto the self. The statement she had read puzzled her and she swore she would remember it for later analysis.

The sun set and shadowed the two in darkness until one of the librarians brought two candles and set them down beside the girls.

They were left alone after that.

Total silence settled over the library until Caya finally snapped her book shut.

"I can't do this anymore. I'm tired. I'm hungry. We can always do this tomorrow."

Lousai nodded wearily and closed her book. She hoped tomorrow wouldn't be too late.

The two girls trudged home.

When they reached their little home, they climbed into their beds.

Snuggled under her blankets, warm and cozy, sleep would not come. Lousai's mind ran over the riddle, over and over, thinking, pondering. "Day sun a fiery ball," she muttered. "Must be somewhere warm." *An island perhaps?* "In the southeast, so maybe the islands near Nutria? Three creatures who live in dying peace..." Lousai rubbed her eyes. "Three creatures, three —" Ogres. The word popped into her head. Her mother had told them the story about the first battle between Good and Evil. The ogres had vanished supposedly going to three islands off the southern coast of Atay.

Excitement racing through her blood, Lousai popped out of bed and scrambled over to her sister's bed, poking Caya in the side. "Get up, Caya! I figured it out!"

"What?" Caya muttered, burying her head under the pillow.

"I can't believe it! It was right under our noses!" Lousai screeched.

Caya sat up, rubbing her face.

"What?"

"I'm so stupid," Lousai continued.

"Lousai!"

"Oh, sorry. I just feel so... sorry. I was thinking about the riddle after you had fallen to sleep. And you know how it says *'three they be, where creatures of once beauty live in dying peace?'*"

Caya yawned. "Yeah."

"It's so simple. There is only one species that can fit the description. Ogres! We must travel to the islands off of Atay," Lousai finished triumphantly.

"Oh." Caya thought a moment. "How did you figure that out?"

"I was thinking over some of the legends mother used to tell us before we went to bed. One of them was about the curse of the ogres."

"Smart," Caya admitted, nodding.

Lousai was pleased with herself. All it was was a word game.

"When are we leaving?"

"Tonight."

"Tonight? Why?" Caya said. "Don't we need to say good-bye?"

Lousai shook her head, tears filling her eyes. They dropped silently to the floor. "Mother knows that for some reason we were picked to help the Dragons. Father knows and Teaa and Jarin will understand. And I don't think I could stand a good-bye."

"Can we at least leave a note?"

"I'll write it. You can pack a few clothes, some food and money into those two bags," Lousai said, pointing to two bags under a table in the corner of their room.

Lousai scrawled a hasty letter as Caya snuck down the stairs to grab some food and money.

Once they had packed and quickly gone down the creaking stairs, they stood in the kitchen.

A tear slid down Caya's cheek. She brushed it off annoyingly with the back of her hand.

They crept out the door.

Having thought through it carefully, Lousai decided they would go south towards Carim, the Warlord's territory. Once in Carim they would get passage on a ship heading for Atay.

Perhaps they would live, perhaps they would die, Lousai prayed all went well and that the Lady of the Light would protect them. It all lay in the hands of fate and the will of the gods.

Chapter 41
How Gods Bicker

"Does it ever bore you to watch them scurry around?" Kard said, lounging on a large blue pillow.

Tghil turned and looked at him, her gray eyes offended. "No. Unlike you, I understand that we did not become gods because of some war. The old gods meant us to become gods. They are the real gods, we are just pawns, like the Warlord is a pawn for you."

Kard shrugged, letting Tghil continue. "Yes, we can change what happens to our liking. We can interfere and twist things to what we want to happen. But we are not in control. Something else is. Something even we, as new gods, cannot grasp."

Kard stared lazily at Tghil. "Very inspiring speech, my dear. But it does little to worry over things, as you said, we cannot control." Kard's thin lips twisted up into a sneer. "By the way, why did you get those two little girls to go after the Seven Pearls of Light?"

"I see their importance. They have a very big role to play even if it looks small," Tghil said, her fingers smoothing out her ever-white dress.

Kard nodded, clearly bored. He conjured up a wine glass filled with dark red wine. He took a sip, savoring the rich taste.

Tghil looked at him. "As much as you talk, you still cannot let go of your human lineage. You enjoy the simple pleasures of their lives."

Kard took another sip. "Yes, I do."

Tghil paused and her face suddenly became concerned. "What's happening to us, love? Why are we fighting?"

Kard stood up, his black clothes looking like the abyss. "We are not fighting, sweet love, but discussing. We are just as caught up in the weavings of Fate and Time as the mortals below us. Yet we understand there is more beyond. We are the tides of Darkness and Light, meant to be battling for eternity. We cannot stop it. It is inevitable. Just like you and I are meant to hate one another, yet we love each other." Kard kissed Tghil gently on the lips. He pulled back. "When we were born in the First Age, we were not meant to fall in love. But when we found each other, we fell in love. Why? I do not know. But we were meant to fall in love." He kissed her again. "Now, we only wait for the third. Once she comes, balance will be restored and the old gods will pass on their rule to the new. They will pass on complete rule of all the Kingdoms to us, not just the west of the Northern Kingdom."

Tghil shivered at his kiss then froze. "What if all the events that we set into happening fail?"

"Then we know they were not meant to be."

"Sometimes I wish we were back in that grove where we first met and true love caged us within its iron bonds," Tghil said, resting her head against Kard's shoulder.

"Love, that grove in A'unat is long dead. A village lies over it now."

"I know, but I can still dream."

Kard started to laugh, a strange sound coming from such a dark man. Tghil glared at him. "What?"

Kard eased his laughter. "We are gods yet we still dream."

Tghil's eyes softened. "Everyone is meant to dream."

They stayed there awhile in each other's embrace. All around them the strange whiteness swirled with pictures of memories springing fourth and hanging in the mist. One picture was of two young people, a boy and a girl. They were in a grove, surrounded by magnificently dark green trees.

"What of the Artifacts? What are we to do with them?" Kard said, breaking the peaceful silence.

Tghil's grin became evil, something rarely seen on the Goddess of Light. "We send the Phoenixes to search for them. They need to meet."

"The Dragons can send their Phoenixes but mine must stay behind. He is too important to leave."

"Then who do we send for the Warlord?" Tghil looked up into Kard's near black eyes. She bit her lower lip. "Who is there to send?"

"Saviak."

"The assassin?" Tghil frowned.

"Yes. She has a spark where the seed of Evil can grow. And who is better to find things hidden than a thief?"

"I see your point. If she goes alone she will probably die. She has way too much importance to die before the world is ready. Should we send Dasher with her?"

Kard nodded.

Tghil frowned again. "If Saviak is to join the Warlord, then won't the Warlord need to win the First Battle?"

"Of course."

"But that would be a blow to the side of Light. It will only harm everything that we have worked to make happen."

"No, if anything it will make the Dragon's power stronger, the Warlord's too. Like you said, we have no control, we are only pawns." Kard smirked down at her, his eyes glinting like black pools in moonlight. "Besides, Calahadar will keep Raxsen from staying too long."

"I don't like this," Tghil said, pouting.

"I know, love, I know." Kard bent down and kissed Tghil again.

She giggled and wrapped her arms around his muscular shoulders.

"A love so strong it will never die," Kard whispered against Tghil's soft lips.

They molded into each other.

Chapter 42
Dragons Meet

ALD 3919 SD July

They had traveled across all of Caendor and part of Selkare to reach Calahar.

Ake was sore. Her bottom was in the shape of a saddle and her back ached to lean against something.

To Ake's right was Kiera.

Kiera was miserable, anyone could tell. Her long white blonde hair was tangled, her blue eyes red and squinted against the sun. Her cheeks and nose were sunburned. Her sunburn had already started to peel, leaving her face rough and dry. Her clothes were her usual, extravagant and pointless. She wore a white dress that spread out from her waist two feet before it reached her feet. It had no straps and Ake wondered how it stayed on. Her dress was low enough for any man to blush. She insisted on having a servant ride next to her and hold an umbrella over her head. In short, she looked ridiculous.

On the other side of Kiera was Riak. Riak, too, was sunburned, but only slightly. Her long brown hair was braided down her back. The Phoenix on her left arm shimmered in the sunlight. Her gray eyes were closed as she attempted to sleep in the saddle. Around her neck was a wreath of flowers. Ake had never seen her take it off. Riak wore simple brown pants and a white sleeveless tunic with a black belt around her plump waist. Her cat sat in front of her, orange eyes filled with panic as the horse moved along.

Ake was dressed in a blue tunic similar to Riak's and black skirt that had slits all the way up to her thighs, revealing a good length of leg. A white belt made of coral hung around her hips and clinked together when she moved. Her short black hair ruffled in the wind and her earrings, nose ring and necklace sparkled in the sunlight. Her darker skin kept her from getting sunburned and she was very comfortable in the sun. She had grown up in much hotter weather than this. Her own Phoenix was shimmering in the daylight. It entwined itself all the way up to her shoulder. It looked very real, like a gold bird.

Janevra sat on the other side of Ake. Her auburn hair was swept back into two braids. Her green shirt was very short sleeved. It did not go past her collarbone. It allowed for the lightning bolt on her right arm to be seen, clear and electric in the light. Janevra's eyes were fixed straight ahead, staring at nothing but rolling grass. Her face was impossible to read, but Ake knew she was thinking of the upcoming battle with the Warlord.

On the other side of Janevra rode Qwaser. He had changed. His bright green eyes were alert and weary. His bow was constantly at hand and his sword was always on his hip. His green attire made it seem like he shifted in and out of focus with the grass plain. The wound he had attained in battle was healed by magic, leaving no scar or limp in his leg.

Behind the five was an army consisting of over three thousand souls, all elves. A thousand were on horses. Janevra had only asked for two thousand but all had volunteered, those on horses bringing their own. They wanted to follow the human woman who had saved them and the woman prophesied to bring them into the world. They wanted to follow the woman with the lightning dancing in her eyes and on her skin.

The wagons carrying food, water and shelter brought up the rear, horses and oxen pulling the large, loaded wagons.

Ake rode her horse closer to Janevra.

"Janevra, where are we going to meet the Lord Dragon?" Ake asked.

Janevra's lips quirked into a small smile. "We are to meet them ten miles south of Calahar."

Ake briefly wondered about the amusement in Janevra's voice. "How close are we?"

"Full of questions today, aren't you? We're five miles off. If you look eastward you will see a small cloud of rising dust. That is the Lord Dragon's army." Ake squinted, trying to see the cloud of dust. Obviously Janevra's eyes were much better than hers.

Janevra's tone became cold. "And if you look southward you will see another cloud of dust. That is the Warlord's army."

Ake glanced up at Janevra. She had never known her friend to fill her voice with so much hate and bitterness.

"Ake, what was your life like before you knew you were to became the Phoenix of Water?" The interest in Janevra's voice was evident.

Ake frowned. Her life before was not much. "I lived in a small house with my brother, mother and father."

Janevra glanced at her. "Let me guess, your father was a drunk and your mother died in child birth."

Ake nodded, not surprised at Janevra's knowledge of her past.

"You'll like him," Janevra said suddenly.

Ake was startled. "Who, my Lady Dragon?"

"Eside Thron, the Phoenix of Fire."

Ake smiled. "Fire and water cancel each other out. We wouldn't go good together."

Janevra smiled wickedly. "Oh, you would be surprised."

Before Ake could answer, Kiera rode up. "My Lady Dragon, may I please ask when we are to meet the Lord Dragon?" Kiera ignored Ake.

Janevra smiled. "Within the next three hours, Kiera."

Kiera's sunburned face grimaced. "Do you think it's possible, my Lady Dragon, to stop before we reach our destination?"

"And why would we do that?" Janevra sounded amused.

Kiera straightened in her saddle. "I must prepare myself. I look absolutely hideous and I want to look my best when we meet the Lord Dragon and his Phoenixes." Kiera patted her hair and smoothed out her dress. "How do I look?"

Janevra looked at Kiera with her eyes half closed. "What do you think?"

Kiera sniffed and rode away, her long white blonde hair flying out behind her.

Janevra rubbed her hands together gleefully. "Oh, it'll be so much fun!"

"What?" Ake asked, rubbing her horse's brown neck.

"When Kiera sees Mat she'll die. Ryen and Eside are not bad looking either. It will be hilarious to watch them try to get away from her."

They rode on for the next three miles in silence. The army behind them at a steady walk, they slowly reached the meeting point.

When the Lady Dragon's army had passed through small villages, the people had come out to stare. They had never seen elves before and the Legend of the Dragons and Warlord was growing. Some of the younger men and women kissed their sweethearts and parents good-bye and joined the army.

The army was divided into two simple sections, archers and swordsmen. The archers out numbered the swordsmen two to one.

As they reached the destination point Qwaser rode up.

His green eyes were troubled and his bow was drawn. Being so close to the enemy made him tense.

"Janevra, the Warlord's army reaches over eight thousand. It's going to be a hard battle. Most of his forces are sylai."

"What are their numbers?" Ake asked. She had grown up with violence. War was second nature to her.

Qwaser thought for a moment. "There's roughly two thousand rogui, three thousand sylai, and over two thousand humans actually capable of fighting."

"Would you like me to ride ahead and meet Mat beforehand?" Qwaser turned towards Janevra. He drew up his hood, hiding his elegant ears.

Janevra nodded. "Take Ake with you. Tell Mat our numbers and strength when you reach him. And if you run into a guard tell him 'it is a good day to die'."

Qwaser nodded, turning his horse. "Come on then," Qwaser said, kicking his mount in the sides and pushing it into a gallop.

Ake quickly followed suit.

They rode through the grassy hills and underneath the crystal sky. *In two days time,* Ake thought as the wind brushed her face, *the land will be covered in blood.*

Ake looked down at the Lord Dragon's army as they rose up over the hill. The Lord Dragon had obviously been around for a while for tents were pitched and cook fires blazing. But what struck Ake as odd was that the Lord Dragon's tent was located around the outside of the camp.

They slowed their horses to a walk as they watched for a guard.

By the time they got half way to the camp, Ake wondered why no guards had been posted.

Suddenly Qwaser had his bow drawn, pointed directly at a young man who seemed to have appeared out of nowhere.

Ake had never seen a man such as the one that stood before her. On his upper left arm was a tattoo of a blazing sun. His only clothing consisted of high boots that reached his knees, and deer hide pants. He was heavily armed. In his hand was a spear and around his waist were several knives. His face was decorated with red paint. He was crouched in a defensive position and his spear was aimed at her. When he spoke, he had a strange accent.

"What business do you have here?" he demanded.

"I came to speak with the Lord Dragon. We are messengers of the Lady Dragon. I am the general of her Elven Army and this woman is the Phoenix of Water." Qwaser pulled down his hood as he spoke, exposing his pointed ears.

At the word elven the man raised his eyebrows. "Elven? I thought they were all dead. Tell me, what is your message?"

Qwaser stiffened. "That is for me to know. I believe I am supposed to say, "it is a good day to die"."

The strange man suddenly looked relieved. "Come, the Lord Dragon is expecting you."

They dismounted and followed the man. Ake did not see any more guards as they followed the man.

The strange man brought them to a tent larger than all of the others. He turned towards them and held up a hand. "Wait," he said. The man slipped into the tent.

He came out very soon and kept the tent flap open for them. Ake and Qwaser walked in.

The inside was cluttered with maps and battle plans. Three men sat in the tent. All three looked up as they entered. One gave a smile and stood up. He hopped over some maps until he was directly in front of Qwaser.

"General of the Elven Army, huh?" The man grinned and Qwaser laughed in return. They hugged, slapping each other on the back.

"It's good to see you again, Mat. The last time you saw me I was an outcast."

The man patted Qwaser on the back. "The last time you saw me, Qwaser, I was only a peasant with a princess as a friend."

The man who had addressed Qwaser was tall for human standards and his black pants seemed to add to his height. His short dark brown hair was not tidy. His hazel eyes sparkled and his handsome face was lit with joy that seemed to rarely shine.

Remembering herself, Ake curtsied. "My Lord Dragon."

The Lord Dragon let go of Qwaser. "No need to call me that, Ake. I'm Mat." He stuck out his hand. She shook his hand, feeling very uncomfortable in the presence of such a dominant male.

Mat smiled. A woman could melt under that smile, with those straight white teeth and dancing hazel eyes. Ake snickered when she thought what Kiera would do. *Poor man,* she thought. *It'll be fun to see the Lord Dragon squirm.*

"Ake, allow me to introduce you to Ryen Dael and Eside Thron, the Phoenixes of Earth and Fire."

Ake looked at the two men standing in front of her, amazed at their stark differences.

Ryen was tall, shorter than Mat but above average height. He had rich brown hair and green eyes a shade so deep they were the color of pine trees. His green shirtsleeves were rolled up, showing the end of the red-gold phoenix on his arm. The pants he wore were a light brown. *If I crossed my eyes just enough,* Ake thought, *he would look like a small tree.*

Ake turned her purple eyes to take in Eside and she wondered why Janevra said she would like him. His eyes were such a light brown they almost looked red. His red hair had touches of brown in it and she could not determine what color it really was. His face had freckles on it, but they were so light they were barely visible. He seemed to have a haunted look about him, as if he had died and come back again. His clothes were simple. *He would be a good smuggler,* she thought. *He's not distinguishable in a crowd.*

Ryen smiled as he shook her hand. "You see, Mat's been waiting a long time to see Janevra and—"

Mat elbowed him in the side, glaring.

Ryen grunted. "Some things are better left unsaid."

Ake and Eside laughed.

The smile changed his face completely. Eside's straight white teeth flashed and his crooked grin stunned her. How could a young man not at all handsome suddenly be the most beautiful one she had ever seen? She decided there was much more to Eside Thron.

"When is she—they coming?" Mat asked, blushing to his hairline. Qwaser grinned. "Soon."

Mat rubbed his chin thoughtfully. He sighed and sank down onto a chair. He started talking to Qwaser in low tones.

Ake turned her attention back to Eside who was sitting down on the floor and was studying the map with Ryen. Ake sat down beside them.

"You see here is an advantage point," Ryen said, pointing to an indication of a hill on the map. "If we could get control of this, the odds would lessen against us."

"True, but the hill is on the side of the Warlord's. It would be suicidal to try to reach it during the battle," Eside pointed out.

"What about before the battle?" Ake asked.

Eside shook his head. "That won't work either. Right there," Eside jabbed a finger at a small cluster of trees, "is around the area the Warlord is going to set up camp." The spot Eside had pointed to was well beyond the hill.

"How could you possibly know where he is going to set up camp?" Ake was unfamiliar with land-based war.

Eside glanced at her, annoyed. "The Warlord is moving north right now. He will not want to tire his troops before a battle. If he marches beyond this point he'll be risking his troop's strength. He'll expect us to bring the battle to him."

"Why would he expect that?" Ake asked.

"Because," Ryen said, "we're the ones defending. He wants Calahar. We don't want him to have it."

Ake was confused. "But if we're the ones defending then should not he bring the battle to us?"

Eside shook his head again. "No, he's the threat. When you feel threatened you must protect yourself."

Ake grinned, suddenly understanding. "So, we're defending but we must attack in order to stop the threat of him attacking."

"You could put it that way," Ryen said.

They sat in silence for a while, trying to catch the low tones of Mat and Qwaser talking.

"Where are you two from?" Ake said, giving up on trying to listen.

Eside looked up from studying the map. "I'm from Sunda, Caroa. I was a dock hand."

Ake smiled. "I'm from Wakee, Zinder Island. I was a serving girl at the Island Tree Inn and..."

"And what?" Eside pushed.

Ake grinned. "I was a smuggler and a pirate."

The astounded looks both men gave her were enough to set her off into a fit of giggles.

Her fit of giggles subsiding, Ryen said, "I'm from Manel, Taymyr. I was a servant. Not as impressive as your past, I'm sorry to admit."

Ake laughed. "It's funny when you think where you can find people who will 'serve at the side under the Dragons'. The Phoenix of Light was also a servant. But I'm afraid the other one of us was close to being a princess."

"The Phoenix of Air was almost a princess?" Ryen raised his eyebrows.

Ake rolled her eyes. "Almost. She thinks she is one. She's very shallow and has a love for men. You could call it her hobby. She only obeys the Lady Dragon." Ake paused, listening. She could hear new voices in the camp. "And it seems like you'll get to meet her very soon."

The sounds of an army were slowly drifting to their ears.

But when the tent flap opened, it was two Ile that had entered.

The woman was dressed in soft leather, which was hard to distinguish from her tanned skin. She wore high boots like the Ile sentry Ake had met on the way in. Brown pants were tucked into the high boots and for a shirt only a band of leather covered her chest. Her red hair was short, stopping at the nape of her neck and her gray eyes held a deep sorrow, much like the sorrow found in Qwaser's eyes. She was tall, as tall as the man standing next to her and heavily guarded. Around her waist were ten knives. A quiver of arrows was slung over her back and in her hand she held a long spear. On the woman's upper left arm was a tattoo of a sun. She was one of the infamous Ile Warriors, the Tar-ten.

The man standing next to her was dressed in only pants and high leather boots. He carried the same tattoo as the woman. His hair was a blonde-red and his gray eyes looked her up and down. His features were sharp and similar to the woman's next to him. He wore red paint on his face and had drawn a strange design on his chest. Like the woman next to him he was heavily armed.

Mat smiled at them. "Ake, this is, Kayzi and Dei. They are very trusted friends of mine. Kayzi, Dei, this is Ake, the Phoenix of Water."

Ake nodded to them. Dei only nodded in return. Kayzi on the other hand came over and shook her hand.

She smiled at him. "I'm pleased to meet both of you."

"And this is Qwaser," Mat said, slapping the elf on the back. Dei smiled at him, a strange thing to appear on her features.

Qwaser smiled at Dei in return. But the look that passed between Kayzi and Qwaser was not lost to Ake. It was instant wariness.

"Come, it is better that we meet outside. This tent is too small for this many people," Mat said.

They filed out of the tent flap and waited for Janevra to approach with Riak and Kiera.

A woman's laughter raced through the gathering crowd of Ile. The laughter seemed to draw them towards her. It was Janevra's laugh.

She came through the crowd looking stunningly beautiful. Ake glanced at Mat and snickered in spite of herself. Mat was awe struck.

Riak and Kiera followed Janevra.

Kiera must have used her magic for her face was not sunburned any more and her puffy white dress was clean of dirt smudges.

When Janevra spotted Mat, she smiled with such brilliance that even Ryen and Eside blushed in pleasure to be honored by her smile.

Janevra stood in front of Mat and something passed between them. Mat cleared his throat and they briefly hugged.

Janevra turned to Dei, sorrow written all over her face.

"Deivenada, I'm so sorry. I know how hard it is to lose someone you love."

The change over Dei was astonishing. Dei's eyes spilled over with tears and she cried into Janevra's shoulder. A tear slid down Janevra's cheek as well.

The impact on the watching crowd was just as amazing. The watching Ile had new respect in their eyes for Janevra. She became more than the Lady Dragon to them. As for the elves, pride shone in their eyes, for this young woman, this Lady Dragon, who they had followed on some strange desire, belonged to them. Now they knew why they followed her if they had not known before.

When Dei's tears stopped, she smiled at Janevra and went and stood next to her brother's side. He put an arm around her shoulder.

The two armies moved on, interested in setting up camp and meeting new people from other lands. Many headed straight for the wagons, intending to unload and scout out a place to put up a tent.

Janevra turned to Qwaser. "Thanks for coming ahead. I assume you and Mat had a pleasant conversation?"

Qwaser bent his head and murmured a few words to Janevra. Janevra grimaced and then smiled once more. Qwaser stepped away.

Janevra glanced at Ake and her eyes slid off of Eside and back to wink at her.

Ake felt herself turn crimson.

Janevra moved over and stood across from Eside and Ryen.

"Ryen, Phoenix of Earth and Eside, Phoenix of Fire, I'm pleased to meet you. I've heard much about you."

Puzzlement crossed both of their faces as they wondered how she could have possibly known about them.

Ryen bowed low. "I, too, am pleased to meet you, my Lady Dragon." When he straightened his face was red, but he grinned.

Janevra smiled in return. "Call me Janevra. I dislike titles."

She turned her attention to Eside. "Is your sister here, Eside?"

Eside shook his head. "No. I decided she would be safer in Daaguwh than with an army."

Janevra nodded then did something very strange, she kissed her fingers and put them on Eside's forehead. "May the Light bless the memory of your parents."

The part of Eside that he had long ago boxed up spilled out. He did not cry but the sorrow was on his face like a picture. "Thank you," he choked.

Ake slipped her hand through Eside's and squeezed it gently. He looked down at her and smiled sadly. The pain on his face was quickly gone, only lingering in his eyes.

"Ryen and Mat, this is Riak, the Phoenix of Light, and Kiera, the Phoenix of Air," Janevra said introducing the two women behind her.

Riak smiled and shook their hands, finding friends immediately. Riak, with her easy smile and twinkling gray eyes was hard not to like. Her rarity at having a familiar, an animal close to her, was another thing that made people interested in her. Ake wished she could charm everyone with a smile and find quick friends.

Kiera on the other hand was fawning over the two young men in front of her. Kiera's low white dress displayed her breasts too much. To Ake it seemed they would pop out.

She stuck out her hand, awaiting a kiss. When none came Kiera smiled. "My Lord, tell me I am not beautiful?"

Eside took a step backwards, bewildered. Ake grinned.

Ryen, born of a high class spoke. "My Lady, your beauty is like a thousand roses. It is like the sun on a rainy day." All, save her, heard his sarcasm.

She sighed and started fanning herself. "Oh, it is hot. Do fetch me a drink."

Ryen looked disgusted. "The only water around here is fetched by one's own hands."

Even Kiera could not miss the dismissal. "Oh, you are right, I—" Kiera stopped as Janevra's face became stern.

Kiera, whipping around, her long white blonde hair catching Ryen in the face, addressed the Lord Dragon. "My Lord Dragon, how wonderful it is to meet you. You are an extraordinarily handsome man. In fact you are the type of man beautiful enough to be close to reaching my own beauty."

Mat flickered a glance at Kiera. "Kiera, tell me, would you spend time with a commoner?"

Kiera scoffed. "Why no, milord, I would never sink so low."

Mat smiled. "A pity, for I was born a commoner."

Kiera looked shocked. "You, milord?"

Mat's smile turned wicked. "Yes, I was a farmer. I slept with the pigs when it got too cold and shoveled cow dung with these hands." He held out his hands. "It's good for the soil."

Kiera backed away, her face more than confused.

Ake giggled along with Riak and Janevra. *The poor girl, she is beyond clueless.*

A woman came swishing through the pitched tents. Her wide skirt brushed the people she walked by and her white blouse was buttoned up to her neck but she wasn't sweating. She looked worn-out.

"Janevra, my child, I'm so pleased to see you again," the woman said, throwing her arms around Janevra's neck.

"Vena, it seems like only yesterday you took Mat from me," Janevra smiled and returned the hug.

"You children must get better acquainted. Janevra, you and Mat must talk. Phoenixes follow me."

Vena swept off and they could only quickly say good-bye to the Dragons before they had to hurry to keep up.

Vena brought them to two tents, slightly smaller than the Lord Dragon's.

"Women in one, men in the other. Kiera, child, I need to talk to you," Vena said.

Kiera went with Vena out of earshot.

"By the Dark Lord is she annoying," Ryen muttered.

Riak laughed. "Yes, that she is." She scratched Curly behind the ear, earning a deep purr.

"She gets worse," Ake said reassuringly.

Eside sighed. "Gods help us."

Ryen looked at the sky. "It's still light enough out, shall we talk out here?"

They all nodded and sat down on the grassy ground.

The warmth of the dying summer sun beat down on them from the horizon. If it were not for the cool north breeze they would have been sweating. The sky was cloudless and darkness slowly spread its fingers across the sky. The flowers put their sweet scent in the night air and birds sang goodnight. The lazy murmur of voices rose from the camping army.

"Where are you from, Riak?" Ryen asked. "I'm from Manel, Taymyr and Eside is from Sunda, Caroa."

Riak gave a low laugh. "I'm from Atii, Istra where I was a servant for a rich noble family. I watched their daughter. Kiera is a lot like her."

Eside shook his head. "I'm sorry for you. You get away from one, then meet another."

"Those kinds of girls aren't that bad. You just need to understand them. Ryen, you seem to know."

Ryen nodded. "I was born of a rich family, not noble though. They thought I was a mistake, so I was their servant. When they entertained nobility, I had to be polite. All noble girls are snots."

Ake frowned. "That's not true."

"Why isn't it?"

"Janevra is the Princess-Queen of Caendor. She is the only heir to the throne and the highest noble in Caendor. And she is anything but a snot."

"The Lady Dragon is a Princess?" Eside sounded amazed.

Riak smiled. "Yes. Her parents are dead and a lunatic now holds the throne. The country is in chaos. But she's the only rightful heir."

Ryen frowned. "I can see how she would be a princess. How did she meet Mat?"

Ake rubbed her hands together. "It's a wonderful story."

Chapter 43
Warlord and Dragons

Janevra watched as Vena took the Phoenixes away. She turned towards Mat and grinned. "What did you think of Kiera?"

Mat winced. "That girl has serious problems."

"I pity her."

"Why?"

"She's always trying to prove that she's good enough. It started when she was a child. And when her parents were forced to forget her...she's alone and no one likes her."

Mat nodded. It made sense.

Janevra looked at Qwaser, Dei, and Kayzi. She grimaced slightly at the looks of hatred passing between the two men.

She studied Kayzi closely. There was something odd about him. She had never met him before but he seemed like a caged animal, as if he was expecting an attack from his enemies. *It probably comes from constant war,* she reflected.

"You've all changed," Janevra said bluntly.

Qwaser looked at her. "It happens when someone you trust betrays you."

Dei wiped her eyes. "Or when the one you love is killed by your enemy."

Janevra watched them for a moment then said, "Betrayal is by far the worst."

Kayzi went pale, his tan face ashen. Qwaser's face hardened.

Dei started crying, her tears sliding silently down her face. Janevra's eyes flickered to Kayzi. His face was as readable as stone. "Kayzi, why don't you take your sister to her tent. I'll send Qwaser to help in a moment."

Kayzi lead his sister towards her tent. When they got out of earshot Janevra addressed Qwaser. "Watch for traitors, my friend. I fear the worst."

Qwaser's bright green eyes sharpened and he nodded. "Don't worry. I feel the betrayal in the air as well."

"I'm afraid someone is passing plans to the Warlord," Janevra said, watching the two siblings step into a tent.

"What?" Mat jumped in, offended. "A traitor? How can you think that? These people are my friends! There is no one in my camp who is a traitor."

Janevra's green eyes flashed. "Sometimes trust can blind us."

Qwaser caressed his sword. "I agree with her."

"You know what? Fine. Watch for the traitor. But there's nothing wrong with anyone here." Mat waved his hands at Qwaser. "Go."

Janevra raised her eyebrows at Mat as Qwaser drew himself up stiffly. "I am not some servant to be ordered around, *my Lord Dragon*. I was the person who brought you this power. If I had not come to Janevra for help, you would still be just Mat Trakall, not Mat Trakall, the Dragon of the Rising Sun, the One to unite the Ile and kill the Destroyer of Dark. No, you would be Mat the farmer. Nobles would scoff at you and you would crawl on the ground if they threw a copper chip. You would sleep with the pigs for warmth," Qwaser spat, his bright green eyes lit with wrath.

Mat stood still, shocked, but Qwaser did not wait for him to answer. "Janevra, I wonder if you deserve him. He seems to be below you. Once I thought he was your equal but it seems as if power has reached his head. Sleep well, my friend." Qwaser paused and stared at Mat. "My Lord Dragon."

Qwaser turned his back on Mat and walked into the surrounding tents, lost in the glare of fire.

Janevra looked coldly at Mat. "I would expect this from someone of Kiera's position, but not from you. I know being the Dragon is stressful, but must you go and destroy the few friends and allies that we have?"

Mat looked miserable. "No."

"How could you do such a thing? I— No?" Janevra crossed her arms. "At least you see your wrong doings."

Mat looked up at her, anger glinting in his hazel eyes. "What he said is right. I would be nothing if you hadn't kept me for a servant."

Janevra was taken back. "That's not true. Every person is something beautiful. Everyone was put on this earth for a reason. Some reasons might be small compared to others but they all fit into a much greater whole. If one person didn't fulfill his destiny, the world would see destruction."

Mat sighed. "I feel like such a fool."

Janevra snickered. "Even the best of us will. Qwaser will forgive you. He's going through a hard time right now."

The rustling of skirts came from behind them and Vena appeared. Her face was very white.

"Vena, what is it?" Mat looked worried. Very few things ever troubled Vena.

"It's Kiera."

The worry disappeared in Mat's eyes. "Has she already lain with half the men in this camp?"

Vena glared at Mat then rounded on Janevra. "You knew! Yet she is still with us!" The woman's hair was in disarray and she drew on her magic.

Janevra quickly summoned her own magic and cut the strings connecting Vena to her magic. Vena gasped, feeling the power drain from her being.

"I did not get rid of her for she is very important." Janevra stared into the eyes of Vena, green fire verse gray ice. "How did you know?"

"I brought her aside to tell her that her flittering was rude and inexcusable when I saw some blood trickling down her neck. I asked her what was wrong and I pulled back her hair to see what it was. I saw a skull." Vena's lips were thin.

Mat blanched. "A skull? That is the sign of the Warlord."

"I know," Janevra snapped. "I let her stay because she is a Phoenix. She will not betray us." *A skull?* Janevra wondered. *I wonder what that does? Why didn't I see it before?*

Vena stepped back. "Forgive me, Janevra, but sometimes I think you are too trusting."

Janevra sighed. "Vena, we shouldn't fight. We only weaken our defenses when we do so. I'm sorry I did not tell you. Ake knows of Kiera and I told her to watch her. Kiera won't betray us." *At least not in the end.* Janevra kept this thought to herself.

Vena nodded her head, more gray-blonde hair falling out of her braid. "I trust your judgment, child." Vena smiled weakly. "Could you please stop cutting off my magic?"

Janevra smiled and released her magical hold on Vena.

"Good night, children, sleep well," Vena said, her rustling skirts drifting off into the distance.

Mat suddenly laughed. "Aren't we getting off to a good start."

Janevra grinned. "Yes, we do seem to be setting people afire don't we?"

They dissolved into giggles.

The enjoyment was quickly stopped as they both felt a magical pull towards the forest. They glanced at each other. The call was cold and icy. It was dark out but they could see the line of magic leading them towards their enemy.

All the mirth left Mat's face. "Raxsen," he hissed. He started running towards the forest but Janevra caught him in a weaving of magic.

"Let me go, woman," he demanded, drawing in on his own magic.

"Do you think it's smart to go charging in there all alone? He's my enemy as well as yours. We go together." Janevra cut the weaving holding Mat. He dropped to the ground.

Mat got up and brushed the leaves off him. He shot a glare at Janevra.

They entered the forest, stopping briefly to allow their eyes to adjust to the sudden faint light.

Their feet crunched on dead leaves and a breeze whispered through the trees calling to the dark.

They followed the magic.

It brought them to a small clearing with a pool of water glittering in the center. The two moons were reflected in the pool, casting eerie shadows all around. The breeze stopped whispering and the night died into silence.

"We meet again," a cold voice came from the other side of the pool.
Raxsen stepped into the two moon's white light. He smiled at them. The
smile was cold and reached his eyes.

Mat's jaw tightened and Janevra stiffened.

Raxsen just smiled. The black he was wearing shifted his form in and
out of the darkness making it hard for Janevra to place his exact location.

"What are you doing here, Raxsen?" Mat spat.

"I love you too, Mat," Raxsen said, his eyes bright orbs of cold blue
light in the moonlight. "I am here because I was weary of talking to weak
minded mortals and, I must admit, I'm meeting someone here."

Raxsen sat down on a large rock, still smiling. "So, how is Kiera?"

"She's fine. Unfortunately you cannot use her for she will never know
the battle plans," Janevra said.

Raxsen shrugged. "It is unavoidable that your own pawn will be your
obliteration."

"We will win," Mat said. "The only obliteration will be you."

Raxsen turned his icy gaze at Mat. "That I doubt."

Janevra lifted her lip in disgust. "What makes you so certain you'll
win? What power do you have that we don't?"

Raxsen put his finger in the moon lit water sending small ripples across
the pond. "I have fear, I have immortality, and I have all the people you
have forgotten."

Mat sneered. "Immortality? No human could—"

Raxsen sliced his hand through the air. "The Darkness and Light were
once humans. They fought each other as we do. I will be the next God of
Darkness. I will rule."

"If you defeat us first," Janevra said.

Raxsen laughed dryly. "If? You are a woman, Janevra, someone
meant only to satisfy the hunger of men. You have no place in society.
That is why you will lose."

Janevra screamed and gathered her magic. She directed it at Raxsen in
an explosion of raw energy. Raxsen shattered her attempt with a simple
shield.

The energy lit up the surrounding forest with a pure white light
brilliance. People from both armies turned and stared at the sudden flash of
white blinding light.

"Is that all you can muster?"

Mat glanced between the two, drawing on his magical power.

Raxsen barely glanced at him.

Janevra smiled grimly. "I can do much more than that, *Warlord*."
Janevra spat the word. *He is such an arrogant fool!*

Raxsen threw back his head and laughed, the sound echoing off the
thick forest trees. Once his mirth died he turned his icy stare back at
Janevra. "What a fiery little cat!"

Mat clenched his teeth but reined his temper.

"I may be a fiery little cat but I also have claws," Janevra said, forcing her magic into a ball of purple blue flame. She blasted it at Raxsen.

The Warlord lurched out of the way as the tree next to him went up in a roar of flame. Raxsen picked himself up from the dirt. His blue eyes became colder and his face seemed to be etched of stone. He smothered his magic on the burning tree and the hot flames went out.

"That was a mistake," the Warlord said. He spread his hands apart, an ugly square of green forming between his hands. "A grave mistake."

The square flew out of his hands and zoomed across the water. Janevra and Mat had only enough time to toss themselves aside before it exploded into a tree, sending bits of burning bark raining down on their heads.

Janevra lay on the ground, glaring at Raxsen over the pond. She pointed a finger at the water and it rose into a large wave looming over Raxsen. With a dull *whoosh*, it cascaded down upon the Warlord before gradually seeping back into the pond.

Choking and sputtering, Raxsen dragged himself out of the water.

Janevra smiled. "Not so grand anymore, are you?"

Raxsen glared at her and fire sprouted behind her, the forest blazing in a magical inferno.

Janevra felt the heat from the fire wash over her, singeing the hair on her arms. Mat rolled away from the fire, getting up close to her. Glancing at Mat, she nodded. They combined their powers, a bright orange orb forming between them. They aimed it at Raxsen. He was no match for their combined powers. Only if he had an Artifact or a Pearl could he overpower them.

"You may be able to threaten me but I, in the end, will win the battle."

Mat smiled but it was devoid of humor. "You may win this battle, but we will win the war. This battle is but a small piece in a much larger puzzle. It will take cunning, genius and strategy to win. We have that, you do not." The orange orb disappeared.

"I may lack one of those but in its place I have power."

Mat scoffed. "Power? Over what?"

Raxsen sneered. "Over the creatures who live on this piece of rock, over the gods who twist things to their liking, over you."

Mat stood straighter. "You will never have power over us. If we die in the Last Battle, our souls will be beyond even your reach."

A moment of silence whirled into the forest. The pool stood frozen in the two moons' light. The trees looked ghostly with alien whitish light. Even the distant armies seemed quiet as if a spell of silence had been cast. The stars shone down, twinkling in soundless silver beauty.

In the short moment of silence, Janevra talked to Mat with her mind.

"He does not threaten us. I think there is something we don't know that we should," Janevra said.

"Kiera?"

"No. He has something planned." Janevra paused. *"He must have*

spies close to us."

Mat jerked. *"Spies? Who could it be?*

"Someone close, someone we should never expect."

Janevra turned her attention to Raxsen who was inspecting them carefully. "Who is it that you managed to twist and warp on your side with threats and promises?"

Raxsen suddenly let loose a wild grin. "Ah, and the conversation gets interesting. That is for you to find out. You managed to find out that Kalioa was a spy. Do it again."

Janevra bit her lip. They had never known Kalioa was a spy until Qwaser had killed her.

"Do you think we should have our own spies?" Janevra asked.

"And risk another life? No. Unless the person volunteers," Mat said.

"An ability that works well," Raxsen said.

They both jumped out of their silent conversation.

"What?" Janevra asked, shocked.

Raxsen waved his hand. "Nothing. I just figured you found some way to communicate without talking."

Mat balled his fists, his hate for Raxsen raging.

"But then that is little compared to what I've accomplished."

"What have you learned?" The interest was plain in Janevra's voice.

Raxsen suddenly looked normal, he smiled a real smile. "I've learned how to bring back the dead."

Janevra took a step backwards. "Is that possible?"

Raxsen rolled his eyes upward. "Obviously."

Mat puffed his chest out. "Bringing something back to life is to disrupt the balance of nature."

Raxsen shook his head. "You really are naive aren't you? If you are even able to bring something back to life then it was made to do so. Therefore I'm not upsetting the balance of nature in any way."

Mat scowled.

Raxsen yawned and made to go. "May your dreams be filled with flowers and meadows." Raxsen laughed mirthlessly at his own humor. He turned and faced them one more time. "Oh and one more thing. If you send anyone in search of the Artifacts or the Pearls of Light, I will kill them."

Raxsen disappeared into the trees.

"I shall face you in battle the day after tomorrow." The Warlord's voice trailed back to them.

Janevra felt his presence walk away and soon he was far enough away she could not feel him at all.

"Damn it!" Mat said.

Janevra looked at him. "What's so special about the Pearls of Light?"

Mat looked at her, his face stony with rage. "Remember when I told you about the Seven Artifacts?"

"Yes."

"The Pearls of Light allow anyone to tap into the Artifact it's connected to, no matter who is in possession of the Artifact."

Janevra clenched her jaw. "So they are unattainable for us then?"

"Unless we want someone else to die."

"But what if we sent the Phoenixes, or at least two of them? They're strong."

"I suppose we could ask one of them." Mat shrugged, dropping the subject.

Janevra took off her boots and sat down, putting her feet in the cool clear water. Mat sat down next to her, throwing small rocks into the pool. The rocks hit the water with a small kplunk, sending ripples across the pond.

"The pressure is unbearable, isn't it?" Mat said. "I don't want the day after tomorrow to come. So many people are going to die at our expense. Just because we were born, they have to die."

"Don't forget all the people who have died already. My mother and father, your mother and father, Zenerax, everyone under Raxsen's control and so many more people we cannot even name."

Mat leaned his own head on top of Janevra's. "Sometimes I wish to be a commoner again," Mat said, pausing. "I had a dream once. It was to be a solider. Now, after seeing so many die, I wonder what made me want to be such a thing. Someone who kills and gets paid. There is no honor in that."

Janevra sighed. "We all had dreams but they were crushed when someone else's dream became reality."

Mat traced a sign on the sandy shore with a finger. "I wonder what would have happened if we had never found each other. If some other two people were the Dragons, if our place in the future would be as important as it is now."

Janevra put her hand over Mat's. "Everything happens for a reason, like Raxsen said. If someone you love dies, you change. You become stronger or weaker. Either way, it was meant to happen. We have no control. We were meant to be the Dragons. Why? I don't know."

Mat's hazel eyes looked into Janevra's. "At least the world still provides gifts."

Janevra blushed and tilted her head to look up at the stars. She was pleased by his words but ignored them. "When a star shines it is in that heat of its glory. But when the star falls, it falls dramatically, shooting across the sky and dying into the night. We are like stars. We rise to power and then when everything seems right, we die and no one remembers us."

Mat hugged Janevra. "We won't be forgotten, if that's what you're afraid of."

"I'm afraid everything we suffer through and all the people who die will be forgotten. Everything we work so hard to accomplish will be but memories in a book hundreds of years from now. You and I will be but names," Janevra said, still looking up at the stars. "People won't know what we and everyone living through this had to go through. They won't understand."

"We may be only names but whatever we do now will change the world. If we lose, the world is bound to darkness and shadow. If we win, the world will live in light. I think that's enough for the people in the future to understand. As long as they see that, I will be happy." Mat stood up, pulling Janevra up with him.

They stood there awhile staring at each other.

Mat coughed, cracking the calm. "We need to go. We have a battle to plan tomorrow."

Janevra smiled up at him.

They turned and walked through the forest arm in arm.

The forest was filled with the sounds of night creatures. Crickets called to each other from under leaves. An owl hooted, the eerie sound echoing off the dark trees. Somewhere a wolf howled to the two moons, its voice carrying a deadly yet reassuring melody. A wind whispered through the branches, shaking the leaves and sending them to land lightly on the ground.

Before they reached Mat's tent, Janevra stopped him.

"Did you ever have a sweetheart?"

Mat frowned. "Once. She was a dark haired girl, pretty. She left me not long before I was caught for theft."

Janevra grinned. "I never had a true sweetheart." She watched him for a moment then went up on her tippy toes and kissed him on the lips.

She pulled away quickly and walked swiftly to where her tent had been set up. She felt like a little girl giving her sweetheart his first kiss. Her stomach seemed to be doing cartwheels.

ঙ্গ   ৫   ৪০

Mat stared after her. When she vanished into the tent, he gawked at the tent flap. The kiss had sent shivers down his back and he was slightly dizzy for some reason. Not even his sweetheart had ever kissed him like that before.

He laughed suddenly, enjoying this newfound desire for Janevra.

Still laughing, Mat went to his tent. He opened the tent flap and glanced back over at Janevra's tent. *By the gods I am lucky.*

He let the flap go and summoned his magic, sending a small glowing light to hover at the center of his tent.

Qwaser was sitting in one of the chairs.

Mat frowned. "Qwaser? What are you doing here?"

Qwaser stood up, a hand resting on the hilt of his sword.

Mat held up his hands. "I'm sorry if I offended you today, Qwaser. You're my friend and I would never insult you on purpose."

Qwaser shook his head. "I forgive you for that. It's about what Janevra wanted me to do."

Mat raised his eyebrows. "Then why did you come to me?"

"You know the Ile better."

Mat clenched his teeth, fearing what he had feared in the beginning to come true. "What is it?"

Qwaser smiled haughtily. "She was right. There is reason to suspect someone."

Mat grimaced. "Tell me."

"I saw him sifting through your battle plans in here. The idiot had a light. Any elven eyes could see that it wasn't you. I waited until he came out then I followed him. He went into the forest. He gave a copy of your battle plans to someone. I couldn't get their face but they worked for the Warlord. I saw a sword on their shoulder."

"Who is it?"

Qwaser stared Mat in the eyes. "Kayzi."

Mat growled. He drew on his magic, as much as he could. "Where is Kayzi?"

Qwaser stepped back, holding open the tent flap. "In his tent, counting the coins given to him."

Mat burst from his tent, his face contorted into a snarl, Qwaser close behind him.

He drew even more magic into his being. He felt it in his veins, dark and raging as it threatened to overtake him. He held so much magic that the Warlord, dozens of miles away, could feel the power and he caught his breath.

Mat marched to Kayzi's tent, not far from his own. Light from the campfires lit his face and his eyes blazed a deep hazel. His eyes seemed to be the color of the ocean with a storm roaring over it.

Mat swatted aside the tent flap of Kayzi's tent.

Kayzi looked up from counting several bags of golden coins. He didn't bother to hide them.

"My Lord Dragon?" he asked, standing up.

"Kayzi, you traitor!" Mat screamed.

Kayzi's gray eyes flashed. "Traitor?"

Mat shot his magic at Kayzi, flinging Kayzi out of the tent and landing him with a thud on the ground. Mat tossed the tent flap out of his way and went after Kayzi.

A crowd had gathered. Most were staring at Mat as if he were crazed. Kayzi could not be a traitor. He was a Djed and the brother of Deivenada.

Janevra, who had felt the awesome power Mat had harnessed, was standing in the front of the crowd, a little apart from everyone else, wearing her nightclothes. Ake, Riak and Kiera had dashed from their tents and were standing by Janevra. They were only half dressed. Eside and Ryen were close behind Qwaser and darting glances between Mat and Kayzi.

Dei ran from the crowd and helped her brother stand up. When he could stand she rounded on Mat.

"What the hell are you doing?" She had drawn her spear and had it aimed at Mat's throat.

Mat paid no attention to it, his gaze hard on Kayzi. "You betrayed us! You betrayed me! You betrayed your people! You betrayed your sister!"

Dei lowed the spear slightly, her eyes confused.

Janevra hurried over to Mat and laid a hand on his shoulder. She twisted towards Qwaser. "Is he a traitor?"

Qwaser nodded. "I was watchful as you asked. I saw him raiding Mat's battle plans. I watched as he gave them to a Dark follower."

The crowed went silent.

"He not only gave it to a Dark follower, he gave it to the Warlord himself. Janevra and I saw him in the forest," Mat said, his eyes locked onto Kayzi's.

Mat felt it as Janevra drew on her own magic and added it to his own stunning power.

Dei dropped her spear, the hurt in her eyes heartbreaking.

Kayzi sneered at her.

"Why?" Dei asked, her gray eyes dry.

Kayzi remained silent.

"Answer her!" Mat shouted. "Or I will make you."

Kayzi swallowed, not wishing to visualize that. He spoke, if hesitantly. "Before our village was attacked, I had talked to a sylai. They said I would get rewarded for my information. I gave them a map of the Edieata nation. Ever since then I've been working for the Warlord. I was the one that let the sylai into the Edieata city after I had killed all the Tar-ten guarding the gate with me. The Warlord has promised me power and riches. I am loyal to him now. You cannot sway me."

Dei caught her breath. "Did you lead the attack on the Daaguwh city?"

Kayzi seemed to regain some of his confidence. "Yes, in fact I killed Zenerax. The arrow that was shot into his back was from my bow. That little bastard was catching on to me. He first got suspicious when you followed me on my hunt, the night we saw the colors in the sky, the night when our village was attacked. And how we miraculously survived unscathed. Yet again he tried to scare me. Before you left to get the Lord Dragon he said, "the Council is watching." Of course they knew nothing except the Djed of the Daaguwh."

Dei went pale.

Janevra exchanged an icy look with Qwaser.

Ryen drew in on his magic followed closely by Eside.

The Ile in the crowd were stony faced, most fingered weapons they had brought with them as if wondering what way they would prefer to see Kayzi die.

Mat clenched his jaw. "In most countries the penalty for being a traitor is death."

Kayzi showed no emotion.

The silence seemed to weigh down upon the crowd, the night seemed heavier and the stars were but dull orbs.

"You can't kill him," Dei said, shocking everyone. Her gray eyes were the color of clouds filled with rain.

"Then what do we do with this traitor?" Mat asked. He did not take his eyes off Kayzi.

"We let him go."

The crowd erupted in an uproar. People yelled and shouted curses. Others aimed their weapons at Kayzi.

Mat lifted his eyes and stared at Dei. Even Janevra looked at her with question.

Dei drew herself up. "I will kill him one day, for killing Zenerax. I will search for him and when I find him he will wish he had died by the hands of the Lord Dragon. He will pay for what he did to my people and me. I will get revenge."

"If you let him live, he'll be able to kill even more people," Janevra said, standing next to Mat.

Dei shook her head. "No, he is my brother. And even if he is nothing but filth, he should not be murdered. I know him too well. He is a coward. He will hover in the background of everything, twisting it to his liking, but he will not fight. He might have killed Zenerax but his own life was at stake."

"I don't think it's smart," Mat said. It wasn't smart, letting a spy go.

Dei's gray eyes turned deadly and she rounded on Kayzi. "I saved his life if only to kill him another day. He will owe a life debt to me, until the day I kill him. No matter how low he sinks, the life debt will always lay between him and his goal. One day, I will kill him." Dei spit in Kayzi's face, who was still lying on the ground. She walked away, disappearing into the crowd.

Mat lifted his lip in disgust. "Get up."

Kayzi pulled his bruised body up, wincing slightly.

Mat looked Kayzi in the eyes, hazel verse gray. Hazel won. Kayzi lowered his eyes and stared at the ground.

Mat cleared his throat and spoke loudly. "We will let him go and Dei will get the revenge she desires upon him. He is an outcast, no longer an Ile."

Kayzi flinched at Mat's words. To become an outcast to the Ile was worse than death itself. He would be branded as an outcast in all Ile nations and never allowed to return. The tattoo on his arm would be scraped off. His honor would be ruined and his status destroyed. In Ile eyes he was dead.

Mat continued. "He will be allowed to leave peacefully. But know this, traitor. I will be looking for you, Janevra will be looking for you, Deivenada will be looking for you, Qwaser will be looking for you, and every Ile who was here tonight will be looking for you and we will find you."

Mat put his hand on Kayzi's arm. A flash of light exploded from his hand. Kayzi screamed, his eyes rolling back in his head.

When Mat removed his hand there was a smudge of black where the tattoo had been.

Tears were rolling down Kayzi's face and his hair stood on end. But his eyes roared hatred and promised revenge.

"Just as you are searching for me, I will be looking for you," he hissed. "I will kill every one of you and *you* will wish you had never done this to me."

The Ile in the crowd moved apart as Kayzi left the camp, making a direct path into the forest and towards the Warlord's camp.

Distain shone in their eyes and most shielded away from him like he was a deadly disease. The hate and loathing radiated from them. Their eyes were blank. He was a curse upon this earth and all they cared was that it was destroyed.

He disappeared into the forest, unarmed and weak.

"Follow him," Mat said, pointing to a young woman experienced in tracking. "Make sure he doesn't circle back."

The young woman nodded and slipped away as silent as an owl on wings.

The crowd moved away after that. They needed to sharpen their weapons for the battle the day after tomorrow and they needed sleep.

Vena pushed her way through the leaving crowd.

"What happened?" she demanded.

Eside sniffed. "Overslept the amusement, huh?"

Vena shot a glare at him then turned her gaze back on Mat and Janevra.

Mat felt Janevra let go of her magic. He did the same.

"Kayzi betrayed us," Mat said.

"I had Qwaser watch him. Kayzi is aligned with the Warlord," Janevra said.

Vena gasped. "No, he wouldn't, not that child."

"Children are always much more then they appear," Ake said. Clearly the Phoenixes thought Vena a pain. Mat sighed inwardly, five hours into their meeting and there was already tension between the two groups. With Qwaser convicting Kayzi and Vena suspicious of Kiera.

Mat summoned his magic once more and minded his memory of the conflict to her.

Vena gasped again. "Dei, that poor child." Vena swished away, her wide skirts brushing the ground.

Riak shook her head, watching Vena hurry away. "I need sleep, Janevra, if I'm to be up tomorrow making battle plans. Good night." She picked up Curly and hurried off.

Ake and Kiera followed Riak.

Eside glanced after them. "I agree." He departed into camp.

Ryen was still standing there, looking at Mat and Janevra.

"I pity you," he said. "You are trying to help people but all they see is someone destroying their lives."

Janevra smiled weakly. "We know, but we try our best."

Ryen turned and ran to catch up to Eside.

"Sleep well, Qwaser," Janevra said. "We depend on you so much."

Qwaser smiled briefly. "I know." He turned to leave.

"Qwaser?" Mat said.

Qwaser looked over his shoulder. "My Lord Dragon?"

"Thanks."

Qwaser nodded and left the two alone.

Janevra looked up at Mat and wrapped her hands around his waist. Tears leaked from her eyes and dripped onto Mat's shirt. Mat laid his head on hers. Her hair smelled of some exotic soap. Mat put his arm around her waist. With the other he lifted Janevra's chin up, to look into her eyes. The two moons seemed to illuminate her eyes and turn them a strange deep dark green. She looked up at him with complete trust. Her lips formed a smile.

"You're beautiful," he whispered.

Janevra blushed and smiled.

Mat bent down and kissed her fully on the lips. "That's for being there for me." Mat dropped his arms and headed for his tent.

"Mat, wait," Janevra said.

He turned around.

"Mat, do you feel for me the way you would a sweetheart?" she asked, holding her breath.

Mat smiled. "More so." He was surprised it was true.

Janevra grinned and fled again to her tent.

Mat breathed in deeply, the smell of the night entering his lungs. Even in the darkest of times, light still found a way to shine through.

Chapter 44
Betrayal

Kiera tossed in her bed. She was not used to sleeping on the floor and never would be. She peered over at Riak and Ake. Both were sleeping peacefully, little snores coming from Riak.

Kiera sighed and got out of her bed. She quickly slipped on a pair of Ake's pants, something she wouldn't be caught dead wearing during the day. *But since I'm just going for a walk, who will see me?*

She quickly ran a brush through her whitish hair for some appearance.

Glancing again at her two companions she slipped out of the tent.

Her tent, like the Dragons, was on the far side of the camp, closest to the Warlord and his army. Kiera would have rather slept in the very center of the camp.

The rest of the encampment was sleeping. Some people were up, elves and Ile talking quietly. She started walking towards the plains, in the direction they had come to meet the Lord Dragon.

Her thoughts became bitter as she walked further away from the camp, long grass brushing against her legs.

Why don't they understand me? Why don't Janevra, Mat, Ake, Riak, Eside, Ryen, Vena, all of them, understand me? They always look at me with scorn, as if I'm a child. I don't understand. And I especially don't understand why the Lord Dragon has not fallen head over heels in love with me. I am ten times prettier than Janevra, Ake, Riak and any other woman for that matter. I am gorgeous. No one can best me. No one.

As Kiera thought, her legs carried her further and further away from safety. The pants allowed her to move so quietly that she had passed by the sentries unnoticed.

The two moons above shone down, their white light sparkling in Kiera's hair. The wind blew gently, swaying the grasses of the plain. The stars shone, covering the sky with glitter.

"Again, nowhere to run," the cold voice struck out, lashing across Kiera's face.

Kiera's eyes went wide and fear was full in them. She knew that voice. She tried to summon her magic but a barrier held her. She was powerless, like last time.

A young man emerged out of the darkness, his bright green eyes laughing. His dark brown hair was ruffled from the wind and his black clothes thrashed around him.

"Pierce," Kiera sneered. She sealed herself up. His beauty could still send her dreaming.

David Pierce smiled. "Ah, but you must call me by my title, the First General, my love."

Kiera ignored him. "Let go of my magic or are you afraid I'll hurt you?"

Pierce laughed. "Hurt me?" He let go of his bind holding her magic.

Kiera's eyes lit with trimph and she lashed out at her enemy.

Pierce cut through her attack as if it were a bug. He then bound her magic again and she was left powerless. "See, what good would it do? I'm powerful, more so than you."

Kiera glared at him, she knew it was useless. He *was* stronger than her.

Pierce crossed his arms across his chest. "Now, I have a proposal to make to you."

"Forget it, there is nothing you can give me."

"That is where you are wrong. I can give you power and riches, something the Dragons will never offer you."

Kiera looked at him, her white blonde hair blowing across her face. "That's not enough."

Pierce gave her an odd look and continued in his deep voice. "My sweet, I can give you love and I can give you friendship."

A shiver went up Kiera's spine. *No one has ever loved me and no one has ever offered me their friendship.* It was her weakness. *I have always wanted to be someone who people love and trust.* But it had never happened and she had gone on wishing.

Pierce's lip twitched. "I can also give you beauty."

That froze Kiera's thoughts. She knew she was not pretty. She had made herself believe she was. Her mind raced. If she accepted she would be turning her back on Janevra and Mat, she would be leaving people she had admired for the enemy. On the other hand, if she was beautiful, if she was desirable by all men, she could also get her revenge. Revenge for the people who had thought her not important enough. People like Ake, Riak, Eside, Ryen and even Mat and Vena. It was only Janevra who had treated her remotely with some respect. But that was only one person.

Moreover she wanted to be powerful. And she knew Janevra and Mat would never completely trust her. Neither would Peirce, but the Dragons had not offered beauty. Or power. Or riches.

Kiera bit her lip. "If you made me beautiful, what would I need to give you in return?"

"Loyalty."

"What would I have to do?" Kiera asked, wishing to the Light that she would not have to spy. She had seen what Mat had done to Kayzi.

Pierce grinned callously. "We shall have none of that now, my sweet, praying to the Light."

Kiera's hand went up and touched the skull on the back of her neck.

"And, yes, you would spy for us. You are right in the inner circle of the Dragons," Pierce continued.

Kiera pushed any thought of doubt aside. "I'll help you."

Peirce smirked. "Of course you will. It was believed long ago that you would help us, my love."

"But there is a problem."

Pierce's eyes became cold and he stared at Kiera.

"Someone suspects I am already a spy."

"Who?"

"You do not know?" Kiera gloated. "It is Vena, the Ile Yria'ti."

Pierce ran a finger along his chin. "Yes, but she is no threat."

"What if I am caught?"

"You will say that you were brainwashed and cannot remember anything."

Kiera nodded but then paused before saying, "Won't they think something is wrong for my face will be different…pretty?"

Pierce gave a dry laugh. "No, you will stay the same in their eyes. The Dragons might be able to see the difference but it will take them awhile. Anyone you meet who is true to the Light that you do not know will see your new beauty. As I said before, the Dragons, the Phoenixes, Qwaser, Vena, and Deivenada won't be able to tell the difference. I will and so will anyone who follows the dark. They will see your new beauty. Just like they will see that you are bound to the Warlord."

Kiera felt hope for the first time in her life that she could actually be beautiful. She didn't listen to the rest of what Pierce was saying.

"Now come with me. The Warlord wishes to see you," Pierce said, summoning his magic.

Kiera felt her insides grow cold. The Warlord? Light help her!

Pierce slipped a hand into her own and muttered a simple spell. Kiera felt the land slip from under her and then be replaced again.

Pierce dropped her hand and Kiera gasped. The Warlord's army was impressive even from what she could make out in the dark.

Black tents surrounded her and Pierce. Blue fires flickered in the night and the sliding of metal could be heard everywhere as the Warlord's army prepared for battle. Some men moved about and others gambled with dice and placed bets on who would kill the most. Strange creatures stared up at her as she followed Pierce to the west side of the camp, closest to the Dragon's army.

The tickling of magic brushed against her mind as she felt shoi wonder who she was. Pierce shoved them away with force as they started to feel threatened.

They soon reached a large tent. A blue fire crackled in front of it, giving off light. No guards stood outside of it.

The tent flap opened and a young man stepped out.

Pierce stood straighter.

The young man was handsome, very much so, Kiera had to admit and if she was in a different situation she would have flirted with him. His blue eyes were icy and no emotion showed on his face. Power seemed to radiate from him and even walking he flowed with deadly grace. The Warlord gazed down upon her.

"She has agreed?"

Pierce glanced at her. "If we give her beauty and riches she will remain loyal, Warlord."

Kiera wanted to shrink down inside herself as these two powerful men scrutinized her. For a brief moment she wondered if the Dragons knew what they were up against, but then the thought passed and she shrugged to herself. It was their problem, not hers.

The Warlord looked at her a moment. "Who shall give her this beauty?"

Kiera quivered as she felt another presence of magic come near her. This one was also powerful. Kiera stared at the young man who had approached. It was not hard to see him in the dark. His clothes were black but his face was very pale.

The man bowed to the Warlord. "Warlord," he said. The Warlord seemed not to notice the man.

"Kard, this is Kiera, the Phoenix of Air," Pierce said.

Kard looked at her. "And I, Kiera, am the Phoenix of Death, Dorl

Kard." Kard extended his hand. Kiera took it, a little hesitantly and was shocked to find it ice cold. She took her hand away quickly and Kard laughed with no humor.

"Let's make her beautiful, each of us adding something we think is necessary in a woman's face and body," Pierce said. Kiera noticed he suggested it to the Warlord for nothing happened until the Warlord nodded.

Kiera gasped as they all gathered the forces of magic into their beings. So much power it was astonishing. And all of it came from three men. The most powerful being the Warlord and the weakest being Pierce and Pierce was stronger than she.

The Warlord went first. "Blue eyes you have, and they are so plain. Sky blue is what is desired." The Warlord focused his magic on her and her head burst into pain.

Kiera screamed and fell to her knees.

Kard followed the Warlord, not letting Kiera overcome her pain. "Your hair is too white. Blonde the color of corn is what is wanted." More power and more pain engulfed her. She screamed again, her head throbbing and darts of agony shooting all over her body.

"Your chin is too pointed. But your body is fine and your breasts are perfect. Your lips will look better if we smooth your chin out," Pierce said.

More pain flowed through her body. This time she did not scream for all her energy was aimed at trying to stay conscious.

When the pain finally stopped, Kiera stood up, her legs shaking, and looked up at the man who now had her loyalty. From the Warlord, she got no reaction. He just stood there, power streaming from him, his blue eyes colder than winter itself.

Kard nodded, obviously satisfied.

It was Pierce who smiled. He summoned his magic and held a mirror in his hand. He handed it to her with the reflection facing down.

Kiera looked down at the mirror in her hands, afraid for what she might see. She took a deep breath and turned the mirror over and lifted it to her face.

She gasped.

The woman staring back at her was beautiful. No, she was beyond beautiful. Rich blonde hair flowed down her back. Blue eyes as pretty as the day sky shone back at her. Her chin, which had always been too pointed, was rounded off, allowing her lips to look full and alluring. Her cheeks were brushed with color and her facial structure was perfectly symmetrical.

Kiera smiled and was pleased to see the dazed look on Pierce's face.

"Take her back to the Dragon's camp, Pierce. Kiera, you will meet Pierce back at that spot tomorrow night, with the information of the battle plans." The Warlord turned his back on them.

Kard followed the Warlord, daring to chance one last look back at Kiera. Her blue eyes met his black ones. She trembled. What she saw in his eyes was unnatural.

Pierce laid a hand on her arm, bringing her attention back to him. "You can call me whenever you want. All you must do is summon your magic and think of me. I will try to get to you if I can."

Kiera smiled, happy to have an admirer.

Pierce embraced his magic yet again and warped them back to the plain near the Dragons' camp.

In the darkness Kiera could barely make out Pierce but she could feel him draw near her.

"Do you see what magic can do when used in the right hands? Ah, but you are beautiful."

Kiera shivered. No one had ever said that to her before. She could feel Pierce's dazzling green eyes caress her face. Her heart fluttered in her chest like a blue bird taking wing. Her breath caught.

"A kiss before I leave?" he asked even as he brought his lips down to hers.

Kiera responded to his kiss. Her body was pressed against his and his arms traveled up from her waist almost to her bosom.

But he pulled away.

Kiera blushed, glad for the dark.

"You, woman, are tempting."

Before she could reply Pierce was gone. She regretted his disappearance.

As she slowly walked back to camp, her heart leapt with joy. She was beautiful now and no one could take it from her. She might be a spy against someone who had trusted her. But they had offered her nothing. Nothing.

When Kiera slipped into her bed, she fell deeply into sleep.

Her dreams were filled with gold and power.

Kiera did not feel the fingers of magic brush against her mind. Nor did she know that some who had once trusted her watched and shook her head. It was a shame when someone could be bought with beauty and riches.

Chapter 45
A Pearl of Light

That next morning dawned in streams of sunlight.

Raxsen stepped outside, breathing in the fresh morning air. He felt so smug. Since Kayzi had failed him as a spy, he now had an even better one. Kiera. The beauty-craving bitch. *She only proves my point that women are weak.* Raxsen laughed evilly. Oh yes, she would do nicely. *She probably does not know she is bound to me now, forever, until the end of eternity.*

He wished he could remember the dream he had of her last night. He had felt something last night that had to do with her, something important. He was starting to feel as if he had made a mistake.

Raxsen cursed to himself. It was no use dwelling on Kiera. He had more important things to do. Raxsen summoned his magic and transported himself to the bedroom of the Queen. He had figured out last night what he needed to get from the Queen of Angarat, something she had managed to keep from him for so long. *I should make her regret it.*

Raxsen looked around. It was a nice room. Maybe too much color but nice. His eyes were directed to a lump lying on the large bed.

Raxsen smiled wickedly.

The woman lying under the silken sheets stirred and pulled the blankets closer around her body.

"It is not polite to keep your Warlord waiting," Raxsen whispered.

The woman in the bed jerked into a sitting position, the silken sheets falling away to bunch around her waist, revealing her white breasts. Her dark eyes were wide and fear filled them. Her hair looked like black water as it fell down her back.

The woman quickly pulled up a sheet to cover her nakedness.

Raxsen moved over to her bed with a feline grace and looked down at the woman. "Get dressed, Syilvia."

The woman shot out of bed and ran behind a curtain.

"What are you doing here, Warlord?" Syilvia asked, her voice muffled from pulling a black gown over her head.

"I came to make sure my Queen was not betraying me." Raxsen conjured up a glass of wine and took a sip.

Syilvia stepped out from behind the curtain, sneering. The tight black gown she wore spread out around her feet like a blanket of midnight. Her red lips were in a thin line and her black eyes were daggers. A bird of prey were the first words that came into his mind when he saw her.

She moved towards him and pressed her body up against his.

"My Warlord," she whispered in his ear, "surely you—"

Raxsen's hand squeezed her arm hard enough to bruise it. "You will *never* attempt to seduce me again."

Syilvia pushed herself away, rubbing her arm.

"Now," Raxsen sat down in one of the chairs, "I believe I need something from you."

Syilvia laughed. "The great Warlord is asking *me* for something?"

Raxsen stared at her with ice in his eyes. His face was stony but when she looked into his eyes, she saw more than just the abyss.

The Queen paled if that was possible but she quickly regained her composure. "What, Warlord?"

Raxsen laced his fingers together. "I need to see your jewelry collection."

Syilvia screwed up her face. "Why?"

"Just let me see it," Raxsen snapped.

All dignity lost, Syilvia jumped up and ran into an adjoining room. She came back carrying a polished dark wood box with gold inlaid on the top.

The Queen thrust the box into his hands. "Here." She sat down opposite him. "I have more boxes if you don't find what you're looking for in there."

Raxsen opened the box. Silver and gold necklaces filled the box along with twisted copper bracelets and sapphire earrings. A dark ruby was hung in a pendant and diamonds adorned rings. What caught his eye was a rosy pink ball attached to a silver necklace chain.

He pulled out the pink pearl. "Where did you get this?"

"I don't know. It was my mother's. She told me she had acquired it from a servant who acquired it in Mauke."

Raxsen fingered the pearl. "Interesting." It was a very powerful little jewel.

"You can have it. It means nothing to me."

"I'm glad you gave it willingly or I would have had to kill you."

Syilvia shuddered.

Raxsen slipped the necklace around his neck. He quietly tucked it into his shirt. "Did you know that this pearl is one of the seven Pearls of Light?"

Syilvia shook her head.

"It allows me to tap into the powers of the Moons of Iwo. An Artifact that will boost my magic by twofold, making me that much more powerful than the Dragons."

Raxsen's eyes lit with a twisted triumph and Syilvia sank lower into her chair at the deadly look in his eyes.

The Warlord abruptly stood up. He leaned down and kissed the Queen on her cheek. "You are one of the few women I will ever trust. Don't tarnish that trust or you will find yourself in a place worse than death."

Raxsen summoned his magic and disappeared, leaving behind a very shaken Queen.

Reappearing back in front of his tent, he smiled even more wickedly. He stuffed his hands into his black trouser pockets. Tomorrow was the battle and the Dragons were in for a big surprise.

"Kard!" Raxsen bellowed.

Kard tumbled out of his tent, tugging on a pair of pants.

"Yes, Warlord?" Kard said, tucking in his black shirt.

"I want to inspect the shoi you have attempted to make into a fighting force."

Kard nodded and hurried away, yelling harsh commands into the tents of his students.

Raxsen watched Kard, his icy blue eyes seeming to see more than the flesh. It impressed Raxsen when Kard had all of his students dressed and ready to present in less than fifteen minutes.

Raxsen stood in front of them. "I have always wondered," Raxsen said, startling them with his voice, "what would happen to a shoi if he were stripped of his magical ability."

The men and women in front of him shifted uneasily.

Raxsen smiled coldly. "We will see the result if we lose this battle." Raxsen paused and enjoyed their pulsing fear for a moment.

"But since that must not happen, I will ask you to do only one thing in preparation of the battle." He paused again. "I want you to trap a small part of your ability into a ball this big." Raxsen summoned his magic and created a ball one inch by one inch. He created twenty-three more and handed them to each member of Kard's army. "Once you do this, hand it to me and you may leave."

When the last student handed him their magic filled balls, Raxsen made the balls vanish with his magic.

Kard came up to him. "What do you plan to do with those, Warlord?"

Raxsen turned his cold gaze on Kard. "Have you ever seen a ball of pure magic hit the ground?"

Kard shook his head, his black eyes confused.

"Of course you haven't." *I do not know how I myself know,* he thought, casting a dark look up at the sky. *I wonder why I know of it?* "When a ball of pure magic drops, it creates an explosion similar to a volcanic blast. Since we do not want to kill ourselves, I made the balls much smaller. They will only damage an area twelve feet by twelve feet. When your enemy is closely packed together, this is a deadly weapon."

Kard smiled, mimicking Raxsen's own grin. He turned to move away.

"Kard." Kard faced the Warlord.

"I want you to do something for me."

Kard raised his eyebrows. "What?"

"Do you know where the Lady Dragon used to live?"

"No."

Rage showed in Raxsen's eyes. "Do you not know anything?"

Kard didn't answer.

"It doesn't matter. The Lady Dragon is the Heir to the Throne of Caendor, the nation with a mad man currently in power. I want you to go to Jariran and persuade him to join my ranks."

"Why do you want a mad man under your control?"

Raxsen smiled but the smile missed his eyes. "He was going to be the next King of Caendor if Janevra had not refused to marry him and run away. He took power into his own hands and killed the Lady Dragon's parents. He is a powerful shoi and I want him on my side. If he does agree to my terms it will also add much land onto my expanding empire. He also has a very impressive army."

"How large is his army?" Kard asked.

Raxsen's lips twisted upwards. "That's the funny thing. It's as big as how many he kills."

Kard winced. "He has created an army of the dead?"

"Yes. He seems to have a remarkable Talent in creating the walking dead."

Silence followed Raxsen's words and for a brief moment a cloud covered the sun and the land turned dark.

"Bring him to me before the sun sets tonight, Kard, or you will regret it."

"Yes, Warlord," Kard said. He summoned his magic and disappeared.

Raxsen's face settled back into the cold mask he always wore.

"General Pierce!" Raxsen yelled as if calling to a faithful dog.

Pierce came walking up, his arrogant smile on his lips. "What?"

"Bring me my twenty-three best warriors."

Pierce sent a message through lines of magic to his best warriors.

They came quickly. Over half of them were men, big and heavily guarded. Each male had some visible scar or wound and stank of wine.

The women on the other hand were skinny but their brawny muscles could not be hidden under baggy clothes. Among the women was Cobrau, the captain of all the women in his army. Her fiery red hair was cut close to her head and her blue eyes lingered on Pierce. The sun shaped scar on her cheek was outlined in red. From her ears hung fire captured in a small ball. She was from Sunda, Caroa and had a temper none could match. She was, next to the Queen of Angarat, one of the few women he dared to trust.

Raxsen summoned his magic and brought forth the balls of magic. He handed each warrior one ball.

"This is a ball of pure magic. When you throw it, it will create an explosion. But make sure you can throw it over twelve feet away for that is the blast radius. You are to use these tomorrow but only if you are in a position where you cannot fight your way out without many losses. And make sure you do not throw it where your own men are fighting."

They all nodded.

Raxsen waved a hand, dismissing them. All the men and woman left but Cobrau and Pierce remained.

Raxsen watched, intending to see sparks fly.

Cobrau walked up to Pierce, her earrings sparkling in the sun.

"Why didn't you come last night?" she demanded.

The smile on Pierce's face disappeared. "The Warlord had something for me to do."

"And it took all night?" Her blue eyes were slits.

"Yes."

"What was it?" the fiery red head asked.

"I had to seduce the Phoenix of Air."

Raxsen winced. Poor Pierce. Cobrau's sharp tongue would skin him.

Cobrau's eyes became icy and her jaw clenched. "Did you show her a good time?"

Pierce looked taken back. "No. It was business."

"Oh, then what did you do? Or shall I not ask?"

Pierce, at least, had the grace to blush. "The Warlord wanted her as a spy and in order to do so, we had to get her to come here."

Cobrau thawed slightly. "Is she pretty?"

"Yes—No! I mean she wasn't!" Pierce swallowed.

Cobrau's eyes became even blacker than before. "Burn in hell," she spat. Cobrau turned around and stalked off. Pierce ran after her and grabbed her arm.

She whirled around, a knife in her hand. She put it up against his throat. "Don't you ever touch me again," she whispered.

"I won't. I swear, Cobrau."

Cobrau looked up at him. "I once had a man who would do anything for me. He would never have thought of cheating on me. I don't know why I left him." She wrenched her arm out of his grasp and sheathed her dagger.

"I believe you, Pierce. But if I ever find out that you lied to me today, I will kill her. And you. The Warlord will pity you for what I will do to you." Cobrau ran, leaving Pierce to stare after her.

Pierce shook his head and walked back to Raxsen, his face pale.

Raxsen bit the inside of his cheek to keep from snickering. Oh, what fun it was to laugh at others' misery.

"Shut up," Pierce said.

"You kissed Kiera didn't you?"

Pierce rubbed his throat. "Yes."

"I like Cobrau. She's got what it takes."

Pierce glared at Raxsen. "If you weren't the Warlord I would wring your neck."

Raxsen's gaze became cold. "But I am the Warlord. And I'm telling you not to mess things up with Cobrau. We need her. I'm also telling you to leave Kiera alone. She's a pawn not a toy."

Pierce spat on the ground and walked away.

Raxsen surveyed his camp. It was time to call a meeting for his generals, captains and lieutenants. First he would think about that strange dream he had had of Kiera last night. That dream where she had... Raxsen frowned, where she had what? "I have to remember!" he mumbled to himself.

Chapter 47
The Plains of Calahar

Janevra nudged Mat awake.

"Get up, Mat. I have something to tell you."

Mat put his head under his pillow. "Just five more minutes. I'm having a wonderful dream."

"Mat," Janevra pulled the pillow off his head and hit him with it. "Get up."

Mat sat up, his hair rumpled. He kept his eyes closed.

"I found something out that— Mat!"

He jerked out of his sleep. He opened one eye. "What?"

Janevra gave an exasperated sigh. "Get dressed." She tossed a shirt at him.

Mat slipped on the shirt and ran a hand through his hair. "Now, what is it that I must know that is so important that I must be deprived of my sleep?"

Janevra's lips thinned. "Last night I tapped into the dreams of the Phoenixes."

"So?"

"Kiera is betraying us," Janevra said grimly.

Mat stood up, fury making him summon his magic. "I'll kill her!" he roared.

Janevra pulled him back down onto the bed. "No."

Mat let his magic go, shocked. "Why not?"

"Because she is perfect." Janevra smiled.

"Perfect?"

Janevra's smile suddenly turned wicked. "Yes. She went to the Warlord last night and if she gave him her loyalty, he would give her beauty."

Mat shrugged.

"Don't you see? Kiera is going to give Raxsen our battle plans. But what we'll do is give her the wrong ones or just say she can't join the war council."

"She's still a spy."

"True. Try looking at it this way. Raxsen had to give her beauty and power in order for her to agree. So therefore she will have some unconscious connection to him. If we can slip into her dreams at night and find the link that connects her to Raxsen, we can find out his *own* battle plans."

"My intelligent Lady Dragon, what would I do without you?" Mat smiled and kissed Janevra on the cheek.

"You wouldn't be able to get out of bed in the morning, that's for sure." Janevra snorted.

"I'm sure it works both ways. I bet Kiera could give us the wrong information," Mat said, getting back on topic.

Janevra looked pensive. "You're probably right. It would be best then to hand her over to Raxsen."

"Yes, it would. But what would Raxsen do to her? He might kill her."

"He might. He probably will if she gets in his way enough."

"Then we can't give her over to him."

"She knew what she was getting herself into when she joined him. We have no responsibility for her now. She is on her own."

Mat nodded then frowned. "You said he gave her beauty?"

"Yes. I've seen her. Well, what she thought was her in her dreams. It's not that much of an improvement. She is beautiful but there's something odd surrounding her new beauty."

"Raxsen can do that?"

"No, he had help. It's a big undertaking to change someone's appearance forever."

Mat's frown grew deeper.

"I think we should tell her that we know. Let her fear us."

Mat's eyes became wide. "Janevra, that's what Raxsen does and—"

Janevra cut him off. "Mat, I don't care if it's like Raxsen or not. Kiera knew what she was doing when she sold her loyalty to the Warlord. All we're going to do is make her feel guilty."

"It's time to pay a visit to our dear Kiera." Janevra felt him summon his magic to make himself look presentable. She was already wearing her day clothes, tan pants and shirt with roses working their way up the sides.

They stepped out of Mat's tent, looking like a king and queen. No, they stepped out of the tent looking like an Emperor and Empress.

They slowly made their way to the Phoenix's tents, talking to people who passed them by or quickly dispatching orders about the war council that was to be held.

When they reached the tent of Ake, Riak and Kiera, Janevra motioned Mat to stop and wait for her outside.

Janevra entered the tent and quickly scanned it. Kiera was not there.

Janevra nodded to the two other women as they awoke. "Ake, Riak, I trust you slept well?"

Ake rubbed her eyes and Riak yawned.

"Have you seen Kiera?" Janevra asked.

Ake shook her head and lay back down on her bed, pulling the blankets around her tightly.

"I think she went out on a walk. She mentioned something about grass and a walk," Riak murmured, falling back asleep.

Janevra thought of a moment. Grass. But...ah, Kiera was going to the plains, the plains they had crossed yesterday. And in the plains Kiera could easily summon her magic and not call the attention of the Dragons.

Janevra brushed the tent flap aside. She grabbed Mat. "She's gone to the plains."

Mat winced slightly as the same thoughts crossed his mind.

The Phoenix's tent was on the northwestern side of the camp so they were able to get out of camp without anyone seeing them.

"We must be quiet," Janevra said.

"Yes and do not draw on your magic. We do not know if she can feel it."

They walked through the long prairie grass, stopping only to tell the sentinel that they would be back soon.

The prairie grass swayed gently in the morning breeze. The blue sky above was dotted with white clouds and the sun shone with joy.

The whispers of magic floated to Janevra and Mat. Both slowed, cocking their heads into the wind. The magic they felt was dark and tainted. Only the slightest trace of light was there but even that was twisted.

Janevra got down on her hands and knees, pulling Mat with her. They crawled through the long grass until the faint sound of voices was clear.

"The Dragons are going to hold a war council today, I'm sure. By tonight I'll have all the information you want," Kiera said.

A deep voice answered Kiera's. "Yes, I know. But why did you call me?"

"I just wanted to see you again. Is there any harm in that?" Kiera pouted.

Deep, seductive laughter sounded. "Of course not, my sweet."

Janevra turned and looked at Mat. Mat nodded. Mat summoned his magic slowly so not to attract the attention of Kiera and her friend. He gradually built up a shield around both of them. When he was finished Janevra embraced her own magic and Mat channeled his full power.

The two people standing in the long grass kissing had not noticed either of them.

Janevra aimed her magic and blocked Kiera and the man from their power.

Kiera screamed, feeling the life filling magic getting ripped from her being. The man whose arms she stood in gaped at them.

Janevra and Mat stood. Magic emitted from their bodies, filling them with power and life.

"Kiera," Janevra said coldly, her green eyes afire.

Kiera turned and looked at Janevra, screaming even louder, her face paling to a remarkable white.

Mat thrust his magic up against her face, silencing her. Kiera's hair was in disarray and her lips pressed tightly together. She looked at Mat with horror.

The Dragons walked up to Kiera and the man, the power the Dragons held stunning them.

Mat pulled Kiera and the man apart with magic, setting them several feet away, tied tightly in the bonds on magic. He then set up a shield around all four of them so no one could hear what was going on.

When Mat finished he turned to Janevra and nodded.

Janevra rounded on Kiera. "What have you done?" Kiera whimpered.

"What have you done, Kiera?" Janevra shouted, destroying the gag Mat had put on the Phoenix of Air.

"N-nothing," Kiera mumbled.

Janevra's lips thinned. "You will either tell me what you did or I'll tell you myself. And I can promise that you will not like it."

Kiera shivered. "I-I'm loyal to the Warlord."

Mat clenched his jaw, the muscles in his neck straining.

Janevra looked Kiera in the eyes. Kiera didn't meet her glance. "Why?"

"Because he offered me beauty."

"You betrayed us Kiera. You betrayed your friends."

Kiera looked up, her new sky blue eyes hard. "You never offered me your friendship, you and your Phoenixes, never!"

Janevra's temper blazed. "Friendship? You accuse us of not offering friendship? Bah! We offered it to you. You didn't accept. You thought yourself too high, too mighty. So we did not offer our friendship again. It is your own fault."

Tear's rolled down Kiera's face.

Janevra stood taller and put her hand on Kiera's arm, the one that held the Phoenix. "I hoped you would not be a problem. I knew you had met the Warlord's minion before you ever met me. I knew you had been tainted. However I had hoped and prayed that you would not betray me. I see I was wrong. I tried to see past your short failings and see the kind of woman you could be. I do not know why I tried. I was originally going to tell you that I knew you had betrayed us. Now I see that your betrayal goes far deeper." Janevra tightened her hold on Kiera's arm. "I gave you this gold Phoenix to make you the Phoenix of Air. I wish I never had to do this Kiera, know that, but because of your actions, I must."

Janevra's grip became even tighter around Kiera's arm. Kiera's eyes widened in fear and tears were bright in her eyes.

Janevra brought even more magic into her person and shot a bolt of cold energy into Kiera's arm.

Kiera screamed and her eyes rolled back into her head. She fainted, her body held in the air from Mat's magic.

Janevra let go of Kiera's arm. "I trusted you. I hate myself for doing what I did to you but I cannot risk the lives of thousands to let you go."

The Phoenix that had once been a beautiful unblemished gold and red was now black. Smoke arose from where Janevra's hands had been.

Janevra stepped away from Kiera's limp form.

Mat turned towards the man who was held from his magic and tied in bands of power. Janevra moved and stood next to him.

"Who are you?" Mat asked.

The man turned his head.

"Tell me who you are," Mat demanded.

The man remained silent.

"If you wish then…" Mat gathered more magic and slipped under the shields the man had put around his mind.

"Pierce, First General in the Warlord's army." Mat smiled darkly.

Pierce looked up at Mat, his dazzling green eyes frosty.

Janevra clutched Pierce's shirt, ripping off the left arm. A sword had been tattooed into his skin.

"I believe," Janevra said, "that if we send a burst of energy through this tattoo, we can get the Warlord here."

"Do it," Mat said. "We need to talk to him."

Janevra laid her hand on Pierce's shoulder, her hands cool. She fired a shock of energy into the tattoo.

Pierce did not scream as the energy ripped through him but he gave a jolt and his hair stood on end.

"He should be here soon," Janevra said.

"Pierce," Mat said, "why did Raxsen wish for Kiera to be his spy?"

Pierce pressed his lips together.

"I do not want to go in your mind again."

Pierce shuddered. "He knew she was the weakest and he knew that he could use her as long as he gave her beauty, riches and power. But I do not know exactly why he wanted her."

There was a loud crack and suddenly the Warlord was striding towards them, his magic crackling around his fingertips. When he reached the shield Mat had erected, Mat quickly destroyed it.

"I knew that woman would be a distraction. I knew it!" Raxsen screamed.

Janevra smiled at the Warlord. "It's nice to finally see you more than calm, Raxsen."

Raxsen sneered at her. He rounded on Pierce. "Did Kiera call you?"

Pierce nodded, his magic still cut from him.

"That fool!" Raxsen screamed again, spittle flying from his mouth. "Now I'm stuck with her!"

Mat gazed at Raxsen. "That's what you get for turning people against us."

Raxsen summoned more of his magic and shot a bolt of black power at Mat.

Mat deflected it with his own bolt of white power.

Raxsen's cold blue eyes stared into Mat's. "It is useless for us to fight each other now."

Mat nodded but did not lower his guard. Janevra regarded Raxsen coolly, not trusting him. He had a way of slipping around her defenses.

"What are we going to do with Kiera?" Raxsen asked, his cold gaze flickering to the unconscious woman.

"She betrayed us and you have a bond with her. You must take her," Janevra said.

"She betrayed me," Raxsen shot back.

Janevra folded her arms. "How?"

"In her dreams. You sneaked into them last night and learned what she had done. She did not guard her dreams closely enough and that tells me she was regretting what she had done," Raxsen answered, his fury at Kiera apparent.

Mat laughed mirthlessly. "So we have a woman on our hands who betrays both the Dragons and the Warlord."

"It seems we do," Raxsen said.

"What do we do with her? Its obvious none of us can trust her. But one of us needs to take her," Janevra pointed out.

Raxsen scrutinized Pierce. "Let him go, Dragon. I'm going to send him back to my camp."

Mat's jaw tightened at taking orders from Raxsen but he did so anyhow.

Pierce fell to the ground. He stood up quickly, his back rigid. "I didn't betray you, Warlord."

"I know, Pierce, I would have felt it if you had done so. Call all my generals together," Raxsen ordered and transported Pierce back to the camp.

Raxsen faced the Dragons. "I'm taking Kiera."

"What? You just accused her of betraying you," Mat said. "What will you use her for?"

The tension between the Warlord and Dragons rose and the ice in Raxsen's eyes became colder as Janevra's blazed as if tinder had been added to the fire.

"We don't want Kiera," Janevra said, looking at Mat. "She betrayed us knowing that it could have destroyed everything. Take her."

Raxsen smiled. "I'm glad you see things my way."

"We don't see them your way," Mat said.

Raxsen sneered at him.

Mat cut his magic binding Kiera. Raxsen and the Phoenix of Air disappeared.

"I hate him," Janevra said with venom.

They made their way back to camp slowly. Janevra kept thinking that she had done something wrong. Within only a few hours time, two people had betrayed them. *Why?* she thought.

"Should we tell the Phoenixes that Kiera betrayed us?" Janevra asked.

"What else can we do? We have no choice," Mat said letting go of his magic.

"People keep betraying us," Janevra said, rubbing the lightning bolt on her arm, tracing its jagged edges. She let the hold on her magic go, sighing when the life-giving power left her.

"They never betrayed us. They betrayed the Light the moment they were born."

"I just hope no one else betrays us."

Mat shook his head. "I don't think anyone else will. The First Battle is upon us and people's hearts should be firmly in place."

"I hope so."

They walked through the long golden prairie grass. The sky above was a timeless blue and birds sung in the bush, their songs promising peace and beauty. This land was not yet touched by war and did not show the signs as other waving plains of grass did.

Janevra and Mat reached the Phoenixs' tents. They found Ryen, Eside, Ake and Riak sitting outside, laughing. When they saw the Dragons approaching the four calmed and stood up.

"Kiera's Phoenix is black," Janevra said.

Riak put her hand on her upper arm and touched the Phoenix. Ake and Eside summoned their magic unconsciously.

"I don't understand," Ryen said, his forest green eyes confused, not surprised.

"She's left us," Mat said simply.

Ake frowned. "Why? We offered her everything."

Janevra sighed. "It wasn't enough for her. She wanted more then what we could give her." *She will always want more,* Janevra realized silently.

"How did she betray us?" Riak asked.

The Dragons' faces became stone and their eyes blazed.

"She bonded herself to the Warlord," Mat said grimly.

"Where is she now?" Eside said, running a hand through his red hair.

"With the Warlord." Janevra's eyes were green fire.

The Phoenixes were silent. The fact that Kiera had betrayed them hit them hard. Even though she was never close to any of them, she was still a Phoenix and that created a link between all of them.

Janevra turned away and Mat followed her.

"We hold a war meeting at noon. Two hours time," Mat said, looking over his shoulder.

CB   CR   BO

The Phoenixes watched the Dragons walk away.

Ake faced Eside. "Why? Why would Kiera do that?"

Eside clenched his jaw. "Because he offered her more."

"I don't understand. She had respect from the Dragons, and she had our friendship if she had wanted to ever befriend us," Riak said.

"Me neither," Eside said.

Ryen frowned. "She never fit. That's why she betrayed us. She didn't feel like she fit in and she felt like an outcast." Cradling Curly in her arms, Riak snuggled her face close to his.

"But that wasn't the case," Ake said.

"She didn't know that," Ryen restored

"There's only four of us left now, the Phoenixes of Life, Earth, Water and Fire. It's barely enough." Eside whispered. "It's barely enough."

"Don't lose hope, never lose hope. Kiera, yes, she was a Phoenix but she was not that strong. We'll make it. We'll complete the destiny that was set out for us," Riak said strongly, renewing the belief in all four of them.

"Yes, we will never lose hope," Ake said, her deep purple eyes glinting. "Never while we live and fight the Darkness."

The Phoenixes looked towards the retreating figures of the Dragons. A deep forest green, an ocean purple, a flaming brown and a misty gray watched the man and woman they followed with undying trust.

"We will not lose hope and we will forever follow the Dragons.

Forever," Riak said, the power of the Light racing through her body.

"We Phoenixes are now a circle of four that can never be broken," Eside said. "And the Dragon of the Rising Sun and the Dragon of the Coming Storm have their four to rule at their side."

Chapter 48
The King

Kard stepped on broken glass, his boots crushing into it, the sound echoing in the ruined hallway.

I do not want to be here. But the Warlord had given him orders and he must obey the Warlord.

Kard was to find Ravften, the King of Jariran. *Not lawfully,* thought Kard bitterly.

As a boy he had always wanted to travel to Jariran, the City of Jewels. He had always wanted to see the Tower of Light, the impregnable black obsidian walls that surrounded the city, the Library of Jariran with its gold roof and most of all he had wanted to see the princess, the girl with her womanly beauty and strange green eyes.

He had never had the chance.

Kard summoned his magic, feeling its protective cloak wrap around him like a heavy blanket.

He walked through the scorched hallways, more broken glass crunching under foot. Smoke hung in the air, as did the smell of death. The clouds outside were so dark that they allowed no light to filter through.

Kard suddenly felt a tug on the weavings of magic. A shoi was near, a powerful one.

The clanking of feet sounded from down the hallway. Kard listened carefully, trying to decide if he should attack or not. He stopped walking and stepped back into a shadowed corner.

Kard peered around the corner and saw to his horror a patrol of skeletons. The white bones of the once living things had tatters of clothing stuck to the bone. Steel helmets were fitted over the heads of most and the bony hands griped cold metal weapons.

Kard pulled away from the wall, in full view of the approaching skeletons.

The lead skeleton stopped and raised a hand, the ones behind him coming to a halt. *"Gedve huvxq kudge?"* the leader said, the guttural sounds coming from its ever-grinning mouth. The language it spoke in was long ago lost in the myths of history. Only the dead would ever know its words.

Kard spread his hands. "I don't speak Dgeu."

The skeleton looked at him and cocked its head, the bones grinding together.

"I do not speak Dgeu," Kard repeated.

The things looked at him.

Kard sighed and gathered his magic into his being.

He blasted the skeletons with a ball of fire.

The skeletons screamed, their bones splitting and popping, their souls finally fleeing their long dead bodies imprisoned by the Dead King.

In seconds there was nothing but dark ash scattering the marble floor of the palace.

Kard walked through the ash, lessening his hold on his magic. He flickered ash off his black coat and continued down the hallway.

Crazed laughter crackled through the hall.

Kard's head whipped up, his coal eyes going to the door at the end of the hallway.

He moved slowly down the hallway, keeping his back to the walls.

More laughter sounded, higher pitched this time.

Kard reached the door and put his ear against it.

"Let them go?" The laughter sounded again.

"But, my lord, they…" the person speaking paused. "They offered the riches of the Thieves Guild."

"The treasures within the Guild are already mine. All I must do is get rid of the rebels protecting it."

"But, my lord—"

"Do not—" the crazed voice broke off. Kard pressed closer to the door and reeled back as he felt the gathering of magic in the room, all its power aimed at…

Kard dove out of the way, a ball of heat and ice just missing his head. The doors that had lead to the room were all blasted away, revealing two men.

Kard jumped up, gathering all the magic his body could hold. He quickly put a shield around himself and stepped into the room.

A man sat on the throne. On top of his black hair a crown rested and his baby blue eyes stared down at Kard. His clothes, dark blue, made his eyes look like the depth of an ocean.

Another man was bowed down in front of the throne, his eyes wide in fear.

"Get away from me," the King said to the man bowed in front of him.

The man scrambled up and stumbled out of the room.

Kard watched the man hurry away and turned his attention to the King. "Ravften," Kard said quietly.

The man jerked visibly. "How did you know me?"

"I'm an ambassador of the Warlord."

"The Warlord, oh?" the man snickered. "And what does the Warlord want with me?"

Kard felt the tendril of dislike brush his mind and he was careful not to speak with scorn. "The Warlord wants an alliance with you."

The man cackled with more high-pitched laughter. "An alliance?"

Kard's coal eyes darkened. "If you were to agree, you would be allied with the most powerful man in history."

Ravften stopped laughing. "I am the most powerful man in history."

Kard stayed silent.

"What would I get in return for following the Warlord?"

Kard didn't know. "More land, riches," Kard paused. "More power."

"I have land, I have riches and I have power," Ravften clenched his fist. "I want something that I don't have."

Kard moved over and stood by a window looking down at the metropolis. Black burned buildings covered every block of the city. Patrols of skeletons marched up and down streets. Smoke gathered and clung to the air creating a misty haze over the city. A skirmish was taking place between a small number of humans and skeletons. The humans were winning.

Kard turned away from the window, a smile playing on his lips. "What do you want in return for your services?"

Ravften sat back in his chair. "I want Janevra. The Princess of Caendor, Heir to the Throne, Princess of the Tower of Light, Daughter to the Nation Caendor and Child of the Old King."

Kard laughed dryly. "You want *her*?"

Ravften roared to his feet, magic snapping around his fingers and in his eyes. "Do not insult my wife to be!" he screamed, spittle flying from his mouth.

Kard stood his ground. "I did not insult her."

Ravften let go of his magic quickly and sat back down.

"Why do you want Janevra?" Kard asked.

Ravften's eyes got lost in the past. "The King wanted me to marry his daughter. He knew I had always admired her and he knew I would be a good King to his land. He set up my marriage to Janevra. But she did not want to marry me. I kept telling her that her love for me would eventually grow. She rejected my advances and insulted me during the Festival of the Stars, humiliating me in front of lords and ladies below my station. When she disappeared, her father was too heart broken to do anything except hand control over to me. I sent armies of men searching for her. When news reached me that she had gone into the Lost Mountains, I called off the search. I knew it would be pointless to search for her in there. I announced that she was dead. The King and Queen were heart broken when I told them that their daughter was dead. I quickly realized that without Janevra I would never be able to become king and the Queen was still of child bearing age, even if she was on her last years. She could still produce another heir. I killed both of them with magic and proclaimed myself the rightful king. No one challenged me and I began my rule. The people themselves did not trust me and I turned to violence in order to control them. Then some of the nobles started to speak about me, how I was unfit to rule and that they should find someone with Royal Blood to take the throne. In anger I destroyed all those not loyal to me and many others fled.

In order for me to regain my kingdom and become the only King of Caendor, I must marry Janevra."

Demented psycho, Kard thought. *No wonder she hates you. Your country is too destroyed to restore. It will never again reach its past splendor.*

"You want Janevra," Kard said. *If I remember correctly, she's taken. In more ways then one.*

Ravften folded his arms. "If you can bring her to me from the Lost Mountains, I will give the Warlord my full loyalty."

"What would you do if I told you I knew exactly where she was and that you could talk to her? Would you still give the Warlord your loyalty?"

"Where is she? When?" Ravften threw himself off the throne, running wildly at Kard.

Kard quickly erected his shield and Ravften bounced off it, sliding across the smooth stone floor.

Ravften stumbled up, the madness lost from his eyes, his dignity regained. He stood stiffly, brushing at his clothes.

"Would you give the Warlord your loyalty if you could see her and speak to her?" Kard asked again.

"I would."

"Good. Do you swear with your life and loyalty that you will be forever devoted to the Warlord?" Kard asked.

"Yes, yes I do. I swear," Ravften said.

Kard twisted his lips. "Do you bind your life to the Warlord's?"

"Yes."

Kard showed his teeth, an evil grin on his face. The spell he summoned he put on Ravften.

Ravften howled as the binding spell hit him. He withered on the floor twisting and turning, screams and curses pouring from his mouth.

When Ravften's screams died away, Kard let go of his magic.

Ravften stood up slowly. "What did you do?" he spat.

"I put the strongest binding spell on you. It binds you to the Warlord and if you ever betray him by allying yourself to others, you will die," Kard said lightly. *I think the Warlord should kill you anyhow. You're not sane if I know what sane is.*

Ravften rubbed his chest. "Do you have binding spell over your heart?"

"In a manner of speaking."

"Why is it different?"

"Because I am the Phoenix of Death. It is my destiny to follow the Warlord."

Ravften stepped back and looked Kard up and down. His blue eyes held no doubt. "What do you want me to do?"

"Come with me back to the Warlord's camp. We are attacking the Dragons tomorrow at dawn."

"The first Battle between the Warlord and the Dragons?"

"Yes," Kard said. *Is the man not in tune with the world?*

"And you will get me Janevra?"

"No."

"You bastard!" Ravften screeched, fury blazing in his blue eyes.

"But I will show you where she is and give you the opportunity to talk to her."

Ravften regarded Kard suspiciously.

"Where is she?" Ravften asked.

"Do you even know who she is?" Kard said, ignoring Ravften's question.

"She is Janevra, the Princess of—" Ravften began but Kard cut him off. "She is the Lady Dragon, the most powerful woman in the world."

Ravften stared at him. "The Lady Dragon is Janevra?"

Kard snickered. "Yes."

"Who is the Lord Dragon?"

"Mat Trakall."

"Mat?" Ravften lifted his lip. "The servant boy?"

"From what I heard, yes, he was once a servant for Janevra," Kard said, watching the jealousy rise up in Ravften's eyes. *And now the servant boy is more powerful than you will ever be.* "Come then, the Warlord is waiting for us." Kard summoned all of his magic.

Ravften eyes became calm again. "Yes, let's go."

Kard pictured the Warlord's camp in his mind. The ground tipped under their feet only to return again.

Warlord was about to meet King.

They found themselves standing among a forest of black tents. Men sat around campfires, sharpening weapons. Women tested their armor in mock battles, men beating on the winner. Sylai and rogui fought over the best bows and others traded armor.

The Warlord's Army was preparing for battle.

Kard brought Ravften to the largest tent in the camp, the tent where the Warlord held his meetings. He strode up to the guard. The guard stepped aside and pulled back the tent flap, casting a look at Ravften.

Raxsen was standing at the head of the table with Pierce on his right and Cobrau on his left.

03   ରେ   ഇ0

Raxsen looked up as Kard and Ravften entered. A cold gleam came into his eyes.

"Ah, Kard, I see you have convinced the King that he was wanted," Raxsen purred dangerously.

"He only agreed if he could see Janevra," Kard said, walking around the table and sitting next to Cobrau.

Ravften stayed in the doorway, looking the Warlord up and down.

"This is the Warlord?" Ravften said, and all of Raxsen's men winced. "This man? He's barely out of childhood."

Raxsen bared his teeth in a cold smile. "I am the Warlord," he said, moving around to stand in front of Ravften. "You did agree to serve?"

"Yes," Ravften said, boredom so clear in his voice.

"Good, then this should not hurt at all."

Raxsen moved with serpent grace and laid a hand on Ravften's arm, summoning his magic.

Ravften fell on his knees, screaming out in pain as a flame was tattooed into his skin with his shirt under it. But Raxsen did not seal it with his normal loyalty curse. He wanted to have some fun first.

Raxsen pulled his hand away, his icy eyes fiery.

"Never call me a child. Never," Raxsen growled, resuming his place at the head of the table. His anger was rising and he would not keep it down.

Ravften stood up on shaking legs and put his weight on the back of an empty chair.

"Bastard," he snarled at Raxsen.

Both men summoned their magic, anger and hate shimmering in their eyes.

"You will never insult me," Raxsen said, his voice a quiet whisper.

"I already did, twice," Ravften said.

Raxsen focused his magic in a small ball of ice. He threw out his hand, the ball of ice flying towards Ravften. Ravften rolled out of the way. The ball of ice hit the tent, freezing the whole side.

The council members ran out of the tent. No one wanted to be in the way of two angry and powerful shoi.

"It seems like too much time in Court has made you soft," Raxsen growled.

Ravften looked at Raxsen over his shoulder, his hands and knees in the dirt. He gathered more magic into his body, standing up.

"It may have made me soft, but it did not make me arrogant," Ravften said, shooting a blast of water at Raxsen.

Raxsen threw his hand out again, wind streaming forth.

The two energies met in mid-air, sending shock waves coursing throughout the countryside.

A loud boom sounded, wind and water disappearing. The tent covering the men blew off, exposing them to the army.

People gathered to watch but kept far back, not wanting to get caught in a gust of magic.

Raxsen felt Kard quickly summon his own magic and put a shield around Raxsen and the King so they could not hurt anyone.

"If you do not back down, you will die," Raxsen snapped.

"I cannot die," Ravften shot back.

"You would be surprised."

The Warlord gathered a little more magic into his being, enough so he was even with Ravften's power.

Ravften threw another blast of air when Raxsen was gathering more magic.

Raxsen flew back and tumbled across the ground. He rolled to a stop. He reached his hand up and wiped the blood from his face, smearing it on the back of his hand.

Standing, pure energy crackled around his fingers. He aimed it at Ravften. Ravften quickly erected a body shield and tried to jump out of the way but the ball of energy hit him in the stomach, throwing him backwards and into a tent.

The tent collapsed under his weight, weapons and pots rolling on the ground. Ravften stood up, his stomach aching from the blast. If he had not put up the body shield, he would have been dead.

Raxsen laughed. "You were right. Death is the easy way out. This is too much fun." He pointed his finger at the Dead King and suddenly over a dozen knives flew from it to thud into a quick barrier Ravften had created.

Ravften snarled a curse and gathered the air surrounding him to his being. He sent the force of air rippling towards Raxsen.

The people watching gasped, as the air seemed to move and twist, its target their Warlord.

But the Warlord just smiled coolly and waved a hand. The current of air disappeared.

Ravften stared as his attack was destroyed. Anger grew afresh in his mind. The King murmured a few words, making his attack stronger. A ball of molten rock formed between his outstretched hands. "Die, Warlord." He fired it at Raxsen.

What happened next caused the watchers to blink several times.

The ball of molten rock seemed to go *through* Raxsen.

Ravften whooped in triumph.

But his success was short lived.

The ball of molten rock did not vanish as it was supposed to. Instead Raxsen had let it go through him, his body only air. When Raxsen's body became solid again, he turned the ball of molten rock back at Ravften.

"See how the tables a' turn?" Raxsen said, no mercy in his voice. The Warlord shot the ball at the King.

Ravften paled as the ball of molten rock came flying at him. He closed his eyes tightly, knowing he could not protect himself from this attack.

When his death didn't come, Ravften opened his eyes. He found the Warlord standing in front of him, his cold eyes furious, magic blazing from them.

"I am stronger than you. I will forever be stronger than you. You were at your highest strength, I was barely at my half."

Ravften flinched. For the first time he knew the awesome power of the Warlord.

He felt Raxsen lay a spell down upon his heart. A loyalty spell. Ravften was trapped.

"You are my servant. You will be my servant until you die."

Ravften nodded, letting his magic go. He had finally met his better.

"Go back to your kingdom and gather up your forces. Start your march towards Calahar. I will be there waiting for you."

"But what of our deal."

"What deal?" Raxsen said, flickering his eyes at Kard.

"I was told that—"

"Yes. I know. You will leave tomorrow right before the battle then."

Ravften nodded.

Raxsen directed his attention at Kard. "Kard, find a place for Ravften to sleep. Then gather up my War Council. We will meet in an hour." *Will I ever get to lay out my battle plans with so many interruptions? First Kiera and the Dragons, now Ravften. Maybe I should let my generals plan it. That way I can save my genius strategies for when it really matters.*

Kard nodded and motioned Ravften to follow him.

Raxsen stared around the camp, the smell of magic stinging the air. Cobrau was helping set up the War Tent. She was a good woman. Loyal.

Raxsen moved his cold eyes around. Pierce was ordering people back to their jobs and Kiera was gods knew where. Kard was leading Ravften away, magic flowing in the Phoenix of Death's veins. The sky above was darkening with rain clouds, the sun hidden from view.

The Warlord himself was not only powerful but his army was filled with powerful men. And women too, Raxsen amended as an afterthought and with much contempt.

Chapter 49
A Job

"We should've brought more money," Caya said, digging into her pocket, searching for coins.

"Should've, would've, could've. But we didn't have that much to bring," Lousai snapped as she sat down on a bench, the hot sun beating down upon her. She threw an arm over her eyes, blocking out the scorching light.

They were in a small village several miles from Jatai. They had walked most of the way from Regigan to Jatai with the occasional ride on a wagon.

Caya's stomach grumbled. "We shouldn't have bought new clothes. We should have spent it on food."

Lousai sighed. "Maybe we could get a traveling job that would take us to Kandang or Carim."

"Carim? But that's the Warlord's land."

"So is Atay."

"Oh. You're right. How will we find a job?"

Lousai got up. "We'll ask around."

They walked down the dirt street, stopping at an inn.

The sun was at mid afternoon, nearing the hottest part of the day. Few people were on the streets, most taking cover from the blistering sun.

They entered the inn to find it empty save for an innkeeper and several maids lounging around one of the tables.

The innkeeper put down the glass he was cleaning and addressed the two girls. "What can I do for ye?"

"We're looking for traveling jobs," Caya said, sitting down at one of the tables.

"Jobs to bring you where?" one of the serving girls asked.

"Carim or Kandang," Lousai said cautiously.

"On what business?" the innkeeper asked.

"That's for us to know," Caya said. "Are there any job offers in this town that might take us there?"

The innkeeper scratched his chin. "Wull, there be a circus passing by here in two weeks, heading towards Kandang. Ye could probably get a job with them. That's it. The next moving job opportunity won't be coming till next month."

Caya looked at Lousai. "We're gonna starve if we don't get some money soon."

The serving girl who had over heard them spoke up. "Wull, I'm sure Sulley would let you work here for two weeks. We need some help."

Sulley shot a glare at the maid, but his face lightened when he looked back at the two girls. "She's right, we do need more help. I'm afraid the pay is little."

"If you provide us with food, a place to stay and a wage, we would be willing to work here for two weeks," Lousai said. She hoped she didn't have to work as a maid.

Caya nodded.

Sulley rubbed his hands together. "Since it's too hot out to drink, we won't be having many customers till after sunset so I'll let ye get accustomed to the place. Cleovia will show ye 'round and explain what you're to do," Sulley said and walked through a door and into the kitchen.

Cleovia, the maid who had spoken up, jumped off the table and walked over to them. She was very beautiful. Her eyes were the color of clear water and her long silvery hair fell down her back in waves like water. Her form fit her red dress well and her smile showed off straight teeth. She looked to be seventeen and was of medium height.

"I'm Cleovia," she said and stuck out her hand.

Caya's callused hands grasped Cleovia's smooth ones. "I'm Caya and this is Lousai, my older sister."

"Wull, pleased to meet you. Now if you'll follow me, I'll show you where you're going to stay."

Cleovia led them out of the inn and into the boiling sun.

They walked down the boardwalk, their feet thunking on the wood.

"So," Cleovia said, "how old are you? Seventeen? Sixteen?"

"Sixteen?" Lousai stopped walking. "I'm fourteen and Caya's thirteen."

Cleovia's eyes went wide. "Really? You both look much older. Oh wull, Sulley'll just change your jobs to washing pots and pans."

They resumed walking again.

"What were our previous jobs?" Caya asked, squinting up at Cleovia.

"Why you was gonna be serving maids."

Lousai choked. "You mean...?"

Cleovia laughed. "Yes."

Lousai felt relief flood through her.

Caya frowned, lost from the flow of conversation.

They walked to the end of the boardwalk where Cleovia turned left and took them along a well-used trail leading into a sparse wood.

"Cleovia, where are you from?" Caya inquired.

Cleovia looked over her shoulder. "Wull, I don't know. I know I'm not from the Northern Kingdom for no one has got silver hair in this land. I think my mother and father were from one of the other Kingdoms, but I don't know which one."

"How did you get here?"

"I don't know. Sulley said he found me one day on his doorstep. And being Sulley he went to Goodwife Clarita and she raised me."

"I like your silver hair, it's very pretty," Lousai said, fingering her own dark hair.

"Thank you, Lousai. Now it's your turn to answer a question. Why are you here?"

Caya glanced at Lousai. Lousai shook her head. "I'll tell her."

Lousai cleared her throat. "Do you believe in the goddess Tghil?"

"So and so."

"When we left Jariran—"

"Jariran? You lived in Jariran? How did you escape Ravften?"

"We were close friends with Princess Janevra. She gave us money so we could leave." Lousai shrugged.

"I thought the Princess was dead," Cleovia said absently.

"She's not dead," Caya blurted out. "She's..."

Cleovia looked down at Caya. "What?"

Caya drew herself up. "She's the Lady Dragon."

"Hmmm and I thought she was dead. But Ravften declared that she—"

"Screw what Ravften said. He's a liar and he killed her parents," Caya snarled.

Cleovia stopped walking and faced the two girls. "He did what?"

"He killed the King and Queen," Lousai said.

Cleovia took a step back. "He killed them? How come you know this?"

"Janevra paid us to keep her in touch with the city after she left. We were spies." Lousai wiped her forehead. She was getting really hot. Even in the shade the sun still manged to scorch the very air she breathed.

"Why don't the people of Caendor know this?"

"Ravften is a shoi and he is powerful enough to smear the truth."

Cleovia stared at them, her eyes wide. "You girls are carrying dangerous secrets. Do not tell me anymore."

They started walking again and hiked down the well-worn path past tall, slender trees. Birds chirped in the oak branches and a small stream on the right gurgled and frothed.

They came into an opening, lush green grasses and flowers filling the meadow. In the center stood a large house. Two women were outside the door, kneading bread.

"This is where all of us maids live most of the time."

Lousai frowned. "Why so far away?"

"Wull, it's a nice place to live and Sulley doesn't have't worry about watching over us. Those two women over there are the town's Goodwives. The one with the brown hair is Clarita, and the other one is Susan. They watch over the eight of us girls and also make the bread for the inn."

"Do we walk to the inn everyday?" Caya asked.

"We do. It's rather refreshing. Every week, two of us stay at the inn overnight just to make sure the customers are doing okay. Come, I'll introduce you to the Goodwives."

Cleovia started running through the meadow and the two girls had to hurry to catch up.

The Goodwives saw them coming and put aside their work, folding their hands and smiling.

"Goodwife Clarita, Susan, this is Caya and Lousai. Caya and Lousai, these two women are the Goodwives Clarita and Susan," Cleovia said.

Goodwife Clarita shook the hands of both Lousai and Caya. "I'm so pleased to meet both of you."

Goodwife Susan hugged both of them, her large frame swallowing the two girls. Goodwife Susan was a fat and jolly middle-aged woman.

Goodwife Clarita was also round with rosy red cheeks and her brown hair was pulled back into a bun. She reached into her pocket and pulled out two sweets and gave them to Caya and Lousai who promptly plopped the sweets in their mouths.

"Now, what brings these two children here?" Goodwife Susan asked.

"They're waiting for the circus. Sulley employed them for two weeks."

"Where do they want to go?" Goodwife Clarita asked glancing down at the two children.

Cleovia winced slightly. "To Kandang or...Carim."

"Carim? What an awful place to go." Goodwife Clarita looked down at the two girls again. "But they look so young. They must only be ten."

Cleovia laughed. "I thought they were sixteen."

"How old are they, then?" Goodwife Susan asked, curious.

"Lousai is fourteen and Caya is thirteen."

"My goodness, we certainly were off," Goodwife Clarita said, pressing a hand to her chest and smiling.

Cleovia shook her silver hair. "Wull, I need to show these two around. You'll probably see them again tonight."

"Tonight?" the Goodwives echoed. "They're not..."

"No, washing pots and pans instead."

Both of the old women let out a breath.

"Caya, Lousai, inside. I need to show you around."

Lousai and Caya followed the silver haired foreigner inside.

The house was simple. On the first floor was a kitchen and living room. Stairs led up to the second floor where there were six rooms. The rooms were small, barely livable for two girls.

Cleovia led them out a back door where they found a stable and a small fenced in area where two spotted horses grazed.

"Wull, this is my home," Cleovia said facing the two sisters.

"It's wonderful," Lousai said. "We never had a permanent home. With our father being a merchant we never had the chance to settle down."

Cleovia looked up at the sun. It was an hour from sunset. "Wull, it's time for us to get back to the inn."

They left the stables and walked through the house, saying good-bye to the Goodwives who were washing clothes in a large tub.

They entered the forest.

"Your life seems so perfect, Cleovia," Caya said.

Cleovia's clear eyes clouded up. "It wasn't always this good."

Caya frowned. "What do you mean? There haven't been any wars with Angarat within your life span. The nation has had no major disasters and until late the King's rule has been fair."

Cleovia looked down at the two young girls. "You know so much but there is so little you understand."

Caya drew herself up. "What don't we understand?"

Cleovia smiled gently. "Do you know what is beyond the seas?"

Lousai and Caya shook their heads.

They walked through the forest in silence. The only sound was the thud of their footsteps.

"Then I shall tell you what lies beyond the seas," Cleovia said finally.

"But how do you know what lies beyond the seas? You've never been there. You said you came here when you were but a babe." Lousai frowned. *I'm confused. I hate being confused.*

"Yes, I did say that. However, my memories hint at something else."

"How is that possible?"

"My memories aren't mine, perhaps."

"Ah," both girls murmured.

"Would you like me to tell you what I know?" Cleovia ducked under a low hanging branch.

"Yes," the two girls chorused together.

"There are four Kingdoms, the Northern Kingdom, the Western Kingdom, the Southern Kingdom and the Eastern Kingdom. We live in the Northern Kingdom, the one that holds the most races and the most humans. In the Western Kingdom lives a civilization of people directly descended from the Ancients. Even though they do not have the long life of the Ancients, they do live much longer than Elves. The Westerners are of human height with light colored skin. Their hair can be black-green, midnight blue, dark red, dark or light purple, sun-kiss orange and the very rare silver."

Lousai glanced at Cleovia's hair. It shone in the dying daylight, sparks of silver glittering.

Cleovia continued, her voice lost among her strange memories. "Their eyes can be sapphire blue, emerald green, amber gold, ruby crimson, ruby violet and water blue clear."

Again Lousai's eyes darted up to Cleovia's face, this time to her eyes. Her eyes were water blue clear.

"The Westerners make strange weapons, weapons that are forged of furipyr and Black Iron. The metal formed is unbreakable and when in battle sings a song of death. This form of metal they gave the name the Metal of Sorrow. It is believed that the sword of Hadar is formed from this dangerous mix. Magic is greatly used by these peoples. But they use something deeper than magic itself and cannot be explained. The land is divided in half, Keani and Naiuri, which are ruled by Empresses. The rulers of these two nations are locked in an endless battle for complete control. Women hold the power. Men are not rejected of high offices and aren't treated differently but they cannot hold the position of Supreme Ruler, Empress."

"The Southern Kingdom is a kingdom of dark skinned people. They have brown or purple eyes, and black hair almost purple in the sunlight. It is believed that they developed a gill system in order to breath under water. They are masters of the ocean and know whenever the breeze is going to change or the tide is altering. Even though these are a sea faring people, they stay close to their homeland, fearful of outsiders. Their weapons are a form of Black Iron, a metal that cuts through wood like butter."

"The Eastern Kingdom is in shadows. The land is controlled by Evil. I know nothing of Evil for one of Good knows nothing of Evil as one of Evil knows nothing of Good."

Lousai lifted her head. "What?"

Cleovia's eyes lost their cloudiness. "What?"

Lousai stopped walking. "What was that last thing you said?"

Cleovia paused. "I spoke of Good knowing nothing of Evil."

"That's what I thought."

"Why do you ask?"

"I've heard that saying before, that's all." Lousai started walking again. *But where have I heard it before?*

Caya touched Cleovia's hair as they exited the forest. "You said that Westerners can have silver hair and water clear blue eyes. Do you think that is where you are from?"

Cleovia sighed. "I wish but I'm only seventeen when these Westerners live thousands of years. I know I'm seventeen too because Goodwife Clarita speaks of me as a child as do Sulley and Susan."

Caya lifted her eyebrows. "You are oddly mature for only being seventeen."

"I know."

They arrived at the outer buildings of the town and stepped onto the boardwalk.

Lousai stamped her foot. "Argh! I can't think of where I've heard that passage before."

Caya giggled. "You'll think of it, you always do. Until then I'm blessed with your silence."

Lousai glared.

They reached the inn, which was still empty of people. There Sulley met them but he was frowning.

"Ah, Cleovia, I thought you were going to get them in more 'appropriate' clothes?" he asked.

Cleovia laughed again. "They're only fourteen and thirteen. We have dish cleaners here, not bar maids."

The barmaids sitting at a nearby table laughed.

Sulley winced. "Wull, I'm sorry for that mistake. Follow me back and I'll show you the rounds for cleaning."

Lousai and Caya followed Sulley while Cleovia joined the other barmaids.

By the time the sun had set, the inn was packed and a bard had come down from his room to sing. The bard told stories and sang several songs. The bar maids moved around serving drinks and attending to other wishes the men had. Sulley directed some foreigners to rooms and collected the money his customers laid on the tables. Lousai and Caya listened to the happiness in the common room and glared at one another, their sleeves pushed past their elbows and their hands in soap.

"Why couldn't we have been maids?" Caya complained, her hair wet and soapy.

Lousai's face reddened. "We're too young." *Why doesn't my sister get it? She can be smart when she wants to and I do not feel like explaining why we can't be serving girls.*

Caya scrubbed a dish and handed it to Lousai to dry. "Too young for serving food?"

"Ah, Caya, I think you're missing the point."

"What point?"

"Um...well... the barmaids just don't serve food, they can... you know." Lousai wiped her arm across her forehead, getting bubbles in her hair.

"No, I don't know," Caya said, annoyed at her sister.

"Ah...they... entertain."

"Entertain? Like singing and dancing? We can do that," Caya said, casting a dark look at the door that led to the common room.

"No, not that kind of entertaining," Lousai said, blushing at the thought.

"What other kind is there?" Caya demanded.

"You know...um...when a—"

The door banged open and Cleovia came in, her face slightly flushed and her hair tangled.

"Sorry for interrupting you girls, but I need a quick drink of water," she said, grabbing a clean glass and pouring herself a drink from the pitcher.

She drank the glass down and handed it to Caya. "Thanks." She left, closing the doors behind her.

"Well, tell me what other kind of entertainment?" Caya demanded again.

Lousai scowled and looked up at the ceiling, her face reddening. "The kind where two people..." She winced then opened her hands and then put them together in a rude gesture.

Caya blushed. "Oh, I see."

Lousai rolled her eyes.

"But then that means Cleovia is a—" Caya started.

"Shhhh. Don't say that word. For all we know she might not be," Lousai interrupted.

"Gods, I hope not. She's so young."

Lousai picked up another plate. "Yes, but she is also very mature for her age, pretty and a foreigner. And that changes several things."

Caya sighed. "Who could live like that?"

"Not me. But then who could live being a thief?"

Caya blanched. "I was never a thief."

"No, but you know things that I could never figure out how you knew them."

A *thunk* above stopped their speaking. Then through the light wood ceiling came a woman's breathless laughter and a man's chuckle.

Both girls looked at each other, their faces strawberry red.

"Oh, dear," Caya said and vigorously started scrubbing a pot.

Chapter 50
The First Battle of the Fifth Battle

The day had come, the day of the First Battle of the Fifth Battle between the Light and the Dark.

The two armies stood facing each other, a field of grass between them as they waited for their leaders to meet and settle what the victor would win.

The Warlord's army of men, sylai, rogui and shoi waited in silent, straight lines, their black armor shining darkly in the sun. They held their spears vertical to the ground and their swords crossed against their chests.

The Dragon's army, elves and Ile, stood in formation. The Ile, the Warriors of the Tar-ten, had red knol painted on their faces. The elves, none wearing armor, held their bows notched.

Both armies stood at the base of two hills, half a mile apart. From the top of the two small hills, the Dragons and the Warlord would direct the battle and send their magic at each other.

Janevra walked through the long grass, her clothing, a gray shirt and black pants fitting for this dire day. Her long auburn hair flew out behind her and her green eyes shone with the power of the stars. The lightning bolt on her arm twisted in the daylight even when hidden from view.

Mat walked by her side. A belt was around his waist holding a sheathed sword. He had summoned his magic, the magic crackling around his fingertips and in his eyes. The sun on his arm shone gold with the power of the sun.

On Janevra's left walked Qwaser, his bow slung across his back, next to his quiver. His face was set in a grim line, his elven features stony.

Next to Qwaser walked Dei. She was dressed in her traditional Ile war clothes and her face was covered in marks of red knol. Two lines had been painted under her eyes and one across her forehead. Two more were vertical on her cheeks. She clutched a spear in her hand. The spear had a foot long blade at the end of it, its black metal glimmering. It was a unique battle weapon for an Ile.

To Mat's right walked the Phoenixes. Ake's jewelry glinted in the sunlight, her nose crystal and star earrings making her seem an exotic goddess. Eside was wearing his own gold earring and his light brown eyes looked of fire. A necklace with a seashell tied to it dangled from his neck. Ryen stood tall, his dark green eyes seeing all. Riak wore a frown, her face crinkled and her cat sat on her shoulders, his claws digging into her shirt.

Vena walked behind them all, her wide skirts swishing the ground and her hair pulled tightly into a bun.

Another Ile walked next to her, carrying a banner. The banner flapped in the gentle wind, the symbol on it glowing white against the red like molten white flame. The symbol was a circle with eight lightning bolts pointing away from it, the symbol of the Light.

Walking towards the Dragons was Raxsen. He was dressed in all black, his cold blue eyes even more vibrant. His high cheekbones and clenched jaw made his face an unreadable mask. A sword was belted to his waist, a skull on the sheath.

Walking behind him was Kard, dressed in his own black clothes. Kard, who had no Phoenix on his arm to flaunt, wore long sleeves. His coal black eyes followed Riak scornfully, his lips in a smirk.

Ravften, with a crown perched on his blonde hair, strutted next to Kard. The crown was gold with rubies and diamonds. He watched Janevra with eyes that burned with desire.

To Raxsen's left and slightly behind walked Cobrau. Her flaming red hair blazed in the sunlight. The scar on her cheek was very visible as were the fire earrings she wore. A sword rode on her waist and a long dagger was next to it.

General Pierce walked next to Cobrau. His vibrant green eyes were alight with glory and power. His lips were in a charming smile no woman could resist.

Kiera was the last. Her head was held high, her blonde hair flowing down her back. Her long sleeved dress covered up her black Phoenix, her only physical appearance of betrayal. Her hair was filled with drops of jewels and around her neck was a necklace of sapphires.

At the very end of the line walked a banner man carrying a black flag with a white skull and blue eyes imprinted on the front.

The two forces gathered in the middle of the two armies, white and black flags flying high and proud.

"I assume you're going to want to fight me," Raxsen said, his cold eyes amused.

Janevra smiled. It was obviously forced. "Of course."

"Janevra," a voice said from behind the Warlord.

Before Raxsen could turn around and stop Ravften, Ravften brushed past him to stand in front of Janevra.

"Janevra, my love, I thought I had lost you," Ravften said, bringing her hand up and kissing it.

Janevra stared at the man in front of her, confused. Those eyes, that charm. That man. She recoiled, hate flashing across her features.

"Get away from me," she spat.

"But, my love—" Ravften began.

"I am not your love!" Janevra screamed. "You killed my parents! You stole the throne from me! You destroyed my Kingdom and my people! I will kill you!"

She started forward, her hands going for Ravften's throat. Mat grabbed her from behind and held her arms. "Don't," he warned. Janevra's eyes blazed with fury but she managed to regain her composure and Mat let her go.

"Ravften," she began, her voice tight.

"My love, Janevra, I—" Ravften interrupted.

"Silence," she hissed. "I am not your love. You are not the King. You only want me to make your rule complete. But it will never be complete, for I will never bow down to your wishes. I despise you. You are filth upon this earth. I hate you and I curse the day you were born."

Ravften's jaw dropped. Kard snickered behind his hand and Raxsen smiled cruelly.

"One day I will kill you. I will hang your corpse from the walls. Maggots will crawl from your flesh and the crows will peck at your eyes. You will never hold the throne of Caendor."

Ravften's eyes went wide. "Janevra, but what of your father's promise that I could have your hand in marriage?"

"My father is dead. Therefore anything he wanted that was not written down will never happen. Perhaps if you had not killed him, things would have been more in your favor."

Ravften sneered, his handsome face twisted. "You will regret your words, my princess. You will be Queen of Caendor when I am the King. You will rule at my side even if it is in chains."

"I will never rule at your side," Janevra snarled.

"We will see."

Raxsen threw up his hands. "Enough of this bickering." He pointed at Ravften. "Get back to Jariran and start your march," he ordered

Ravften nodded. He summoned his magic and disappeared.

Raxsen folded his arms across his chest. "We must decide what the victor of this battle gains. One of my Captains has drawn out the details." Raxsen motioned for Cobrau to step forward.

Cobrau moved up next to Raxsen and unrolled the scroll she was carrying.

"The Warlord," she read, "has decided that the victor of this battle will get Calahar, and all the land two miles before reaching Surat. The border will then continue along the Riyad border and the Zayen border eventually reaching the Angarat border. It will follow along these lines and then the Eastern Caendor border defining the winner's prize."

Cobrau lowered the scroll and rolled it back up. Her blue eyes looked behind the Dragons at the Phoenixes and what she saw made her face burst in joy.

"Eside?"

Eside looked around Mat. "Cobrau?"

They both laughed and ran to each other, embracing.

Raxsen lifted his lip in disgust and the Dragons frowned.

Eside and Cobrau were oblivious of everyone else.

"How did you get here?" Eside asked, his arms around her waist.

"My ship landed in Carim after the Warlord conquered it. I needed a job so I joined his army. Why are you here?"

"I'm the Phoenix of Fire."

Cobrau laughed. "It's so good to see you. I thought I would never lay eyes on you again."

Eside smiled and quickly kissed her. "I see you're still wearing the earrings I gave you."

"And you are wearing my necklace."

"Dark hell," Raxsen cursed. "Is this a time for everyone to get reunited? We are about to start a battle. You two are enemies. You are supposed to hate the other, not reminisce about an old love."

Raxsen summoned his magic and pulled Cobrau and Eside apart.

"Eside, if I live through the battle, I'll find you and we'll talk," Cobrau said, smiling at Eside.

"No. You will not see him again," Raxsen shouted. "He is on the side of Light, you on Dark. It doesn't work."

Eside moved to go to Cobrau but Ake touched his arm and shook her head.

Raxsen's eyes suddenly became coldly amused. "Besides, you two have already found someone else."

Cobrau jerked. "Warlord, no—"

"Quiet," Raxsen snapped. "Did you know, Eside, that Cobrau has found someone else?" Raxsen laughed at Eside's crushed look. "And did you know, Cobrau, that Eside has his eyes on another?"

Eside looked ashen. "Cobrau, I'm sorry, but you left me."

"Yes, but you promised you would wait for me," she said stiffly.

"I promised, yes, but you said you would never come back. I wasn't going to wait forever," Eside shot back.

Cobrau's temper cracked. "Shut it! I've only loved you."

Eside's jaw clenched. "If you loved me, then you would have never left."

Cobrau screamed her frustration. She reached up and pulled the earrings out of her ears, tearing the skin. She flung them on the ground. "Take these back. We're done."

Eside's brown eyes burned like a firestorm. He yanked the necklace off his neck and threw it in the grass. "Fine."

Cobrau's eyes blazed. "If I hadn't left, I would never have been a captain and realized my full potential."

"Oh, so living peacefully isn't enough?" Eside spat. "You would rather destroy the world and follow a murderer? For what reason would you want this? Power? Congratulations, Cobrau, you've succeeded in life. You've got everything."

"Yes, I do. What do you have? Nothing. For once, Eside, things won't be going good for you. This time you've made a costly mistake. You not only joined with the wrong side but you angered me. You will regret what you have said. I will make sure your Dragons lose this battle."

Cobrau grabbed her dagger and with the stealth of a cat she was standing next to him, the dagger at his throat.

Dei had been standing next to Ake and when Cobrau had pulled out her knife, Dei had pulled out her own dagger and moved forward and placed the cold steel on Cobrau's throat.

Qwaser had acted just as quickly and had pulled an arrow from his quiver, aiming it at Cobrau's heart.

"Don't move," Dei said. "Or my dagger might slip."

Cobrau's face twisted in rage. She pulled her dagger away from Eside's throat and sheathed it.

Qwaser lowered his bow.

Dei sheathed her own weapon and she and Eside stepped back.

The Dragons and Warlord faced each other.

"Do you agree to the terms?" Raxsen asked.

"Yes," Janevra said. "We do."

Raxsen smiled, but it did not touch his eyes. "Good. I hope your troops are assembled, because the battle starts when my horns sound."

Raxsen turned and walked away, back to his troops, Cobrau, Pierce and Kard following. Kiera remained. She looked at Janevra and then followed the Warlord.

The Dragons faced the Phoenixes and the Ile. "Battle comes. Get ready," Mat said. "Qwaser, align your archers. Dei, get your Tar-ten ready. Vena, prepare your strength for the end. We need you to heal. Phoenixes, summon your magic together. Go."

The Phoenixes, Vena, Qwaser and Dei, along with the banner carrier, fled, hurrying to carry out orders.

Janevra looked at Mat and smiled weakly. They summoned their magic. The Dragons disappeared only to re-emerge at the head of their army, the Phoenixes and the others quickly reaching them.

Qwaser ran to his archers, mostly elves. He motioned for half of them to move up to the front and draw their bows. He then directed the other half to march to the back, surrounding the Ile. Telling Danlk and Tasawer to go to the back and fire from there. Qwaser joined the front of the line. The elves that were on horses waited next to him, their horses moving restlessly with fear while a group of one hundred archers broke off from the main group and faded into the trees surrounding the large clearing. During the battle they would fire upon the enemy and help out warriors of the Light.

Dei stood in front of the Ile. She raised her spear and shouted, *"A'shaing te kra de naum!"*

The painted Ile shouted in return, thudding their *khrieths* on the ground and screaming death chants. Those that stood in chariots banged their weapons on the chariots. The weapons hit the ground with a repeated *thunk-thunk*. Their cries carried over to the Warlord's army, inflicting fear in the hearts of men. *"A'shaing te kra de naum!"*

Vena moved to stand behind the back archers, the banner carrier with her.

Janevra looked at Riak as the woman summed her magic. "Go with Vena."

Riak scowled. "Why? I can fight."

"You are needed to heal," Janevra said.

"But I want to fight." Curly meowed at Riak, plainly bothered by her argument.

"You are the Phoenix of Life, Riak. You do not kill. You will go with Vena and when the battle is over you will save lives."

Riak nodded and joined Vena in the back.

Janevra then turned towards Eside, Ake, and Ryen. "Good luck," she said and turned away.

The Phoenixes summoned their magic.

The army of the Dragons waited. Fear and eagerness were thick in the air.

଄   ଈ   ଞ

Raxsen leered as he watched the Dragons prepare. He would win. He could feel it.

Raxsen summoned his own magic and with it his mind soared above the clouds. He looked at the Dragon's army and then at his own huge force split in half.

He laughed as he let his magic go.

"Pierce," Raxsen said to his general, "prepare my forces. And when that cloud covers the sun, blow the horns." Raxsen pointed to a cloud in the sky.

Pierce nodded curtly and started shouting orders at captains and lieutenants. Cobrau was ordering her own force into position, her dagger in hand. Kard was standing in front of his twenty-three shoi.

Raxsen grinned to himself, remembering the small balls of magic he had given to twenty-three of his best warriors.

Oh, yes, today would be a day filled with death and glory.

Raxsen glanced at the sun. The cloud that was going to cover it was minutes away from doing so.

Raxsen fingered the necklace encircling his throat. His eyes became cold and hate burned with in them. He *would* win this battle.

The cloud covered the sun, the shadow setting over the plain.

The horns of the Warlord sounded. It was a sound of a dying animal in the throes of pain. The sound carried across the plain, lifting the hair of the enemy. The eerie sound was answered by silver elven horns and screaming Ile.

The First Battle of the Fifth Battle had come.

Raxsen nodded to Cobrau and Pierce. Cobrau's face twisted in a nasty smile and Pierce pulled out his sword. Raxsen looked at the Phoenix of Death. Dorl Kard was smiling, his magic shimmering around him. Kiera was nowhere to be found. She had run back to camp to hide in her tent.

Raxsen raised his arm then dropped it, signaling the charge. He summoned his magic again, the dark power filling his body. He spread his hands wide, energy forming in between. "Let's see how good they are," he whispered as his forces ran to meet the Dragon's.

The Warlord targeted the Dragons and shot his ball of black energy at them.

One of them quickly countered his attack with a ball of white light, the two energies smashing together and blinding everyone with a flash as they began to annihilate one another.

Raxsen smiled a smile of pure joy. "The game begins."

ଓଃ   ଓଃ   ଅଠ

Qwaser watched as the sylai in black armor, rogui, and men on foot ran towards him. He checked Brytaya's sword at his side, ready for what came after his arrows were depleted. He pulled an arrow from his quiver, three thousand elves following suit.

He notched the arrow.

The enemy came closer.

Suddenly the forces of Dark split in thirds. The two outside thirds turned and positioned themselves to attack on either side of the forces of Light. The middle third charged in the original direction, heading directly towards them.

The archers quickly moved to adjust to the change in attack, each side swinging their bows to point at the on-coming side.

Qwaser drew the arrow, the fletching touching his cheek. He could hear the straining of the strings behind and next to him.

"Aim!" he yelled over the sound of pounding feet.

Qwaser looked down the shaft, aiming at a sylai in black armor, its black eyes gleaming death.

"Fire!" Qwaser bellowed.

Three thousand arrows, each with deadly aim, slammed into the first five rows of the Warlord's ranks.

Men and creatures fell down screaming.

The shafts were not as deadly as they were intended. Only a quarter of the arrows got past the heavy black armor, piercing the eyes or neck. Most of the arrows bounced off, mere twigs on the ground.

Qwaser slid another arrow out of his quiver. He quickly took aim and fired again, three thousand elves doing the same.

Again deadly shafts rained down from the sky. Only a few out of many actually took the enemy down.

Qwaser cursed and fitted another arrow to his bow. He aimed. The enemy was seventy feet away. He loosened his arrow and drew another one, knowing his target had been hit.

Again and again he shot, his shafts one of the few always driving into the enemy target.

He reached down again to grab another arrow, but his quiver was empty. He slung his bow over his back, along with his quiver. He unsheathed his sword, metal sliding against leather.

"Archers, drop back!" he yelled. Any elf that couldn't use a sword or spear would be needed later.

Qwaser tensed.

He heard Dei yelling. "Ile! Charge! *A'shaing te kra de naum!*"

Qwaser ran, his sword held out in front of him like a deadly snake. Out of the corner of his eye he saw Dei, her spear held tightly in her hands, her painted face smiling in enthusiasm.

The forces of Good collided into the forces of Evil.

ༀ ༀ ༀ

Eside winced, hearing battle cries and the painful sounds of the dying.

He glanced at Ake. Her eyes were closed but her hands moved in front of her, creating intricate patterns in the air. His eyes shifted to Ryen. Ryen had his hand pressed against the ground. A green glow surrounded his fingers. Beads of sweat were on his brow and his jaw was clenched so hard, his teeth were grinding together.

Eside felt the power of fire magic in his veins. He would have to use his magic to kill.

Eside's eyes followed the path of the battle. The forces of Dark were evenly matched against the forces of Light. Even though the forces of Dark had on heavy black armor.

Armor.

Eside smiled. He would heat the armor. He took a deep breath, and spread his hands wide. He drew from the heat of the sun that burned down on his back. He drew it from the heat shimmering off the black armor, he drew it from the still warm bodies of the dead and he drew it from the heat of the inner earth.

Eside brought his hands together.

A loud *boom!* sounded.

Cries of pain tore from the throats among the ranks of Evil, their skin popping and boiling under the quickly heating metal, body fluids sizzling.

ༀ ༀ ༀ

Raxsen cursed. That damned Phoenix of Fire was smart.

Raxsen swiveled around and glared at Kard. "Make your shoi useful," he snapped.

Kard paled. "Yes, Warlord." Kard fixed his eyes upon the Warlord's army. "Shoi, make it rain." The shoi turned as one and focused their attention on the army below.

Clouds had formed above the battle, their dark, threatening presence darkening the day even more than the hate and the blood.

It began to rain and the forces of Evil battled with renewed vigor.

Ω Ω Ω

Ake continued tracing the complex patterns in the air. Rainwater ran down her face.

She dropped her hands, the symbols in the air disappearing. The rain stopped.

"There," she murmured, "now, let's play."

A fine mist covered the battle, obscuring the enemies from each other.

She nodded to Eside. "Make the armor of the Dark glow."

Sparks flew from Eside's fingers, thousands of sparks. They darted around and into the mist.

Glowing clumps of men, rogui and sylai could be seen, the forces of Light still hidden from view.

Ω Ω Ω

Qwaser shook his head, shaking off the rainwater. His sword sliced into a human, blood splattering.

An ugly sylai came running at him, its curved blade slick with blood. Qwaser blocked the attacker's thrust. He stared into the thing's black eyes and spat. The sylai snarled, its pointed teeth yellow.

Qwaser drew his knife and jabbed it into the thing's neck. He pulled his knife out, the creature falling down and dying.

Blood spattered on his face as he spun his sword through the air.

Suddenly a heavy mist surrounded everything, the battle slowing.

Then the black armor of the enemy appeared, glowing.

Qwaser grinned, his face covered in blood.

He looked at Dei, standing next to him, her face paint still on. "Phoenixes," he said, than ran to the closest glowing thing, knowing it could not see him.

Dei followed him, her spear slipping between the armor and dealing lethal wounds.

Soon all that they could see around them were dead and dying sylai and rogui. The sounds of battle could still be heard but only faintly, the mist suppressing the crash of war.

Dei let out a breath. "I say we take a moment of rest then start fighting again."

Qwaser nodded. He walked over to a dead rogui, its gray skin already rotting from the heated metal. He pulled out four arrows lodged in the thing's thick skin. He slipped the arrows in his quiver.

Qwaser griped his sword and glanced at Dei. "Come," he said, running towards the sounds of battle.

The wind starting blowing and the blood on Qwaser's face began to dry.

The mist began to lift.

ଓଃ   ଓଃ   ଓ

"Must I do everything myself?" Raxsen snarled, watching as the thick mist enfolded his forces and fire illuminated them.

The ground tipped under his feet only to return as he transported himself back to camp.

Raxsen ran through the abandoned camp, the black tents fluttering. Crows sat on top of the tents, their black eyes glinting with malicious secrets.

"Kiera!" Raxsen yelled.

Kiera came out of one of the tents, her blonde hair sparkling and her blue eyes matching the sky.

Raxsen grabbed onto her hand and they disappeared. Raxsen and Kiera emerged next to Kard.

Kiera looked around wildly. Then she spotted the battle below and her face went very pale.

"You will be of some use to me," Raxsen said. "Summon the wind and blow away the mist."

Kiera held her chin up. "Why didn't you do it, or Kard? You're strong enough."

Raxsen's eyes became dangerously cold.

Kiera winced and summoned her magic. A wind came down from the North. Soon the mist vanished. And the battlefield was revealed, the Light having the upper hand.

Raxsen clenched his hands. "Damn it." He turned around, his back to the battle. He strode down the hill, the sounds of battling quieting.

The Warlord walked up to a sylai commander, standing before a thousand sylai. "Kill them."

The sylai commander made a fist and pounded it into his chest, where the heart would be. The sylai raised its curved sword. It bared its teeth and spoke in the harsh language of the sylai.

Raxsen led the force up the hill, his black clothes snapping around him in the strong wind Kiera had created.

Raxsen topped the hill, a line of sylai behind him.

He raised his arm and dropped it.

The sylai stormed down the hill.

ଓଃ   ଓଃ   ଓ

Janevra grew sick as she watched the new force of sylai charge down the hill. She turned her eyes towards Mat. Mat returned her glance, calm and considering possibilities.

They had not used their magic yet, except at the very beginning when Raxsen had shot a ball of energy at them.

The magic ran through Janevra's veins, its music singing in her blood. She drew into her complete power.

Mat did the same.

"What should we do?" Mat asked, putting his trust in her. She was the one who knew how to rule, not him.

"We make lightning and sun."

They gathered all the power they could hold, taking some from the ground, the sky, the sun, and even from the attacking army.

Janevra lifted her hands, facing her palms to the sky. Lightning exploded from them straight up into the clouds.

Mat lifted his own hands up, pure beams of fire blasting from his fingertips.

The two energies intertwined, creating a column of brilliant white light, barbs of electricity shooting out of the edges.

The beam disappeared, vanishing into the Dragon's hands. The Dragon's eyes blazed with power, both pairs of eyes locked on their target. They brought down their hands, aiming them right at Raxsen. Power ejected forward, sun racing over lightning.

The power was greeted by another force, one oily black.

The two forces hit and the loudest sound echoed from the impact. The armies fighting below were knocked off their feet. The Phoenixes toppled to the ground. The Warlord and the Dragons only remained standing, their focus and power centered on one thing.

Janevra faltered when she felt Raxsen draw his magic from somewhere else. From something he had not created, from something that held an ancient magic.

An Artifact. Raxsen had an Artifact. Janevra pushed harder, panicking. She wondered if Mat had noticed it. When his ray of magic jerked slightly, she had her answer.

Raxsen did indeed have an Artifact.

03   03   80

The armies below staggered to their feet and resumed fighting.

Dei could feel the blood caked to her skin.

She blocked a sword thrust from an attacker, her spear dancing deadly circles. She deflected another jab of the sword.

Her attacker smiled, obviously pleased. They didn't know who Dei was.

Dei smiled back. She brought her spear up in the same instant, jabbing it into her foe.

The man jolted, his body doubling over. He clutched his stomach, blood seeping out of his mouth.

Dei pulled out a knife with her free hand and slit the man's throat. No mercy. Never. Not in war.

Dei whipped around, a second instinct telling her someone was coming. She drove her spear into a sylai's neck, the only place they could easily be killed.

The Ile maiden jumped away before the dead thing crashed into her.

The sylai were hard to fight. They were stronger than the rogui and more sadistic.

Dei quickly rubbed a hand across her face, smearing the blood out of her eyes. Her dagger drawn and her spear wet with blood, Deivenada fought on.

She killed many sylai, her weapon putting fear into their hearts. She felt a shiver work its way up her back. The tides of war were changing.

A new wave of sylai swept down the hill, their wicked swords drawn and wanting blood.

Then a flash of blinding light hit and fighting ceased for a moment. The Dragons had drawn on the power of the day. The Warlord in response drew on the forces of night and blasted his own power.

Dei felt fear flicker across her heart. So much magic. Too much magic was at work here. She felt the hair on the back of her neck rise with the static in the air and the barbs of magic blazing. Yet as a veteran warrior she did not pause in her killing as did the sylai and rogui. She dispatched them, her spear and dagger circles of death. She killed over a dozen before the creatures came out of their magic inflicted fear.

The fighting resumed.

Dei smiled grimly to herself. She did not kill to kill; she killed to avenge the death of her beloved and her home. The forces of Dark had ruined her life and she would do all she could to make their quest for the world impossible.

She blinked away tears, memories of Zenerax suddenly overwhelming her. She screamed in grief and plunged her spear into a black armored solider.

Tears fled unchecked down her face, washing away the blood.

The forces of Dark backed away from her, fearing her hate and anger. Dei followed, her spear ripping skin yet she herself untouchable.

Blood dribbled from her mouth she had bitten it so hard. She danced a dance of death.

CZ   CR   ଧ

Cobrau's sword flashed. Her hair was sweat drenched and her wounds blossomed blood. She fought like a beast that was possessed. Her sword bit any enemy who came too close to her.

Pulling an Ile from the back of a chariot, she slit his throat, warm blood spraying in her face and soaking down her front.

She was trying to make her way to the Ile woman, the one who had threatened Cobrau before the battle.

Cobrau saw the Ile maiden fighting, killing dozens of sylai and rogui. The maiden was good, but could she best Cobrau's sword? Doubtfully.

Cobrau brought her sword up and sliced an elf across the chest. The elf tumbled backwards, blood budding forth and staining his teeth red.

She cut her way through the masses, her only goal the Ile maiden warrior.

The magic above her head crackled, the beams of light and dark battling. Dark had the upper hand.

Cobrau reached the Ile warrior and smiled. Her smile left her features as she saw rage blazing in the maiden's eyes, tears streaming down her face and blood leaking from her mouth. The Ile warrior had a clear space around her, the masses of Dark fearful.

The Ile warrior slid a knife across a rogui's throat and turned her gray eyes towards Cobrau.

Cobrau stepped into that circle, blood splattered down the front of her shirt from the rogui. She held her sword out in front of her, daring the woman to attack. The woman crouched down, her spear parallel to the ground.

"We dance," Cobrau whispered so only the maiden warrior would hear her.

The woman smirked.

The two began to circle each other, sizing up their opponent. Their eyes were locked onto each other, their bodies tense.

Cobrau lunged forward. The maiden jerked back, her spear still parallel to the ground. Cobrau planted her left foot and lunged to the right, past the Ile woman. Calculating that the Ile would see a fault, Cobrau lifted her left foot, twisted and felt wind brush against her back.

The woman's momentum carried her past Cobrau and Cobrau took this moment to jab her sword into the Ile's back.

But the maiden had somehow foreseen the attack and had dropped to the ground, her feet tripping Cobrau.

Cobrau crashed to the ground, her sword spinning out of her grasp. She scrambled back. The Ile rose quickly and thrust her spear at Cobrau.

Cobrau kicked out her feet, the weapon whirling out of the maiden's hands.

Both women unsheathed their daggers and leapt at each other.

They joined with a clang and the daggers birthed sparks.

Cobrau pushed with all her force and managed to knock the dagger out of the Ile's hands. She kicked the woman to the ground and drove her dagger down. But her dagger hit only earth.

Cobrau screamed and grabbed the Ile woman by her shirt and dragged her back. She drove her knife down again. The woman's hands came up and clutched Cobrau's wrists.

Cobrau pushed down and the woman pushed up. Sweat ran down their foreheads.

The Ile brought her legs up and put her feet against Cobrau's stomach. The maiden grinned. She kicked her legs out.

Cobrau went flying backwards and the woman flipped, rising before Cobrau hit the ground.

The woman picked up Cobrau's dagger.

Fear struck Cobrau's heart and she tried to get back up.

The Ile came for her.

The warrior maiden made a fearsome appearance. Dirt was smudged on her face and clothes. Red war paint was painted under her eyes and on her forehead. Blood was sprayed on her arms.

Cobrau blinked the sweat out of her eyes.

The Ile warrior held the dagger by the tip; she was going to throw it.

A bolt of magic came through the air and knocked the dagger from the maiden's hands. Cobrau could not tell who had released the bolt, but she scrambled up into a fighting stance.

The Ile warrior charged forward, her hands bleeding.

Suddenly a burst of magical light lit the world. A large boom shook the ground. Cobrau and the woman fell to the ground and the earth underneath their feet rippled.

Another explosion sounded and more light danced across their eyes. They struggled up, still fighting.

They gripped each other at the forearms, staring at the ball of fire coming at them. They pushed off, each from the other.

The ball of fire whizzed past them, blowing up a group of fighting elves and rogui. Fire whooshed up from the ground and spread, running right between the duelists.

Cobrau watched the maiden on the other side of the fire. Heat made the sweat glisten on their bodies.

Their eyes met for a moment then the Ile woman bent down and picked up a spear, a sylai running to attack her.

Cobrau would meet the woman in battle again, and next time she would win.

Cobrau located her sword and went back into battle, her sword giving death.

ଔ   ଔ   ଯ

Pierce ground his teeth, taking a step back from his attacker.

The painted man he was fighting was good. All the painted men and women were good.

Pierce and a few other good fighters were in a tight circle trying to keep the forces of Light at bay.

He blocked a spear thrust with his sword.

The General concentrated. He wanted to draw on his magic but he couldn't. His mind was too focused on the man attacking him.

A knife whistled past Pierce's ear and thudded into the back of a man behind him. His face became grim as he fought with renewed effort. This time his attacker took a step back.

Pierce switched hands, his sword now in his right. He was better with his right. His sword lashed out, cutting the man's spear in half.

Pierce hit the man on the head with the flat of his sword, knocking him out.

Grabbing a knife from his belt, he flung it and it buried itself to the hilt in an elven rider's chest. The elf fell off her horse only to be trampled by the beast.

The man next to Pierce fell over, an arrow growing from his chest. A small ball fell out of the man's pocket and rolled to Pierce's feet.

Pierce hurriedly picked it up. The words Raxsen had said came to his mind. *"This is a ball of pure magic. When you throw it, it will create an explosion. But make sure you can throw it over twelve feet away for that is the blast radius. You are to use these tomorrow and only if you are in a position where you cannot fight your way out without many losses. And make sure you do not throw it where your own men are fighting."*

Pierce looked down at the ball in his hands, ignoring the fighting around him. The ball had a purple black power pulsing inside of it. Pierce stared into its center fire and his eyes were filled with pure magic. Raxsen had created something that the world had not seen for thousands of years. Something that only the Ancients knew how to handle.

The General swiftly scanned the battlefield. He saw a large cluster of elves and Ile. Pierce quickly summoned his magic and put a shield around him, protecting himself from sword thrusts and arrows.

He threw the ball, sending it flying through the air on wings of magic.

The ball hit ground in the center of the group of elves and Ile.

It exploded.

Light burst forth, fiery red light that threw fireballs in every direction.

Pierce smiled and glanced up at the sky. The powers of Light and Dark fought, the beams of lightning-sun and dark power smashing in the air.

The dark power was winning.

           03   03   80

Sweat ran down Mat's face as he used all of his power to keep Raxsen from beating them.

Janevra stood next to him, her face glistening with perspiration. Her hands shook, the lightning blasting out from them wavering.

"We—can't do this!" she hissed. "He has too much power."

Mat's hazel eyes hardened. "We must beat him."

Janevra looked at him. "What do we do?"

"We draw our power from the Earth, Water, Fire and Air."

Janevra nodded.

They both let the beams coming from their hands stop.

Raxsen who had not foreseen them letting go stumbled as his blast of dark energy became too much.

The Dragons quickly gathered their magic around themselves again. They drew it from the four elements, power filling their bodies.

Again they lifted their hands into the heavens, Earth, Water, Fire and Air coming together. The four elements became one.

φ   φ   φ

Raxsen snarled as he watched the Dragons. He yanked the Pearl of Light off his neck, grasping it in his hand. He summoned his full power and the full power of the Pearl.

The Warlord waited for the Dragons to harness their own power, watching with contempt. He would win this battle.

A ball of magic formed in his hands. He was tired of waiting. He shot it at them.

The ball of magic blasted across the battlefield, hurtling at the Dragons.

Tghil must have been with them for the ball bounced off a shield.

Raxsen spat, put the Pearl back around his neck, and transported himself.

He reappeared next to Janevra. She jumped back at his appearance, a sword of lightning emerging in her hand.

Raxsen summoned his own dark fire sword.

"Enough. We battle now. Not with magic balls and beams but with magic wrought swords. You and me." He pointed at Janevra. Raxsen sneered at Mat. "It looks like you're going to have to let your Lady Dragon fight the battle for you."

"I know how to use a sword," Mat said. "I was taught not that long ago by the Ile."

Raxsen scowled and then grinned evilly. "I will fight both of you then."

Mat shrugged and a sword of flame appeared in his hand. "First blood," he said.

Raxsen nodded once. "Agreed."

Raxsen crouched; his feet spread apart, his balance perfect. His cold blue eyes became a winter's frost.

Janevra swung her sword in a wide arch, leaving a trail of lightning behind it. "I believe the Ile refer to sword fighting as dancing."

Mat's hazel eyes stared into Raxsen's. "Let's dance."

The Warlord twirled his blade in his hands, the dark fire mesmerizing those watching. He carried it down towards Janevra.

She brought her sword up and met Raxsen's attack with a crackling cling as the swords clashed.

Mat lunged forward, his sun sword aiming at Raxsen's back.

Raxsen, with a burst of strength, pushed Janevra off and spun around to rally Mat's attack. He blocked it with his sword. Mat's blade slid down Raxsen's, stopping at the hilt.

Raxsen smiled coldly. He said a quick spell and Mat stumbled back, his vision clouded.

Raxsen brought his sword downward, close to killing Mat but Janevra darted between them and deflected it, her green eyes blazing. Their swords pushed against each other.

"You said nothing but the swords. You said no magic!" she seethed.

"I lied," Raxsen said, pushing down with his sword, making Janevra drop to her knees next to Mat. "Oh, I'm sorry, but did you actually trust that I would keep my word?" He laughed. "By the abyss, I thought you were smarter than that."

Janevra growled and whispered a spell that cleared Mat's vision. Mat scrambled up, his sword clutched in his hand. "Then we play by your rules," Mat snarled.

Mat summoned his magic and threw forth a gust of wind that hit Raxsen in the stomach, tossing him to the ground.

Raxsen rolled and jumped up, his blade in front of him. A ball of magic formed in his palm. He jerked his fingers and the ball sprung out from them.

Janevra repelled the ball with her sword. The ball soared off into the sky, forever lost.

Janevra pointed a finger at Raxsen. Lightning grew out of her finger-tips, flying towards Raxsen.

Raxsen brought his own hand up and the bolt hit him in the palm. But it didn't do anything. Raxsen caught the bolt in his hand. He shot it back.

Janevra wasn't prepared for his quick counterattack. The bolt hit her in the collarbone. The force of the bolt knocked her backwards. The sword in her hands vanished. Crumpling to the ground, she fainted.

"I grow bored of your puny attempts to try to beat me. This ends now." Raxsen drew from the power of the Pearl hanging around his neck. He started murmering words, dark words. Powerful words.

The sky above grew dark, lightning flashed and thunder boomed. The clouds boiled and rolled.

Mat held Janevra tight, her body limp in his arms.

Arcane words drifted to Mat's ears, words that the Warlord should not have uttered. All the blood drained from Mat's face. He stood up with Janevra in his arms and faced the battlefield.

The forces of Light had been pushed back, their numbers small. Out of five thousand that had attacked, just over a thousand remained. They were trying to retreat.

Mat looked over at Ake, Eside and Ryen. They were doing their best to work their magic but they were afraid they would hit their own troops.

"Ake! You, Eside and Ryen transport the rest of the army to Surat! Tell Riak and Vena to find any that have a chance then transport the wounded to Surat! Save any supplies you can from the camp!" he yelled over the screaming wind.

The Phoenixes stared at him.

"Now!" he shouted.

They departed on the wing of magic and a short time later Mat saw a flash where the battle was being fought and another flash. At least they had managed to save some.

Mat faced Raxsen again.

Raxsen's eyes had rolled back in his head. His hair was plastered to his head from the rain, water dripping down his face. Through his shirt the skull on his arm glowed.

Fear twisted in Mat's stomach. He had to stop Raxsen.

"Raxsen!" Mat screamed, trying to get the Warlord's attention. "If you summon that monster you'll bring the world down upon our heads!"

Raxsen didn't listen to him.

Wind lashed at Mat's face and rain soaked his clothes. Janevra hung limp in his arms, her wet garments sticking to her body.

The ground trembled underneath Mat's feet. Raxsen had been successful in his casting. The earth cracked and trembled, deep trenches splitting the land.

Raxsen looked at Mat, his eyes glowing a blue ice. "Die, Dragon!" he pointed his finger at Mat.

Mat took a step back, clutching Janevra.

Out of the ground burst a monster. It towered above all, standing some eight feet above the tallest tree. It had two extended black arms with two-foot long claws at the end. It had a long snout from which fangs were sticking out. Red eyes with elongated pupils stared at Mat. Its tail slashed back and forth. The thing's body glittered with black and gray scales. Steam rose from its nose.

"What has he done? What has he done?" Mat whispered.

Janevra stirred in his arms. "Mat," she murmured. "Pray to Tghil." She fainted again, a dead weight in his arms.

Mat took another step back, the creature sniffing the air.

Raxsen laughed. "You cannot hide from it, Dragon! It will find you!"

Thunder sounded and lightning burst.

Mat took another step back but his foot caught on a rock and he fell over, Janevra still cradled in his arms.

"Tghil! Help us!" Mat said, hating himself for showing weakness in front of Raxsen.

The monster raised a giant claw and brought it down, thirsting for man blood. Mat squeezed his eyes shut, waiting for the pain.

It was the creature that screamed in pain and Mat's eyes tore open.

A beam of light had hit the creature between the eyes.

Raxsen stopped laughing. "No." He stared at the monster. "No!"

The beam of light disappeared as did the monster and in place stood two gods.

Mat stumbled up, Janevra growing heavier in his arms. They were safe.

Tghil and Kard stood between the Warlord and Dragons.

Raxsen's eyes went from disbelief to a raging cold hate. "You!" he snarled. "You told me to kill the Dragons and yet you let her destroy my beast?" He pointed a finger at the Lady of Light.

The Lord of the Dark remained silent, his black eyes staring at Raxsen.

"You ruined my plans!" Raxsen raged on. "I was this close to controlling the world." He held his thumb and forefinger an inch apart. "This close," he hissed.

Rage blazed in the Lord of Dark's eyes. "You ignorant fool! You cannot kill them until the end of the Fifth Battle! Fate and Time forbid it! You and the Dragons must have a power struggle to prove if you are worthy."

Raxsen immediately became curious. "Worthy of what?"

Kard waved an elegant hand. "Time will reveal all to you soon."

Tghil glided over to Mat and Janevra. She laid a hand on Janevra's forehead and pure white light burst forth.

Tghil removed her hand, the light sinking into Janevra's forehead.

Janevra's eyes opened. She blinked several times and looked at Mat. "What?"

Mat nodded at Tghil, letting Janevra stand on her own.

Janevra faced Tghil. "Thank you."

Tghil smiled but a shadow fell upon her. The Lord of the Dark and Raxsen were behind her. Tghil slipped her arm through Kard's, her face sad.

Kard smiled coldly. "The victor of this battle is the Warlord."

Raxsen's lips curled up into a cruel smile. "I told you I would win."

Kard cuffed Raxsen on the head.

Raxsen glared at the god. "I must go and reassemble my troops," he said. "I have a city awaiting me."

Raxsen walked down the small hill and into the battlefield where the wounded groaned.

Tghil smiled at the Dragons. "Get to Surat and unite the remaining nations. Most of the wounded have been taken there. Your people need you. Go."

"What of the other wounded?" Janevra asked.

"They will come with me."

"May the Light bless them," Janevra said.

The Dragons summoned their magic and slipped into the air.

଼ଷ   ଢ଼   ଅ

Tghil and Kard looked down on the battlefield, both remembering the days when they fought in war.

The ground was filled with the wounded and the dead. Broken spears and swords stuck out of the land. Dead horses were scattered across the battlegrounds and chariot wheels spun, creaking. One overturned chariot burned. Smoke rose from the brown grass and small fires smoldered. The wounded cried out for help. Blood was everywhere, on the ground, on the living and the dead. The stench of death clung to the rain washed air. The dark clouds above roiled with dangerous energy. The Warlord's men, those standing, cared for the wounded but killed their enemies and those too badly injured. Cobrau and Pierce walked side-by-side, surveying the battleground. The Phoenix of Death was directing his shoi to gather up the wounded. Kiera was sitting on a small rise, her arms folded across her stomach, tears running down her face. Raxsen barked orders at his captains and lieutenants.

Of all the Warlord's six thousand men, women, sylai and rogui, only two thousand lived. The Dragons were not the only ones who had lost many men. But the Warlord was a military genius. The forces that he had used in battle were only one third of what he had. An hour's march behind, a force of twelve thousand rogui and sylai, and over six thousand men and women marched. All the humans were mounted on horseback and a huge wagon train ladled with supplies plodded along behind the army. They marched towards the old battlefield, ready to conquer Calahar and follow the Warlord.

Tghil and Kard vanished.

଼ଷ   ଢ଼   ଅ

Raxsen, giving the final orders to his men, walked through the battlefield, his boots squelching in the blood soaked ground. The crows and ravens had already begun feasting on the bodies.

Pierce rode up, Raxsen's horse pulled along behind. "Warlord," Pierce said. "Calahar awaits. There will be a small resistance, nothing Kard's mages cannot handle."

Raxsen nodded absently, gazing at the field of battle. Many of the dead would be left where they had fallen, he did not have time for burials. The birds could clean up the mess.

"Where is Selkare's army?" he asked.

"They've vanished. We think they fled into the Iwo Mountains but we can't be sure."

Raxsen took his horse's reins from Pierce. "Find them. An army does not vanish. Especially one the size of Selkare's."

Pierce bowed from his saddle. "Yes, Warlord." He galloped away, shouting orders.

Casting a final glance at the battlefield, Raxsen smiled, his frozen blue eyes laughing. Before climbing onto his horse, he looked at the hill he had battled on with the Dragons. "The world is mine," he said and his laughter rang across the battleground.

The End of Book 1

Glossary

Adea (A-de-a) de'Ralla- mother of Lousai, Caya, Teaa and Jarin

Aivon (Ai-ve-on) Valynier (Val-in-ir)- A young man fighting to restore Jariran to its past splendor

Ake (A-ke)- Phoenix of Water

Brytaya (Bra-tay-a)- elf who lives with Qwaser, also an outcast

Caya (Kay-a) de'Ralla- works for Janevra, sister of Lousai, Teaa, Jarin and daughter to Adea and Joea de'Ralla

Cobrau (Cobra-u)- Captain in the Warlord's army, has a sun shaped scar on her cheek

Danlk (Dan-ilk)- a young elf who survives the attack on Andaon

Dasher- the leader of the Thieves Guild in Calahar

David Pierce- Originally Second General in the Warlord's Army, later promoted to First General

Deivenada (Dei-vin-a-da)- goes by the name Dei, young Ile woman of the Edieata, of the warrior class Tar-ten, later becomes Djed of the Edieata

Dorl Kard- Phoenix of Death, descendant of the Goddess of Light and the Dark Lord

Eside (E-side) Thron- Phoenix of Fire

General Andrews- General in the Warlord's army

Hasaxta (Has-axe-ta)- General of the Elven Army

Janevra (Jan-eve-ra)- Princess of Caendor and the Lady Dragon

Jarin (Jar-in) de'Ralla- older brother of Teaa, Lousai and Caya, soon to be married

Joea de'Ralla- husband of Adea and father of Lousai, Caya, Teaa, and Jarin, runs the family business

Kalioa (Kay-lo-a)- an elf survives the attack on Andaon

Kard (Card)- God of Dark, the Dark Lord

Kayzi (Kay-zye)- brother of Deivenada, of the Ile warriors class Tar-ten, one of the Edieata., later becomes Djed of the Edieata

Kiera (Kyi-ee-ra) Aade (A-ade)- Phoenix of Air

Lana Thron- Eside's sister

Leama (Le-am-a)- Djed of the Daaguwh

Lord Dimsenlos (Dim-sen-los)- Elven Lord who is an ambassador

Lord Ravften (Ravef—ten)- son of the High Lord Darquin, has been promised Janevra's hand in marriage

Lousai (Lou-sigh-a) de'Ralla- a young girl who works for Janevra, sister of Caya, Teaa, Jarin and daughter to Adea and Joea de'Ralla

Mat Trakall (Tra-call) - a farmer living twenty miles from Jariran and the Lord Dragon

Queen Eliza- Queen of Caendor, mother of Janevra

Qwaser (Qu-ways-ar) Silverglow- An elf outcast by his people for speaking to a human, he is a survivor of Andaon. Later becomes the Head General of the Elven Army.

Ryen (Ri-yen) Dael (Day-el)- Phoenix of Earth

Raxsen (Rax-sen)- the Warlord

Riak (Rye-a-k) Tghil- Phoenix of Life, descendant of the Goddess of Light and the Dark Lord

Saviak (Sa-vi-a-ka)- thief and assassin

Tasawer (Ta-say-were)- a young elf who survives the attack on Andaon

Teaa (Tea-a) de'Ralla- older sister of Lousai and Caya, daughter to Adea and Joea de'Ralla

Tghil (T-ghil)- the Goddess of the Light,

The King of Caendor (Ca-en-dor)- father of Janevra, married to Queen Eliza, also known as Richard

Vena (V-en-a)- a Yria'ti of the Daaguwh Ile

Zenerax (Zen-er-ax)- of the Ile warrior class Tar-ten, of the Edieata, later Djed of the Edieata

Ages of the Northern Kingdom
* = Battle at beginning of Age
^= Birth of Dragons

The First Age, Age of Magic- two thousand years long (0-2000)

*The Second Age, Age of War- Five hundred years long (2000-2500) Tghil
and Kard fight in the first 20 years, the rest are spent deciding who owns
what

*The Third Age, the First Battle- three hundred years long (2500-2800)

*The Fourth Age, the Second Battle, the Age of Evil- four hundred years
(2800-3200)

^The Fifth Age, the Third Battle- six hundred years long (3200-3800) Called
the Age of the First Dragons (they ruled for forty years (3200-3240))

*The Sixth Age, the Fourth Battle- one hundred years (3800-3900) The Age
of Prophecies

^The Seventh Age, the Age of the Second Dragons- current age (3900-_)

Abbreviations:

AP- Ancient Peoples
BA- Before Ancients
BG- Before Gods
ALD- After Light and Dark
FA- First Age
SA- Second Age
TA- Third Age
AE- Fourth Age, Age of Evil
FD- Fifth Age, First Dragons
P- Sixth Age, Prophecies
SD- Seventh Age, Second Dragons

Don't miss the second book of the Fifth Battle Trilogy. Check
www.iysofwar.com for publication updates.